The Best Alternate History Stories of the 20th Century

THE

BEST

ALTERNATE

HISTORY STORIES

OF THE

20TH

CENTURY

**EDITED BY HARRY TURTLEDOVE
WITH MARTIN H. GREENBERG**

**THE RANDOM HOUSE PUBLISHING GROUP
NEW YORK**

A Del Rey® Book
Published by The Random House Publishing Group

Introduction and compilation copyright © 2001 by Harry Turtledove

Published in the United States by Del Rey Books, an imprint of The Random House Publishing Group, a division of Random House, Inc., New York, and simultaneously in Canada by Random House of Canada Limited, Toronto.

Del Rey is a registered trademark and the Del Rey colophon is a trademark of Random House, Inc.

Owing to limitations of space, permission acknowledgments can be found on page 416, which constitutes an extension of this copyright page.

www.delreybooks.com

Library of Congress information available upon request

Manufactured in the United States of America in 2009

Cover design by David Stevenson
Cover art: Russian flag © Cathy Crawford; Adolf Hitler © Corbis; Abraham Lincoln © Oscar White/Corbis; Confederate flag © David Stevenson

ISBN-13: 978-0-307-29167-7

9 8 7 6 5 4 3 2 1

CONTENTS

INTRODUCTION

Harry Turtledove

WHAT IF . . .

Most science-fiction ideas don't come naturally. Most take a degree of intellectual sophistication that came only with the Industrial Revolution. It's hard to write about the effects of technology before there's much in the way of technology to write about. But alternate history isn't like that. It's as natural as those two mournful little words up there. What if . . .

What if I'd married Lucy instead of Martha, George instead of Fred? What would my life be like? Would I be richer? Happier? What would our kids have been like, if we'd had kids? What if there hadn't been that traffic accident that clogged three lanes of the freeway, so I wasn't late to the interview? How would things have looked if I'd got that job? Or—let's not think small—what if I won the lottery? How would I live if I had sixty million dollars in the bank?

In our own lives, we endlessly imagine these scenarios. We can't help it. There's always the feeling that we're inside God's pinball machine, bouncing through life and off bumpers at random, and that we could have ended up elsewhere as easily as where we did.

It's certainly true for me. If I hadn't read a particular book—*Lest Darkness Fall*, by L. Sprague de Camp—when I was about fourteen years old, I wouldn't have ended up with the degree I have (a doctorate in, God help me, Byzantine history), wouldn't have written much of what I've written (I surely wouldn't be working on this introduction now), wouldn't have met the lady I'm married to, wouldn't have the kids I have. Other than that, it didn't change my life a bit. If someone else had taken that novel out of the secondhand bookstore where I found it . . .

And from there, from the sense that individuals' lives might be plastic, mutable, comes the sense that the wider world might work the same way. "A horse! A horse! My kingdom for a horse!" Richard III cried. What if he'd got that horse, instead of going down to defeat and death because he didn't? What would England be like today? No different at all? A little different? A lot different? How can we know?

Well, we can't *know*, not in any absolute sense. Whatever else history may be, it's not an experimental science. How can we make plausible guesses, interesting guesses, entertaining guesses? This is the way in which the alternate-history story was born.

The subgenre is a lot older than you might think, too. As I've noted, alternate history doesn't require a relatively high-tech background. All it requires is the ability to extrapolate from the individual to the wider world, the intuitive leap that lets you see that, just as small things can change individual lives, they can also change wider affairs.

The first person of whom I'm aware who made this leap was the Roman historian Livy, who wrote about the time of Christ. In Book IX, sections 17–19, of his monumental (so monumental that it was frequently abridged and extracted, and does not survive complete) *History of Rome from Its Foundation,* Livy wonders what would have happened if Alexander the Great had turned his attention to the west and attacked the Roman Republic in the late fourth century B.C. With fine Roman patriotism, he tries to show that his countrymen could and would have beaten the Macedonian king. My own opinion is that Livy was an optimist, but that's neither here nor there. He clearly invented the game of alternate history—not a small achievement for a man who has been criticized for the past two thousand years as one who made his history with scissors and paste, taking it all from the works of those who went before him and piecing those works together into a continuous narrative as best he could.

Livy proved to be ahead of his time, as inventors sometimes are. In his case, he was further ahead of his time than most: about eighteen hundred years ahead. Not till the aftermath of Napoleon's downfall did alternate history rear its head again, with several French novelists wondering what might have been had the defeated emperor proved triumphant.

It is not till the twentieth century that most—not all, but most—

alternate history came to be reckoned part of that new and sometimes strange kid on the literary block, science fiction. To this day, some people wonder why this identification was made. I have a couple of reasons to propose. For one thing, people who wrote other forms of science fiction also came to write alternate-history stories. And, for another, alternate history plays by some of the same rules as (other) varieties of science fiction. In many science-fiction stories, the author changes one thing in the present or nearer future, and speculates about what would happen in the more distant future as a result of the change. Alternate history goes down the same road, but from a different starting point. It usually changes one thing in the more distant past and speculates about what would have happened in the nearer past or the present. The relationship seems obvious.

The American Civil War has offered aficionados of the subgenre a playground full of toys ever since a still fell at Appomattox. In fact, many Civil War officers' memoirs read as if they were alternate history, with the authors trying to seize credit for everything that went right anywhere near them and blaming incompetent subordinates and superiors for everything that went wrong. But, as their purpose was to make themselves look good rather than really to examine what might have been, they cannot in fact be included among early alternate historians.

The crowded, chaotic twentieth century saw the true rise of alternate history. Murray Leinster's seminal story, "Sidewise in Time" (after which the Sidewise Award for alternate history is named), introduced this type of story to the science-fiction pulp magazines. But alternate history was also the province of intellectuals on a lark. In 1931, for example, Winston Churchill's essay "If Lee Had Not Won the Battle of Gettysburg" examined the possible consequences of a Northern victory in the Civil War in a world where the South won it—a neat double twist. And, in the second volume of his A Study of History, Arnold Toynbee, in "The Forfeited Birthright of the Abortive Far Western Christian Civilization," postulated a world in which Celtic Christianity had survived along with the Roman variety, and in which the Muslims defeated the Franks at the Battle of Tours in 732.

This latter speculation was later fictionalized by L. Sprague de Camp in his classic novella, "The Wheels of If," which imagined a modern lawyer from our world transported to the twentieth century of that one. That novella, along with de Camp's even more important novel, Lest Darkness Fall, in which an archaeologist is dropped back into the

Rome of the sixth century A.D., and seeks to keep the Dark Ages from descending on Europe by propping up the Ostrogothic Kingdom of Italy against the resurgent Byzantine Empire and by improving technology, finished the job begun by Leinster's story and brought alternate-historical speculation into the orbit of science fiction.

In the years following World War II, a few writers followed de Camp's lead and produced thoughtful alternate histories of their own. H. Beam Piper's Paratime stories and Poul Anderson's tales of the Time Patrol (and, in a different vein, his stories collected in *Operation Chaos*, in which magic reappeared in the world as a technology around the beginning of the twentieth century) stand out among these.

For the centennial of the War Between the States, Pulitzer Prize winner MacKinlay Kantor wrote *If the South Had Won the Civil War*, an optimistic scenario in which the severed parts of our nation reunite in the 1960s. Also coming into prominence during the decades following the end of the Second World War were stories in which the Axis won, which have challenged stories of Confederate victories in the Civil War for popularity. Three of the best of the earlier ones were Sarban's *The Sound of His Horn*, C. M. Kornbluth's great novella, "Two Dooms," and Philip K. Dick's Hugo-winning novel, *The Man in the High Castle*.

In the 1960s, two Englishmen, John Brunner and Keith Roberts, produced stimulating alternate histories on a subject particularly relevant to British hearts: a successful invasion by the Spanish Armada. Brunner's *Times Without Number* examined why travel between different time lines doesn't happen more often, while Roberts' beautiful *Pavane* looked at, among other things, the consequences of slowing down technological growth (strictly speaking, *Pavane* isn't an alternate history, but a first cousin: a recursive future). At about the same time, Keith Laumer, in *Worlds of the Imperium* and its two sequels, did a first-rate job of combining alternate history with fast-moving adventure.

But alternate history really became a more prominent subgenre in the last two decades of the twentieth century. There are a couple of reasons for this. One is that, with our much greater knowledge of the true nature of the solar system, we have found that it looks much less inviting than it did a couple of generations ago. There are no canals on Mars, and no Martians, either; nor are there oceans on Venus full of reptilian monsters. Before the space probes went out, these were scientifically plausible speculations. No more; brute facts have killed such possibilities. Furthermore, more people trained in history have begun writing science fiction, and have naturally gravitated to areas with which they find themselves familiar: S. M. Stirling, with a law degree and an undergraduate degree in history; Susan Shwartz and Judith Tarr, both with doctorates in western medieval studies; and myself, with a doctorate in Byzantine history (a subject I was inspired to study, as I've said, by *Lest Darkness Fall*).

Stirling's Draka universe, commencing with *Marching Through Georgia*, is as thoroughly unpleasant a place as any ever envisioned by an alternate historian, but, especially in *Under the Yoke*, alarmingly convincing as well. His more recent trilogy, beginning with *Island in the Sea of Time*, drops the entire island of Nantucket back to about 1250 B.C. and examines the consequences with fine writing, splendid research, and careful logic.

Shwartz and Tarr have both combined fantasy and alternate history in intriguingly different ways. Shwartz's series that begins with *Byzantium's Crown* looks at a magical medieval world that might have sprung from Cleopatra's victory over Octavian, while Tarr's beautifully written the Hound and the Falcon trilogy and other succeeding books examine what the world might have been like if immortal elves were real rather than mythical.

My own book-length work includes *Agent of Byzantium*, set in a world where Muhammad did not found Islam; *A Different Flesh*, in which *Homo erectus* rather than American Indians populated the New World; *A World of Difference*, which makes the planet in Mars's orbit different enough to support life; the Worldwar series, which imagines an alien invasion in 1942; *The Guns of the South*, in which time-traveling South Africans give Robert E. Lee AK-47s; and *How Few Remain* and the Great War books, which embroil an independent Confederacy and the United States of America in World War I.

In a slightly different vein, Kim Newman has imagined the Victorian age and the early years of this century controlled by vampires in *Anno Dracula* and *The Bloody Red Baron*. The really frightening thing about the latter book is that the World War I he imagines is no bloodier than the one we really had. Newman's entertaining *Back in the USSA* looks at a Red revolution in the United States rather than Russia, with Al Capone in the role of Stalin.

And alternate history has not become the sole province of escaped history buffs. Aerospace engineer Stephen Baxter's *Voyage* looks at a journey to Mars in 1986 that might have happened had John Kennedy not been assassinated. This is hard science fiction at its best, as is Gregory Benford's award-winning *Timescape*, which touches on ecological disaster along with its main theme of communicating across time lines.

Nor has alternate history remained the sole province of science-fiction writers. Spymaster Len Deighton produced *SS-GB*, a chilling account of a Nazi-occupied Britain. And journalist Robert Harris's *Fatherland* became an international best-seller—certainly a breakthrough for alternate history. *Fatherland*, another tale of Germany triumphant, is carefully researched; its principal flaw seems to be a conviction that the discovery of the Holocaust twenty years after the fact would be a world-shaking event rather than a nine days' wonder, if even that.

Several anthologies have also highlighted alternate history in recent years. Gregory Benford edited, with Martin H. Greenberg, *Hitler Victorious* and the four volumes titled *What Might Have Been*, which examined different ways in which the past might have changed. And the prolific Mike Resnick edited and wrote for a series of *Alternate* anthologies, including such titles as *Alternate Kennedys* and *Alternate Tyrants*. Alternate-history stories have found homes in magazines as diverse as *Omni* and *Analog*.

And there is a renewed interest in alternate history outside the confines of science fiction and fantasy. Articles on the topic have appeared in such mainstream publications as *USA Today* and *American Heritage*, and academic alternate histories, the parlor game of the 1930s, are respectable once again. Serious historians have played the game in two collections of essays edited by Kenneth Macksey, *Invasion: The Alternate History of the German Invasion of England, July 1940* and *The Hitler Options: Alternate Decisions of World War II*. Peter Tsouras's recent *Disaster at D-Day: The Germans Defeat the Allies, June 1944* and *Gettysburg: An Alternate History* recall, in their detail and fictional critical apparatus, Robert Sobel's classic *For Want of a Nail*, which imagines a failed American Revolution and the subsequent 180 years of history from the perspective of a college history text.

The stories in this collection, in their quality and their variety, show where the field went during the last century. I have no doubt that, with so many talented writers wondering what might have been, we will continue to see many more fascinating, thought-provoking stories in the century just being born. The purpose of any good fiction, after all, is not to examine the created world alone, but to hold up that created world as a mirror to the reality we all experience. Alternate history gives us a fun-house mirror that lets us look at reality in ways we cannot get from any other type of story. That, to me, is its principal attraction—along with the joys of storytelling. Have fun!

Kim Stanley Robinson

Kim Stanley Robinson's monumental Mars trilogy (Red Mars, Green Mars, Blue Mars)—*a future history of the Red Planet from its colonization through its struggle for independence from Earth—has been hailed a modern classic and acknowledged a landmark of twentieth-century science fiction. Robinson's first published story appeared in 1976, and since that time he has earned the Hugo, Nebula, World Fantasy, and John W. Campbell Memorial Awards for his short fiction and novels. His first novel,* The Wild Shore, *published in 1984, produced two thematic sequels,* The Gold Coast *and* Pacific Edge, *which form the Orange County trilogy, about the future development of the California coast in the aftermath of nuclear holocaust. Robinson's other novels include* The Memory of Whiteness, A Short, Sharp Shock, *and* Antarctica, *the story of a future Antarctica society threatened by ecological saboteurs. His short fiction has been collected in* Escape from Kathmandu, Remaking History, *and* Down and Out in the Year 2000. *His doctoral dissertation has been published as the critically acclaimed* The Novels of Philip K. Dick.

THE LUCKY STRIKE

Kim Stanley Robinson

WAR BREEDS STRANGE PASTIMES. In July of 1945 on Tinian Island in the North Pacific, Captain Frank January had taken to piling pebble cairns on the crown of Mount Lasso — one pebble for each B-29 takeoff, one cairn for each mission. The largest cairn had four hundred stones in it. It was a mindless pastime, but so was poker. The men of the 509th had played a million hands of poker, sitting in the shade of a palm around an upturned crate sweating in their skivvies, swearing and betting all their pay and cigarettes, playing hand after hand after hand, until the cards got so soft and dog-eared you could have used them for toilet paper. Captain January had gotten sick of it, and after he lit out for the hilltop a few times some of his crewmates started trailing him. When their pilot Jim Fitch joined them it became an official pastime, like throwing flares into the compound or going hunting for stray Japs. What Captain January thought of the development he didn't say. The others grouped near Captain Fitch, who passed around his battered flask. "Hey, January," Fitch called. "Come have a shot."

January wandered over and took the flask. Fitch laughed at his pebble. "Practicing your bombing up here, eh, Professor?"

"Yah," January said sullenly. Anyone who read more than the funnies was Professor to Fitch. Thirstily January knocked back some rum. He could drink it any way he pleased up here, out from under the eye of the group psychiatrist. He passed the flask on to Lieutenant Matthews, their navigator.

"That's why he's the best," Matthews joked. "Always practicing."

Fitch laughed. "He's best because I make him be best, right, Professor?"

January frowned. Fitch was a bulky youth, thick-featured, pig-eyed—a thug, in January's opinion. The rest of the crew were all in their mid-twenties like Fitch, and they liked the captain's bossy roughhouse style. January, who was thirty-seven, didn't go for it. He wandered away, back to the cairn he had been building. From Mount Lasso they had an overview of the whole island, from the harbor at Wall Street to the north field in Harlem. January had observed hundreds of B-29s roar off the four parallel runways of the north field and head for Japan. The last quartet of this particular mission buzzed across the width of the island, and January dropped four more pebbles, aiming for crevices in the pile. One of them stuck nicely.

"There they are!" said Matthews. "They're on the taxiing strip."

January located the 509th's first plane. Today, the first of August, there was something more interesting to watch than the usual Super-fortress parade. Word was out that General Le May wanted to take the 509th's mission away from it. Their commander Colonel Tibbets had gone and bitched to Le May in person, and the general had agreed the mission was theirs, but on one condition: one of the general's men was to make a test flight with the 509th, to make sure they were fit for combat over Japan. The general's man had arrived, and now he was down there in the strike plane, with Tibbets and the whole first team. January sidled back to his mates to view the takeoff with them.

"Why don't the strike plane have a name, though?" Haddock was saying.

Fitch said, "Lewis won't give it a name because it's not his plane, and he knows it." The others laughed. Lewis and his crew were naturally un-popular, being Tibbets' favorites.

"What do you think he'll do to the general's man?" Matthews asked.

The others laughed at the very idea. "He'll kill an engine at takeoff, I bet you anything," Fitch said. He pointed at the wrecked B-29s that marked the end of every runway, planes whose engines had given out on takeoff. "He'll want to show that he wouldn't go down if it happened to him."

" 'Course he wouldn't!" Matthews said.

"You hope," January said under his breath.

"They let those Wright engines out too soon," Haddock said seri-ously. "They keep busting under the takeoff load."

"Won't matter to the old bull," Matthews said. Then they all started in about Tibbets' flying ability, even Fitch. They all thought Tibbets was the greatest. January, on the other hand, liked Tibbets even less than he liked Fitch. That had started right after he was assigned to the 509th. He had been told he was part of the most important group in the war, and then given a leave. In Vicksburg a couple of fliers just back from England had bought him a lot of whiskies, and since January had spent several months stationed near London they had talked for a good long time and gotten pretty drunk. The two were really curious about what January was up to now, but he had stayed vague on it and kept returning the talk to the blitz. He had been seeing an English nurse, for instance, whose flat had been bombed, family and neighbors killed. . . . But they had really wanted to know. So he had told them he was onto something special, and they had flipped out their badges and told him they were Army Intelligence, and that if he ever broke security like that again he'd be transferred to Alaska. It was a dirty trick. January had gone back to Wendover and told Tibbets so to his face, and Tibbets had turned red and threatened him some more. January despised him for that. The upshot was that January was effectively out of the war, because Tibbets really played his favorites. January wasn't sure he really minded, but during their year's training he had bombed better than ever, as a way of showing the old bull he was wrong to write January off. Every time their eyes had met it was clear what was going on. But Tibbets never backed off no matter how precise January's bombing got. Just thinking about it was enough to cause January to line up a pebble over an ant and drop it.

"Will you cut that out?" Fitch complained. "I swear you must hang from the ceiling when you take a shit so you can practice aiming for the toilet." The men laughed.

"Don't I bunk over you?" January asked. Then he pointed. "They're going."

Tibbets' plane had taxied to runway Baker. Fitch passed the flask around again. The tropical sun beat on them, and the ocean surrounding the island blazed white. January put up a sweaty hand to aid the bill of his baseball cap.

The four props cut in hard, and the sleek Superfortress quickly trundled up to speed and roared down Baker. Three-quarters of the way down the strip the outside right prop feathered.

"Yow!" Fitch crowed. "I told you he'd do it!"

The plane nosed off the ground and slewed right, then pulled back on course to cheers from the four young men around January. January pointed again. "He's cut number three, too."

The inside right prop feathered, and now the plane was pulled up by the left wing only, while the two right props windmilled uselessly. "Holy smoke!" Haddock cried. "Ain't the old bull something?"

They whooped to see the plane's power, and Tibbets' nervy arrogance.

"By God, Le May's man will remember this flight," Fitch hooted. "Why, look at that! He's banking!"

Apparently taking off on two engines wasn't enough for Tibbets; he banked the plane right until it was standing on its dead wing, and it curved back toward Tinian.

Then the inside left engine feathered.

War tears at the imagination. For three years Frank January had kept his imagination trapped, refusing to give it any play whatsoever. The dangers threatening him, the effects of the bombs, the fate of the other participants in the war, he had refused to think about any of it. But the war tore at his control. That English nurse's flat. The missions over the Ruhr. The bomber just below him blown apart by flak. And then there had been a year in Utah, and the viselike grip that he had once kept on his imagination had slipped away.

So when he saw the number two prop feather, his heart gave a little jump against his sternum and helplessly he was up there with Ferebee, the first team bombardier. He would be looking over the pilots' shoulders. . . .

"Only one engine?" Fitch said.

"That one's for real," January said harshly. Despite himself he *saw* panic in the cockpit, the frantic rush to power the two right engines. The plane was dropping fast and Tibbets leveled it off, leaving them on a course back toward the island. The two right props spun, blurred to a shimmer. January held his breath. They needed more lift; Tibbets was trying to pull it over the island. Maybe he was trying for the short runway on the south half of the island.

But Tinian was too tall, the plane too heavy. It roared right into the jungle above the beach, where 42nd Street met their East River. It exploded in a bloom of fire. By the time the sound of the explosion struck them they knew no one in the plane had survived.

Black smoke towered into white sky. In the shocked silence on Mount Lasso insects buzzed and creaked. The air left January's lungs with a gulp. He had been with Ferebee there at the end, he had heard the desperate shouts, seen the last green rush, been stunned by the dentist-drill-all-over pain of the impact.

"Oh my God," Fitch was saying. "Oh my God." Matthews was sitting. January picked up the flask, tossed it at Fitch.

"C-come on," he stuttered. He hadn't stuttered since he was sixteen. He led the others in a rush down the hill. When they got to Broadway a jeep careened toward them and skidded to a halt. It was Colonel Scholes, the old bull's exec. "What happened?"

Fitch told him.

"Those damned Wrights," Scholes said as the men piled in. This time one had failed at just the wrong moment; some welder stateside had kept flame to metal a second less than usual—or something equally minor, equally trivial—and that had made all the difference.

They left the jeep at 42nd and Broadway and hiked east over a narrow track to the shore. A fairly large circle of trees was burning. The fire trucks were already there.

Scholes stood beside January, his expression bleak. "That was the whole first team," he said.

"I know," said January. He was still in shock, in imagination crushed, incinerated, destroyed. Once as a kid he had tied sheets to his arms and waist, jumped off the roof and landed right on his chest; this felt like that had. He had no way of knowing what would come of this crash, but he had a suspicion that he had indeed smacked into something hard.

Scholes shook his head. A half hour had passed, the fire was nearly out. January's four mates were over chattering with the Seabees. "He was going to name the plane after his mother," Scholes said to the ground. "He told me that just this morning. He was going to call it *Enola Gay*."

AT NIGHT the jungle breathed, and its hot wet breath washed over the 509th's compound. January stood in the doorway of his Quonset barracks hoping for a real breeze. No poker tonight. Voices were hushed, faces solemn. Some of the men had helped box up the dead crew's gear. Now most lay on their bunks. January gave up on the breeze, climbed onto his top bunk to stare at the ceiling.

He observed the corrugated arch over him. Cricketsong sawed through his thoughts. Below him a rapid conversation was being carried on in guilty undertones, Fitch at its center.

"January is the best bombardier left," he said. "And I'm as good as Lewis was."

"But so is Sweeney," Matthews said. "And he's in with Scholes."

They were figuring out who would take over the strike. January scowled. Tibbets and the rest were less than twelve hours dead, and they were squabbling over who would replace them.

January grabbed a shirt, rolled off his bunk, put the shirt on.

"Hey, Professor," Fitch said. "Where you going?"

"Out."

Though midnight was near it was still sweltering. Crickets shut up as he walked by, started again behind him. He lit a cigarette. In the dark the MPs patrolling their fenced-in compound were like pairs of walking armbands. The 509th, prisoners in their own army. Fliers from other groups had taken to throwing rocks over the fence. Forcefully January expelled smoke, as if he could expel his disgust with it. They were only kids, he told himself. Their minds had been shaped in the war, by the war, and for the war. They knew you couldn't mourn the dead for long; carry around a load like that and your own engines might fail. That was all right with January. It was an attitude that Tibbets had helped to form, so it was what he deserved. Tibbets would *want* to be forgotten in favor of the mission, all he had lived for was to drop the gimmick on the Japs, he was oblivious to anything else, men, wife, family, anything.

So it wasn't the lack of feeling in his mates that bothered January. And it was natural of them to want to fly the strike they had been training a year for. Natural, that is, if you were a kid with a mind shaped by fanatics like Tibbets, shaped to take orders and never imagine consequences. But January was not a kid, and he wasn't going to let men like Tibbets do a thing to his mind. And the gimmick . . . the gimmick was not natural. A chemical bomb of some sort, he guessed. Against the Geneva Convention. He stubbed his cigarette against the sole of his sneaker, tossed the butt over the fence. The tropical night breathed over him. He had a headache.

For months now he had been sure he would never fly a strike. The dislike Tibbets and he had exchanged in their looks (January was acutely aware of looks) had been real and strong. Tibbets had understood that January's record of pinpoint accuracy in the runs over the Salton Sea had been a way of showing contempt, a way of saying *you can't get rid of me even though you hate me and I hate you.* The record had forced Tibbets to keep January on one of the four second-string teams, but with the fuss they were making over the gimmick January had figured that would be far enough down the ladder to keep him out of things.

Now he wasn't so sure. Tibbets was dead. He lit another cigarette, found his hand shaking. The Camel tasted bitter. He threw it over the fence at a receding armband, and regretted it instantly. A waste. He went back inside.

Before climbing onto his bunk he got a paperback out of his foot-locker. "Hey, Professor, what you reading now?" Fitch said, grinning.

January showed him the blue cover. *Winter's Tales*, by an Isak Dine-sen. Fitch examined the little wartime edition. "Pretty racy, eh?"

"You bet," January said heavily. "This guy puts sex on every page." He climbed onto his bunk, opened the book. The stories were strange, hard to follow. The voices below bothered him. He concentrated harder.

As a boy on the farm in Arkansas, January had read everything he could lay his hands on. On Saturday afternoons he would race his father down the muddy lane to the mailbox (his father was a reader too), grab the *Saturday Evening Post* and run off to devour every word of it. That meant he had another week with nothing new to read, but he couldn't help it. His favorites were the Hornblower stories, but anything would do. It was a way off the farm, a way into the world. He had become a man who could slip between the covers of a book whenever he chose.

But not on this night.

THE NEXT DAY the chaplain gave a memorial service, and on the morn-ing after that Colonel Scholes looked in the door of their hut right after mess. "Briefing at eleven," he announced. His face was haggard. "Be there early." He looked at Fitch with bloodshot eyes, crooked a finger. "Fitch, January, Matthews—come with me."

January put on his shoes. The rest of the men sat on their bunks and watched them wordlessly. January followed Fitch and Matthews out of the hut.

"I've spent most of the night on the radio with General Le May," Scholes said. He looked them each in the eye. "We've decided you're to be the first crew to make a strike."

Fitch was nodding, as if he had expected it.

"Think you can do it?" Scholes said.

"Of course," Fitch replied. Watching him January understood why they had chosen him to replace Tibbets: Fitch was like the old bull, he had that same ruthlessness. The young bull.

"Yes, sir," Matthews said.

Scholes was looking at him. "Sure," January said, not wanting to think about it. "Sure." His heart was pounding directly on his sternum. But Fitch and Matthews looked serious as owls, so he wasn't going to stick out by looking odd. It was big news, after all; anyone would be taken aback by it. Nevertheless, January made an effort to nod.

"Okay," Scholes said. "McDonald will be flying with you as copilot." Fitch frowned. "I've got to go tell those British officers that Le May doesn't want them on the strike with you. See you at the briefing."

"Yes, sir."

As soon as Scholes was around the corner Fitch swung a fist at the sky. "Yow!" Matthews cried. He and Fitch shook hands. "We did it!" Matthews took January's hand and wrung it, his face plastered with a goofy grin. "We did it!"

"Somebody did it, anyway," January said.

"Ah, Frank," Matthews said. "Show some spunk. You're always so cool."

"Old Professor Stoneface," Fitch said, glancing at January with a trace of amused contempt. "Come on, let's get to the briefing."

The briefing hut, one of the longer Quonsets, was completely surrounded by MPs holding carbines. "Gosh," Matthews said, subdued by the sight. Inside it was already smoky. The walls were covered by the usual maps of Japan. Two blackboards at the front were draped with sheets. Captain Shepard, the naval officer who worked with the scientists on the gimmick, was in back with his assistant Lieutenant Stone, winding a reel of film onto a projector. Dr. Nelson, the group psychiatrist, was already seated on a front bench near the wall. Tibbets had recently sicced the psychiatrist on the group—another one of his great ideas, like the spies in the bar. The man's questions had struck January as stupid. He hadn't even been able to figure out that Easterly was a flake, something that was clear to anybody who flew with him, or even played him in a single round of poker. January slid onto a bench beside his mates.

The two Brits entered, looking furious in their stiff-upper-lip way. They sat on the bench behind January. Sweeney's and Easterly's crews filed in, followed by the other men, and soon the room was full. Fitch and the rest pulled out Lucky Strikes and lit up; since they had named the plane only January had stuck with Camels.

Scholes came in with several men January didn't recognize, and went to the front. The chatter died, and all the smoke plumes ribboned steadily into the air.

Scholes nodded, and two intelligence officers took the sheets off the blackboards, revealing aerial reconnaissance photos.

"Men," Scholes said, "these are the target cities."

Someone cleared his throat.

"In order of priority they are Hiroshima, Kokura, and Nagasaki. There will be three weather scouts: *Straight Flush* to Hiroshima, *Strange Cargo* to Kokura, and *Full House* to Nagasaki. *The Great Artiste* and *Number 91* will be accompanying the mission to take photos. And *Lucky Strike* will fly the bomb."

There were rustles, coughs. Men turned to look at January and his mates, and they all sat up straight. Sweeney stretched back to shake Fitch's hand, and there were some quick laughs. Fitch grinned.

"Now listen up," Scholes went on. "The weapon we are going to deliver was successfully tested stateside a couple of weeks ago. And now we've got orders to drop it on the enemy." He paused to let that sink in. "I'll let Captain Shepard tell you more."

Shepard walked to the blackboard slowly, savoring his entrance. His forehead was shiny with sweat, and January realized he was excited or nervous. He wondered what the psychiatrist would make of that.

"I'm going to come right to the point," Shepard said. "The bomb you are going to drop is something new in history. We think it will knock out everything within four miles."

Now the room was completely still. January noticed that he could see a great deal of his nose, eyebrows, and cheeks; it was as if he were receding back into his body, like a fox into its hole. He kept his gaze rigidly on Shepard, steadfastly ignoring the feeling. Shepard pulled a sheet back over a blackboard while someone else turned down the lights.

"This is a film of the only test we have made," Shepard said. The film started, caught, started again. A wavery cone of bright cigarette smoke speared the length of the room, and on the sheet sprang a dead gray landscape: a lot of sky, a smooth desert floor, hills in the distance. The projector went *click-click-click-click, click-click-click-click.* "The bomb is on top of the tower," Shepard said, and January focused on the pinlike object sticking out of the desert floor, off against the hills. It was between eight and ten miles from the camera, he judged; he had gotten good at calculating distances. He was still distracted by his face.

Click-click-click-click, click—then the screen went white for a second, filling even their room with light. When the picture returned the desert floor was filled with a white bloom of fire. The fireball coalesced and then quite suddenly it leaped off the earth all the way into the *stratosphere,* by God, like a tracer bullet leaving a machine gun, trailing a whitish pillar of smoke behind it. The pillar gushed up and a growing ball of smoke billowed outward, capping the pillar. January calculated the size of the cloud, but was sure he got it wrong. There it stood. The picture flickered, and then the screen went white again, as if the camera had melted or that part of the world had come apart. But the flapping from the projector told them it was the end of the film.

January felt the air suck in and out of his open mouth. The lights came on in the smoky room and for a second he panicked, he struggled to shove his features into an accepted pattern, the psychiatrist would be looking around at them all — and then he glanced around and realized he needn't have worried, that he wasn't alone. Faces were bloodless, eyes were blinky or bug-eyed with shock, mouths hung open or were clamped whitely shut. For a few moments they all had to acknowledge what they were doing. January, scaring himself, felt an urge to say, "Play it again, will you?" Fitch was pulling his curled black hair off his thug's forehead uneasily. Beyond him January saw that one of the Limeys had already reconsidered how mad he was about missing the flight. Now he looked sick. Someone let out a long *whew*, another whistled. January looked to the front again, where the psychiatrist watched them, undisturbed.

Shepard said, "It's big, all right. And no one knows what will happen when it's dropped from the air. But the mushroom cloud you saw will go to at least thirty thousand feet, probably sixty. And the flash you saw at the beginning was hotter than the sun."

Hotter than the sun. More licked lips, hard swallows, readjusted baseball caps. One of the intelligence officers passed out tinted goggles like welder's glasses. January took his and twiddled the opacity dial.

Scholes said, "You're the hottest thing in the armed forces, now. So no talking, even among yourselves." He took a deep breath. "Let's do it the way Colonel Tibbets would have wanted us to. He picked every one of you because you were the best, and now's the time to show he was right. So — so let's make the old man proud."

The briefing was over. Men filed out into the sudden sunlight. Into the heat and glare. Captain Shepard approached Fitch. "Stone and I will be flying with you to take care of the bomb," he said.

Fitch nodded. "Do you know how many strikes we'll fly?"

"As many as it takes to make them quit." Shepard stared hard at all of them. "But it will only take one."

*   *   *

WAR BREEDS STRANGE DREAMS. That night January writhed over his sheets in the hot wet vegetable darkness, in that frightening half sleep when you sometimes know you are dreaming but can do nothing about it, and he dreamed he was walking . . .

. . . *walking through the streets when suddenly the sun swoops down, the sun touches down and everything is instantly darkness and smoke and silence, a deaf roaring. Walls of fire. His head hurts and in the middle of his vision is a bluewhite blur as if God's camera went off in his face. Ah— the sun fell, he thinks. His arm is burned. Blinking is painful. People stumbling by, mouths open, horribly burned—*

He is a priest, he can feel the clerical collar, and the wounded ask him for help. He points to his ears, tries to touch them but can't. Pall of black smoke over everything, the city has fallen into the streets. Ah, it's the end of the world. In a park he finds shade and cleared ground. People crouch under bushes like frightened animals. Where the park meets the river red and black figures crowd into steaming water. A figure gestures from a copse of bamboo. He enters it, finds five or six faceless soldiers huddling. Their eyes have melted, their mouths are holes. Deafness spares him their words. The sighted soldier mimes drinking. The soldiers are thirsty. He nods and goes down to the river in search of a container. Bodies float downstream.

Hours pass as he hunts fruitlessly for a bucket. He pulls people from the rubble. He hears a bird screeching and he realizes that his deafness is the roar of the city burning, a roar like the blood in his ears but he is not deaf, he only thought he was deaf because there are no human cries. The people are suffering in silence. Through the dusky night he stumbles back to the river, pain crashing through his head. In a field men are pulling potatoes out of the ground that have been baked well enough to eat. He shares one with them. At the river everyone is dead—

—and he struggled out of the nightmare drenched in rank sweat, the taste of dirt in his mouth, his stomach knotted with horror. He sat up and the wet rough sheet clung to his skin. His heart felt crushed between lungs desperate for air. The flowery rotting jungle smell filled him and images from the dream flashed before him so vividly that in the dim hut he saw nothing else. He grabbed his cigarettes and jumped off the bunk, hurried out into the compound. Trembling he lit up, started pacing around. For a moment he worried that the idiot psychiatrist might see him, but then he dismissed the idea. Nelson would be asleep. They were all asleep. He shook his head, looked down at his right arm and almost dropped his cigarette—but it was just his stove scar, an old scar, he'd had it most of his life, since the day he'd pulled the frypan off the stove and onto his arm, burning it with oil. He could still remember the round O of fear that his mother's mouth had made as she rushed in to see what was wrong. Just an old burn scar, he thought, let's not go overboard here. He pulled his sleeve down.

For the rest of the night he tried to walk it off, cigarette after cigarette. The dome of the sky lightened until all the compound and the jungle beyond it was visible. He was forced by the light of day to walk back into his hut and lie down as if nothing had happened.

Two days later Scholes ordered them to take one of Le May's men over Rota for a test run. This new lieutenant colonel ordered Fitch not to play with the engines on takeoff. They flew a perfect run. January put the dummy gimmick right on the aiming point just as he had so often in the Salton Sea, and Fitch powered the plane down into the violent bank that started their 150-degree turn and flight for safety. Back on Tinian the lieutenant colonel congratulated them and shook each of their hands. January smiled with the rest, palms cool, heart steady. It was as if his body were a shell, something he could manipulate from without, like a bombsight. He ate well, he chatted as much as he ever had, and when the psychiatrist ran him to earth for some questions he was friendly and seemed open.

"Hello, doc."

"How do you feel about all this, Frank?"

"Just like I always have, sir. Fine."

"Eating well?"

"Better than ever."

"Sleeping well?"

"As well as I can in this humidity. I got used to Utah, I'm afraid." Dr. Nelson laughed. Actually January had hardly slept since his dream. He was afraid of sleep. Couldn't the man see that?

"And how do you feel about being part of the crew chosen to make the first strike?"

"Well, it was the right choice, I reckon. We're the b—the best crew left."

"Do you feel sorry about Tibbets' crew's accident?"

"Yes, sir, I do." You better believe it.

After the jokes and firm handshakes that ended the interview January walked out into the blaze of the tropical noon and lit a cigarette. He allowed himself to feel how much he despised the psychiatrist and his blind profession at the same time he was waving good-bye to the man.

Ounce brain. Why couldn't he have seen? Whatever happened it would be his fault. . . . With a rush of smoke out of him January realized how painfully easy it was to fool someone if you wanted to. All action was no more than a mask that could be perfectly manipulated from somewhere else. And all the while in that somewhere else January lived in a *click-click-click* of film, in the silent roaring of a dream, struggling against images he couldn't dispel. The heat of the tropical sun—ninety-three million miles away, wasn't it?—pulsed painfully on the back of his neck.

As he watched the psychiatrist collar their tail-gunner Kochenski, he thought of walking up to the man and saying *I quit*. I don't want to do this. In imagination he saw the look that would form in the man's eye, in Fitch's eye, in Tibbets' eye, and his mind recoiled from the idea. He felt too much contempt for them. He wouldn't for anything give them a means to despise him, a reason to call him coward. Stubbornly he banished the whole complex of thought. Easier to go along with it.

And so a couple of disjointed days later, just after midnight of August 9th, he found himself preparing for the strike. Around him Fitch and Matthews and Haddock were doing the same. How odd were the every-day motions of getting dressed when you were off to demolish a city, to end a hundred thousand lives! January found himself examining his hands, his boots, the cracks in the linoleum. He put on his survival vest, checked the pockets abstractedly for fishhooks, water kit, first aid package, emergency rations. Then the parachute harness, and his coveralls over it all. Tying his bootlaces took minutes; he couldn't do it when watching his fingers so closely.

"Come on, Professor!" Fitch's voice was tight. "The big day is here."

He followed the others into the night. A cool wind was blowing. The chaplain said a prayer for them. They took jeeps down Broadway to runway Able. *Lucky Strike* stood in a circle of spotlights and men, half of them with cameras, the rest with reporter's pads. They surrounded the crew; it reminded January of a Hollywood premiere. Eventually he escaped up the hatch and into the plane. Others followed. Half an hour passed before Fitch joined them, grinning like a movie star. They started the engines, and January was thankful for their vibrating, thought-smothering roar. They taxied away from the Hollywood scene and January felt relief for a moment until he remembered where they were going. On runway Able the engines pitched up to their twenty-three hundred rpm whine, and looking out the clear windscreen he saw the runway paint-marks move by ever faster. Fitch kept them on the runway till Tinian had run out from under them, then quickly pulled up. They were on their way.

WHEN THEY GOT TO ALTITUDE January climbed past Fitch and McDonald to the bombardier's seat and placed his parachute on it. He leaned back. The roar of the four engines packed around him like cotton batting. He was on the flight, nothing to be done about it now. The heavy vibration was a comfort, he liked the feel of it there in the nose of the plane. A drowsy, sad acceptance hummed through him.

Against his closed eyelids flashed a black eyeless face and he jerked awake, heart racing. He was on the flight, no way out. Now he realized how easy it would have been to get out of it. He could have just said he didn't want to. The simplicity of it appalled him. Who gave a damn what the psychiatrist or Tibbets or anyone else thought, compared to this? Now there was no way out. It was a comfort, in a way. Now he could stop worrying, stop thinking he had any choice.

Sitting there with his knees bracketing the bombsight January dozed, and as he dozed he daydreamed his way out. He could climb the step to Fitch and McDonald and declare he had been secretly promoted to major and ordered to redirect the mission. They were to go to Tokyo and drop the bomb in the bay. The Jap War Cabinet had been told to watch this demonstration of the new weapon, and when they saw that fireball boil the bay and bounce into heaven they'd run and sign surrender papers as fast as they could write, kamikazes or not. They weren't crazy, after all. No need to murder a whole city. It was such a good plan that the generals back home were no doubt changing the mission at this very minute, desperately radioing their instructions to Tinian, only to find out it was too late . . . so that when they returned to Tinian January would become a hero for guessing what the generals really wanted, and for risking all to do it. It would be like one of the Hornblower stories in the *Saturday Evening Post*.

Once again January jerked awake. The drowsy pleasure of the fantasy was replaced with desperate scorn. There wasn't a chance in hell that he could convince Fitch and the rest that he had secret orders superseding theirs. And he couldn't go up there and wave his pistol around and *order* them to drop the bomb in Tokyo Bay, because he was the one who had to actually drop it, and he couldn't be down in front dropping the bomb and up ordering the others around at the same time. Pipe dreams.

Time swept on, slow as a second hand. January's thoughts, however, matched the spin of the props; desperately they cast about, now this way now that, like an animal caught by the leg in a trap. The crew was silent. The clouds below were a white scree on the black ocean. January's knee vibrated against the squat stand of the bombsight. He was the one who had to drop the bomb. No matter where his thoughts lunged they were brought up short by that. He was the one, not Fitch or the crew, not Le May, not the generals and scientists back home, not Truman and his advisors. Truman—suddenly January hated him. Roosevelt would have done it differently. If only Roosevelt had lived! The grief that had filled January when he learned of Roosevelt's death reverberated through him again, more strongly than ever. It was unfair to have worked so hard and then not see the war's end. And FDR would have ended it differently. Back at the start of it all he had declared that civilian centers were never to be bombed, and if he had lived, if, if, if. But he hadn't. And now it was smiling bastard Harry Truman, ordering *him*, Frank January, to drop the sun on two hundred thousand women and children. Once his father had taken him to see the Browns play before twenty thousand, a giant crowd—"I never voted for you," January whispered viciously, and jerked to realize he had spoken aloud. Luckily his microphone was off. But Roosevelt would have done it differently, he *would have*.

The bombsight rose before him, spearing the black sky and blocking some of the hundreds of little cruciform stars. *Lucky Strike* ground on toward Iwo Jima, minute by minute flying four miles closer to their target. January leaned forward and put his face in the cool headrest of the bombsight, hoping that its grasp might hold his thoughts as well as his forehead. It worked surprisingly well.

His earphones crackled and he sat up. "Captain January." It was Shepard. "We're going to arm the bomb now, want to watch?"

"Sure thing." He shook his head, surprised at his own duplicity. Stepping up between the pilots, he moved stiffly to the roomy cabin behind the cockpit. Matthews was at his desk taking a navigational fix on the radio signals from Iwo Jima and Okinawa, and Haddock stood beside him. At the back of the compartment was a small circular hatch, below the larger tunnel leading to the rear of the plane. January opened it, sat down and swung himself feet first through the hole.

The bomb bay was unheated, and the cold air felt good. He stood facing the bomb. Stone was sitting on the floor of the bay; Shepard was laid out under the bomb, reaching into it. On a rubber pad next to Stone were tools, plates, several cylindrical blocks. Shepard pulled back, sat up, sucked a scraped knuckle. He shook his head ruefully: "I don't dare wear gloves with this one."

"I'd be just as happy myself if you didn't let something slip," January joked nervously. The two men laughed.

"Nothing can blow till I change those green wires to the red ones," Stone said.

"Give me the wrench," Shepard said. Stone handed it to him, and he stretched under the bomb again. After some awkward wrenching inside it he lifted out a cylindrical plug. "Breech plug," he said, and set it on the mat.

January found his skin goose-pimpling in the cold air. Stone handed Shepard one of the blocks. Shepard extended under the bomb again. "Red ends toward the breech." "I know." Watching them January was reminded of auto mechanics on the oily floor of a garage, working under a car. He had spent a few years doing that himself, after his family moved to Vicksburg. Hiroshima was a river town. One time a flatbed truck carrying bags of cement powder down Fourth Street hill had lost its brakes and careened into the intersection with the River Road, where despite the driver's efforts to turn it smashed into a passing car. Frank had been out in the yard playing, had heard the crash and saw the cement dust rising. He had been one of the first there. The woman and child in the passenger seat of the Model T had been killed. The woman driving was okay. They were from Chicago. A group of folks subdued the driver of the truck, who kept trying to help at the Model T, though he had a bad cut on his head and was covered with white dust.

"Okay, let's tighten the breech plug." Stone gave Shepard the wrench. "Sixteen turns exactly," Shepard said. He was sweating even in the bay's chill, and he paused to wipe his forehead. "Let's hope we don't get hit by lightning." He put the wrench down and shifted onto his knees, picked up a circular plate. Hubcap, January thought. Stone connected wires, then helped Shepard install two more plates. Good old American know-how, January thought, goose pimples rippling across his skin like cat's paws over water. There was Shepard, a scientist, putting together a bomb like he was an auto mechanic changing oil and plugs. January felt a tight rush of rage at the scientists who had designed the bomb. They had worked on it for over a year down there in New Mexico; had none of them in all that time ever stopped to think what they were doing?

But none of them had to drop it. January turned to hide his face from Shepard, stepped down the bay. The bomb looked like a big long trash can, with fins at one end and little antennae at the other. Just a bomb, he thought, damn it, it's just another bomb.

Shepard stood and patted the bomb gently. "We've got a live one now." Never a thought about what it would do. January hurried by the man, afraid that hatred would crack his shell and give him away. The pistol strapped to his belt caught on the hatchway and he imagined shooting Shepard—shooting Fitch and McDonald and plunging the controls forward so that *Lucky Strike* tilted and spun down into the sea like a spent tracer bullet, like a plane broken by flak, following the arc of all human ambition. Nobody would ever know what had happened to them, and their trash can would be dumped at the bottom of the Pacific where it belonged. He could even shoot everyone and parachute out, and perhaps be rescued by one of the Superdumbos following them. . . .

The thought passed and remembering it January squinted with disgust. But another part of him agreed that it was a possibility. It could be done. It would solve his problem. His fingers explored his holster snap.

"Want some coffee?" Matthews asked.

"Sure," January said, and took his hand from the gun to reach for the cup. He sipped: hot. He watched Matthews and Benton tune the loran equipment. As the beeps came in Matthews took a straightedge and drew lines from Okinawa and Iwo Jima on his map table. He tapped a finger on the intersection. "They've taken the art out of navigation," he said to January. "They might as well stop making the navigator's dome," thumbing up at the little Plexiglas bubble over them.

"Good old American know-how," January said.

Matthews nodded. With two fingers he measured the distance between their position and Iwo Jima. Benton measured with a ruler.

"Rendezvous at five thirty-five, eh?" Matthews said. They were to rendezvous with the two trailing planes over Iwo.

Benton disagreed: "I'd say five-fifty."

"What? Check again, guy, we're not in no tugboat here."

"The wind—"

"Yah, the wind. Frank, you want to add a bet to the pool?"

"Five thirty-six," January said promptly.

They laughed. "See, he's got more confidence in me," Matthews said with a dopey grin.

January recalled his plan to shoot the crew and tip the plane into the sea, and he pursed his lips, repelled. Not for anything would he be able to shoot these men, who, if not friends, were at least companions. They passed for friends. They meant no harm.

Shepard and Stone climbed into the cabin. Matthews offered them coffee. "The gimmick's ready to kick their ass, eh?" Shepard nodded and drank.

January moved forward, past Haddock's console. Another plan that wouldn't work. What to do? All the flight engineer's dials and gauges showed conditions were normal. Maybe he could sabotage something? Cut a line somewhere?

Fitch looked back at him and said, "When are we due over Iwo?"

"Five-forty, Matthews says."

"He better be right."

A thug. In peacetime Fitch would be hanging around a pool table giving the cops trouble. He was perfect for war. Tibbets had chosen his men well—most of them, anyway. Moving back past Haddock, January stopped to stare at the group of men in the navigation cabin. They joked, drank coffee. They were all a bit like Fitch: young toughs, capable and thoughtless. They were having a good time, an adventure. That was January's dominant impression of his companions in the 509th; despite all the bitching and the occasional moments of overmastering fear, they were having a good time. His mind spun forward and he saw what these young men would grow up to be like as clearly as if they stood before him in businessmen's suits, prosperous and balding. They would be tough and capable and thoughtless, and as the years passed and the great war receded in time they would look back on it with ever-increasing nostalgia, for they would be the survivors and not the dead. Every year of this war would feel like ten in their memories, so that the war would always remain the central experience of their lives—a time when history lay palpable in their hands, when each of their daily acts affected it, when moral issues were simple, and others told them what to do—so that as more years passed and the survivors aged, bodies falling apart, lives in one rut or another, they would unconsciously push harder and harder to thrust the world into war again, thinking somewhere inside themselves that if they could only return to world war then they would magically be again as they were in the last one—young, and free, and happy. And by that time they would hold the positions of power, they would be capable of doing it.

So there would be more wars, January saw. He heard it in Matthews' laughter, saw it in their excited eyes. "There's Iwo, and it's five thirty-one. Pay up! I win!" And in future wars they'd have more bombs like the gimmick, hundreds of them no doubt. He saw more planes, more young crews like this one, flying to Moscow no doubt or to wherever, fireballs in every capital, why not? And to what end? To what end? So that the old men could hope to become magically young again. Nothing more sane than that.

They were over Iwo Jima. Three more hours to Japan. Voices from *The Great Artiste* and *Number 91* crackled on the radio. Rendezvous accomplished, the three planes flew northwest, toward Shikoku, the first Japanese island in their path. January went aft to use the toilet. "You okay, Frank?" Matthews asked. "Sure. Terrible coffee, though." "Ain't it always." January tugged at his baseball cap and hurried away. Kochenski and the other gunners were playing poker. When he was done he returned forward. Matthews sat on the stool before his maps, readying his equipment for the constant monitoring of drift that would now be required. Haddock and Benton were also busy at their stations. January maneuvered between the pilots down into the nose. "Good shooting," Matthews called after him.

Forward it seemed quieter. January got settled, put his headphones on and leaned forward to look out the ribbed Plexiglas.

Dawn had turned the whole vault of the sky pink. Slowly the radiant shade shifted through lavender to blue, pulse by pulse a different color. The ocean below was a glittering blue plane, marbled by a pattern of puffy pink cloud. The sky above was a vast dome, darker above than on the horizon. January had always thought that dawn was the time when you could see most clearly how big the earth was, and how high above it they flew. It seemed they flew at the very upper edge of the atmosphere, and January saw how thin it was, how it was just a skin of air really, so that even if you flew up to its top the earth still extended away infinitely in every direction. The coffee had warmed January, he was sweating. Sunlight blinked off the Plexiglas. His watch said six. Plane and hemisphere of blue were split down the middle by the bombsight. His earphones crackled and he listened in to the reports from the lead planes flying over the target cities. Kokura, Nagasaki, Hiroshima, all of them had six-tenths cloud cover. Maybe they would have to cancel the whole mission because of weather. "We'll look at Hiroshima first," Fitch said. January peered down at the fields of miniature clouds with renewed interest. His parachute slipped under him. Readjusting it he imagined putting it on, sneaking back to the central escape hatch under the navigator's cabin, opening the hatch . . . he could be out of the plane and gone before anyone noticed. Leave it up to them. They could bomb or not but it wouldn't be January's doing. He could float down onto the world like a puff of dandelion, feel cool air rush around him, watch the silk canopy dome hang over him like a miniature sky, a private world.

An eyeless black face. January shuddered; it was as though the nightmare could return any time. If he jumped nothing would change, the bomb would still fall—would he feel any better, floating on his Inland Sea? Sure, one part of him shouted; maybe, another conceded; the rest of him saw that face. . . .

Earphones crackled. Shepard said, "Lieutenant Stone has now armed the bomb, and I can tell you all what we are carrying. Aboard with us is the world's first atomic bomb."

Not exactly, January thought. Whistles squeaked in his earphones. The first one went off in New Mexico. Splitting atoms: January had heard the term before. Tremendous energy in every atom, Einstein had said. Break one, and—he had seen the result on film. Shepard was talking about radiation, which brought back more to January. Energy released in the form of X rays. Killed by X rays! It would be against the Geneva Convention if they had thought of it.

Fitch cut in. "When the bomb is dropped Lieutenant Benton will record our reaction to what we see. This recording is being made for history, so watch your language." Watch your language! January choked back a laugh. Don't curse or blaspheme God at the sight of the first atomic bomb incinerating a city and all its inhabitants with X rays!

Six-twenty. January found his hands clenched together on the headrest of the bombsight. He felt as if he had a fever. In the harsh wash of morning light the skin on the backs of his hands appeared slightly translucent. The whorls in the skin looked like the delicate patterning of waves on the sea's surface. His hands were made of atoms. Atoms were the smallest building block of matter, it took billions of them to make those tense, trembling hands. Split one atom and you had the fireball. That meant that the energy contained in even one hand . . . he turned up a palm to look at the lines and the mottled flesh under the transparent skin. A person was a bomb that could blow up the world. January felt that latent power stir in him, pulsing with every hard heart-knock. What beings they were, and in what a blue expanse of a world!— And here they spun on to drop a bomb and kill a hundred thousand of these astonishing beings.

When a fox or raccoon is caught by the leg in a trap, it lunges until the leg is frayed, twisted, perhaps broken, and only then does the animal's pain and exhaustion force it to quit. Now in the same way January wanted to quit. His mind hurt. His plans to escape were so much crap—stupid, useless. Better to quit. He tried to stop thinking, but it was hopeless. How could he stop? As long as he was conscious he would be thinking. The mind struggles longer in its traps than any fox.

Lucky Strike tilted up and began the long climb to bombing altitude. On the horizon the clouds lay over a green island. Japan. Surely it had gotten hotter, the heater must be broken, he thought. Don't think. Every few minutes Matthews gave Fitch small course adjustments. "Two seventy-five, now. That's it." To escape the moment January recalled his childhood. Following a mule and plow. Moving to Vicksburg (rivers). For a while there in Vicksburg, since his stutter made it hard to gain friends, he had played a game with himself. He had passed the time by imagining that everything he did was vitally important and determined the fate of the world. If he crossed a road in front of a certain car, for instance, then the car wouldn't make it through the next intersection before a truck hit it, and so the man driving would be killed and wouldn't be able to invent the flying boat that would save President Wilson from kidnappers—so he had to wait for that car because everything afterward depended on it. Oh damn it, he thought, damn it, think of something *different*. The last Hornblower story he had read—how would *he* get out of this? The round O of his mother's face as she ran in and saw his arm—The Mississippi, mud-brown behind its levees— Abruptly he shook his head, face twisted in frustration and despair, aware at last that no possible avenue of memory would serve as an escape for him now, for now there was no part of his life that did not apply to the situation he was in, and no matter where he cast his mind it was going to shore up against the hour facing him.

Less than an hour. They were at thirty thousand feet, bombing altitude. Fitch gave him altimeter readings to dial into the bombsight. Matthews gave him windspeeds. Sweat got in his eye and he blinked furiously. The sun rose behind them like an atomic bomb, glinting off every corner and edge of the Plexiglas, illuminating his bubble compartment with a fierce glare. Broken plans jumbled together in his mind, his breath was short, his throat dry. Uselessly and repeatedly he damned the scientists, damned Truman. Damned the Japanese for causing the whole mess in the first place, damned yellow killers, they had brought this on themselves. Remember Pearl. American men had died under bombs when no war had been declared; they had started it and now it was coming back to them with a vengeance. And they deserved it. And an invasion of Japan would take years, cost millions of lives—end it now, end it, they deserved it, they deserved it steaming river full of charcoal people silently dying damned stubborn race of maniacs!

"There's Honshu," Fitch said, and January returned to the world of the plane. They were over the Inland Sea. Soon they would pass the secondary target, Kokura, a bit to the south. Seven-thirty. The island was draped more heavily than the sea by clouds, and again January's heart leaped with the idea that weather would cancel the mission. But they did deserve it. It was a mission like any other mission. He had dropped bombs on Africa, Sicily, Italy, all Germany. . . . He leaned forward to take a look through the sight. Under the X of the crosshairs was the sea, but at the lead edge of the sight was land. Honshu. At two hundred and thirty miles an hour that gave them about a half hour to Hiroshima. Maybe less. He wondered if his heart could beat so hard for that long.

Fitch said, "Matthews, I'm giving over guidance to you. Just tell us what to do."

"Bear south two degrees," was all Matthews said. At last their voices had taken on a touch of awareness, even fear.

"January, are you ready?" Fitch asked.

"I'm just waiting," January said. He sat up, so Fitch could see the back of his head. The bombsight stood between his legs. A switch on its side would start the bombing sequence; the bomb would not leave the plane immediately upon the flick of the switch, but would drop after a fifteen-second radio tone warned the following planes. The sight was adjusted accordingly.

"Adjust to a heading of two sixty-five," Matthews said. "We're coming in directly upwind." This was to make any side-drift adjustments for the bomb unnecessary. "January, dial it down to two hundred and thirty-one miles per hour."

"Two thirty-one."

Fitch said, "Everyone but January and Matthews, get your goggles on."

January took the darkened goggles from the floor. One needed to protect one's eyes or they might melt. He put them on, put his forehead on
the headrest. They were in the way. He took them off. When he looked
through the sight again there was land under the crosshairs. He checked
his watch. Eight o'clock. Up and reading the papers, drinking tea.

"Ten minutes to AP," Matthews said. The aiming point was Aioi
Bridge, a T-shaped bridge in the middle of the delta-straddling city.
Easy to recognize.

"There's a lot of cloud down there." Fitch nodded. "Are you going to
be able to see?"

"I won't be sure until we try it," January said.

"We can make another pass and use radar if we need to," Matthews said.

Fitch said, "Don't drop it unless you're sure, January."

"Yes, sir."

Through the sight a grouping of rooftops and gray roads was just
visible between broken clouds. Around it green forest. "All right," Matthews exclaimed, "here we go! Keep it right on this heading, Captain!
January, we'll stay at two thirty-one."

"And same heading," Fitch said. "January, she's all yours. Everyone
make sure your goggles are on. And be ready for the turn."

January's world contracted to the view through the bombsight. A stip-
pled field of cloud and forest. Over a small range of hills and into Hiroshima's watershed. The broad river was mud brown, the land pale
hazy green, the growing network of roads flat gray. Now the tiny rectangular shapes of buildings covered almost all the land, and swimming
into the sight came the city proper, narrow islands thrusting into a dark
blue bay. Under the crosshairs the city moved island by island, cloud by
cloud. January had stopped breathing, his fingers were rigid as stone on
the switch. And there was Aioi Bridge. It slid right under the crosshairs,
a tiny T right in a gap of clouds. January's fingers crushed the switch.
Deliberately he took a breath, held it. Clouds swam under the
crosshairs, then the next island. "Almost there," he said calmly into his
microphone. "Steady." Now that he was committed his heart was humming like the Wrights. He counted to ten. Now flowing under the
crosshairs were clouds alternating with green forest, leaden roads. "I've
turned the switch, but I'm not getting a tone!" he croaked into the mike.
His right hand held the switch firmly in place. Fitch was shouting
something—Matthews' voice cracked across it—"Flipping it b-back

and forth," January shouted, shielding the bombsight with his body from the eyes of the pilots. "But *still*—wait a second—"

He pushed the switch down. A low hum filled his ears. "That's it! It started!"

"But where will it land?" Matthews cried.

"Hold steady!" January shouted.

Lucky Strike shuddered and lofted up ten or twenty feet. January twisted to look down and there was the bomb, flying just below the plane. Then with a wobble it fell away.

The plane banked right and dove so hard that the centrifugal force threw January against the Plexiglas. Several thousand feet lower Fitch leveled it out and they hurtled north.

"Do you see anything?" Fitch cried.

From the tailgun Kochenski gasped "Nothing." January struggled upright. He reached for the welder's goggles, but they were no longer on his head. He couldn't find them. "How long has it been?" he said.

"Thirty seconds," Matthews replied.

January clamped his eyes shut.

The blood in his eyelids lit up red, then white.

On the earphones a clutter of voices: "Oh my God. Oh my God." The plane bounced and tumbled, metallically shrieking. January pressed himself off the Plexiglas. "Nother shockwave!" Kochenski yelled. The plane rocked again, bounced out of control, this is it, January thought, end of the world, I guess that solves my problem.

He opened his eyes and found he could still see. The engines still roared, the props spun. "Those were the shockwaves from the bomb," Fitch called. "We're okay now. Look at that! Will you look at that son-ofabitch go!"

January looked. The cloud layer below had burst apart, and a black column of smoke billowed up from a core of red fire. Already the top of the column was at their height. Exclamations of shock clattered painfully in January's ears. He stared at the fiery base of the cloud, at the scores of fires feeding into it. Suddenly he could see past the cloud, and his fingernails cut into his palms. Through a gap in the clouds he saw it clearly, the delta, the six rivers, there off to the left of the tower of smoke: the city of Hiroshima, untouched.

"We missed!" Kochenski yelled. "We missed it!"

January turned to hide his face from the pilots; on it was a grin like a rictus. He sat back in his seat and let the relief fill him.

Then it was back to it. "God damn it!" Fitch shouted down at him. McDonald was trying to restrain him. "January, get up here!"

"Yes, sir." Now there was a new set of problems.

January stood and turned, legs weak. His right fingertips throbbed painfully. The men were crowded forward to look out the Plexiglas. January looked with them.

The mushroom cloud was forming. It roiled out as if it might continue to extend forever, fed by the inferno and the black stalk below it. It looked about two miles wide, and a half mile tall, and it extended well above the height they flew at, dwarfing their plane entirely. "Do you think we'll all be sterile?" Matthews said.

"I can taste the radiation," McDonald declared. "Can you? It tastes like lead."

Bursts of flame shot up into the cloud from below, giving a purplish tint to the stalk. There it stood: lifelike, malignant, sixty thousand feet tall. One bomb. January shoved past the pilots into the navigation cabin, overwhelmed.

"Should I start recording everyone's reaction, Captain?" asked Benton.

"To hell with that," Fitch said, following January back. But Shepard got there first, descending quickly from the navigation dome. He rushed across the cabin, caught January on the shoulder. "You bastard!" he screamed as January stumbled back. "You lost your nerve, coward!"

January went for Shepard, happy to have a target at last, but Fitch cut in and grabbed him by the collar, pulled him around until they were face to face—

"Is that right?" Fitch cried, as angry as Shepard. "Did you screw up on purpose?"

"No," January grunted, and knocked Fitch's hands away from his neck. He swung and smacked Fitch on the mouth, caught him solid. Fitch staggered back, recovered, and no doubt would have beaten January up, but Matthews and Benton and Stone leaped in and held him back, shouting for order. "Shut up! Shut up!" McDonald screamed from the cockpit, and for a moment it was bedlam, but Fitch let himself be restrained, and soon only McDonald's shouts for quiet were heard. January retreated to between the pilot seats, right hand on his pistol holster.

"The city was in the crosshairs when I flipped the switch," he said. "But the first couple of times I flipped it nothing happened—"

"That's a lie!" Shepard shouted. "There was nothing wrong with the switch, I checked it myself. Besides, the bomb exploded *miles* beyond

Hiroshima, look for yourself! That's *minutes*." He wiped spit from his chin and pointed at January. "You did it."

"You don't know that," January said. But he could see the men had been convinced by Shepard, and he took a step back. "You just get me to a board of inquiry, quick. And leave me alone till then. If you touch me again," glaring venomously at Fitch and then Shepard, "I'll shoot you." He turned and hopped down to his seat, feeling exposed and vulnerable, like a treed raccoon.

"They'll shoot *you* for this," Shepard screamed after him. "Disobeying orders—treason—" Matthews and Stone were shutting him up.

"Let's get out of here," he heard McDonald say. "I can taste the lead, can't you?"

January looked out the Plexiglas. The giant cloud still burned and roiled. One atom . . . Well, they had really done it to that forest. He almost laughed but stopped himself, afraid of hysteria. Through a break in the clouds he got a clear view of Hiroshima for the first time. It lay spread over its islands like a map, unharmed. Well, that was that. The inferno at the base of the mushroom cloud was eight or ten miles around the shore of the bay and a mile or two inland. A certain patch of forest would be gone, destroyed—utterly blasted from the face of the earth. The Japs would be able to go out and investigate the damage. And if they were told it was a demonstration, a warning—and if they acted fast—well, they had their chance. Maybe it would work.

The release of tension made January feel sick. Then he recalled Shepard's words and he knew that whether his plan worked or not he was still in trouble. In trouble! It was worse than that. Bitterly he cursed the Japanese, he even wished for a moment that he *had* dropped it on them. Wearily he let his despair empty him.

A long while later he sat up straight. Once again he was a trapped animal. He began lunging for escape, casting about for plans. One alternative after another. All during the long grim flight home he considered it, mind spinning at the speed of the props and beyond. And when they came down on Tinian he had a plan. It was a long shot, he reckoned, but it was the best he could do.

THE BRIEFING HUT was surrounded by MPs again. January stumbled from the truck with the rest and walked inside. He was more than ever aware of the looks given him, and they were hard, accusatory. He was too tired to care. He hadn't slept in more than thirty-six hours, and had slept very little since the last time he had been in the hut, a week before. Now the room quivered with the lack of engineer vibration to stabilize it, and the silence roared. It was all he could do to hold on to the bare essentials of his plan. The glares of Fitch and Shepard, the hurt incomprehension of Matthews, they had to be thrust out of his focus. Thankfully he lit a cigarette.

In a clamor of question and argument the others described the strike. Then the haggard Scholes and an intelligence officer led them through the bombing run. January's plan made it necessary to hold to his story: ". . . and when the AP was under the crosshairs I pushed down the switch, but got no signal. I flipped it up and down repeatedly until the tone kicked in. At that point there was still fifteen seconds to the release."

"Was there anything that may have caused the tone to start when it did?"

"Not that I noticed immediately, but—"

"It's impossible," Shepard interrupted, face red. "I checked the switch before we flew and there was nothing wrong with it. Besides, the drop occurred over a minute—"

"Captain Shepard," Scholes said. "We'll hear from you presently."

"But he's obviously lying—"

"Captain Shepard! It's not at all obvious. Don't speak unless questioned."

"Anyway," January said, hoping to shift the questions away from the issue of the long delay, "I noticed something about the bomb when it was falling that could explain why it stuck. I need to discuss it with one of the scientists familiar with the bomb's design."

"What was that?" Scholes asked suspiciously.

January hesitated. "There's going to be an inquiry, right?"

Scholes frowned. "This is the inquiry, Captain January. Tell us what you saw."

"But there will be some proceeding beyond this one?"

"It looks like there's going to be a court-martial, yes, Captain."

"That's what I thought. I don't want to talk to anyone but my counsel, and some scientist familiar with the bomb."

"*I'm* a scientist familiar with the bomb," Shepard burst out. "You could tell me if you really had anything, you—"

"I said I need a scientist!" January exclaimed, rising to face the scarlet Shepard across the table. "Not a G-God damned mechanic." Shepard started to shout, others joined in and the room rang with argument.

While Scholes restored order January sat down, and he refused to be drawn out again.

"I'll see you're assigned counsel, and initiate the court-martial," Scholes said, clearly at a loss. "Meanwhile you are under arrest, on suspicion of disobeying orders in combat." January nodded, and Scholes gave him over to the MPs.

"One last thing," January said, fighting exhaustion. "Tell General Le May that if the Japs are told this drop was a warning, it might have the same effect as—"

"I told you!" Shepard shouted. "I told you he did it on purpose!"

Men around Shepard restrained him. But he had convinced most of them, and even Matthews stared at him with surprised anger.

January shook his head wearily. He had the dull feeling that his plan, while it had succeeded so far, was ultimately not a good one. "Just trying to make the best of it." It took all of his remaining will to force his legs to carry him in a dignified manner out of the hut.

His CELL was an empty NCO's office. MPs brought his meals. For the first couple of days he did little but sleep. On the third day he glanced out the office's barred window, and saw a tractor pulling a tarpaulin-draped trolley out of the compound, followed by jeeps filled with MPs. It looked like a military funeral. January rushed to the door and banged on it until one of the young MPs came.

"What's that they're doing out there?" January demanded.

Eyes cold and mouth twisted, the MP said, "They're making another strike. They're going to do it right this time."

"No!" January cried. "No!" He rushed the MP, who knocked him back and locked the door. "*No!*" He beat the door until his hands hurt, cursing wildly. "You don't *need* to do it, it isn't *necessary.*" Shell shattered at last, he collapsed on the bed and wept. Now everything he had done would be rendered meaningless. He had sacrificed himself for nothing.

A day or two after that the MPs led in a colonel, an iron-haired man who stood stiffly and crushed January's hand when he shook it. His eyes were a pale, icy blue.

"I am Colonel Dray," he said. "I have been ordered to defend you in court-martial." January could feel the dislike pouring from the man. "To do that I'm going to need every fact you have, so let's get started."

"I'm not talking to anybody until I've seen an atomic scientist."

"I am your *defense* counsel—"

"I don't care who you are," January said. "Your defense of me depends on you getting one of the scientists *here*. The higher up he is, the better. And I want to speak to him alone."

"I will have to be present."

So he would do it. But now January's lawyer, too, was an enemy.

"Naturally," January said. "You're my lawyer. But no one else. Our atomic secrecy may depend on it."

"You saw evidence of sabotage?"

"Not one word more until that scientist is here."

Angrily the colonel nodded and left.

Late the next day the colonel returned with another man. "This is Dr. Forest."

"I helped develop the bomb," Forest said. He had a crew cut and dressed in fatigues, and to January he looked more Army than the colonel. Suspiciously he stared back and forth at the two men.

"You'll vouch for this man's identity on your word as an officer?" he asked Dray.

"Of course," the colonel said stiffly, offended.

"So," Dr. Forest said. "You had some trouble getting it off when you wanted to. Tell me what you saw."

"I saw nothing," January said harshly. He took a deep breath; it was time to commit himself. "I want you to take a message back to the scientists. You folks have been working on this thing for years, and you must have had time to consider how the bomb should have been used. You know we could have convinced the Japs to surrender by showing them a demonstration—"

"Wait a minute," Forest said. "You're saying you didn't see anything? There wasn't a malfunction?"

"That's right," January said, and cleared his throat. "It wasn't *necessary*, do you understand?"

Forest was looking at Colonel Dray. Dray gave him a disgusted shrug. "He told me he saw evidence of sabotage."

"I want you to go back and ask the scientists to intercede for me," January said, raising his voice to get the man's attention. "I haven't got a chance in that court-martial. But if the scientists defend me then maybe they'll let me live, see? I don't want to get shot for doing something every one of you scientists would have done."

Dr. Forest had backed away. Color rising, he said, "What makes you think that's what we would have done? Don't you think we considered it? Don't you think men better qualified than you made the decision?" He waved a hand. "God damn it—what made you think you were competent to decide something as important as that!"

January was appalled at the man's reaction; in his plan it had gone differently. Angrily he jabbed a finger at Forest. "Because *I* was the man doing it, *Doctor* Forest. You take even one step back from that and suddenly you can pretend it's not your doing. Fine for you, but *I was there.*"

At every word the man's color was rising. It looked like he might pop a vein in his neck. January tried once more. "Have you ever tried to imagine what one of your bombs would do to a city full of people?"

"I've had enough!" the man exploded. He turned to Dray. "I'm under no obligation to keep what I've heard here confidential. You can be sure it will be used as evidence in Captain January's court-martial." He turned and gave January a look of such blazing hatred that January understood it. For these men to admit he was right would mean admitting that they were wrong—that every one of them was responsible for his part in the construction of the weapon January had refused to use. Understanding that, January knew he was doomed.

The bang of Dr. Forest's departure still shook the little office. January sat on his cot, got out a smoke. Under Colonel Dray's cold gaze he lit one shakily, took a drag. He looked up at the colonel, shrugged. "It was my best chance," he explained. That did something—for the first and only time the cold disdain in the colonel's eyes shifted to a little, hard, lawyerly gleam of respect.

The court-martial lasted two days. The verdict was guilty of disobeying orders in combat and of giving aid and comfort to the enemy. The sentence was death by firing squad.

For most of his remaining days January rarely spoke, drawing ever further behind the mask that had hidden him for so long. A clergyman came to see him, but it was the 509th's chaplain, the one who had said the prayer blessing the *Lucky Strike*'s mission before they took off. Angrily January sent him packing.

Later, however, a young Catholic priest dropped by. His name was Patrick Getty. He was a little pudgy man, bespectacled and, it seemed, somewhat afraid of January. January let the man talk to him. When he returned the next day January talked back a bit, and on the day after that he talked some more. It became a habit.

Usually January talked about his childhood. He talked of plowing mucky black bottom land behind a mule. Of running down the lane to the mailbox. Of reading books by the light of the moon after he had been ordered to sleep, and of being beaten by his mother for it with a high-heeled shoe. He told the priest the story of the time his arm had been burnt, and about the car crash at the bottom of Fourth Street. "It's the truck driver's face I remember, do you see, Father?"

"Yes," the young priest said. "Yes."

And he told him about the game he had played in which every action he took tipped the balance of world affairs. "When I remembered that game I thought it was dumb. Step on a sidewalk crack and cause an earthquake—you know, it's stupid. Kids are like that." The priest nodded. "But now I've been thinking that if everybody were to live their whole lives like that, thinking that every move they made really was important, then . . . it might make a difference." He waved a hand vaguely, expelled cigarette smoke. "You're accountable for what you do."

"Yes," the priest said. "Yes, you are."

"And if you're given orders to do something wrong, you're still accountable, right? The orders don't change it."

"That's right."

"Hmph." January smoked a while. "So they say, anyway. But look what happens." He waved at the office. "I'm like the guy in a story I read—he thought everything in books was true, and after reading a bunch of westerns he tried to rob a train. They tossed him in jail." He laughed shortly. "Books are full of crap."

"Not all of them," the priest said. "Besides, you weren't trying to rob a train."

They laughed at the notion. "Did you read that story?"

"No."

"It was the strangest book—there were two stories in it, and they alternated chapter by chapter, but they didn't have a thing to do with each other! I didn't get it."

". . . Maybe the writer was trying to say that everything connects to everything else."

"Maybe. But it's a funny way to say it."

"I like it."

And so they passed the time, talking.

So IT WAS the priest who was the one to come by and tell January that his request for a Presidential pardon had been refused. Getty said awkwardly, "It seems the President approves the sentence."

"That bastard," January said weakly. He sat on his cot.

Time passed. It was another hot, humid day.

"Well," the priest said. "Let me give you some better news. Given your situation I don't think telling you matters, though I've been told not to. The second mission—you know there was a second strike?"

"Yes."

"Well, they missed too."

"What?" January cried, and bounced to his feet. "You're kidding!"

"No. They flew to Kokura, but found it covered by clouds. It was the same over Nagasaki and Hiroshima, so they flew back to Kokura and tried to drop the bomb using radar to guide it, but apparently there was a—a genuine equipment failure this time, and the bomb fell on an island."

January was hopping up and down, mouth hanging open, "So we n-never—"

"We never dropped an atom bomb on a Japanese city. That's right." Getty grinned. "And get this—I heard this from my superior—they sent a message to the Japanese government telling them that the two explosions were warnings, and that if they didn't surrender by September first we would drop bombs on Kyoto and Tokyo, and then wherever else we had to. Word is that the Emperor went to Hiroshima to survey the damage, and when he saw it he ordered the Cabinet to surrender. So . . ."

"So it worked," January said. He hopped around, "It worked, it worked!"

"Yes."

"Just like I said it would!" he cried, and hopping before the priest he laughed.

Getty was jumping around a little too, and the sight of the priest bouncing was too much for January. He sat on his cot and laughed till the tears ran down his cheeks.

"So—" he sobered quickly. "So Truman's going to shoot me anyway, eh?"

"Yes," the priest said unhappily. "I guess that's right."

This time January's laugh was bitter. "He's a bastard, all right. And proud of being a bastard, which makes it worse." He shook his head. "If Roosevelt had lived . . ."

"It would have been different," Getty finished. "Yes. Maybe so. But he didn't." He sat beside January. "Cigarette?" He held out a pack, and January noticed the white wartime wrapper. He frowned.

"Oh. Sorry."

"Oh well. That's all right." January took one of the Lucky Strikes, lit up. "That's awfully good news." He breathed out. "I never believed Truman would pardon me anyway, so mostly you've brought good news. Ha. They *missed*. You have no idea how much better that makes me feel."

"I think I do."

January smoked the cigarette.

". . . So I'm a good American after all. I *am* a good American," he insisted, "no matter what Truman says."

"Yes," Getty replied, and coughed. "You're better than Truman any day."

"Better watch what you say, Father." He looked into the eyes behind the glasses, and the expression he saw there gave him pause. Since the drop every look directed at him had been filled with contempt. He'd seen it so often during the court-martial that he'd learned to stop looking; and now he had to teach himself to see again. The priest looked at him as if he were . . . as if he were some kind of hero. That wasn't exactly right. But seeing it . . .

January would not live to see the years that followed, so he would never know what came of his action. He had given up casting his mind forward and imagining possibilities, because there was no point to it. His planning was ended. In any case he would not have been able to imagine the course of the post-war years. That the world would quickly become an armed camp pitched on the edge of atomic war, he might have predicted. But he never would have guessed that so many people would join a January Society. He would never know of the effect the Society had on Dewey during the Korean crisis, never know of the Society's successful campaign for the test ban treaty, and never learn that thanks in part to the Society and its allies, a treaty would be signed by the great powers that would reduce the number of atomic bombs year by year, until there were none left.

Frank January would never know any of that. But in that moment on his cot looking into the eyes of young Patrick Getty, he guessed an inkling of it—he felt, just for an instant, the impact on history.

And with that he relaxed. In his last week everyone who met him carried away the same impression, that of a calm, quiet man, angry at Truman and others, but in a withdrawn, matter-of-fact way. Patrick Getty, a strong force in the January Society ever after, said January was talkative for some time after he learned of the missed attack on Kokura. Then he became quieter and quieter, as the day approached. On the morning that they woke him at dawn to march him out to a hastily constructed execution shed, his MPs shook his hand. The priest was with him as he smoked a final cigarette, and they prepared to put the hood over his head. January looked at him calmly. "They load one of the guns with a blank cartridge, right?"

"Yes," Getty said.

"So each man in the squad can imagine he may not have shot me?"

"Yes. That's right."

A tight, unhumorous smile was January's last expression. He threw down the cigarette, ground it out, poked the priest in the arm. "But I *know*." Then the mask slipped back into place for good, making the hood redundant, and with a firm step January went to the wall. One might have said he was at peace.

Nicholas A. DiChario

A prolific writer of short fiction, Nicholas A. DiChario has published more than two dozen stories in the past decade. His short fiction, some of it written in collaboration with Mike Resnick, has appeared in The Magazine of Fantasy and Science Fiction, Starshore, *and* Science Fiction Age, *and been anthologized in* The Ultimate Alien, Universe Three, Witch Fantastic, Christmas Ghosts, *and numerous other anthologies. DiChario's special interest in alternate history is on display in his contributions to* Alternate Tyrants, Alternate Warriors, *and* The Way It Wasn't. *"The Winterberry," which appeared in the anthology* Alternate Kennedys, *was selected for inclusion in the Writers of the Future series.*

THE WINTERBERRY

Nicholas A. DiChario

MAY, 1971

IT WAS UNCLE TEDDY who taught me how to read and write. I think it took a long time but I'm not sure. I heard him arguing with Mother about it one night a few years ago when I wasn't supposed to be out of my room, but I was very excited with the next day being my birthday and I couldn't sleep.

"He can do it," Uncle Teddy had said.

And Mother said, "He doesn't care whether he reads or writes. It's you who cares. Why do you torture yourself? Let him be."

"He's fifty-four years old," Uncle Teddy said.

"*Let him be!*" Mother sounded very angry.

I listened to Uncle Teddy walk across the room. "If you feel that way," he said, "why didn't you just let him die?"

There was a long silence before Mother said, "I don't know," and another long silence after that.

Something in their voices frightened me so I returned to my room. I became very ill, and for several weeks Dr. Armbruster came to see me every day but he wouldn't let anyone else come in because he said I was too weak to have visitors.

But sometime after, when I was much better, Uncle Teddy came to visit and he brought a picture book with him which made me remember his talk with Mother. I'm glad Uncle Teddy got his way because now I read and write a lot even though I throw most of my writing away. I hide some of it though and keep it just for myself, and it's not because I'm being sneaky, it's more because some of the things I write are my own personal secrets and I don't want to tell anyone, just like people don't want to tell me things sometimes when I ask them questions.

DECEMBER, 1977

I am very excited about Christmas almost being here. I am looking forward to Uncle Teddy's stay because he always has something fun in mind. Yesterday after he arrived he walked me through the house and showed me all of the decorations—wreaths and flowers and a huge Christmas tree near the front hall, strung with tinsel and candles. He brought with him several boxes full of gifts, all shapes and sizes, wrapped in bright colors—red and green and blue and silver with bows and ribbons—and I knew they were all for me because he put them under my tree upstairs.

Our house is very large. Mother calls it a mansion. She doesn't allow me to go anywhere except the room on my floor. She says I have everything I need right here.

That's why sometimes at night I'll walk around when everything is dark and everyone is asleep or in their rooms for the night. I don't think I'm being sneaky, it's just that I am very curious and if I ask about things no one tells me what I want to know. I've come to know this house very well. There are many hidden passageways behind the walls and I know them all by heart. I will hear things every once in a while that mother would not like me to hear.

There was a big happening in the house last night and the servants were very busy, although it did not look to be a planned thing because everyone appeared disorganized and Mother didn't come to lock me in my room.

I went through one of my passageways that led to the main entrance of the house and I peeked through a tiny opening in the wall and saw a very beautiful woman with dark hair standing inside the door. She was so beautiful that I held my breath. It must have been very cold outside because she was wearing a long black winter coat and there were flakes of snow on her hair. When she spoke, it was the most soft and delicate voice I had ever heard. She said, "Merry Christmas."

I wanted to stay and watch the woman forever but I knew that Mother would be up to check on me so I ran back to my room and pretended to be asleep. Mother came in and kissed my head and said,

"Sleep well, child," like she did every night. I listened very closely for a long time hoping to hear the voice of the woman again, but next thing I knew it was morning, and she was gone.

OCTOBER, 1982

I heard Mother and Dr. Armbruster arguing yesterday. They were just talking pleasantly for a while and I was listening in my passageway to the low, pleasant sound of their voices. The doctor was saying things I did not understand about sickness and diets and so on, when all of a sudden he said, "But John is doing fine," and Mother just about exploded with anger.

"His name is not John, do you understand me? Don't you ever call him by that name again! John is dead! *My* John is dead!" I had never heard Mother get so angry except for that one time with Uncle Teddy. She made the doctor leave right away and told him he could be replaced, but I hoped that she wouldn't do that because I sort of liked Dr. Armbruster.

I don't know who John is, but I felt very bad for Mother. I had never really thought about my own name before. Uncle Teddy and everyone calls me Sonny because it's short for Sonny Boy, and that's good enough for me. But it made me wonder how someone could get a name like John. Uncle Teddy was probably named after a teddy bear. Mother was just Mother.

MAY, 1987

Today was a very special day. It was my seventieth birthday. Uncle Teddy came to visit and I was very excited because I hadn't seen him in such a long time. We had a big cake and a lot of food and we played checkers for an hour. Then Uncle Teddy took me outside for a walk!

I'll never forget it as long as I live. I think Mother was not happy about it because she did not want to let me go at first, but Uncle Teddy talked her into it and we went outside surrounded by men in black suits and ties and shoes. Uncle Teddy asked me if I minded if his friends went with us, and of course I didn't care. They came to my party and they had a right to have fun. In fact, I told them that if they smiled more they might have a nicer time all around, but Uncle Teddy said they were usually very serious people and were happy that way.

It was a sunny day. The wind blew in my face and stung my eyes at first, but it felt good. Uncle Teddy took me all around the yard and into the garden where I smelled the roses and touched the bushes and the vines. I listened to the birds calling and the insects buzzing. I never dreamed they would sound so loud and so near.

I touched the winterberry hollies which were very special to me because I could always see their bright red berries from my window, even during the cold cold winters.

After a short time I caught a chill and had to go inside, and I was weak for the rest of the day. But I didn't care—I had such fun! I'll always remember it.

AUGUST, 1996

One night I entered a storage room through my passageway where there were a lot of tools and brooms and rags and buckets and things. I rummaged around in the dark and my hands found a flashlight. I thought this would be a wonderful thing to have so I took it with me hoping that no one would miss it. Now I can sit in bed at night and read and write as long as I like and not have to worry about someone seeing my light.

I have not seen Mother in a very long time. I wondered if she was angry with me even though I didn't think she knew about my passageways or my late-night writing. Mother would have yelled at me if she knew.

I've been seeing more and more of Uncle Teddy, so I asked him about Mother today and he said that she went away on a very long trip and I wouldn't be seeing her for a while.

I asked him how long that might be and he said not long, he said soon we'd all be seeing her and then maybe we'd find out whether we did the right thing, whether the choices we'd made over the years had been the proper ones. He looked very sad when he said this, and then he said, "I think there is such a place, Sonny Boy, a place where we learn why everything is the way it is."

I asked him if Dr. Armbruster had gone with Mother since I hadn't seen him in so long and I was seeing Dr. Morelande almost every day now, and Uncle Teddy told me yes.

I thought about how lucky Mother was to visit this place, a place where every time you asked a question you got an answer, and I could not blame her if she didn't want to come back for a while. I told Uncle Teddy so, and he seemed to cheer up. We played cards for the rest of the afternoon.

MAY, 1997

Today was my eightieth birthday. I have been very sick and I was afraid that I might not be able to have my party, but Dr. Morelande said it was OK so we had cake and games with Uncle Teddy and I had a very nice time even though I had to stay in bed.

It was after my party that I had a scare. I was very weak, and I probably should have just gone to sleep, but being so excited all day and not being allowed to get up, I turned restless after dark, so I decided to take a short walk through my passageways.

I followed a path that led to the back of a closet in Uncle Teddy's room, and I saw some light coming through the darkness so I went up to it. That's all I was going to do—peek and go away—until I saw Uncle Teddy crying. I'd never seen Uncle Teddy cry before. He was in bed. He had a large, green book on his lap, and every so often he would turn a page and cry some more.

I watched him for a while, waiting for him to be all right, but he didn't stop crying and I couldn't stand to watch him any longer, so I did a foolish thing and I entered his room through the closet.

"Sonny Boy," he said, "what are you doing here?"

I thought he might be angry with me so I wanted to say that I saw him crying, and that I only wanted to help him and be a friend, but before I could say anything he said, "So you know about the passages," and he didn't seem to be upset at all.

"Come over here, Sonny," he said.

I went and sat on the edge of his bed. He was looking at a photo album. Mother had shown me some photo albums years ago, and I thought they were interesting and we had a lot of fun even though I didn't recognize any of the faces. I don't ever remember crying over them. But Uncle Teddy's album was different. There were newspaper pictures, and headlines, and articles.

Uncle Teddy was looking at a picture of a man and a woman. The man seemed very serious-looking, and his right hand was raised like an Indian chief's, but he had on a suit and tie and no headdress. The man's eyes were closed.

The woman had short black hair with long bangs, and she was looking down.

And then all of a sudden I just about screamed. I knew that woman. I remembered her from . . . from somewhere.

Uncle Teddy said, "You know her, don't you? Think, Sonny Boy, think very hard. What do you remember?"

I did think very hard, and then I remembered where I had seen her. She was the beautiful black-haired woman I had seen at Christmastime in the main entrance of the house years ago.

But then there was more. As I looked at the woman in the picture something very strange came into my head. I had a passing thought of this same woman in a pretty white gown, with a white veil over her face. It was just a piece of a thought that I could not keep in my mind for very long, but I'll never forget it. I reached out and touched the picture.

"Always grand," Uncle Teddy said. "She was wearing a very dignified, raspberry-colored suit that day."

But that's not what I had seen. I had seen the white gown. I had seen something that happened before my room and my house and my passageways and Mother and Uncle Teddy. Was there anything before them? Yes, I think there was. It was more than a passing thought—it was a *memory*.

"Was I married, Uncle Teddy?" I asked him.

He smiled. "Yes, you were. You proposed to her by telegram, you know, from Paris."

I thought this was interesting, but nothing more than that. Uncle Teddy started to cry again.

"Please, don't cry," I said.

He held my hand then. "I'm sorry we couldn't tell her you were alive. We couldn't tell your children, not anyone, not even Father because we couldn't be sure of his reaction. Mother was adamant about that. No one could know. Just Bobby and Mother and myself—and the doctors, of course. Now there's just me.

"It was for the good of the country. Those were critical times. The eyes of the world were watching us. We could not afford hesitancy. We felt you would have wanted it that way. Do you understand?"

I didn't, but I nodded anyway to stop Uncle Teddy from crying. He was clutching my arm very hard.

He traced the newspaper picture with his finger. "She was a strong woman, Sonny Boy. You would have been proud of her. I remember her standing right next to Lyndon, solid as a rock, little more than an hour after you were pronounced dead."

I was very confused about Uncle Teddy calling me dead, and about what the woman in the picture had to do with any of it, so I closed the book and placed it on the floor. I remembered what Mother used to do to make me feel better, so I thought that maybe the same thing might help Uncle Teddy feel better too.

I pulled his bed covers up to his chin, brushed back his hair, kissed him on the forehead, and turned out his light. "Sleep well, child," I said, and then I went back to my room. I was sure Uncle Teddy would be just fine in the morning. It had always worked for me.

DECEMBER, 2008

Dr. Morelande is the only one who comes to see me anymore. He says that Uncle Teddy is so busy he can't find time to stop by. But I don't think that's exactly true. I think Uncle Teddy went on vacation with Mother and Dr. Armbruster, and he is having so much fun that he is not coming back at all.

Dr. Morelande has tried very hard to make this a good Christmas, but I am sorry to say I am not very happy. I am tired all of the time, and I can't even move out of bed. Dr. Morelande asked me if I wanted anything for Christmas, but if I couldn't have Mother or Uncle Teddy, then there was nothing to ask for.

But then I thought about it and thought about it for a long time, and I remembered the pictures Uncle Teddy had shown me many years ago. I told Dr. Morelande about the green photo album in Uncle Teddy's room and asked him if he could find it for me. A little while later Dr. Morelande returned with the book.

Together we went through the pictures, and when we got to the one Uncle Teddy had shown me, the one with the man and the beautiful dark-haired woman, I made him stop.

"There *is* something I want for Christmas," I told him. "There is something I want very much."

I decided to tell Dr. Morelande about the passageways then. I didn't think that I would get in trouble. I made him put me in my wheelchair and take me for a walk behind the walls. He argued with me at first, but I refused to be put off.

I told him exactly which path to follow. He wheeled me all the way down to the wall at the main entrance. I looked through the small opening. I was sure that the beautiful dark-haired woman would be standing at the door in her winter coat. I was disappointed that she wasn't there. I thought that if I waited long enough she would certainly show up—she would come back like the winterberry, bright and strong even in the cold cold winter. There would be snowflakes in her hair, and she would say "Merry Christmas" in her lovely voice. So we waited.

Finally Dr. Morelande said that if I agreed to go to bed, he would wait for the woman, and bring her directly to me as soon as she arrived. I thought that this would be a good idea since I was so tired.

When she arrives, we will have many things to discuss. I have decided to make her my new friend. I think I will show her my book of writings. I think I will ask her about the white gown to show her that I have not forgotten, and then I'll ask her about the children Uncle Teddy mentioned. I won't tell her about the vacation place where everyone has gone without me, and not because I'm being sneaky, but only because I am very lonely and I would like her to stay with me for a while.

Harry Turtledove .

Harry Turtledove first came to prominence as a writer of alternate world fantasy with The Misplaced Legion, *the first volume in his multibook Videssos series of novels about the experiences of a Roman Legion translated to a world that runs on magic. Since then, he has explored the impact of altered historical events in a variety of works, including* Agent of Byzantium, *set in medieval times, the acclaimed* Guns of the South, *in which time travelers manipulate a southern victory in the American Civil War, and the first two volumes of* The Great War *saga,* American Front *and* Walk in Hell, *which envisions an America in which the United States and the Confederacy support opposing sides in World War I. His ambitious* Worldwar *series—which includes* In the Balance, Tilting the Balance, Striking the Balance, *and* Upsetting the Balance—*projects an alternate World War II in which an alien invasion forges alliances between Axis and Allied opponents. Turtledove has also co-edited the anthology* Alternate Generals. *His many other works include the short-fiction collection* Departures, *the comic fantasy* The Case of the Toxic Spell Dump, *and the linked novels* Into the Darkness *and* Darkness Descending, *epic tales of empire building set in a fantasy world where cataclysmic wars are fought with magic.*

ISLANDS IN THE SEA

Harry Turtledove

INTRODUCTION

Islam exploded out of Arabia in the seventh century. The triumphant armies of the caliphs overthrew the Persian Empire and took Syria, Palestine, Egypt, and North Africa from the East Roman or Byzantine Empire. Muslim forces twice besieged Constantinople, in 674–78 and 717–18. In our history, the Byzantine capital held and the Byzantine Empire survived as Christianity's eastern bulwark, holding Islam out of Anatolia and the Balkans for centuries to come and converting the Bulgars and Russians to faith in Christ. But what if the Empire had fallen in the eighth century instead of the fifteenth? The still-pagan folk to the north of Constantinople would have had new choices to make. . . .

A.H. 152 (A.D. 769)

The Bulgar border guards had arrows nocked and ready as the Arab horsemen rode up from the south. Jalal ad-Din as-Stambuli, the leader of the Arab delegation, raised his right hand to show it was empty. "In the name of Allah, the Compassionate, the Merciful, I and my men come in peace," he called in Arabic. To be sure the guards understood, he repeated himself in Greek.

The precaution paid off. The guards lowered their bows. In Greek much worse than Jalal ad-Din's, one of them asked, "Why for you come in peace, whitebeard?"

Jalal ad-Din stroked his whiskers. Even without the Bulgar's mockery, he knew they were white. Not many men who had the right to style themselves *as-Stambuli*, the Constantinopolitan, still lived. More than fifty years had passed since the army of Suleiman and Maslama had taken Constantinople and put an end to the Roman Empire. Then Jalal ad-Din's beard had not been white. Then he could hardly raise a beard at all.

He spoke in Greek again: "My master the caliph Abd ar-Rahman asked last year if your khan Telerikh would care to learn more of Islam, of submission to the one God. This past spring Telerikh sent word that he would. We are the embassy sent to instruct him."

The Bulgar who had talked with him now used his own hissing language, Jalal ad-Din supposed to translate for his comrades. They answered back, some of them anything but happily. Content in their paganism, Jalal ad-Din guessed—content to burn in hell forever. He did not wish that fate on anyone, even a Bulgar.

The guard who knew Greek confirmed his thought, saying, "Why for we want your god? Gods, spirits, ghosts good to us now."

Jalal ad-Din shrugged. "Your khan asked to hear more of Allah and Islam. That is why we are here." He could have said much more, but deliberately spoke in terms a soldier would understand.

"Telerikh want, Telerikh get," the guard agreed. He spoke again with his countrymen, at length pointed at two of them. "This Iskur. This Omurtag. They take you to Pliska, to where Telerikh is. Iskur, him know Greek a little, not so good like me."

"Know little your tongue too," Iskur said in halting Arabic, which surprised Jalal ad-Din and, evidently, the Bulgar who had been doing all the talking till now. The prospective guide glanced at the sun, which was a couple of hours from setting. "We ride," he declared, and started off with no more fanfare than that. The Bulgar called Omurtag followed.

So, more slowly, did Jalal ad-Din and his companions. By the time Iskur called a halt in deepening twilight, the mountains that made the northern horizon jagged were visibly closer.

"Those little ponies the Bulgars ride are ugly as mules, but they go and go and go," said Da'ud ibn Zubayr, who was a veteran of many skirmishes on the border between the caliph's land and Bulgaria. He stroked the mane of his elegant, Arab-bred mare.

"Sadly, my old bones do not." Jalal ad-Din groaned with relief as he slid off his own horse, a soft-gaited gelding. Once he had delighted in fiery stallions, but he knew that if he took a fall now he would shatter like glass.

The Bulgars stalked into the brush to hunt. Da'ud bent to the laborious business of getting a fire going. The other two Arabs, Malik ibn Anas and Salman al-Tabari, stood guard, one with a bow, the other with a spear. Iskur and Omurtag emerged into firelight carrying partridges and rabbits. Jalal ad-Din took hard unleavened bread from a saddlebag: no feast tonight, he thought, but not the worst of fare either.

Iskur also had a skin of wine. He offered it to the Arabs, grinned when they declined. "More for me, Omurtag," he said. The two Bulgars drank the skin dry, and soon lay snoring by the fire.

Da'ud ibn Zubayr scowled at them. "The only use they have for wits is losing them," he sneered. "How can such folk ever come to acknowledge Allah and his Prophet?"

"We Arabs were wine-bibbers too, before Muhammad forbad it to us," Jalal ad-Din said. "My worry is that the Bulgars' passion for such drink will make khan Telerikh less inclined to accept our faith."

Da'ud dipped his head to the older man. "Truly it is just that you lead us, sir. Like a falcon, you keep your eye ever on our quarry."

"Like a falcon, I sleep in the evening," Jalal ad-Din said, yawning. "And like an old falcon, I need more sleep than I once did."

"Your years have brought you wisdom." Da'ud ibn Zubayr hesitated, as if wondering whether to go on. Finally he plunged: "Is it true, sir, that you once met a man who had known the Prophet?"

"It is true," Jalal ad-Din said proudly. "It was at Antioch, when Suleiman's army was marching to fight the Greeks at Constantinople. The grandfather of the innkeeper with whom I was quartered lived with him still: he was a Medinan, far older then than I am now, for he had soldiered with Khalid ibn al-Walid when the city fell to us. And before that, as a youth, he accompanied Muhammad when the Prophet returned in triumph from Medina to Mecca."

"*Allahu akbar*," Da'ud breathed: "God is great. I am further honored to be in your presence. Tell me, did—did the old man grant you an *hadith*, any tradition, of the Prophet that you might pass on to me for the sake of my enlightenment?"

"Yes," Jalal ad-Din said. "I recall it as if it were yesterday, just as the old man did when speaking of the journey to the Holy City. Abu Bakr, who was not yet caliph, of course, for Muhammad was still alive, started beating a man for letting a camel get loose. The Prophet began to smile, and said, 'See what this pilgrim is doing.' Abu Bakr was abashed, though the Prophet did not actually tell him to stop."

Da'ud bowed low. "I am in your debt." He repeated the story several times; Jalal ad-Din nodded to show him he had learned it perfectly. In the time-honored way, Da'ud went on, "I have this *hadith* from Jalal ad-Din as-Stambuli, who had it from—what was the old man's name, sir?"

"He was called Abd al-Qadir."

"—who had it from Abd al-Qadir, who had it from the Prophet. Think of it—only two men between Muhammad and me." Da'ud bowed again.

Jalal ad-Din returned the bow, then embarrassed himself by yawning once more. "Your pardon, I pray. Truly I must sleep."

"Sleep, then, and Allah keep you safe till the morning comes."

Jalal ad-Din rolled himself in his blanket. "And you, son of Zubayr."

"THOSE ARE NO mean works," Da'ud said a week later, pointing ahead to the earthen rampart, tall as six men, that ringed Pliska, Telerikh's capital.

"That is a child's toy, next to the walls of Constantinople," Jalal ad-Din said. "A double wall, each one twice that height, all steep stone, well-ditched in front and between, with all the Greeks in the world, it seemed, battling from atop them." Across half a century, recalling the terror of the day of the assault, he wondered still how he had survived.

"I was born in Constantinople," Da'ud reminded him gently.

"Of course you were." Jalal ad-Din shook his head, angry at himself for letting past obscure present that way. It was something old men did, but who cares to remember he is old?

Da'ud glanced around to make sure Iskur was out of earshot, lowered his voice. "For pagan savages, those are no mean works. And see how much land they enclose—Pliska must be a city of greater size than I had supposed."

"No." Jalal ad-Din remembered a talk with a previous envoy to Telerikh. "The town itself is tiny. This earthwork serves chiefly to mark off the grazing lands of the khan's flocks."

"His flocks? Is that all?" Da'ud threw back his head and laughed. "I feel as though I am transported to some strange new world, where nothing is as it seems."

"I have had that feeling ever since we came through the mountain passes," Jalal ad-Din said seriously. Da'ud gave him a curious look. He tried to explain: "You are from Constantinople. I was born not far from

Damascus, where I dwell yet. A long journey from one to the other, much longer than from Constantinople to Pliska."

Da'ud nodded.

"And yet it is a journey through sameness," Jalal ad-Din went on. "Not much difference in weather, in crops, in people. Aye, more Greeks, more Christians in Constantinople still, for we have ruled there so much less time than in Damascus, but the difference is of degree, not of kind."

"That is all true," Da'ud said, nodding again. "Whereas here —"

"Aye, here," Jalal ad-Din said with heavy irony. "The olive will not grow here, the sun fights its way through mists that swaddle it as if it were a newborn babe, and even a Greek would be welcome, for the sake of having someone civilized to talk to. This is a different world from ours, and not one much to my liking."

"Still, we hope to wed it to ours through Islam," Da'ud said.

"So we do, so we do. Submission to the will of God makes all men one." Now Jalal ad-Din made sure Iskur was paying no attention. The nomad had ridden ahead. Jalal ad-Din went on, "Even Bulgars." Da'ud chuckled.

Iskur yelled something at the guards lounging in front of a wooden gate in Pliska's earthen outwall. The guards yelled back. Iskur shouted again, louder this time. With poor grace, the guards got up and opened the gate. They stared as they saw what sort of companions Iskur led.

Jalal ad-Din gave them a grave salute as he passed through the gate, as much to discomfit them as for any other reason. He pointed ahead to the stone wall of Pliska proper. "You see?"

"I see," Da'ud said. The rectangular wall was less than half a mile on a side. "In our lands, that would be a fortress, not a capital."

The gates of the stone wall were open. Jalal ad-Din coughed as he followed Iskur and Omurtag into the town: Pliska stank like — stank worse than — a big city. Jalal ad-Din shrugged. Sooner or later, he knew, he would stop noticing the stench.

Not far inside the gates stood a large building of intricately carven wood. "This Telerikh's palace," Iskur announced.

Tethered in front of the palace were any number of steppe ponies like the ones Iskur and Omurtag rode and also, Jalal ad-Din saw with interest, several real horses and a mule whose trappings did not look like Arab gear. "To whom do those belong?" he asked, pointing.

"Not know," Iskur said. He cupped his hands and yelled toward the palace—yelling, Jalal ad-Din thought wryly, seemed the usual Bulgar approach toward any problem. After a little while, a door opened. The Arab had not even noticed it till then, so lost was its outline among carvings.

As soon as they saw someone come out of the palace, Iskur and Omurtag wheeled their horses and rode away without a backwards glance at the ambassadors they had guided to Pliska. The man who had emerged took a moment to study the new arrivals. He bowed. "How may I help you, my masters?" he asked in Arabic fluent enough to make Jalal ad-Din sit up and take notice.

"We are envoys of the caliph Abd ar-Rahman, come to your fine city"—Jalal ad-Din knew when to stretch a point—"at the bidding of your khan to explain to him the glories of Islam. I have the honor of addressing—?" He let the words hang.

"I am Dragomir, steward to the mighty khan Telerikh. Dismount; be welcome here." Dragomir bowed again. He was, Jalal ad-Din guessed, in his late thirties, stocky and well-made, with fair skin, a full brown beard framing rather a wide face, and gray eyes that revealed nothing whatever—a useful attribute in a steward.

Jalal ad-Din and his companions slid gratefully from their horses. As if by magic, boys appeared to hitch the Arabs' beasts to the rails in front of the palace and carry their saddlebags into it. Jalal ad-Din nodded at the other full-sized horses and the mule. "To whom do those belong, pray?" he asked Dragomir.

The steward's pale but hooded eyes swung toward the hitching rail, returned to Jalal ad-Din. "Those," he explained, "are the animals of the delegation of priests from the Pope of Rome at the bidding of my khan to expound to him the glories of Christianity. They arrived earlier today."

LATE THAT NIGHT, Da'ud slammed a fist against a wall of the chamber the four Arabs shared. "Better they should stay pagan than turn Christian!" he shouted. Not only was he angry that Telerikh had also invited Christians to Pliska as if intending to auction his land to the faith that bid highest, he was also short-tempered from hunger. The evening's banquet had featured pork. (It had *not* featured Telerikh; some heathen Bulgar law required the khan always to eat alone.)

"This is not so," Jalal ad-Din said mildly.

"And why not?" Da'ud glared at the older man.

"As Christians they would be *dhimmis*—people of the Book—and thus granted a hope of heaven. Should they cling to their pagan practices, their souls will surely belong to Satan till the end of time."

"Satan is welcome to their souls, whether pagan or Christian," Da'ud said. "But a Christian Bulgaria, allied to Rome, maybe even allied to the Franks, would block the true faith's progress northwards and could be the spearpoint of a thrust back toward Constantinople."

Jalal ad-Din sighed. "What you say is true. Still, the true faith is also true, and the truth surely will prevail against Christian falsehoods."

"May it be so," Da'ud said heavily. "But was this land not once a Christian country, back in the days before the Bulgars seized it from Constantinople? All the lands the Greeks held followed their usages. Some folk hereabouts must be Christian still, I'd wager, which might incline Telerikh toward their beliefs."

A knock on the door interrupted the argument. Da'ud kept one hand on his knife as he opened the door with the other. But no enemies stood outside, only four girls. Two were colored like Dragomir—to Jalal ad-Din's eyes, exotically fair. The other two were dark, darker than Arabs, in fact; one had eyes that seemed set at a slant. All four were pretty. They smiled and swayed their way in.

"Telerikh is no Christian," Jalal ad-Din said as he smiled back at one of the light-skinned girls. "Christians are not allowed concubines."

"The more fools they," Da'ud said. "Shall I blow out the lamps, or leave them burning?"

"Leave them," Jalal ad-Din answered. "I want to see what I am doing . . ."

JALAL AD-DIN BOWED low to khan Telerikh. A pace behind him, Da'ud did the same. Another pace back, Malik ibn Anas and Salman al-Tabari went to one knee, as suited their lower rank.

"Rise, all of you," Telerikh said in passable Arabic. The khan of the Bulgars was about fifty, swarthy, broad-faced, wide-nosed, with a thin beard going from black to gray. His eyes were narrow, hard, and shrewd. He looked like a man well able to rule a nation whose strength came entirely from the ferocity of its soldiers.

"Most magnificent khan, we bring the greetings of our master the caliph Abd ar-Rahman ibn Marwan, his prayers for your health and prosperity, and gifts to show that you stand high in his esteem," Jalal ad-Din said.

He waved Salman and Malik forward to present the gifts: silver plates from Persia, Damascus-work swords, fine enamelware from Constantinople, a robe of glistening Chinese silk, and, last but not least, a *Qu'ran* bound in leather and gold, its calligraphy the finest the scribes of Alexandria could provide.

Telerikh, though, seemed most interested in the robe. He rose from his wooden throne, undid the broad bronze belt he wore, shrugged out of his knee-length fur caftan. Under it he had on a linen tunic and trousers and low boots. Dragomir came up to help him put on the robe. He smiled with pleasure as he ran a hand over the watery-smooth fabric.

"Very pretty," he crooned. For a moment, Jalal ad-Din hoped he was so taken by the presents as to be easily swayed. But Telerikh, as the Arab had guessed from his appearance, was not so simple. He went on, "The caliph gives lovely gifts. With his riches, he can afford to. Now please take your places while the envoys of the Pope of Rome present themselves."

Dragomir waved the Arab delegation off to the right of the throne, close by the turbaned boyars—the great nobles—who made up Telerikh's court. Most were of the same stock as their khan; a few looked more like Dragomir and the fair girl Jalal ad-Din had so enjoyed the night before. Fair or dark, they smelled of hard-run horses and ancient sweat.

As he had with the caliph's embassy, Dragomir announced the papal legates in the throaty Bulgarian tongue. There were three of them, as Jalal ad-Din had seen at the banquet. Two were gorgeous in robes that reminded him of the ones the Constantinopolitan grandees had worn so long ago as they vainly tried to rally their troops against the Arabs. The third wore a simple brown woolen habit. Amid the Bulgar chatter, meaningless to him, Jalal ad-Din picked out three names: Niketas, Theodore, and Paul.

The Christians scowled at the Arabs as they walked past them to approach Telerikh. They bowed as Jalal ad-Din had. "Stand," Telerikh said in Greek. Jalal ad-Din was not surprised he knew that language; the Bulgars had dealt with Constantinople before the Arabs took it, and many refugees had fled to Pliska. Others had escaped to Italy, which no doubt explained why two of the papal legates bore Greek names.

"Excellent khan," said one of the envoys (Theodore, Jalal ad-Din thought it was), also in Greek, "we are saddened to see you decked in raiment given you by our foes as you greet us. Does this mean you hold

us in contempt, and will give us no fair hearing? Surely you did not invite us to travel so far merely for that?"

Telerikh blinked, glanced down at the silk robe he had just put on.
"No," he said. "It only means I like this present. What presents have you
for me?"

Da'ud leaned forward, whispered into Jalal ad-Din's ear: "More
avarice in that one than fear of hell." Jalal ad-Din nodded. That made
his task harder, not easier. He would have to play politics along with ex-
pounding the truth of Islam. He sighed. Ever since he learned Telerikh
had also bid the men from Rome hither, he'd expected no less.

The Christians were presenting their gifts, and making a great show
of it to try to disguise their not being so fine as the ones their rivals had
given—Jalal ad-Din's offerings still lay in a glittering heap beside Telerikh's throne. "Here," Theodore intoned, "is a copy of the Holy Scriptures, with a personal prayer for you inscribed therein by his holiness
the Pope Constantine."

Jalal ad-Din let out a quiet but scornful snort. "The words of Allah
are the ones that count," he whispered to Da'ud ibn Zubayr, "not those
of any man." It was Da'ud's turn to nod.

As he had with the *Qu'ran*, Telerikh idly paged through the Bible.
Perhaps halfway through, he paused, glanced up at the Christians. "You
have pictures in your book." It sounded almost like an accusation; had
Jalal ad-Din said it, it would have been.

But the Christian in the plain brown robe, the one called Paul, answered calmly, "Yes, excellent khan, we do, the better to instruct the
many who cannot read the words beside them." He was no longer
young—he might have been close to Jalal ad-Din's age—but his voice
was light and clear and strong, the voice of a man sure in the path he
has chosen.

"Beware of that one," Da'ud murmured. "He has more holiness in
him than the other two put together." Jalal ad-Din had already reached
the same conclusion, and did not like it. Enemies, he thought, ought by
rights to be rogues.

He got only a moment to mull on that, for Telerikh suddenly shifted
to Arabic and called to him, "Why are there no pictures in your book, to
show me what you believe?"

"Because Allah the one God is infinite, far too mighty for our tiny
senses to comprehend, and so cannot be depicted," he said, "and man
must not be depicted, for Allah created him in his image from a clot of

blood. The Christians' own scriptures say as much, but they ignore any law which does not suit them."

"Liar! Misbeliever!" Theodore shouted. Torchlight gleamed off his tonsured pate as he whirled to confront Jalal ad-Din.

"No liar I," Jalal ad-Din said; not for nothing had he studied with men once Christian before they saw the truth of Muhammad's teaching. "The verse you deny is in the book called Exodus."

"Is this true?" Telerikh rumbled, scowling at the Christians.

Theodore started to reply; Paul cut him off. "Excellent khan, the verse is as the Arab states. My colleague did not wish to deny it." Theodore looked ready to argue. Paul did not let him, continuing, "But that law was given to Moses long ago. Since then, Christ the Son of God has appeared on earth; belief in him assures one of heaven, regardless of the observance of the outdated rules of the Jews."

Telerikh grunted. "A new law may replace an old, if circumstances change. What say you to that, envoy of the caliph?"

"I will quote two verses from the *Qu'ran*, from the *sura* called The Cow," Jalal ad-Din said, smiling at the opening Paul had left him. "Allah says, 'The Jews say the Christians are astray, and the Christians say it is the Jews who are astray. Yet they both read the Scriptures.' Which is to say, magnificent khan, that they have both corrupted God's word. And again, 'They say: "Allah has begotten a son." Allah forbid!' "

When reciting from the *Qu'ran*, he had naturally fallen into Arabic. He was not surprised to see the Christians following his words without difficulty. They too would have prepared for any eventuality on this mission.

One of Telerikh's boyars called something to the khan in his own language. Malik ibn Anas, who was with Jalal ad-Din precisely because he knew a little of the Bulgar speech, translated for him: "He says that the sacred stones of their forefathers, even the pagan gods of the Slavs they rule, have served them well enough for years upon years, and calls on Telerikh not to change their usages now."

Looking around, Jalal ad-Din saw more than a few boyars nodding. "Great khan, may I speak?" he called. Telerikh nodded. Jalal ad-Din went on, "Great khan, you need but look about you to see proof of Allah's might. Is it not true that my lord the caliph Abd ar-Rahman, peace be unto him, rules from the Western Sea to India, from your borders to beyond the deserts of Egypt? Even the Christians, who know the one God imperfectly, still control many lands. Yet only you here in this small country follow your idols. Does this not show you their strength is a paltry thing?"

"There is more, excellent khan." Niketas, who had been quiet till then, unexpectedly spoke up. "Your false gods isolate Bulgaria. How, in dealing with Christians or even Muslims, can your folk swear an oath that will be trusted? How can you put the power of God behind a treaty, to ensure it will be enforced? In what way can one of you lawfully marry a Christian? Other questions like these will surely have occurred to you, else you would not have bid us come."

"He speaks the truth, khan Telerikh," Jalal ad-Din said. He had not thought a priest would have so good a grasp of matters largely secular, but Niketas did. Since his words could not be denied, supporting them seemed better than ignoring them.

Telerikh gnawed on his mustaches. He looked from one delegation to the other, back again. "Tell me," he said slowly, "is it the same god both groups of you worship, or do you follow different ones?"

"That is an excellent question," Jalal ad-Din said; no, Telerikh was no fool. "It is the same god: there is no God but God. But the Christians worship him incorrectly, saying he is Three, not One."

"It is the same God," Paul agreed, once more apparently overriding Theodore. "Muhammad is not a true prophet and many of his preachings are lies, but it is the same God, who gave his only begotten Son to save mankind."

"Stop!" Telerikh held up a hand. "If it is the same God, what difference does it make how I and my people worship him? No matter what the prayers we send up to him, surely he will know what we mean."

Jalal ad-Din glanced toward Paul. The Christian was also looking at him. Paul smiled. Jalal ad-Din found himself smiling back. He too felt the irony of the situation: he and Paul had more in common with each other than either of them did with the naive Bulgar khan. Paul raised an eyebrow. Jalal ad-Din dipped his head, granting the Christian permission to answer Telerikh's question.

"Sadly, excellent khan, it is not so simple," Paul said. "Just as there is only one true God, so there can be only one true way to worship him, for while he is merciful, he is also just, and will not tolerate errors in the reverence paid him. To use a homely example, sir, would it please you if we called you 'khan of the Avars'?"

"It would please me right well, were it true," Telerikh said with a grim chuckle. "Worse luck for me, though, the Avars have a khan of their own. Very well, priest, I see what you are saying."

The Bulgar ruler rubbed his chin. "This needs more thought. We will all gather here again in three days' time, to speak of it further. Go now in peace, and remember"—he looked sternly from Christians to Muslims—"you are all my guests here. No fighting between you, or you will regret it."

Thus warned, the rival embassies bowed their way out.

JALAL AD-DIN SPENT more time before his next encounter with the priests exploring Pliska than he had hoped to. No matter how delightful he found his fair-skinned pleasure girl, he was not a young man: for him, between rounds meant between days.

After the barbarous richness of Telerikh's wooden palace, the Arab found the rest of the town surprisingly familiar. He wondered why until he realized that Pliska, like Damascus, like Constantinople, like countless other settlements through which he had passed at one time or another, had been a Roman town once. Layout and architecture lingered long after overlords changed.

Jalal ad-Din felt like shouting when he found a bath house not only still standing but still used; from what his nose had told him in the palace, he'd doubted the Bulgars even suspected cleanliness existed. When he went in, he found most of the bathers were of the lighter-colored folk from whom Dragomir and his mistress had sprung. They were, he'd gathered, peasant Slavs over whom the Bulgars proper ruled.

He also found that, being mostly unacquainted with either Christianity or Islam, they let in women along with the men. It was scandalous; it was shocking; in Damascus it would have raised riots. Jalal ad-Din wished his eyes were as sharp as they'd been when he was forty, or even fifty.

He was happily soaking in a warm pool when the three Christian envoys came in. Theodore hissed in horror when he saw the naked women, spun on his heel, and stalked out. Niketas started to follow, but Paul took hold of his arm and stopped him. The older man shrugged out of his brown robe, sank with a sigh of pleasure into the same pool Jalal ad-Din was using. Niketas, by his expression still dubious, joined him a moment later.

"Flesh is flesh," Paul said calmly. "By pledging yourself to Christ, you have acknowledged that its pleasures are not for you. No point in fleeing, then."

Jalal ad-Din nodded to the Christians. "You have better sense, sir, than I would have looked for in a priest," he told Paul.

"I thank you." If Paul heard the undercurrent of irony in the Arab's voice, he did not let it affect his own tone, which briefly shamed Jalal ad-Din. Paul went on, "I am no priest in any case, only a humble monk, here to advise my superiors if they care to listen to me."

"Only!" Jalal ad-Din scoffed. But, he had to admit to himself, the monk sounded completely sincere. He sighed; hating his opponents would have been much easier were they evil. "They would be wise to listen to you," he said. "I think you are a holy man."

"You give me too much credit," Paul said.

"No, he does not," Niketas told his older colleague. "Not just by words do you instruct the barbarians hereabouts, but also through the life you live, which by its virtues illuminates your teachings."

Paul bowed. From a man squatting naked in waist-deep water, the gesture should have seemed ludicrous. Somehow it did not.

Niketas turned to Jalal ad-Din. "Did I hear correctly that you are styled as-Stambuli?"

"You did," the Arab answered proudly.

"How strange," Niketas murmured. "Perhaps here God grants me the chance to avenge the fall of the Queen of Cities."

He spoke as if the caliph's armies had taken Constantinople only yesterday, not long before he was born. Seeing Jalal ad-Din's confusion, Paul said, "Niketas' mother is Anna, the daughter of Leo."

"Yes?" Jalal ad-Din was polite, but that meant nothing to him. "And my mother was Zinawb, the daughter of Mu'in ibn Abd al-Wahhab. What of it?"

"Ah, but your grandfather, however illustrious he may have been (I do not slight him, I assure you), was never *Basileus ton Rhomaion*— Emperor of the Romans."

"*That* Leo!" Jalal ad-Din thumped his forehead with the heel of his hand. He nodded to Niketas. "Your grandfather, sir, was a very devil. He fought us with all he had, and sent too many brave lads to paradise before their time."

Niketas raised a dark eyebrow. His tonsured skull went oddly with those bushy brows and the thick beard that covered his cheeks almost to the eyes. "Too many, you say; I would say, not enough."

"So you would," Jalal ad-Din agreed. "Had Leo beaten us, you might be Roman Emperor yourself now. But Abd ar-Rahman the commander of the faithful rules Constantinople, and you are a priest in a foreign land. It is as Allah wills."

"So I must believe," Niketas said. "But just as Leo fought you with every weapon he had, I shall oppose you with all my means. The Bulgars must not fall victim to your false belief. It would be too great a blow for Christendom to suffer, removing from us all hope of greater growth."

Niketas' mind worked like an emperor's, Jalal ad-Din thought—unlike many of his Christian colleagues, he understood the long view. He'd shown that in debate, too, when he pointed out the problems attendant on the Bulgars' staying pagan. A dangerous foe—Pope Constantine had sent to Pliska the best the Christians had.

Whether that would be enough . . . Jalal ad-Din shrugged. "It is as Allah wills," he repeated.

"And Telerikh," Paul said. When Jalal ad-Din looked at him in surprise, the monk went on, "Of course, Telerikh is in God's hands too. But God will not be influenced by what we do. Telerikh may."

"There is that," Jalal ad-Din admitted.

"No telling how long all this arguing will go on," Telerikh said when the Christian and Muslim embassies appeared before him once more. He spoke to Dragomir in his own language. The steward nodded, hurried away. A moment later, lesser servants brought in benches, which they set before Telerikh's throne. "Sit," the khan urged. "You may as well be comfortable."

"How would you have us argue?" Jalal ad-Din asked, wishing the bench had a back but too proud to ask for a chair to ease his old bones.

"Tell me of your one god," Telerikh said. "You say you and the Christians follow him. Tell me what you believe differently about him, so I may choose between your beliefs."

Jalal ad-Din carefully did not smile. He had asked his question to seize the chance to speak first. Let the Christians respond to him. He began where any Muslim would, with the *shahada*, the profession of faith: " '*La illaha ill'Allah: Muhammadun rasulu'llah*—There is no God but Allah; Muhammad is the prophet of Allah.' Believe that, magnificent khan, and you are a Muslim. There is more, of course, but that is of the essence."

"It is also a lie," Theodore broke in harshly. "Excellent khan, the books of the Old Testament, written hundreds of years before God's Son became flesh, foretold His coming. Neither Old nor New Testament speaks one word of the Arab charlatan who invented this false creed because he had failed as a camel-driver."

"There is no prophecy pertaining to Muhammad in the Christians' holy book because it was deliberately suppressed," Jalal ad-Din shot back. "That is why God gave the Prophet his gifts, as the seal of prophecy."

"The seal of trickery is nearer the truth," Theodore said. "God's only begotten Son Jesus Christ said prophecy ended with John the Baptist, but that false prophets would continue to come. Muhammad lived centuries after John and Jesus, so he must be false, a trick of the devil to send men to hell."

"Jesus is no son of God. God is one, not three, as the Christians would have it," Jalal ad-Din said. "Hear God's own words in the *Qu'ran*: 'Say, God is one.' The Christians give the one God partners in the so-called Son and Holy Spirit. If he has two partners, why not three, or four, or more? Foolishness! And how could God fit into a woman's womb and be born like a man? More foolishness!"

Again it was Theodore who took up the challenge; he was a bad-tempered man, but capable all the same. "God is omnipotent. To deny the possibility of the Incarnation is to deny that omnipotence."

"That priest is twisty as a serpent," Da'ud ibn Zubayr whispered to Jalal ad-Din. The older man nodded, frowning. He was not quite sure how to respond to Theodore's latest sally. Who was he to say what Allah could or could not do?

Telerikh roused him from his unprofitable reverie by asking, "So you Arabs deny Jesus is the son of your one god, eh?"

"We do," Jalal ad-Din said firmly.

"What do you make of him, then?" the khan said.

"Allah commands us to worship none but himself, so how can he have a son? Jesus was a holy man and a prophet, but nothing more. Since the Christians corrupted his words, Allah inspired Muhammad to recite the truth once more."

"Could a prophet rise from the dead on the third day, as God's Son did?" Theodore snorted, clapping a dramatic hand to his forehead. "Christ's miracles are witnessed and attested in writing. What miracles did Muhammad work? None, the reason being that he could not."

"He flew to Jerusalem in the course of a night," Jalal ad-Din returned, "as the *Qu'ran* records—in writing," he added pointedly. "And the crucifixion and resurrection are fables. No man can rise from the dead, and another was set on the cross in place of Jesus."

"Satan waits for you in hell, blasphemer," Theodore hissed. "Christ healed the sick, raised the dead, stopped wind and rain in their tracks. Anyone who denies Him loses all hope of heaven, and may garner for his sin only eternal torment."

"No, that is the fate reserved for those who make One into Three," Jalal ad-Din said. "You—"

"Wait, both of you." Telerikh held up a hand. The Bulgar khan, Jalal ad-Din thought, seemed more stunned than edified by the arguments he had heard. The Arab realized he had been quarreling with Theodore rather than instructing the khan. Telerikh went on. "I cannot find the truth in what you are saying, for each of you and each of your books makes the other a liar. That helps me not at all. Tell me instead what I and my people must do, if we follow one faith or the other."

"If you choose the Arabs' false creed, you will have to abandon both wine-drinking and eating pork," Theodore said before Jalal ad-Din could reply. "Let him deny it if he may." The priest shot the Arab a triumphant look.

"It is true," Jalal ad-Din said stoutly. "Allah has ordained it."

He tried to put a bold face on it, but knew Theodore had landed a telling blow. The mutter that went up from Telerikh's boyars confirmed it. A passion for wine inflamed most non-believers, Jalal ad-Din thought; sadly, despite the good counsel of the *Qu'ran*, it could capture Muslims as well. And as for pork—judging from the meals they served at Pliska, the Bulgars found it their favorite flesh.

"That is not good," Telerikh said, and the Arab's heart sank.

A passion for wine . . . passion! "Magnificent khan, may I ask without offense how many wives you enjoy?"

Telerikh frowned. "I am not quite sure. How many is it now, Dragomir?"

"Forty-seven, mighty khan," the steward replied at once, competent as usual.

"And your boyars?" Jalal ad-Din went on. "Surely they also have more than one apiece."

"Well, what of it?" the khan said, sounding puzzled.

Now Jalal ad-Din grinned an unpleasant grin at Theodore. "If you become a Christian, magnificent khan, you will have to give up all your wives save one. You will not even be able to keep the others as concubines, for the Christians also forbid that practice."

"What?" If Telerikh had frowned before, the scowl he turned on the Christians now was thunderous. "Can this be true?"

"Of course it is true," Theodore said, scowling back. "Bigamy is a monstrous sin."

"Gently, my brother in Christ, gently," Paul said. "We do not wish to press too hard upon our Bulgar friends, who after all will be newly come to our observances."

"That one is truly a nuisance," Da'ud whispered.

"You are too right," Jalal ad-Din whispered back.

"Still, excellent khan," Paul went on, "you must not doubt that Theodore is correct. When you and your people accept Christianity, all those with more than one wife—or women with more than one husband, if any there be—will be required to repudiate all but their first marriages, and to undergo penance under the supervision of a priest."

His easy, matter-of-fact manner seemed to calm Telerikh. "I see you believe this to be necessary," the khan said. "It is so strange, though, that I do not see why. Explain further, if you will."

Jalal ad-Din made a fist. He had expected Christian ideas of marriage to appall Telerikh, not to intrigue him with their very alienness. Was a potential monk lurking under those fur robes, under that turban?

Paul said, "Celibacy, excellent khan, is the highest ideal. For those who cannot achieve it, marriage to a single partner is an acceptable alternative. Surely you must know, excellent khan, how lust can inflame men. And no sin is so intolerable to prophets and other holy men as depravity and sexual license, for the Holy Spirit will not touch the heart of a prophet while he is engaged in an erotic act. The life of the mind is nobler than that of the body; on this Holy Scripture and the wise ancient Aristotle agree."

"I never heard of this, ah, Aristotle. Was he a shaman?" Telerikh asked.

"You might say so," Paul replied, which impressed Jalal ad-Din. The Arab knew little of Aristotle, hardly more than that he had been a sage before even Roman times. He was certain, however, that Aristotle had been a civilized man, not a barbarous pagan priest. But that was surely the closest equivalent to sage within Telerikh's mental horizon, and Paul deserved credit for recognizing it.

The Bulgar khan turned to Jalal ad-Din. "What have you to say about this?"

"The Qu'ran permits a man four lawful wives, for those able to treat them equally well," Jalal ad-Din said. "For those who cannot, it enjoins only one. But it does not prohibit concubines."

"That is better," the khan said. "A man would get bored, bedding the same woman night after night. But this business of no pork and no wine is almost as gloomy." He gave his attention back to the priests. "You Christians allow these things."

"Yes, excellent khan, we do," Paul said.

"Hmm." Telerikh rubbed his chin. Jalal ad-Din did his best to hide his worry. The matter still stood balanced, and he had used his strongest weapon to incline the khan to Islam. If the Christians had any good arguments left, he—and the fate of the true faith in Bulgaria—were in trouble.

Paul said, "Excellent khan, these matters of practice may seem important to you, but in fact they are superficial. Here is the key difference between the Arab's faith and ours: the religion Muhammad preached is one that loves violence, not peace. Such teaching can only come from Satan, I fear."

"That is a foul, stinking lie!" Da'ud ibn Zubayr cried. The other two Arabs behind Jalal ad-Din also shouted angrily.

"Silence!" Telerikh said, glaring at them. "Do not interrupt. I shall give you a chance to answer in due course."

"Yes, let the Christian go on," Jalal ad-Din agreed. "I am sure the khan will be fascinated by what he has to say."

Glancing back, he thought Da'ud about to burst with fury. The younger man finally forced out a strangled whisper: "Have you gone mad, to stand by while this infidel slanders the Prophet (may blessings be upon his head)?"

"I think not. Now be still, as Telerikh said. My ears are not what they once were; I cannot listen to you and Paul at once."

The monk was saying, "Muhammad's creed urges conversion by the sword, not by reason. Does not his holy book, if one may dignify it by that title, preach the holy war, the *jihad*"—he dropped the Arabic word into his polished Greek—"against all those who do not share his faith? And those who are slain in their murderous work, says the false prophet, attain to heaven straightaway." He turned to Jalal ad-Din. "Do you deny this?"

"I do not," Jalal ad-Din replied. "You paraphrase the third *sura* of the Qu'ran."

"There, you see?" Paul said to Telerikh. "Even the Arab himself admits the ferocity of his faith. Think also on the nature of the paradise Muhammad in his ignorance promises his followers—"

"Why do you not speak?" Da'ud ibn Zubayr demanded. "You let this man slander and distort everything in which we believe."

"Hush," Jalal ad-Din said again.

"—rivers of water and milk, honey and wine, and men reclining on silken couches and being served—served in all ways, including pandering to their fleshly lusts (as if souls could have such concerns!)—by females created especially for the purpose." Paul paused, needing a moment to draw in another indignant breath. "Such carnal indulgences—nay, excesses—have no place in heaven, excellent khan."

"No? What does, then?" Telerikh asked.

Awe transfigured the monk's thin, ascetic face as he looked within himself at the afterlife he envisioned. "Heaven, excellent khan, does not consist of banquets and wenches: those are for gluttons and sinners in this life, and lead to hell in the next. No: paradise is spiritual in nature, with the soul knowing the eternal joy of closeness and unity with God, peace of spirit and absence of all care. That is the true meaning of heaven."

"Amen," Theodore intoned piously. All three Christians made the sign of the cross over their breasts.

"That is the true meaning of heaven, you say?" Telerikh's blunt-featured face was impassive as his gaze swung toward Jalal ad-Din. "Now you may speak as you will, man of the caliph. Has this Christian told accurately of the world to come in his faith and in yours?"

"He has, magnificent khan." Jalal ad-Din spread his hands and smiled at the Bulgar lord. "I leave it to you, sir, to pick the paradise you would sooner inhabit."

Telerikh looked thoughtful. The Christian clerics' expressions went from confident to concerned to horrified as they gradually began to wonder, as Jalal ad-Din had already, just what sort of heaven a barbarian prince might enjoy.

Da'ud ibn Zubayr gently thumped Jalal ad-Din on the back. "I abase myself before you, sir," he said, flowery in apology as Arabs so often were. "You saw further than I." Jalal ad-Din bowed on his bench, warmed by the praise.

His voice urgent, the priest Niketas spoke up: "Excellent khan, you need to consider one thing more before you make your choice."

"Eh? And what might that be?" Telerikh sounded distracted. Jalal ad-Din hoped he was; the delights of the Muslim paradise were worth being distracted about. Paul's version, on the other hand, struck him as a boring way to spend eternity. But the khan, worse luck, was not altogether ready to abandon Christianity on account of that. Jalal ad-Din saw him focus his attention on Niketas. "Go on, priest."

"Thank you, excellent khan." Niketas bowed low. "Think on this, then: in Christendom the most holy Pope is the leader of all things spiritual, true, but there are many secular rulers, each to his own state: the Lombard dukes, the king of the Franks, the Saxon and Angle kings in Britain, the various Irish princes, every one a free man. But Islam knows only once prince, the caliph, who reigns over all Muslims. If you decide to worship Muhammad, where is there room for you as ruler of your own Bulgaria?"

"No one worships Muhammad," Jalal ad-Din said tartly. "He is a prophet, not a god. Worship Allah, who alone deserves it."

His correction of the minor point did not distract Telerikh from the major one. "Is what the Christian says true?" the khan demanded. "Do you expect me to bend the knee to your khan as well as your god? Why should I freely give Abd ar-Rahman what he has never won in battle?"

Jalal ad-Din thought furiously, all the while damning Niketas. Priest, celibate the man might be, but he still thought like a Greek, like a Roman Emperor of Constantinople, sowing distrust among his foes so they defeated themselves when his own strength did not suffice to beat them.

"Well, Arab, what have you to say?" Telerikh asked again.

Jalal ad-Din felt sweat trickle into his beard. He knew he had let silence stretch too long. At last, picking his words carefully, he answered, "Magnificent khan, what Niketas says is not true. Aye, the caliph Abd ar-Rahman, peace be unto him, rules all the land of Islam. But he does so by right of conquest and right of descent, just as you rule the Bulgars. Were you, were your people, to become Muslim without warfare, he would have no more claim on you than any brother in Islam has on another."

He hoped he was right, and that the jurists would not make a liar of him once he got back to Damascus. All the ground here was uncharted: no nation had ever accepted Islam without first coming under the control of the caliphate. Well, he thought, if Telerikh and the Bulgars did convert, that success in itself would ratify anything he did to accomplish it.

If . . . Telerikh showed no signs of having made up his mind. "I will meet with all of you in four days," the khan said. He rose, signifying the end of the audience. The rival embassies rose too, and bowed deeply as he stumped between them out of the hall of audience.

"If only it were easy." Jalal ad-Din sighed.

* * *

THE LEATHER PURSE WAS SMALL but heavy. It hardly clinked as Jalal ad-Din pressed it into Dragomir's hand. The steward made it disappear. "Tell me, if you would," Jalal ad-Din said, as casually as if the purse had never existed at all, "how your master is inclined toward the two faiths about which he has been learning."

"You are not the first person to ask me that question," Dragomir remarked. He sounded the tiniest bit smug: *I've been bribed twice,* Jalal ad-Din translated mentally.

"Was the other person who inquired by any chance Niketas?" the Arab asked.

Telerikh's steward dipped his head. "Why, yes, now that you mention it." His ice-blue eyes gave Jalal ad-Din a careful once-over: men who could see past their noses deserved watching.

Smiling, Jalal ad-Din said, "And did you give him the same answer you will give me?"

"Why, certainly, noble sir." Dragomir sounded as though the idea of doing anything else had never entered his mind. Perhaps it had not: "I told him, as I tell you now, that the mighty khan keeps his own counsel well, and has not revealed to me which faith—if either—he will choose."

"You are an honest man." Jalal ad-Din sighed. "Not as helpful as I would have hoped, but honest nonetheless."

Dragomir bowed. "And you, noble sir, are most generous. Be assured that if I knew more, I would pass it on to you." Jalal ad-Din nodded, thinking it would be a sorry spectacle indeed if one who served the caliph, the richest, mightiest lord in the world, could not afford a more lavish bribe than a miserable Christian priest.

However lavish the payment, though, it had not bought him what he wanted. He bowed his way out of Telerikh's palace, spent the morning wandering through Pliska in search of trinkets for his fair-skinned bed-mate. Here too he was spending Abd ar-Rahman's money, so only the finest goldwork interested him.

He went from shop to shop, sometimes pausing to dicker, sometimes not. The rings and necklaces the Bulgar craftsmen displayed were less intricate, less ornate than those that would have fetched highest prices in Damascus, but had a rough vigor of their own. Jalal ad-Din finally chose a thick chain studded with fat garnets and pieces of polished jet.

He tucked the necklace into his robe, sat down to rest outside the jeweler's shop. The sun blazed down. It was not as high in the sky, not as hot, really, as it would have been in Damascus at the same season, but this was muggy heat, not dry, and seemed worse. Jalal ad-Din felt like a boiled fish. He started to doze.

"*Assalamu aleykum*—peace to you," someone said. Jalal ad-Din jerked awake, looked up. Niketas stood in front of him. Well, he'd long since gathered that the priest spoke Arabic, though they'd only used Greek between themselves till now.

"*Aleykum assalamu*—and to you, peace," he replied. He yawned and stretched and started to get to his feet. Niketas took him by the elbow, helped him rise. "Ah, thank you. You are generous to an old man, and one who is no friend of yours."

"Christ teaches us to love our enemies," Niketas shrugged. "I try to obey His teachings, as best I can."

Jalal ad-Din thought that teaching a stupid one—the thing to do with an enemy was to get rid of him. The Christians did not really believe what they said, either; he remembered how they'd fought at Constantinople, even after the walls were breached. But the priest had just been kind—no point in churlishly arguing with him.

Instead, the Arab said, "Allah be praised, day after tomorrow the khan will make his choice known." He cocked an eyebrow at Niketas. "Dragomir tells me you tried to learn his answer in advance."

"Which can only mean you did the same." Niketas laughed drily. "I suspect you learned no more than I did."

"Only that Dragomir is fond of gold," Jalal ad-Din admitted.

Niketas laughed again, then grew serious. "How strange, is it not, that the souls of a nation ride on the whim of a man both ignorant and barbarous. God grant that he choose wisely."

"From God comes all things," Jalal ad-Din said. The Christian nodded; that much they believed in common. Jalal ad-Din went on, "That shows, I believe, why Telerikh will decide for Islam."

"No, you are wrong there," Niketas answered. "He must choose Christ. Surely God will not allow those who worship Him correctly to be penned up in one far corner of the world, and bar them forever from access to whatever folk may lie north and east of Bulgaria."

Jalal ad-Din started to answer, then stopped and gave his rival a respectful look. As he had already noticed, Niketas' thought had formidable depth to it. However clever he was, though, the priest who might have been Emperor had to deal with his weakness in the real world. Jalal ad-Din drove that weakness home: "If God loves you so well, why has he permitted us Muslims dominion over so many of you, and why has he let us drive you back and back, even giving over Constantinople, your imperial city, into our hands?"

"Not for your own sake, I'm certain," Niketas snapped.

"No? Why then?" Jalal ad-Din refused to be nettled by the priest's tone.

"Because of the multitude of our own sins, I'm sure. Not only was— is—Christendom sadly riddled with heresies and false beliefs, even those who believe what is true all too often lead sinful lives. Thus your eruption from the desert, to serve as God's flail and as punishment for our errors."

"You have answers to everything—everything but God's true will. He will show that day after tomorrow, through Telerikh."

"That He will." With a stiff little bow, Niketas took his leave. Jalal ad-Din watched him go, wondering if hiring a knifeman would be worthwhile in spite of Telerikh's warnings. Reluctantly, he decided against it; not here in Pliska, he thought. In Damascus he could have arranged it and never been traced, but he lacked those sorts of connections here. Too bad.

Only when he was almost back to the khan's palace to give the pleasure girl the trinket did he stop to wonder whether Niketas was thinking about sticking a knife in *him*. Christian priests were supposed to be above such things, but Niketas himself had pointed out what sinners Christians were these days.

TELERIKH'S SERVANTS summoned Jalal ad-Din and the other Arabs to the audience chamber just before the time for mid-afternoon prayers. Jalal ad-Din did not like having to put off the ritual; it struck him as a bad omen. He tried to stay serene. Voicing the inauspicious thought aloud would only give it power.

The Christians were already in the chamber when the Arabs entered. Jalal ad-Din did not like that either. Catching his eye, Niketas sent him a chilly nod. Theodore only scowled, as he did whenever he had anything to do with Muslims. The monk Paul, though, smiled at Jalal ad-Din as if at a dear friend. That only made him worry more.

Telerikh waited until both delegations stood before him. "I have decided," he said abruptly. Jalal ad-Din drew in a sudden, sharp breath. From the number of boyars who echoed him, he guessed that not even the khan's nobles knew his will. Dragomir had not lied, then.

The khan rose from his carven throne, stepped down between the rival embassies. The boyars muttered among themselves; this was not common procedure. Jalal ad-Din's nails bit into his palms. His heart pounded in his chest till he wondered how long it could endure.

Telerikh turned to face southeast. For a moment, Jalal ad-Din was too keyed up to notice or care. Then the khan sank to his knees, his face turned toward Mecca, toward the Holy City. Again Jalal ad-Din's heart threatened to burst, this time with joy.

"*La illaha ill'Allah; Muhammadun rasulu'llah,*" Telerikh said in a loud, firm voice. "There is no God but Allah; Muhammad is the prophet of Allah." He repeated the *shahada* twice more, then rose to his feet and bowed to Jalal ad-Din.

"It is accomplished," the Arab said, fighting back tears. "You are a Muslim now, a fellow in submission to the will of God."

"Not I alone. We shall all worship the one God and his prophet." Telerikh turned to his boyars, shouted in the Bulgar tongue. A couple of nobles shouted back. Telerikh jerked his arm toward the doorway, a peremptory gesture of dismissal. The stubborn boyars glumly tramped out. The rest turned toward Mecca and knelt. Telerikh led them in the *shahada*, once, twice, three times. The khan faced Jalal ad-Din once more. "Now we are all Muslims here."

"God is most great," the Arab breathed. "Soon, magnificent khan, I vow, many teachers will come from Damascus to instruct you and your people fully in all details of the faith, though what you and your nobles have proclaimed will suffice for your souls until such time as the *ulama*—those learned in religion—may arrive."

"It is very well," Telerikh said. Then he seemed to remember that Theodore, Niketas, and Paul were still standing close by him, suddenly alone in a chamber full of the enemies of their faith. He turned to them. "Go back to your Pope in peace, Christian priests. I could not choose your religion, not with heaven as you say it is—and not with the caliph's armies all along my southern border. Perhaps if Constantinople had not fallen so long ago, my folk would in the end have become Christian. Who can say? But in this world, as it is now, Muslims we must be, and Muslims we shall be."

"I will pray for you, excellent khan, and for God's forgiveness of the mistake you made this day," Paul said gently. Theodore, on the other hand, looked as if he were consigning Telerikh to the hottest pits of hell.

Niketas caught Jalal ad-Din's eye. The Arab nodded slightly to his defeated foe. More than anyone else in the chamber, the two of them understood how much bigger than Bulgaria was the issue decided here today. Islam would grow and grow, Christendom continue to shrink. Jalal ad-Din had heard that Ethiopia, far to the south of Egypt, had Christian rulers yet. What of it? Ethiopia was so far from the center of affairs as hardly to matter. And the same fate would now befall the isolated Christian countries in the far northwest of the world.

Let them be islands in the Muslim sea, he thought, if that was what their stubbornness dictated. One day, *inshallah*, that sea would wash over every island, and they would read the *Qu'ran* in Rome itself.

He had done his share and more to make that dream real, as a youth helping to capture Constantinople and now in his old age by bringing Bulgaria the true faith. He could return once more to his peaceful retirement in Damascus.

He wondered if Telerikh would let him take along that fair-skinned pleasure girl. He turned to the khan. It couldn't hurt to ask.

Susan Shwartz

Susan Shwartz has been writing fantasy and science fiction for more than twenty years. She is the author of the extraplanetary adventure Heritage of Flight, as well as the Heirs to Byzantium alternate world fantasy trilogy, comprised of Byzantium's Crown, The Woman of Flowers, and Queensblade. The Heirs to Byzantium series lays the groundwork for her recent Shards of Empire and its sequel Cross and Crescent, sword-and-sorcery epics set in the eleventh century at the twilight of the Byzantine empire, which explore the clash of cultures during the First Crusade. Shwartz has collaborated on the Star Trek novels Vulcan's Forge and Vulcan's Heart with Josepha Sherman, and on Empire of Eagles with Andre Norton, for whom she also compiled the tribute anthology Moonsinger's Friends. She has edited the Arabesque anthologies and is a co-editor for the Sisters in Fantasy anthology series.

SUPPOSE THEY GAVE A PEACE

Susan Shwartz

TWENTY-FIVE YEARS AFTER the war, and my damned sixth sense about the phone still wakes me up at 3:00 A.M. Just as well. All Margaret needs is for me to snap awake, shout, and jump out of bed, grabbing for my pants and my .45. I don't have it anymore. She made me sell it as soon as the kids were old enough to poke into the big chest of drawers. I don't interfere when she makes decisions like that. The way things are going to the dogs, though, I'd feel a whole lot better about her safety if I had the gun.

So I stuck my feet into my slippers—the trench foot still itches—and snuck downstairs. If Margaret woke up, she'd think I was raiding the icebox and go back to sleep. I like being up and alone in my house, kind of guard duty. I don't do much. I straighten towels or put books back on the shelves—though with Steff gone, that's not a problem anymore. I don't like seeing the kids' rooms so bare.

Barry's models and football are all lined up, and Margaret dusts them. No problem telling the boys from the girls in our family. Barry's room is red and navy, and Steff's is all blue and purply, soft-like, with ruffles and a dressing table she designed herself. Now that she's at school, we don't trip on clothes all over the place. And I keep reminding myself we ought to yank out the Princess phone she got when she turned thirteen. Light on the dial's burned out, anyway.

I wish she hadn't taken down the crewelwork she did her freshman year. The flower baskets were a whole lot prettier than these "Suppose They Gave a War and Nobody Came" posters. But that's better than the picture of that bearded Che-guy. I put my foot down about that thing, I can tell you. Not in *my* house, I said.

I'm proud of our house: two-floor brick Tudor with white walls and gold carpet and a big ticking grandfather's clock in the hall. Classy taste, my wife has. Who'd have thought she'd look at someone like me?

Besides, dinner was pretty good. Some of that deli rye and that left-over steak . . .

As the light from the icebox slid across the wall phone it went off, almost like it had been alerted. I grabbed it before it could ring twice.

"Yeah?" I snapped the way I used to in Germany, and my gut froze. My son Barry's in Saigon. If anything goes wrong, they send a telegram. No. That was last war. Now they send a car. God forbid.

But Steff, my crazy daughter—every time the phone rings at night I'm scared. Maybe she's got herself arrested in one of her goddamn causes and I'm going to have to bail her out like I did in Chicago. Or it could be worse. Two years ago this month, some kids were in the wrong place at the wrong time up at Kent. Damn shame about them and the National Guard; it'll take us years to live it down. Hell of a thing to happen in Ohio.

I thought my kid was going to lose her mind about it. The schools shut down all over the place, all that tuition money pissed away, and God only knows what she got into.

Not just God. Margaret. Steff would call up, say "put Mom on," and Margaret would cry and turn into the phone so I couldn't hear what she was saying. I think she sent money on the sly-like, so I wouldn't make an issue of it. You don't send kids to college so they can get shot at. Steff would say you don't send anyone anywhere so they can get shot at. She's just a kid, you know. She doesn't really believe all that stuff. The kids shouldn't have been there. Anyone could tell you that.

"Hey, that you, Joey?" The voice on the other end was thick with booze. "It's Al. Remember me?"

"You son of a bitch, what're you doing calling this hour of night?" I started to bellow, then piped down. "You wanna wake up my whole damn family?"

"Thought you'd be up, Joey. Like we were . . . the time when . . ."

"Yeah . . . yeah . . ." Sure I remembered. Too well. So did Al, my old army buddy. It happens from time to time. One of us gets to remembering, gets the booze out—Scotch for me these days now that my practice is finally paying off—then picks up the phone. Margaret calls it "going visiting" and "telephonitis" and only gets mad at the end of the month when the bills come in.

But Al wasn't from my outfit at the Battle of the Bulge. Weren't many of them left. Not many had been real close friends to start with: when you run away from home and lie about your age so you can go fight, you're sort of out of place, soldier or not.

Damn near broke my own dad's heart; he'd wanted me to follow him into school and law school and partnership. So I did that on GI bills when I got out. Got married and then there was Korea. I went back in, and that's where I met Al.

"Remember? We'd run out of fuel for the tank and were burning grain alcohol . . . rather drink torpedo juice, wouldn't you? And pushing that thing south to the 38th parallel, scared shitless the North Koreans'd get us if the engine fused . . ."

"Yeah . . ." How far was Korea from Saigon? My son, the lance corporal, had wangled himself a choice slot as Marine guard. I guess all Margaret's nagging about posture and manners had paid off. Almost the only time it had with the Bear. God, you know you'd shed blood so your kids don't turn out as big damn fools as you. I'd of sent Barry through school, any school. But he wanted the service. Not Army, either, but the Marines. Well, Parris Island did what I couldn't do, and now he was "yes sir"–ing a lot of fancypants like Ambassador Bunker over in Vietnam. At least he wasn't a chicken or a runaway . . .

"You there, Joey?" I was staring at the receiver. "I asked you, how's your family?"

"M'wife's fine," I said. How long had it been since Al and I spoke— three years? Five? "So're the kids. Barry's in the Marines. My son the corporal. Stationed in Saigon. The Embassy, no less." I could feel my chest puffing out even though I was tired and it was the middle of the night.

Car lights shone outside. I stiffened. What if . . . The lights passed. All's quiet on the Western Front. Thank God.

Al and the beer hooted approvingly.

"And Steffie's in college. Some damn radical Quaker place. I wanted her to stay in Ohio, be a nurse or a teacher, something practical in case, God forbid, she ever has to work, but my wife wanted her near her own people."

"She getting plenty of crazy ideas at that school?"

"Steff's a good kid, Al. Looks like a real lady now."

What do you expect me to say? That after a year of looking and acting like the big-shot debs my wife admires in the *New York Times*, my

Steffie's decided to hate everything her dad fought for? Sometimes I think she's majoring in revolution. It wasn't enough she got arrested in 1968 campaigning for McCarthy—clean up for Gene, they called it. Clean? I never saw a scruffier bunch of kids till I saw the ones she's taken up with now. Long hair, dirty—and the language? Worse than an army barracks.

She's got another campaign now. This McGovern. I don't see what they have against President Nixon or what they see in this McGovern character. Senator from South Dakota, and I tell you, he's enough to make Mount Rushmore cry. I swear to God, the way these friends of Steff's love unearthing and spreading nasty stories—this Ellsberg character Steff admires, you'd think he was a hero instead of some nutcase who spilled his guts in a shrink's office, so help me. Or this My Lai business: things like that happen in war. You just don't talk about them. Still, what do you expect of a bunch of kids? We made it too easy.

I keep hoping. She's such a good girl, such a pretty girl; one of these days, she'll come around and say "Daddy, I was wrong. I'm sorry."

Never mind that.

Al had got onto the subject of *jo-sans*. Cripes, I hadn't even thought of some of them for twenty years, being an old married man and all. What if Margaret had walked in? I'd of been dead. Sure, I laughed over old times, but I was relieved when he switched to "who's doing what" and "who's died," and then onto current events. We played armchair general, and I tell you, if the Pentagon would listen to us, we'd win this turkey and have the boys home so damned fast . . .

About the time we'd agreed that this Kissinger was a slippery so-and-so and that bombing Haiphong was one of the best things we could have done, only we should have done it a whole lot earlier . . . hell of a way to fight a war, tying General Westmoreland's hands, I heard footsteps on the stairs.

"Do you have any idea what time it is?" Margaret asked me.

I gestured *he called me*! at the phone, feeling like a kid with his hand in the cookie jar. My wife laughed. "Going visiting, is he? Well, let his wife give him aspirin for the hangover I bet he's going to have. You have to go to the office tomorrow and . . ." she paused for emphasis like I was six years old, "you need your sleep."

She disappeared back up the stairs, sure that I'd follow.

"That was the wife," I told Al, my old good buddy. "Gotta go. Hey, don't wait five years to call again. And if you're ever in town, come on over for dinner!"

God, I hope she hadn't heard that stuff about the *jo-sans*. Or the dinner invitation. We'd eat cold shoulder and crow, that was for sure.

FALL OF '72, we kept hearing stories. That Harvard guy that Kissinger was meeting with Le Duc Tho in Paris, and he was encouraged, but then they backed down: back and forth, back and forth till you were ready to scream. "Peace is at hand," he says, and they say it in Hanoi, too. I mean what's the good of it when the commies and your own leaders agree, and the army doesn't? No news out of Radio Hanoi can be any good. And the boys are still coming home in bags, dammit.

Meanwhile, as I hear from Margaret, Stephanie is doing well in her classes. The ones she attends in between campaigning for this McGovern. At first I thought he was just a nuisance candidate. You know, like Stassen runs each time? Then, when they unearthed that stuff about Eagleton, and they changed VP candidates, I thought he was dead in the water for sure. But Shriver's been a good choice: drawn in even more of the young, responsible folk and the people who respect what he did in the Peace Corps. But the real reason McGovern's moving way up in the polls is that more and more people get sick and tired of the war. We just don't believe we can win it, anymore. And that hurts.

I get letters from Barry, too. He's good at that. Writes each one of us. I think he's having a good time in Saigon. I hope he's careful. *You* know what I mean.

Barry says he's got a lot of respect for Ambassador Bunker. Says he was cool as any Marine during Tet, when the VC attacked the Embassy. Says the Ambassador's spoken to him a couple of times, asked him what he wants to do when he gets out of the service. Imagine: My boy, talking to a big shot like that.

And Margaret sent Stephanie a plane ticket home in time for the election. Sure, she could vote at school, but "my vote will make more of a difference in Ohio," she said to me. She was getting a fancy accent.

"You gonna cancel out my vote, baby?" I asked her.

"I sure am, Dad. D'you mind?"

"Hey, kid, what am I working for if it isn't for you and your mom? Sure, come on home and give your fascist old dad a run for his money."

That got kind of a watery laugh from her. We both remembered the time she went to Washington for that big march in '69. I hit the ceiling and Margaret talked me down. "She didn't have to tell us, Joe," she reminded me.

No, she didn't. But she had. Just in case something happened, she admitted that Thanksgiving when she came home from school.

I didn't like the idea of my girl near tear gas and cops with nightsticks when I wasn't around, so I pulled a few strings and sent her Congressman Kirwan's card. *Mike,* the Congressman says I should call him when he comes to the lawyers' table at the Ohio Hotel. And I wrote down on it the home phone number of Miss Messer, his assistant. If anything goes wrong, I told her, she should call there. And I drew a peace sign and signed the letter, "Love and peace, your fascist father."

She says I drew it upside down. Well, what do you expect? Never drew one before.

Anyhow, she'll be home for Election Day, and Barry'll vote by absentee ballot. I'm proud that both my kids take voting seriously. Maybe that school of hers hasn't been a total waste: Steff still takes her responsibilities as a citizen very seriously.

Meanwhile, things—talking and fighting both—slowed down in Paris and Saigon. I remember after Kennedy won the election, Khrushchev wouldn't talk to President Eisenhower's people because Ike was a lame duck. As if he weren't one of the greatest generals we ever had. I tried to listen to some of the speeches by this McGovern Stephanie was wild for. Mostly, I thought he promised pie-in-the-sky. Our boys home by June, everyone working hard and off welfare—not that I'd mind, but I just didn't see how he was going to pull any of it off. I really wanted to ask Barry what he thought, but I didn't. Might be bad for morale.

Then things started to get worse. They stepped up the bombing. Tried to burn off the jungle, too. And the pictures . . . Dammit, I wish I could forget the one of that little girl running down the road with no clothes on screaming in pain. Sometimes at night, it gets messed up in my mind with that thing from Kent, with the girl kneeling and crying over that boy's body. Damn things leap out at you from the newspaper or the news, but I can't just stick my head in the sand.

Maybe the kids . . . maybe this McGovern . . . I've *been* under attack, and I tell you, there comes a time when you just want it to *stop.* Never mind what it costs you. You've already paid enough. I think the whole country's reached that point, and so McGovern's moving way up in the polls.

ELECTION DAY STARTED out really well. The day before, letters had come from Barry. One for me. One for his mother. And even one for Stephanie. I suppose she'd told him she was going to be home, and APO delivery to the Embassy in Saigon is pretty regular. We all sort of went off by ourselves to read our letters. Then Margaret and I traded. I hoped Stephanie would offer to show us hers, too, but she didn't. So we didn't push.

You don't push, not if you want your kids to trust you. Besides, my son and daughter have always had something special between them. He's a good foot taller than she is, but she always looked out for her "baby brother" in school. He never minded that she was the bright one, the leader. Not till he decided not to go to college, and he overheard one of the family saying that Stephanie should have been the boy. So our Bear joined up, not waiting for the draft or anything. I expected Stephanie to throw a fit—Margaret certainly did, but all my girl said was, "He needs to win at something of his own."

I wouldn't have expected her to understand what that means to a boy. Maybe she's growing up.

But it's still all I can do to keep a decent tongue in my head toward my brother-in-law with the big fat mouth.

Election Day, it's a family tradition that everyone comes over to watch the returns on TV. There were going to be some hot words over the cold cuts, if things ran true to speed. And I couldn't see Steff sitting in the kitchen putting things on trays and talking girl talk with her aunts. Steff calls that sort of thing sexist. That's a new word she's got. Don't see why it bothers her. It's not like sometimes the women aren't talking the most interesting things.

For a while, I really thought we were going to make it through the evening without a fight. Stephanie came in, all rosy-faced and glowing from voting, then marching outside the poll all day. She'd left her protest signs in the garage, and she was wearing one of the good skirts and coats she took to school. When everyone said so, she laughed and went up to change into a workshirt and jeans.

"But you looked so pretty, just like a real college girl," her aunt told her.

"That was just window dressing," Stephanie said. "Can I help set the food out now? I'm famished."

She'd wolfed down about half a corned beef sandwich when the phone rang, and she flew up the stairs. "You're kidding. Massachusetts *already*? Oh wow! How's it look for Pennsylvania? I'm telling you, I think we're going to be lucky here, but I'm worried about the South . . ."

"You want another beer, Ron?" I asked my brother-in-law, who was turning red, pretending like he had swallowed something the wrong way and would choke if he didn't drink real fast. Personally, I think he voted for Wallace in the last election, but you can't pry the truth out of him about that with a crowbar.

We settled down to watch TV. Margaret and my sister Nance turned on the portable in the kitchen. I kind of hoped Stephanie would go in there, but she helped clear the table, then came in and sat beside me.

You could have knocked me over with a feather. Maybe the kids were right and people were sick of the bombings, the deaths, the feeling that Vietnam was going to hang around our necks till we choked on it. But state after state went to McGovern . . . "There goes Ohio! Straight on!" Stephanie shouted, raising a fist.

I don't know when all hell broke loose. One moment we were sitting watching John Chancellor cut to President Nixon's headquarters (and my daughter was doing this routine, like a Chatty Cathy doll, about Tricia Nixon). The next moment, she'd jumped up and was stamping one foot as she glared at her uncle.

"How *dare* you use that word?" she was saying to Ron, my brother-in-law. "They're *not* gooks. They're *Asians*. And it's their country, not ours, but we're destroying it for them. We've turned the kids into fugitives, the women into bar girls . . . and they all had fathers, too, till we killed them! What kind of a racist pig . . ."

"Who you calling a racist, little Miss Steff & Nonsense?" asked Ron. By then, he'd probably had at least two beers too many and way too many of my daughter's yells of "straight on." "Why, when I was in the war, there was this Nee-grow sergeant . . ."

"It's 'black'!" she snapped. "You call them *black*! How can you expect me to stay in the same house as this . . ."

She was out of the living room, and the front door slammed behind her before I could stop her.

"That little girl of yours is out of control," Ron told me. "That's what you get, sending her off to that snob school. OSU wasn't good enough, oh no. So what happens? She meets a bunch of radicals there and picks up all sorts of crazy ideas. Tell you, Joey, you better put a leash on that kid, or she'll get into real trouble."

I got up, and he shut up. Margaret came in from the kitchen. I shook my head at her: *everything under control.* I wanted to get a jacket or something. Stephanie had run out without her coat, and the evening was chilly.

"I'd teach her a good lesson, that's what I'd do," said Ron.

Damn! Hadn't I warned her, "I know you think it's funny calling your uncle Ronnie the Racist. But one of these days, it's going to slip out, and then there'll be hell to pay." But she'd said what I should have said. And that made me ashamed.

"She shouldn't have been rude to you," I said. "I'm going to tell her that. But you know how she feels about words like that. I don't much like them either. Besides, this is her house, too."

Ron was grumbling behind my back like an approaching thunderstorm, when I went into the front hall, took out a jacket from the closet, and went outside. Steffie was on the stoop, her face pressed against the cold brick. I put the jacket over her and closed my hands on hers. They were trembling. "Don't rub your face against the brick, baby. You could cut yourself."

She turned around and hugged me. I could feel she was crying with anger and trying hard not to. "I'm not going in there and apologizing," she told me.

"Not even for me?" I coaxed her. There'd been a time she'd do anything in the world for her old dad.

She tried to laugh and cry together, and sounded like the way she used to gurgle when she was a baby.

"I'll promise not to start any fights," she said. "But I won't promise to keep quiet if . . ."

"I told him you shouldn't have been rude to an elder and a guest . . ."

She hissed like the teenager she wasn't. Not anymore.

"I also told him this was your house and you had a right to have your wishes respected, too. Now, will you come in and behave like a lady?"

"It's *woman,* Daddy," she told me.

I hugged her. "You know what I mean. Lady or woman, you're still my little girl. You're supposed to be for peace. Can you try to keep it in your own home?"

She looked up, respect in her eyes. "Ooh, that was a *nice* one," she told me.

"Then remember, tantrums don't win any arguments. Now, you go in. Maybe your mother needs help with the dishes."

"He ought to help," she muttered. "You do. It wouldn't hurt."

"No, it wouldn't." To my surprise, I agreed. "But if we wait for him to get off his butt, your mother's going to be stuck with all of them."

The gift of her obedience hit me in the face like a cold wind when you've had too much to drink. My eyes watered, and the lights up and down Outlook Avenue flickered. Everyone was watching the returns. Some of them had promised to drop in later. The Passells' younger boy had gone to school with Steff. He was the only boy on the street still in school, studying accounting. The Carlsons' middle son, who'd played varsity football, but always took time to coach our Bear, had left OSU and was in the Army. So was the oldest Bentfield, who'd been our paperboy. Fine young men, all of them. And the girls had turned out good, too, even Reenie, who'd got married too young.

Just a one-block street, but you had everything on it. Even a black family had moved in. Maybe I'd had my worries to start off with, but I was real proud we'd all greeted them like neighbors. On some streets when that happened, the kids dumped garbage on the lawn or TP'ed the house.

It was a nice street, a good block, and we'd all lived on it a long time. Nothing fancy, but solid. I wished my father could have seen my house. We'd come back since he'd lost everything in the Depression. But that's the way of it. Each generation does a little bit better than the last one and makes things a little easier for the ones next in line.

We've been five generations in Youngstown. I like to think our name counts for something. Now, this is sort of embarrassing. I don't go to church much, but I looked out over that street and *hoped*, that's a better word for it, that my kids would make that name even more respected. My daughter, the whatever-she-wanted-to-be. A lawyer, maybe. And my son. Who knew? Maybe he'd come home and go back to school, and then this Ambassador—I couldn't see my Bear as a diplomat, but . . .

"How many beers did *you* have?" I asked the sky, gave myself a mental shake, and went back in in time to watch President Nixon's concession speech. It wasn't, not really. You remember how close the race was against JFK. And the 1962 California election when he told the press, "You won't have Nixon to kick around any more."

I don't know. Man's a fighter, but he's not a good loser. I tell you, I don't know what a recount's going to do to this country just when we need a strong leader in place.

"Country's going to hell in a handbasket," Ron grumbled. "I'm going home. Hey, Nancy? You going to yak all night? C'mon!"

After he left, my wife and daughter came back into the living room. Margaret brought out a pot of coffee.

Stephanie sat down to watch McGovern's victory speech. She was holding her mother's hand.

"I admit I am distressed at this demand for a recount at just the time when our country needs to be united. But I am confident that the count will only reaffirm the judgment of the great American people as the bombing has gone on, pounding our hearts as well as a captive nation, that it is enough!

"Now, I have heard it said," the man went on with shining eyes, "that I do not care for honor. Say, rather, that I earn my honor where it may be found. Not in throwing lives after lives away in a war we should never have entered, but in admitting that we have gone as far as we may, and that now it is time for our friends the South Vietnamese to take their role as an independent people, not a client state. Accordingly, my first act as Commander in Chief will be . . ." his voice broke, "to bring them home. Our sons and brothers. The young fathers and husbands of America. Home."

Tears were pouring down the women's faces. I walked over to Margaret. All the years we've been married, she's never been one to show affection in front of the kids. Now she leaned her head against me. "Our boy's coming home!"

Stephanie's face glowed like the pictures of kids holding candles in church or the big protest marches. She could have been at McGovern headquarters; that school of hers has enough pull to put her that high, but she'd chosen to come home instead.

I put a hand on her hair. It was almost as silky as it had been when she was in diapers. Again, my hand curved around her head. It was so warm, just like when she'd been little. "Baby, it looks like you and your friends have won. I just hope you're right."

SOMETHING WOKE ME EARLY that morning. Not the house. Margaret's regular breathing was as always, and I could sense the presence of Stephanie, a now-unfamiliar blessing. I went downstairs, ran some water in the sink, and washed off the serving dishes Margaret had set to soak overnight. Nice surprise for her when she got up.

Of course, I wasn't surprised when the phone rang.

"Hey, Al," I greeted him. Drunk again. "What's the hurry? It's only six months, not five years between calls this time."

"How d'you like it, Joe?" he demanded. "Those little bastards pulled it off. They don't want to go, so, by God, they stop the war. Can you believe it? Not like us, was it. I tell you, ol' buddy, we were suckers. Go where we were told, hup two three four, following orders like goddamn fools, and these kids change the rules on us and get away with it."

Maybe it would be better. Margaret and Steff had held hands and cried for joy. I had to believe it was better, that I wasn't just bitching because other men's sons wouldn't have to go through what I had. I started to talk Al down like I had in Korea, but my heart wasn't in it.

The sky was gray. All the houses on Outlook were dark. Soon it would be dawn and the streetlights would go out, regular as an army camp.

But what were those lights going on? I levered up from my chair — damn, my bones were creaking — and peered out. Lights on at Bentfield's? And, oh my God, Johnny Bentfield . . . no. Oh no. *Not my son, thank God!* Dammit, what kind of a man was I to thank God like that? Sometimes I make myself want to puke.

"Al!" I broke into his ramblings. "I gotta hang up *now.* Something's going on on the street."

"Probably a bunch of stoned kids, celebrating the new age. Well, they're welcome to it. Let 'em come running to me when it blows up in their faces. I'll laugh."

"Yeah, Al. Sure. But I gotta go."

Moving more quietly than I had since Korea, I slipped upstairs and slid open drawers for undershorts, slacks, a sports shirt. Very cautiously, listening to see if they'd wake up, I dressed in the bathroom, then left the house, moving as cautiously as if I were scouting out my own neighborhood. I sneaked over to Bentfield's and peered in the window. At least they didn't have a dog. If what I feared was true, they'd have more on their minds than listening for prowlers. And if I were wrong, please God, if I were wrong, they were good enough friends I could always make up something.

But they were in robes in the living room. Alma Bentfield sat hunched over, hands over her face, while Stan came in, gray-faced, with coffee. The two little girls clutched each other, too sleepy to feel yet how badly they were going to hurt.

God *damn*! Just a little longer, and we'd have brought Johnny home safe. Someone must have called from Vietnam. Unauthorized. Don't ask me how.

I slipped out of their yard and back home.

"What's wrong?" Margaret's voice was sharp and came from outside Stephanie's room. She must have heard what she thought was a prowler, found me gone, and run to see if our daughter needed help.

"Better get dressed," I told her. "There's a light on at Bentfield's. I've had a crazy feeling. I went over and looked. It's about as bad as it can get."

My wife's face twisted, and she clenched her hands.

"I'll wake Steff, too," she said. "She's grown up enough to help out."

I went upstairs to change into a suit. It was almost time to get dressed for work anyhow. But long after I should have left, I sat in the kitchen drinking coffee. Margaret was cooking something. A casserole to take over, maybe. A knife fell into the metal sink. We both jumped and she spilled the milk she was pouring.

"Shit!"

In twenty-five years of marriage, I don't think I'd ever heard her cuss like that.

She mopped up, and I poured myself another cup. I sat staring at the birds and butterflies on the wallpaper mural she took such care of. Different from birds in Southeast Asia, that was for sure: nice tame birds and pale colors. They call it a green hell there.

"It's time to go," she reminded me. I picked up the phone to call my office and tell my secretary I wouldn't be in just yet.

"Hope you're feeling all right," Mary-Lynn wished me, almost laughing.

"I'm fine," I almost snapped. No point taking it out on her. She'd gone to high school with my kids. I remember how old I felt the day I interviewed her—and found out that her mother had been my secretary when I'd started out in practice.

"That's good." She was almost singing. Guess she was relieved too about how the vote had gone. Her husband—the first one was no damn good, but this guy seems to be treating her okay—would be coming home. Vet or no vet, he damn well better be good to her. She's a nice kid, and besides, big as he is, I'll beat the crap out of him.

I drank my coffee and looked out at the street till the olive-drab Army car I was expecting pulled up outside Bentfield's and the long-legged uniformed men strode up the neat walk to the front door. It opened, so reluctantly. All over the street, doors opened, and the women started coming out. Each one carried a covered bowl or baking dish.

Margaret kissed me on the cheek. Her lips were cold. Then she and Stephanie went out. My daughter carried the casserole. She had on her good clothes again and lipstick the color of bubble gum. It looked fake against her pale face, and I wanted to tell her to wipe it off, but I didn't. Her legs, under the short, dark skirt, looked like a little girl's, heading into the doctor's office to get a shot. It was Johnny Bentfield who'd gotten shot.

My womenfolk went to Bentfield's and the door shut behind them.

All down the street, cars pulled out of the driveways like we were escaping.

WHEN I GOT HOME that night, Steffie was in her jeans again, sitting in the living room.

"You shouldn't sit in the dark." I switched on some lights.

"Mom's upstairs with a headache. Took two Fiorinal." Margaret never took more than one.

I headed for the liquor cabinet and pulled out the Scotch.

"I'll do that," said my daughter. She mixed me a double the way I like them. To my surprise, she poured a stiff one for herself.

"I don't know, kitten," I began.

"I'm legal," she said flatly. "And I was there. You weren't. God!" She sat down too fast and lifted her glass. But she knows better than to belt down good Scotch.

"You did the right thing," I praised her. She'd done a good job, the sort of thing nice women like the ones on our street do without even thinking about it.

She wrapped her arms about her shoulders and hunched in. In her jeans and workshirt, she looked like a veteran of some army I'd never seen before. A vet who'd lost a buddy.

Finally, she looked up. The big brown eyes under their floppy bangs held my attention. "They brought her a flag. It was for John, they said. She didn't want to take it, but they put it in her hands. Her knees caved in, but she had to take the flag. We all sat around her. All day. Even after the soldiers left. They had other houses to visit. God *damn!*"

"Don't swear, baby. It's not nice."

"Wasn't nice to be there. Or to have to be there. What if . . ."

"Don't think about it!"

What kind of a father was I, leaving her alone like that? But I couldn't help it. I got up and went outside to check the garage door. Saw a neighbor.

"You hear about Bentfield?" he asked. Carefully, he bent and broke a dead branch off the hedge that divides our property.

I nodded. "My daughter's pretty shook up."

"It's worse than that. Stan told me, and I'm not telling the family. It wasn't VC that got his boy. 'Friendly fire,' they call it. He was stationed in front of the regular troops and, well, someone screwed up."

That's what happens when you cut and run. You get stuck facing something even worse. I had to go in and face Steffie like nothing had happened. She wasn't crying, at least, but she'd turned the lights off again.

"You want dinner? Mom said to heat stuff up."

I shook my head.

"Me neither."

"Let's not tell her we skipped dinner. She'd get mad."

We sat in the dark for a long time. After a while, the house got chilly, and it was time to go to bed.

Well, Nixon had his recount. It was close. Even closer than when he'd lost against Kennedy. I don't know, if I'd have thought he'd be such a bad loser, maybe I wouldn't have voted for him the first time. And the grins on the faces of those guys who look like Ho Chi Minh's grandsons at the UN made me want to wipe them out with my fist.

"It's face, y'know," Al said. After all these years, he'd finally made it to Youngstown on a business trip. Some of us got together at his Holiday Inn. These days, Al sells steel pipe. Frankly, I think he drinks through them—the gut he's got on him now! "Now that we're pulling out, they don't respect us. Not that they ever did, all that much. Talk about yellow . . . I know who's yellow, those little yellow . . ."

"Al." Father Klein picked his beer bottle out of his hand. "You've had enough. We've all had enough."

Al lurched onto his feet, his face red. Peanuts scattered across the table. I swept them back into the bowl. Didn't think Al would take on Father Klein. He was wearing his collar, for one thing. For another, he'd always been able to punch out anyone in our outfit.

"I wanted us to win," Al said. The fight drained out of him. "You know what happens when you retreat. Remember what we'd have got if they'd caught us in Korea? Tiger cages and bamboo under our fingernails. This isn't going to be a retreat. It's a goddamn rout. Who's holding the fort while everyone's pulling out? You mark my words, it's going to be a bloodbath."

"It's okay, Al," Father Klein said. "Joey and I'll walk you back to your room and you can stick your head in the john."

PRO-WAR OR PEACENIK, we all went sort of crazy that spring. The atlas from our *Britannica* fell open at the mark of Southeast Asia as I showed Margaret just where our men were pulling back from.

"It's so green. Can't they just jump out?" Our dining room is white and gold: formal, Margaret calls it. If she likes it, fine, I'm happy. It seemed weird to be talking about weapons and jungles as we sat at a table covered by a cloth, eating off real silver.

"McGovern won't let us burn off the jungle. It's a no-no. Like DDT. Damn! It's all tunnels underneath. The VC can pop out of a tunnel, strike from behind, then disappear. Or hide in a village. You can't tell VC from rice farmers. And there's no good aerial cover."

"I don't want to talk about this at dinner," she said, and closed the atlas. She didn't ever want to talk about it. Well, she wasn't a vet. God forbid we ever use our women like that, though those nurses . . . you've really got to hand it to them. They've got guts. Day after day, nurses flew out with their patients. The big, silent planes flew out too, with the flags and the coffins. But the news wasn't showing them much anymore.

McGovern called it peace with honor. Withdrawal with honor, someone had tried to call it at a press conference; the reporters had cracked up. They'd had to fade to black real fast. Besides, you couldn't say that around the kids. McGovern still had them in the palm of his hand. They had a lot of influence, and they wanted our boys out. McGovern always had a bunch of them following him around, as interns or admirers or something. They were beginning to look a little frantic.

It was Father Klein who called it the long defeat. We were fighting to lose. It reminded me of something. Once I had to help the Bear with his history homework, and I read this thing about a Children's Crusade. They wanted to do what their elders couldn't—free the Holy Land, miracles, that sort of thing. So they left home and went on Crusade. And none of 'em ever made it back.

Every time the phone rang, I dreaded it. Sometimes it was Steff. She'd turned expert, like all the kids. We talked over the withdrawal, and she said the exotic names in tones I hadn't heard for years. Sometimes it was relief operations. Everyone wanted a check. Once it was Steff's school—some lady from development assuring us that no, the school wasn't planning to close down as it had in 1970 so everyone could go do relief work. Oddly enough, I don't think I'd have minded if it had. Let the college kids do their share. But while she had me on the phone, could she possibly convince me to donate . . .

Yeah, sure.

Al never called. After a while that sort of worried me, I picked up the phone one evening at a decent hour and called him. Got his Mrs. And the cold shoulder, too, till I explained. Al was resting, she said. He'd been working too hard lately. No, he couldn't come to the phone.

Drying out, I thought. Not all the casualties of a war happen in combat.

Used to be, letters from the Bear were a surprise—a treat to top off a good deal or a reward to make up for a lousy one. Now, I started calling home about the time the mail usually came. "Any news?" I'd ask. Usually, there wasn't. If there was, Margaret would read Bear's letters to me. Steffie said he was still writing her, but she didn't offer.

Don't know when he had time. He said he was helping out when he was off-duty in one of the orphanages. Run by French nuns. Didn't know he'd learned some French, too. Maybe he wouldn't mind if his dad stuck his nose into his business when he came back and suggested going to college on a GI bill. There *had* to be a GI bill or something, didn't there? I mean, we owe those boys a lot.

Well, he always had been good with kids. He sent us one snapshot. There he was, all spit and polish, with these cute little round-faced kids with their bright eyes crawling all over him, scuffing up those patent shoes.

At least he got to keep clean and dry. I remembered how your feet felt like they'd rot off if you couldn't get them out of those stinking boots. In the jungle, you get mold on everything, it's so damp. I didn't like it when the Bear would complain that he had it soft, compared to most of the men. I was scared he'd try to transfer out. But I guess someone talked to him, and he thought of what he owed to his mom and sister, because after a while, he didn't talk about that anymore.

And meanwhile, those goddamn VC were getting closer to Saigon. The whole fucking—sorry, I never swear like that, must be thinking back to my army days—country was falling apart. Hated to admit it, but Al was right. As long as we came on like Curtis Le May and threatened, at least, to bomb 'em back to the Stone Age, they'd at least respected what we could do to them if we really set our minds to it. Now, "paper tiger" was the kindest name they had for us.

President McGovern began to look haunted. He'd be a one-term president, that was for sure. And when he came down with cardiac arrhythmia, some of us wondered if he'd even manage that. The kids who surrounded his staff looked pretty grim, too. Like the kids who get caught stealing cars and suddenly realize that things are not going to be much fun anymore.

The anchormen on the evening news sounded like preachers at a funeral. I'm not making this up; it happened at Da Nang. You saw a plane ready for takeoff. Three hundred people crowded in, trampling on women and children, they were so panicky. Then the crew wanted to close the doors and get out of there, but the people wouldn't get off the runway, clear the stairs. They pulled some off the wheels and took off anyway. And you could see little black specks as people fell off where they'd hung on to the rear stairway.

Did McGovern say anything? Sure. "We must put the past behind us. Tragic as these days are, they are the final throes of a war we never should have entered. In the hard days to come, I call upon the American people to emulate the discipline and courage of our fine servicemen who are withdrawing in good order from Vietnam."

I'd of spat, but Margaret was watching the news with me. We couldn't *not* watch. Funny, neither of us had ever liked horror films, but we had to watch the news.

Some people waded into the sea, the mothers holding their babies over their heads. They overloaded fishing boats, and the Navy found them floating. Or maybe the boats hadn't overloaded. Those people mostly hadn't much, but it wouldn't have been hard to take what they had, hit them on the head, and throw them overboard.

Refugees were flooding Saigon. The Bear's French orphanage was mobbed, and the grounds of all the embassies were full. Would the VC respect the embassies? How could they? Human life means nothing to them, or else they wouldn't treat their own people the way they do. And Cambodia's even worse, no matter what Steffie's poli-sci profs say.

In a letter I didn't show my wife, Barry told me he could hear the cluster bombs drop. The North Viets were at Xuanloc, thirty-five miles northwest of Saigon, on the way to Bien Hoa airfield, heading south, always heading south.

"If our allies had fought as well as they did at Xuanloc, maybe we wouldn't be in this fix, Dad," Barry wrote me. "It doesn't look good. Don't tell Mom. But the Navy's got ships standing offshore in the Gulf of Thailand and a fleet of choppers to fly us out to them. I hope . . ."

I crumpled the letter in my hand. Later, I smoothed it out and made myself read it, though. My son was out in that green hell, and I was scared to read his letter? That wasn't how I'd want to greet him when the choppers finally brought him out. He'd be one of the last to leave, I knew that. Probably pushing the ambassador ahead of him.

I wrote I was proud of him. I didn't say the half of what I meant. I don't know if he got the letter.

THEN ONE MORNING Mary-Lynn met me at the door of my office, and she'd been crying.

She wouldn't let me inside. "Mrs. Black called. You have to go home, she says. Right away. Oh, Mr. Black, I'm so sorry!" She wiped at her nose. I was in shock. I pulled my handkerchief from my suit jacket and handed it to her.

She put her hands out as if I was going to pass out. "There's a . . . there's a *car* out there . . ."

"Not . . ." I couldn't say the word. It would make it real. My boy. Never coming home? I couldn't make myself believe it.

"They've got a car there and Marines—oh, your wife says please, please come straight home . . ."

The spring sun hit my shoulders like something I'd never felt before. What right did the sun have to shine here? The trees in Crandall Park were fresh and green, and the gardens at the big corner house where they always spent a mint on flowers looked like something out of the first day of the world. How did they dare? My boy had been shot. Other men's sons had been shot in a green hell they should have burnt down to ash.

A voice broke in on the radio.

". . . the American Embassy has closed its gates, and the Ambassador . . . Ambassador Bunker has refused evacuation . . ."

He'd have been there, my son. Firing into the enemy, not wanting to fire, I knew that, but there'd be a wall of Marines between the VC and the panicked crowd and the diplomats they had sworn to protect. . . .

I had people to protect too. I put my foot hard on the gas, peeled round a slowpoke station wagon with three kids and their mom in it, and roared up Fifth Avenue.

". . . We interrupt this program . . . there is a rumor that Ambassador Bunker has been shot. . . . We repeat, this is a rumor, no one has seen his body . . ."

Sweet suffering Christ! Damn that red light, no one was around, so it wouldn't matter if I crashed it. Didn't want to smear myself all over the landscape before I got home; Margaret would never forgive me if I got myself killed coming home to her now, of all times.

*God*damn siren! I thought of giving the cop a run for his money, but you don't do that in Youngstown. Not ever, and especially not if you're a lawyer.

The man who got out of the car recognized me. "Hey, Counselor, what you think you're doing? You were going seventy and you crashed that light . . ." He sniffed at my breath, then pulled out his pad. "You know better than that. Now I wish I could let you off with a warning . . ."

A fist was squeezing my throat. Finally, it let up long enough for me to breathe. "It's my boy . . ." I said. Then I laid my head down on the steering wheel.

A hand came in over my shoulder and took the keys. "I'm driving you home. The way you're driving, you could get yourself . . . Come on, Counselor."

I made him let me off up the street. No telling what Margaret would have thought if she'd seen a cop car roll up to the door. The Marine car was in the drive. The men got out of the car and followed me. I made it up the front walk, feeling like I was walking off a three-day binge. Toni Carlson opened the door. She was crying, but Margaret wasn't. Sure enough, the living room and kitchen were full of women with their covered dishes.

"I called Steffie's school," Margaret said before I could even get to her. She had Barry's service photo out like they do in the newspapers. His face grinned under his hat. God, he was a good-looking boy. "Her plane gets in this afternoon."

"I'm going to pick her up," said a voice from behind me.

"Sir," began one of the Marines. A fine young man. I had ... I have ... a son like him.

He shook my hand and bravely said the things they're supposed to say. "Sir, the President of the United States and the Secretary of Defense have asked me to inform you that your son ..." The boy's voice faltered, and he went on in his own words.

Missing. Presumed dead. My son was ... is ... a hero. But presumed dead. After Ambassador Bunker died (that wasn't supposed to get out yet, but he supposed I had a right to know), the surviving Marines were supposed to withdraw. But Barry gave his seat to a local woman and a child.

"Probably knew them from the orphanage," I muttered.

"No doubt, sir," said the Marine. It wasn't his business to comment. He'd be glad to get out, even if he had more families' hearts to break that day. Lord, I wished I could.

At least he didn't have a damn flag. As long as you don't get the flag, you can still hope.

HER SCHOOL SENT Steffie home, the way these schools do when there's been a death in the family. Pinkos they may be, but I've got to admit each of her professors and the college president wrote us nice letters. Take as much time as you need before coming back to class, they told Steff. Better than she got from some of her friends. Once or twice, when she thought I wasn't looking, I saw her throw out letters. And I heard her shouting on the phone at someone, then hang up with a bang. All she ever said was, "You never know who's really your friend."

I thought she'd do better to stick out the term, but she decided to take the semester off. Seeing how Margaret brightened at that news, I didn't insist she go back. And when my wife threw a major fit and screamed, "I can't bear to lose *both* the men in our family!" at the dinner table and practically *ordered* me to get an EKG, I kept the appointment with our doctor that she'd made.

Oddly enough, now that the worst had happened, I slept like a baby right through the next time the phone rang at 3:00 A.M.

Steffie came into our room. She spoke to Margaret. "It's from Frankfurt. West Germany."

Why would she be getting a call from West Germany of all places?

Margaret got up and threw on a robe. "It's in, then?"

My daughter nodded. I stared at both women. Beyond family resemblance, their faces wore the same expression: guilt, fear, and a weird kind of anticipation under the sorrow that had put circles under their eyes.

Like the damn fool husbands on TV, I waited for my womenfolk to explain what was going on. It didn't much matter. After all, when your country's lost a war and a son, what else can happen?

"We have to talk," Margaret said in *that* tone of voice. "I'll make us some coffee."

So at three in the morning, we sat down to a family conference. Margaret poured coffee. To my surprise, she looked imploringly at Steffie.

"The call from Frankfurt came through on my line," she said.

That stupid Princess phone!

"That's where they evacuate the refugees and process them."

My hand closed on the spoon till it hurt. How did that rate a transatlantic phone call?

Stephanie took a deep, deep breath and drew herself up. For a moment, I thought I could see her brother, making up his mind at the Embassy to give up his place to a woman and a child.

Our eyes met. She'd been thinking of Barry too.

"You know that woman and kid Barry pushed onto the helicopter in his place?"

"The ones he knew from the orphanage?"

"Where'd you get that idea?" Margaret broke in.

"Mom, he *did* meet Nguyen at the orphanage."

"Now wait a damn minute, both of you. Maybe it's too early, but no one's making sense!"

Margaret set down her coffee cup. "Joe, please listen."

"Dad, about a year ago, Barry wrote me. He'd met a girl who worked at the French Embassy. She's from Saigon and her name is Nguyen."

I held up a hand. I wanted to be stupid. I wanted to be Ward Cleaver and have this episode end. Margaret would switch off the TV set, the show would be over, we could all go back to bed, and none of this, *none* of the whole past miserable year would have happened.

So my boy had sacrificed himself for a friend. . . .

"She's his *wife*, Daddy. And the child . . ."

When you're on the front lines and you get hit bad, it doesn't hurt at first. You go into shock.

"You knew about this?" I asked Margaret. She looked down, ashamed.

"And didn't tell me?" Both women looked down.

"My son *married*—how do we know it's true?—he says he *married* this goddamn gook! Her people *killed* him, and you have the nerve to say . . ."

"If you say that word, I'll never speak to you again!" Stephanie was on her feet, her big flannel nightgown billowing in flowers and hearts about her. "Nguyen's not a bar girl. Barry said she's a lady. She worked at the French Embassy. She speaks French and Vietnamese . . . some English."

"They seem to have communicated just fine without it!" I snapped, hating myself.

They'd hidden this from me! Barry had written to Stephanie, and all those calls when she'd said, "I need to talk to Mom," they were talking about this unknown girl. This gook girl. Who my son had planned to bring home. I could just see Ronnie the Racist's face.

They'd hidden this from me.

"Oh Mom, I'm making such a mess of this!" Steffie cried. "I didn't really believe he'd take it like this . . ."

"Give him some time, darling," said my wife. "We were caught by surprise, too."

"*You* give him some time," my daughter burst into tears. "The only grandkid he may ever have, and all he can think of is to ask, 'Are they really married?' and call the mother a gook and a bar girl! I haven't got time for this! I have to pack and go to Washington to meet Nguyen, and then I have to go . . ."

I reached up and grasped my daughter's wrist.

"Just where do you think you're going?"

That little bit of a thing faced me down. "I'm joining the Red Cross relief effort." She laughed, shakily. "I wish I'd listened to you and become a nurse after all. It's a hell of a lot more useful than a poli-sci major for what I need to do. We're going over there."

"That hellhole's already swallowed one of my kids!"

"That's right. So I'm going over there to look for him."

I shook my head at her. Just one small girl in the middle of a war zone. What did she think she could do?

"Daddy, you know I've *always* looked after my brother. No matter how big he got. Except with this . . . this mess about the war. I did what I thought was right, and see how it worked out." She wiped at her eyes.

"Somehow, I have to make up for that. All of us do. So I'm going to look for him. And if I . . . when I find him . . . so help me, I am going to beat the crap out of him for scaring us this way!" She was sobbing noisily now, and when I held out my arms, she flung herself into them.

"Oh Daddy, I was wrong, it all went wrong and it got so fucked up!"

"Don't use words like that," I whispered, kissing my girl's hair. "Not in front of your mother."

"It's all right," said Margaret. "I feel the same way."

"Unless I find him, Nguyen and the little boy are all we've got of Barry. And we're all *they've* got. But all you can do is call them bad words and . . . and . . ."

I patted her back and met my wife's eyes. She nodded, and I knew we'd be having guests in the house. No, scratch that. We'd be having new family members come to live here. And if my sister's husband even *thought* of opening his big fat mouth, I'd shut it for him the way I'd wanted to for the past thirty years.

Stephanie pulled out of my arms and pushed her bangs out of her eyes. I sighed and picked my words. If I said things wrong, I was scared I'd lose her.

"We've been in this town for five generations," I began slowly. "I think our family has enough of a reputation so people will welcome . . . what did you say her name was?"

"Nguyen," Margaret whispered. Her eyes were very bright. "I'll brush up on my French." She used to teach it before we got married. "And the little boy—our grandson—is Barry, Jr. I can't imagine how that sounds in a Vietnamese accent, can you?"

A tiny woman in those floaty things Vietnamese women wore. A little lady. My son's wife . . . or widow. And one of those cute little black-eyed kids, unless he looked like Bear. Family. Just let anyone *dare* say anything.

"We can put them in Barry's room," I stammered. "I suppose."

"Nguyen can have mine," said Steffie. "I won't need it. Oh, Daddy, I was wrong about so many things. But I was right about you after all."

She kissed me, then ran upstairs, a whirlwind in a flowered night-gown. I could hear closets and drawers protesting and paper ripping.

"I wish she'd been right about all of them," I told Margaret. She took my hand.

"I'm going with Stephanie to pick up . . . Nguyen," my wife informed me.

It would get easier, I sensed, for both of us to think of her and the boy as family once we met them. My son's wife. My son's son. This wasn't how I'd thought that would be.

In a few minutes, once the shock wore off, I supposed I'd get to see the pictures. I knew there had to be pictures. But you don't live with a woman for this many years without knowing when she has more to say. And having a pretty good idea of what it is—most of the time.

This time, though, my guess was right. "Joe, I want you to come with us to Washington so we can all meet as a family. Nguyen must be terrified. She's lost everything and, and everyone."

Her voice trembled, but she forced it to calm. "It would mean a lot to her. Steff says the Vietnamese are Confucian. If the head of our family were there to greet her, she'd *know* she was welcome, she and the little one."

A smile flickered across her face. "I wonder where we can get a crib," she mused. "All our friends' children are grown and haven't started having babies yet. We'll be the first to have a grandchild."

I bent over and hugged her. "Did you make a third plane reservation?"

She smiled at me. "What do you think?"

"I'LL CARRY YOUR SUITCASE downstairs for you, baby," I told my daughter.

"Oh, Dad, you know I'll have to lug my own stuff once I go overseas . . ."

"As long as you're in *my house*, young lady—"

"It's on my bed." I went into her room to get it. She'd taken a cheap plaid fabric thing, not one of the good, big Samsonite cases she'd gotten for high school graduation. Her room wasn't just clean: it was sterile. She'd even torn down her posters and hung the crewelwork back up. I wondered what this strange new daughter-in-law of mine would make of the pretty blue and lilac room.

My foot sent something spinning and rolling. I bent to retrieve the thing, which promptly jagged my finger. One of Stephanie's protest buttons, hurled away as if in despair, poor girl. "Suppose they gave a war and nobody came?" it asked.

Suppose they did? It had never happened yet.

Suppose, instead, they gave a peace? That hadn't worked, either.

But I can always hope, can't I?

After all, I have a grandson to look out for.

Larry Niven

Larry Niven established his credentials as a provocative writer of hard sci-ence fiction with his Nebula Award–winning novel Ringworld, *about an artificial ring-shaped planetary body with a million-mile radius and six-hundred-million-mile circumference that poses unusual technical prob-lems in navigation and escape for its human inhabitants. The novel, and its sequels* Ringworld Engineers *and* The Ringworld Throne, *are part of Niven's vast Tales of Known Space saga, an acclaimed future history of interstellar space that has accommodated a wide variety of themes includ-ing alien culture, immortality, time travel, terraforming, genetic engineer-ing, teleportation, and exotic alien cultures in such novels as* The World of Ptavvs *and* A Gift from Earth, *and the short-fiction collections* Neu-tron Star, The Shape of Space, *and* Tales of Known Space. *Between 1988 and 1991 the series spun off a quartet of shared-world anthologies,* The Man-Kzin Wars, *concerned with human and extraterrestrial conflict. Niven's collaborations extend to novel-length works of fiction and include* The Mote in God's Eye, Inferno, Oath of Fealty, *and* Lucifer's Ham-mer, *all co-authored with Jerry Pournelle, and the Dream Park series, written with Steve Barnes. Niven has also written a series of fantasies con-cerned with primitive concepts of magic, including* The Magic Goes Away *and the collection* Time of the Warlock. *A representative sampling of his short fiction and nonfiction can be found in* N-Space.

ALL THE MYRIAD WAYS

Larry Niven

THERE WERE TIMELINES branching and branching, a mega-universe of universes, millions more every minute. Billions? Trillions? Trimble didn't understand the theory, though God knows he'd tried. The universe split every time someone made a decision. Split, so that every decision ever made could go both ways. Every choice made by every man, woman and child on Earth was reversed in the universe next door. It was enough to confuse any citizen, let alone Detective-Lieutenant Gene Trimble, who had other problems.

Senseless suicides, senseless crimes. A city-wide epidemic. It had hit other cities too. Trimble suspected that it was worldwide, that other nations were simply keeping it quiet.

Trimble's sad eyes focused on the clock. Quitting time. He stood up to go home, and slowly sat down again. For he had his teeth in the problem, and he couldn't let go.

Not that he was really accomplishing anything.

But if he left now, he'd only have to take it up again tomorrow.

Go, or stay?

And the branchings began again. Gene Trimble thought of other universes parallel to this one, and a parallel Gene Trimble in each one. Some had left early. Many had left on time, and were now halfway home to dinner, out to a movie, watching a strip show, racing to the scene of another death. Streaming out of police headquarters in all their multitudes, leaving a multitude of Trimbles behind them. Each of these trying to deal, alone, with the city's endless, inexplicable parade of suicides.

Gene Trimble spread the morning paper on his desk. From the bottom drawer he took his gun-cleaning equipment, then his .45. He began to take the gun apart.

The gun was old but serviceable. He'd never fired it except on the target range, and never expected to. To Trimble, cleaning his gun was like knitting, a way to keep his hands busy while his mind wandered off. Turn the screws, don't lose them. Lay the parts out in order.

Through the closed door to his office came the sounds of men hurrying. Another emergency? The department couldn't handle it all. Too many suicides, too many casual murders, not enough men.

Gun oil. Oiled rag. Wipe each part. Put it back in place.

Why would a man like Ambrose Harmon go off a building?

IN THE EARLY MORNING light he lay, more a stain than a man, thirty-six stories below the edge of his own penthouse roof. The pavement was splattered red for yards around him. The stairs were still wet. Harmon had landed on his face. He wore a bright silk dressing gown and a sleeping jacket with a sash.

Others would take samples of his blood, to learn if he had acted under the influence of alcohol or drugs. There was little to be learned from seeing him in his present condition.

"But why was he up so early?" Trimble wondered. For the call had come in at 8:03, just as Trimble arrived at headquarters.

"So late, you mean." Bentley had beaten him to the scene by twenty minutes. "We called some of his friends. He was at an all-night poker game. Broke up around six o'clock."

"Did Harmon lose?"

"Nope. He won almost five hundred bucks."

"That fits," Trimble said in disgust. "No suicide note?"

"Maybe they've found one. Shall we go up and see?"

"We won't find a note," Trimble predicted.

EVEN THREE MONTHS earlier Trimble would have thought, *How incredible!* or, *Who could have pushed him?* Now, riding up in the elevator, he thought only, *Reporters.* For Ambrose Harmon was news. Even among this past year's epidemic suicides, Ambrose Harmon's death would stand out like Lyndon Johnson in a lineup.

He was a prominent member of the community, a man of dead and wealthy grandparents. Perhaps the huge inheritance, four years ago, had gone to his head. He had invested tremendous sums to back harebrained, quixotic causes.

Now, because one of the harebrained causes had paid off, he was richer than ever. The Crosstime Corporation already held a score of patents on inventions imported from alternate time tracks. Already those inventions had started more than one industrial revolution. And Harmon was the money behind Crosstime. He would have been the world's next billionaire—had he not walked off his balcony.

They found a roomy, luxuriously furnished apartment in good order, and a bed turned down for the night. The only sign of disorder was the clothing—slacks, sweater, a silk turtleneck shirt, knee-length shoesocks, no underwear—piled on a chair in the bedroom. The toothbrush had been used.

He got ready for bed, Trimble thought. He brushed his teeth, and then he went out to look at the sunrise. A man who kept late hours like that, he wouldn't see the sunrise very often. He watched the sunrise, and when it was over he jumped.

Why?

They were all like that. Easy, spontaneous decisions. The victim/killers walked off bridges or stepped from their balconies or suddenly flung themselves in front of subway trains. They strolled halfway across a freeway, or swallowed a full bottle of laudanum. None of the methods showed previous planning. Whatever was used, the victim had had it all along; he never actually went out and *bought* a suicide weapon. The victim rarely dressed for the occasion, or used makeup, as an ordinary suicide would. Usually there was no note.

Harmon fit the pattern perfectly.

"Like Richard Cory," said Bentley.

"Who?"

"Richard Cory, the man who had everything. 'And Richard Cory, one calm summer night, went home and put a bullet through his head.' You know what I think?"

"If you've got an idea, let's have it."

"The suicides all started about a month after Crosstime got started. I think one of the Crosstime ships brought back a new bug from some alternate timeline."

"A suicide bug?"

Bentley nodded.

"You're out of your mind."

"I don't think so. Gene, do you know how many Crosstime pilots have killed themselves in the last year? More than twenty percent!"

"Oh?"

"Look at the records. Crosstime has about twenty vehicles in action now, but in the past year they've employed sixty-two pilots. Three disappeared. Fifteen are dead, and all but two died by suicide."

"I didn't know that." Trimble was shaken.

"It was bound to happen sometime. Look at the alternate worlds they've found so far. The Nazi world. The Red Chinese world, half bombed to death. The ones that are so totally bombed, that Crosstime can't even find out who did it. The one with the Black Plague mutation, and no penicillin until Crosstime came along. Sooner or later—"

"Maybe, maybe. I don't buy your bug, though. If the suicides are a new kind of plague, what about the other crimes?"

"Same bug."

"Uh uh. But I think we'll check up on Crosstime."

Trimble's hands finished with the gun and laid it on the desk. He was hardly aware of it. Somewhere in the back of his mind was a prodding sensation: the *handle*, the piece he needed to solve the puzzle.

He'd spent most of the day studying Crosstime, Inc. News stories, official handouts, personal interviews. The incredible suicide rate among Crosstime pilots could not be coincidence. He wondered why nobody had noticed it before.

It was slow going. With Crosstime travel, as with relativity, you had to throw away reason and use only logic. Trimble had sweated it out. Even the day's murders had not distracted him.

They were typical, of a piece with the preceding eight months' crime wave. A man had shot his foreman with a gun bought an hour earlier, then strolled off toward police headquarters. A woman had moved through the back row of a dark theater, using an ice pick to stab members of the audience through the backs of their seats. She had chosen only young men. They had killed without heat, without concealment; they had surrendered without fear or bravado. Perhaps it was another kind of suicide.

Time for coffee, Trimble thought, responding unconsciously to dry throat plus a muzziness in the mouth plus slight fatigue. He set his hands to stand up, and—

The image came to him of an endless row of Trimbles, lined up like the repeated images in facing mirrors. But each image was slightly different. He would go get the coffee *and* he wouldn't *and* he would send somebody for it *and* someone was about to bring it without being asked. Some of the images were drinking coffee, a few had tea or milk, some were smoking, some were leaning too far back with their feet on the desks (and a handful of these were toppling helplessly backward), some were, like this present Trimble, introspecting with their elbows on the desk.

Damn Crosstime anyway.

He'd have had to check Harmon's business affairs, even without the Crosstime link. There might have been a motive there, for suicide or for murder, though it had never been likely.

In the first place, Harmon had cared nothing for money. The Crosstime group had been one of many. At the time that project had looked as harebrained as the rest: a handful of engineers and physicists and philosophers determined to prove that the theory of alternate time tracks was reality.

In the second place, Harmon had no business worries.

Quite the contrary.

Eleven months ago an experimental vehicle had touched one of the worlds of the Confederate States of America, and returned. The universes of alternate choice were within reach. And the pilot had brought back an artifact.

From that point on, Crosstime travel had more than financed itself. The Confederate world's "stapler," granted an immediate patent, had bought two more ships. A dozen miracles had originated in a single, technologically advanced timeline, one in which the catastrophic Cuba War had been no more than a wet firecracker. Lasers, oxygen-hydrogen rocket motors, computers, strange plastics—the list was still growing. And Crosstime held all the patents.

In those first months the vehicles had gone off practically at random. Now the pinpointing was better. Vehicles could select any branch they preferred. Imperial Russia, Amerindian America, the Catholic Empire, the dead worlds. Some of the dead worlds were hells of radioactive dust and intact but deadly artifacts. From these worlds Crosstime pilots brought strange and beautiful works of art which had to be stored behind leaded glass.

The latest vehicles could reach worlds so like this one that it took a week of research to find the difference. In theory they could get even closer. There was a phenomenon called "the broadening of the bands.". . .

And that had given Trimble the shivers.

When a vehicle left its own present, a signal went on in the hangar, a signal unique to that ship. When the pilot wanted to return, he simply cruised across the appropriate band of probabilities until he found the signal. The signal marked his own unique present.

Only it didn't. The pilot always returned to find a clump of signals, a broadened band. The longer he stayed away, the broader was the signal band. His own world had continued to divide after his departure, in a constant stream of decisions being made both ways.

Usually it didn't matter. Any signal the pilot chose represented the world he had left. And since the pilot himself had a choice, he naturally returned to them all. But—

There was a pilot by the name of Gary Wilcox. He had been using his vehicle for experiments, to see how close he could get to his own timeline and still leave it. Once, last month, he had returned twice.

Two Gary Wilcoxes, two vehicles. The vehicles had been wrecked: their hulls intersected. For the Wilcoxes it could have been sticky, for Wilcox had a wife and family. But one of the duplicates had chosen to die almost immediately.

Trimble had tried to call the other Gary Wilcox. He was too late. Wilcox had gone skydiving a week ago. He'd neglected to open his parachute.

Small wonder, thought Trimble. At least Wilcox had had motive. It was bad enough, knowing about the other Trimbles, the ones who had gone home, the ones drinking coffee, et cetera. But—suppose someone walked into the office right now, and it was Gene Trimble?

It could happen.

Convinced as he was that Crosstime was involved in the suicides, Trimble (some other Trimble) might easily have decided to take a trip in a Crosstime vehicle. A short trip. He could land *here*.

TRIMBLE CLOSED HIS EYES and rubbed at the corners with his fingertips. In some other timeline, very close, someone had thought to bring him coffee. Too bad this wasn't it.

It didn't do to think too much about these alternate timelines. There were too many of them. The close ones could drive you buggy, but the ones further off were just as bad.

Take the Cuba War. Atomics had been used, *here*, and now Cuba was uninhabited, and some American cities were gone, and some Russian. It could have been worse.

Why wasn't it? How did we luck out? Intelligent statesmen? Faulty bombs? A humane reluctance to kill indiscriminately?

No. There was no luck anywhere. Every decision was made both ways. For every wise choice you bled your heart out over, you made all the other choices too. And so it went, all through history.

Civil wars unfought on some worlds were won by either side on others. Elsewhen, another animal had first done murder with an antelope femur. Some worlds were still all nomad; civilization had lost out. If every choice was cancelled elsewhere, why make a decision at all?

Trimble opened his eyes and saw the gun.

That gun, too, was endlessly repeated on endless desks. Some of the images were dirty with years of neglect. Some smelled of gunpowder, fired recently, a few at living targets. Some were loaded. All were as real as this one.

A number of these were about to go off by accident.

A proportion of these were pointed, in deadly coincidence, at Gene Trimble.

See the endless rows of Gene Trimble, each at his desk. Some are bleeding and cursing as men run into the room following the sound of the gunshot. Many are already dead.

Was there a bullet in there? Nonsense.

He looked away. The gun was empty.

Trimble loaded it. At the base of his mind he felt the touch of the *handle*. He would find what he was seeking.

He put the gun back on his desk, pointing away from him, and he thought of Ambrose Harmon, coming home from a late night. Ambrose Harmon, who had won five hundred dollars at poker. Ambrose Harmon, exhausted, seeing the lightening sky as he prepared for bed. Going out to watch the dawn.

Ambrose Harmon, watching the slow dawn, remembering a two-thousand-dollar pot. He'd bluffed. In some other branching of time, he had lost.

Thinking that in some other branching of time that two thousand dollars included his last dime. It was certainly possible. If Crosstime hadn't paid off, he might have gone through the remains of his fortune in the past four years. He liked to gamble.

Watching the dawn, thinking of all the Ambrose Harmons on that roof. Some were penniless this night, and they had not come out to watch the dawn.

Well, why not? If he stepped over the edge, here and now, another Ambrose Harmon would only laugh and go inside.

If he laughed and went inside, other Ambrose Harmons would fall to their deaths. Some were already on their ways down. One changed his mind too late, another laughed as he fell. . . .

Well, why not? . . .

Trimble thought of another man, a nonentity, passing a firearms store. Branching of timelines, he thinks, looking in, and he thinks of the man who took his foreman's job. Well, why not? . . .

Trimble thought of a lonely woman making herself a drink at three in the afternoon. She thinks of myriads of alter egos, with husbands, lovers, children, friends. Unbearable, to think that all the might-have-beens were as real as herself. As real as this ice pick in her hand. Well, why not? . . .

And she goes out to a movie, but she takes the ice pick.

And the honest citizen with a carefully submerged urge to commit rape, just once. Reading his newspaper at breakfast, and there's another story from Crosstime: they've found a world line in which Kennedy the First was assassinated. Strolling down a street, he thinks of world lines and infinite branchings, of alter egos already dead, or jailed, or President. A girl in a miniskirt passes, and she has nice legs. Well, why not? . . .

Casual murder, casual suicide, casual crime. Why not? If alternate universes are a reality, then cause and effect are an illusion. The law of averages is a fraud. You can do anything, and one of you will, or did.

Gene Trimble looked at the clean and loaded gun on his desk. Well, why not? . . .

And he ran out of the office shouting, "Bentley, listen, I've got the answer . . ."

And he stood up slowly and left the office shaking his head. This was the answer, and it wasn't any good. The suicides, murders, casual crimes would continue. . . .

And he suddenly laughed and stood up. Ridiculous! Nobody dies for a philosophical point! . . .

And he reached for the intercom and told the man who answered to bring him a sandwich and some coffee. . . .

And picked the gun off the newspapers, looked at it for a long moment, then dropped it in the drawer. His hands began to shake. On a world line very close to this one . . .

And he picked the gun off the newspapers, put it to his head and

fired. The hammer fell on an empty chamber.

fired. The gun jerked up and blasted a hole in the ceiling.

fired.

The bullet tore a furrow in his scalp.

took off the top of his head.

Greg Bear

The topics of Greg Bear's science fiction have ranged from nanotechnology run amok in Blood Music, to the translation of souls into awesome energy fields in the SF-horror hybrid Psycholone, and future evolution in Darwin's Radio. He is the author of the Songs of Earth and Power heroic diptych, comprised of The Infinity Concerto and The Serpent Mage, and two collections of short fiction, The Wind from a Burning Woman and Tangents, which include his stories "Hardfought" and "Blood Music," each of which won both the Hugo and Nebula Awards. Renowned for his hard science-fiction epics, Bear has written the trilogy that includes Legacy, Eon, and Eternity, which features a multiplicity of alternate worlds and timelines accessed through the interior of a hollow asteroid. Novels of equally impressive scope include the alien contact story The Forge of God and its sequel, Anvil of Stars; the nanotechnology opus Queen of Angels, and its follow-up, Slant; and the Nebula Award–winning Moving Mars, which chronicles the fifty-year history of Earth's Mars colony and its revolt against the mother planet. Bear has also written Dinosaur Summer, a sequel to Sir Arthur Conan Doyle's The Lost World, and Foundation and Chaos, which builds on the concepts of Isaac Asimov's Foundation trilogy.

THROUGH ROAD
NO WHITHER

Greg Bear

THE LONG BLACK MERCEDES rumbled out of the fog on the road south from Dijon, moisture running in cold trickles across its windshield. Horst von Ranke moved the military pouch to one side and carefully read the maps spread on his lap, eyeglasses perched low on his nose, while Waffen Schutzstaffel Oberleutnant Albert Fischer drove. "Thirty-five kilometers," von Ranke said under his breath. "No more."

"We are lost," Fischer said. "We've already come thirty-six."

"Not quite that many. We should be there any minute now."

Fischer nodded and then shook his head. His high cheekbones and long, sharp nose only accentuated the black uniform with silver death's heads on the high, tight collar. Von Ranke wore a broad-striped gray suit; he was an undersecretary in the Propaganda Ministry, now acting as a courier. They might have been brothers, yet one had grown up in Czechoslovakia, the other in the Ruhr; one was the son of a coal miner, the other of a brewer. They had met and become close friends in Paris, two years before.

"Wait," von Ranke said, peering through the drops on the side window. "Stop."

Fischer braked the car and looked in the direction of von Ranke's long finger. Near the roadside, beyond a copse of young trees, was a low thatch-roofed house with dirty gray walls, almost hidden by the fog.

"Looks empty," von Ranke said.

"It is occupied; look at the smoke," Fischer said. "Perhaps somebody can tell us where we are."

They pulled the car over and got out, von Ranke leading the way across a mud path littered with wet straw. The hut looked even dirtier close up. Smoke rose in a darker brown-gray twist from a hole in the peak of the thatch. Fischer nodded at his friend and they cautiously approached. Over the crude wooden door letters wobbled unevenly in some alphabet neither knew, and between them they spoke nine languages. "Could that be Rom?" von Ranke asked, frowning. "It does look familiar—Slavic Rom."

"Gypsies? Romany don't live in huts like this, and besides, I thought they were rounded up long ago."

"That's what it looks like," von Ranke said. "Still, maybe we can share some language, if only French."

He knocked on the door. After a long pause he knocked again, and the door opened before his knuckles made the final rap. A woman too old to be alive stuck her long, wood-colored nose through the crack and peered at them with one good eye. The other was wrapped in a sunken caul of flesh. The hand that gripped the door edge was filthy, its nails long and black. Her toothless mouth cracked into a wrinkled, round-lipped grin. "Good evening," she said in perfect, even elegant German. "What can I do for you?"

"We need to know if we are on the road to Dôle," von Ranke said, controlling his repulsion.

"Then you're asking the wrong guide," the old woman said. Her hand withdrew and the door started to close. Fischer kicked out and pushed her back. The door swung open and began to lean on worn-out leather hinges.

"You do not treat us with the proper respect," he said. "What do you mean, 'the wrong guide'? What kind of guide are you?"

"So *strong*," the old woman crooned, wrapping her hands in front of her withered chest and backing away into the gloom. She wore colorless, ageless gray rags. Worn knit sleeves extended to her wrists.

"Answer me!" Fischer said, advancing despite the strong odor of urine and decay in the hut.

"The maps I know are not for this land," she sang, stopping before a cold and empty hearth.

"She's crazy," von Ranke said. "Let the local authorities take care of her later. Let's be off." But a wild look was in Fischer's eye. So much filth, so much disarray, and impudence as well; these made him angry.

"What maps do you know, crazy woman?" he demanded.

"Maps in time," the old woman said. She let her hands fall to her side and lowered her head, as if, in admitting her specialty, she was suddenly humble.

"Then tell us where we are," Fischer sneered.

"Come, we have important business," von Ranke said, but he knew it was too late. There would be an end, but it would be on his friend's terms, and it might not be pleasant.

"You are on a through road no whither," the old woman said.

"What?" Fischer towered over her. She stared up as if at some prodigal son returned home, her gums shining spittle.

"If you wish a reading, sit," she said, indicating a low table and three battered wood chairs. Fischer glanced at her, then at the table.

"Very well," he said, suddenly and falsely obsequious. Another game, von Ranke realized. Cat and mouse.

Fischer pulled out a chair for his friend and sat across from the old woman. "Put your hands on the table, palms down, both of them, both of you," she said. They did so. She lay her ear to the table as if listening, eyes going to the beams of light coming through the thatch. "Arrogance," she said. Fischer did not react.

"A road going into fire and death," she said. "Your cities in flame, your women and children shriveling to black dolls in the heat of their burning homes. The death camps are found and you stand accused of hideous crimes. Many are tried and hanged. Your nation is disgraced, your cause abhorred." Now a peculiar light came into her eye. "And many years later, a comedian swaggers around on stage, in a movie, turning your Führer into a silly clown, singing a silly song. Only psychotics will believe in you, the lowest of the low. Your nation will be divided among your enemies. All will be lost."

Fischer's smile did not waver. He pulled a coin from his pocket and threw it down before the woman, then pushed the chair back and stood. "Your maps are as crooked as your chin, hag," he said. "Let's go."

"I've been suggesting that," von Ranke said. Fischer made no move to leave. Von Ranke tugged on his arm but the SS Oberleutnant shrugged free of his friend's grip.

"Gypsies are few, now, hag," he said. "Soon to be fewer by one." Von Ranke managed to urge him just outside the door. The woman followed and shaded her eye against the misty light.

"I am no gypsy," she said. "You do not even recognize the words?" She pointed at the letters above the door.

Fischer squinted, and the light of recognition dawned in his eyes. "Yes," he said. "Yes, I do, now. A dead language."

"What are they?" von Ranke asked, uneasy.

"Hebrew, I think," Fischer said. "She is a Jewess."

"No!" the woman cackled. "I am no Jew."

Von Ranke thought the woman looked younger now, or at least stronger, and his unease deepened.

"I do not care what you are," Fischer said quietly. "I only wish we were in my father's time." He took a step toward her. She did not retreat. Her face became almost youthfully bland, and her bad eye seemed to fill in. "Then, there would be no regulations, no rules—I could take this pistol"—he tapped his holster—"and apply it to your filthy Kike head, and perhaps kill the last Jew in Europe." He unstrapped the holster. The woman straightened in the dark hut, as if drawing strength from Fischer's abusive tongue. Von Ranke feared for his friend. Rashness would get them in trouble.

"This is not our fathers' time," he reminded Fischer.

Fischer paused, the pistol half in his hand, his finger curling around the trigger. "Old woman"—though she did not look half as old, perhaps not even old at all, and certainly not bent and crippled—"you have had a very narrow shave this afternoon."

"You have no idea who I am," the woman half-sang, half-moaned.

"*Scheisse*," Fischer spat. "Now we will go, and report you and your hovel."

"I am the scourge," she breathed, and her breath smelled like burning stone even three strides away. She backed into the hut but her voice did not diminish. "I am the visible hand, the pillar of cloud by day and the pillar of fire by night."

Fischer's face hardened, and then he laughed. "You are right," he said to von Ranke, "she isn't worth our trouble." He turned and stomped out the door. Von Ranke followed, with one last glance over his shoulder into the gloom, the decay. *No one has lived in this hut for years*, he thought. Her shadow was gray and indefinite before the ancient stone hearth, behind the leaning, dust-covered table.

In the car von Ranke sighed. "You *do* tend toward arrogance, you know that?"

Fischer grinned and shook his head. "You drive, old friend. *I'll* look at the maps." Von Ranke ramped up the Mercedes's turbine until its whine was high and steady and its exhaust cut a swirling hole in the fog behind. "No wonder we're lost," Fischer said. He shook out the Pan-Deutschland map peevishly. "This is five years old — 1979."

"We'll find our way," von Ranke said. "I wouldn't miss old Krumnagel's face when we deliver the plans. He fought so long against the antipodal skip bombers. . . . And you delay us by fooling with an old woman."

"It is my way," Fischer said. "I hate disarray. Do you think he will try to veto the Pacific Northwest blitz?"

"He won't dare. He will know his place after he sees the declarations," von Ranke said. The Mercedes whined its way toward Dôle.

From the door of the hut the old woman watched, head bobbing. "I am not a Jew," she said, "but I loved them, too, oh, yes. I loved all my children." She raised her hand as the long black car roared into the fog.

"I will bring you to justice, whatever line you live upon, and all your children, and their children's children," she said. She dropped a twist of smoke from her elbow to the dirt floor and waggled her finger. The smoke danced and drew black figures in the dirt. "As you wished, into the time of your fathers." The fog grew thinner. She brought her arm down, and forty years melted away with the mist.

High above a deeper growl descended on the road. A wide-winged shadow passed over the hut, wings flashing stars, invasion stripes and cannon fire.

"Hungry bird," the shapeless figure said. "Time to feed."

Gregory Benford

A professor of physics at the University of California at Irvine, Gregory Benford is also regarded as one of science fiction's "killer B's" for the award-winning novels and short fiction he has written since 1965. His novel Timescape, *winner of the Nebula and John W. Campbell Awards, mixed the themes of alternate history and time travel in its account of a physicist attempting to avert global disaster by manipulating events that happen decades earlier. Benford is considered one of the preeminent modern writers of hard science fiction for such novels as* Eater, *which works cutting-edge astronomy into its story of first human contact with aliens in the 21st century. He has also been praised for his explorations of humanist themes, notably in his Galactic Center sextet of novels of human-alien contact and human-machine interface comprised of* In the Ocean of Night, Across the Sea of Suns, The Stars in Shroud, Great Sky River, Tides of Light, *and* Furious Gulf. *His short fiction has been collected in* In Alien Flesh *and* Matter's End. *He is the author of* Foundation's Fear, *a novel set in Isaac Asimov's Foundation milieu; has collaborated on* Beyond the Fall of Night, *a sequel to Arthur C. Clarke's* Against the Fall of Night; *and has written a popular science book* Deep Time: How Humanity Communicates Across Millennia. *His work as an anthologist includes* Nuclear War, *the alternate history compilation* Hitler Victorious, *and four volumes in the* What Might Have Been *series. The publication of his novel* The Martian Race, *about the first manned mission to the Red Planet, was timed to coincide with the 1999 touchdown of the Mars Polar Lander.*

MANASSAS, AGAIN

Gregory Benford

THERE WERE WORSE THINGS than getting swept up in the first battle of the first war in over a century, but Bradley could not right away think of any.

They had been out on a lark, really. Bradley got his buddy Paul to go along, flying low over the hills to watch the grand formations of men and machines. Bradley knew how to keep below the radar screens, sometimes skimming along so close to the treetops that branches snapped on their understruts. They had come in before dawn, using Bradley's dad's luxury, ultraquiet cruiser—over the broad fields, using the sunrise to blind the optical sensors below.

It had been enormously exciting. The gleaming columns, the acrid smoke of ruin, the distant muffled coughs of combat.

Then somebody shot them down.

Not a full, square hit, luckily. Bradley had gotten them over two ranges of hills, lurching through shot-racked air. Then they came down heavily, air bags saving the two boys.

They had no choice but to go along with the team that picked them out of their wreckage. Dexter, a big, swarthy man, seemed to be in charge. He said, "We got word a bunch of mechs are comin' along this road. You stick with us, you can help out."

Bradley said irritably, "Why should we? I want to —"

"Cause it's not safe round here, kid," Dexter said. "You joyriding rich kids, maybe you'll learn something about that today."

Dexter grinned, showing two missing teeth, and waved the rest of his company to keep moving into the slanting early-morning glow.

Nobody had any food and Bradley was pretty sure they would not have shared it out if they had. The fighting over the ridge to the west had disrupted whatever supply lines there were into this open, once agricultural land.

They reached the crossroads by midmorning and right away knocked out a servant mech by mistake. It saw them come hiking over the hill through the thick oaks and started chuffing away, moving as fast as it could. It was an R class, shiny and chromed.

A woman who carried one of the long rods over her shoulder whipped the rod down and sighted along it and a loud boom startled Bradley. The R mech went down. "First one of the day," the woman named Angel said.

"Musta been a scout," Dexter said.

"For what?" Bradley asked, shocked as they walked down the slope toward the mech in air still cool and moist from the dawn.

Paul said tentatively, "The mech withdrawal?"

Dexter nodded. "Mechs're on their way through here. Bet they're scared plenty."

They saw the R mech had a small hole punched through it right in the servo controls near the back. "Not bad shootin'," a man said to Angel.

"I *tole* you these'd work," Angel said proudly. "I sighted mine in fresh this mornin'. It helps."

Bradley realized suddenly that the various machined rods these dozen people carried were all weapons, fabrications turned out of factories exclusively human-run. *Killing tools*, he thought in blank surprise. *Like the old days. You see them in dramas and stuff, but they've been illegal for a century.*

"Maybe this mech was just plain scared," Bradley said. "It's got software for that."

"We sent out a beeper warning," Dexter said, slapping the pack on his back. "Goes out of this li'l rig here. Any mech wants no trouble, all they got to do is come up on us slow and then lie down so we can have a look at their programming cubes."

"Disable it?"

"Sure. How else we going to be sure?"

"This one ran clear as anything," Angel said, reloading her rifle.

"Maybe it didn't understand," Bradley said. The R models were deft, subtle, terrific at social graces.

"It knew, all right," Angel said, popping the mech's central port open and pulling out its ID cube. "Look, it's from Sanfran."

"What's it doing all the way out here, then, if it's not a rebel?" a black man named Nelson asked.

"Yeah," Dexter said. "Enter it as reb." He handed Bradley a wrist comm. "We're keepin' track careful now. You'll be busy just takin' down score today, kid."

"Rebel, uh, I see," Bradley said, tapping into the comm. It was reassuring to do something simple while he straightened out his feelings.

"You bet," Nelson said, excitement lacing his voice. "Look at it. Fancy mech, smarter than most of them, tryin' to save itself. It's been runnin' away from our people. They just broke up a big mech force west of here."

"I never could afford one of these chrome jobs," Angel said. "They knew that, too. I had one of these classy R numbers meanmouth me in the market, try to grab a can of soybean stew." She laughed sarcastically. "That was when there was a few scraps left on the shelves."

"Elegant thing, wasn't it?" Nelson kicked the mech, which rolled farther downhill.

"You messed it up pretty well," Bradley said.

Dexter said, "Roll it down into that hollow so nobody can see it from the road." He gestured at Paul. "You go with the other party. Hey, Mercer!"

A tall man ambled over from where he had been carefully trying to pick the spines off a prickly pear growing in a gully. Everybody was hungry. Dexter said to him, "Go down across the road and set up shot. Take this kid—Paul's your name, right?—he'll help with the gruntwork. We'll catch 'em in a crossfire here."

Mercer went off with Paul. Bradley helped get the dead mech going and with Angel rolled it into the gully. Its flailing arms dug fresh wet gouges in the spring grass. The exposed mud exhaled moist scents. They threw manzanita brush over the shiny carcass to be sure, and by that time Dexter had deployed his people.

They were setting up what looked like traps of some kind well away from the blacktop crossroads. Bradley saw that this was to keep the crossroads from looking damaged or clogged. They wanted the mechs to come in fast and keep going.

As he worked he heard rolling bass notes, like the mumbles of a giant, come from the horizon. He could see that both the roads leading to the crossroads could carry mechs away from the distant battles. Dexter was everywhere, barking orders, Bradley noted with respect.

The adults talked excitedly to each other about what the mechs would make of it, how easy they were to fool about real-world stuff, and even threw in some insider mech slang—codes and acronyms that meant very little to mechs, really, but had gotten into the pop culture as hip new stuff. Bradley smiled at this. It gave him a moment of feeling superior to cover his uneasiness.

It was a crisp spring morning now that the sun had beamed up over the far hill at their backs. The perfect time for fresh growth, but the fields beyond had no plowing or signs of cultivation. Mechs should be there, laying in crops. Instead they were off over the rumpled ridgeline, clashing with the main body of humans and, Bradley hoped secretly, getting their asses kicked. Though mechs had no asses, he reminded himself.

Dexter and Bradley laid down behind a hummock halfway up the hill. Dexter was talking into his hushmike headset, face jumping with anticipation and concern. Bradley savored the rich scents of the sweet new grass and thought idly about eating some of it.

Dexter looked out over the setup his team was building and said, "Y'know, maybe we're too close, but I figure you can't be in too close as long as you have the firepower. These weapons, we need close, real close. Easier to hit them when they're moving fast but then it's easier for them to hit you, too."

Bradley saw that the man was more edgy here than he had been with his team. Nobody had done anything like this within living memory. Not in the civilized world, anyway.

"Got to be sure we can back out of this if it gets too hot," Dexter went on.

Bradley liked Dexter's no-nonsense scowl. "How did you learn how to fight?"

Dexter looked surprised. "Hobby of mine. Studied the great Roman campaigns in Africa."

"They used ambushes a lot?"

"Sometimes. Of course, after Sygnius of Albion invented the steam-driven machine gun, well sir, then the Romans could dictate terms to any tribes that gave them trouble." Dexter squinted at him. "You study history, kid?"

"I'm Bradley, sir. My parents don't let me read about battles very much. They're always saying we've gotten beyond that."

"Yeah, that Universal Peace Church, right?"

"Yessir. They say—"

"That stuff's fine for people. Mechs, they're different."

"Different how?"

Dexter sucked on his teeth, peering down the road. "Not human. Fair game."

"Think they'll be hard to beat?"

Dexter grinned. "We're programmed for this by a couple million years of evolution. They been around half a century."

"Since 1800? I thought we'd always had mechs."

"Geez, kids never know any history."

"Well, sir, I know all the big things, like the dates of American secession from the Empire, and the Imperial ban on weapons like the ones you've got here, and how—"

"Dates aren't history, son. They're just numbers. What's it matter when we finally got out from under the Romans? Bunch of lily-livers, they were. 'Peace Empire'—contradiction in terms, kid. Though the way the 3D pumps you kids full of crap, not even allowin' any war shows or anything, except for prettified pussy historicals, no wonder you don't know which end of a gun does the business."

This seemed unfair to Bradley but he could see Dexter wasn't the kind of man he had known, so he shut up. *Fair game?* What did that mean? A fair game was where everybody enjoyed it and had a chance to win.

Maybe the world wasn't as simple as he had thought. There was something funny and tingly about the air here, a crackling that made his skin jump, his nerves strum.

Angel came back and lay beside them, wheezing, lugging a heavy contraption with tripod legs they had just assembled.

Nelson was downslope, cradling his rifle. He arranged the tripod and lifted onto it a big array of cylinders and dark, brushed-steel sliding parts unlike anything Bradley had ever seen. Sweating, Nelson stuck a long, curved clip into all this freshly made metal and worked the clacking mechanism. Nelson smiled, looking pleased at the way the parts slid easily.

Bradley was trying to figure out what all the various weapons did when he heard something coming fast down the road. He looked back along the snaky black line that came around the far hills and saw a big shape flitting among the ash trees.

It was an open-topped hauler filled with copper-jacketed mechs. They looked like factory hands packed like gleaming eggs in a carton.

Dexter talked into his hushmike and pointed toward three chalk-white stones set up by the road as aiming markers. The hauler came racing through the crossroads and plunged up the straight section of the road in front of Bradley. The grade increased here so they would slow as they passed the stones.

Bradley realized they had no way of knowing what the mechs were doing there, not for sure, and then he forgot that as a pulse-quickening sensation coursed through him. Dexter beside him looked like a cat that knows he has a canary stashed somewhere and can go sink his teeth into it any time he likes.

When the hauler reached the marker stones Angel opened fire. The sound was louder than anything Bradley had ever heard and his first reaction was to bury his face in the grass. When he looked up the hauler was slewing across the road and then it hit the ditch and rolled.

The coppery mechs in the back flew out in slow motion. Most just smacked into the grass and lay still. The hauler thumped solidly and stopped rolling. A few of the factory mechs got up and tried to get behind the hauler, maybe thinking that the rifle fire was only from Angel, but then the party from across the road opened up and the mechs pitched forward into the ditch and did not move. Then there was quiet in the little valley. Bradley could hear the hauler's engine still humming with electric energy and then some internal override cut in and it whined into silence.

"I hit that hauler square in the command dome, you see that?" Angel said loudly.

Bradley hadn't seen it but he said, "Yes ma'am, right."

Dexter said, "Try for that every time. Saves ammo if we don't have to shoot every one of them."

Nelson called up the slope, "Those're factory mechs, they look like Es and Fs, they're pretty heavy-built."

Angel nodded, grinning. "Easier just to slam 'em into that ditch."

Dexter didn't hear this as he spoke into his hushmike next to Bradley. "Myron, you guys get them off the road. Use those power-override keys and make them walk themselves into that place where the gully runs down into the stream. Tell 'em to jump right in the water."

"What about the hauler?" Bradley asked, and then was surprised at his own boldness.

Dexter frowned a moment. "The next batch, they'll think we hit it from the air. There was plenty of that yesterday to the west."

"I didn't see any of our planes today," Bradley said.

"We lost some. Rest are grounded because some mechs started to catch on just about sunset. They knocked three of our guys right out of the sky. Mechs won't know that, though. They'll figure it's like yesterday and that hauler was just unlucky." Dexter smiled and checked his own rifle, which he had not fired.

"I'll go help them," Bradley said, starting to get up.

"No; we only got so many of those keys. The guys know how to use 'em. You watch the road."

"But I'd like to—"

"Shut up," Dexter said in a way that was casual and yet was not.

Bradley used his pocket binoculars to study the road. The morning heat sent ripples climbing up from the valley floor and he was not sure at first that he saw true movement several kilometers away and then he was. Dexter alerted the others and there was a mad scramble to get the mechs out of sight.

They were dead, really, but the humans could access their power reserves and make them roll down the road on their wheels and treads and then jounce down the gully and pitch into the stream. Bradley could hear laughter as the team across the road watched the mechs splash into the brown water. Some shorted out and started flailing their arms and rotors around, comic imitations of humans swimming. That lasted only a few seconds and then they sank like the rest.

Nelson came running back up the hill, carrying on his back a long tube. "Here's that launcher you wanted. Rensink, he didn't look too happy to let go of it."

Dexter stood and looked down the road with his own binoculars. "Leave it here. We got higher elevation than Rensink."

Dexter took the steel tube, which looked to Bradley exactly like the telescopes he and his friends used to study the sky. Tentatively Bradley said, "If you're not going to use that rifle, uh, sir, I'd . . ."

Dexter grinned. "You want in, right?"

"Well, yes, I thought that since you're—"

"Sure. Here. Clip goes like this," he demonstrated, "you hold it so, sight along that notch. I machined that so I know it's good. We had to learn a whole lot of old-timey craft to make these things."

Bradley felt the heft and import of the piece and tentatively practiced sighting down at the road. He touched the trigger with the caution of a virgin lover. If he simply pulled on the cool bit of metal a hole would—well, might—appear in the carapace of fleeing mech. A mech they would not have to deal with again in the chaos to come. It was a simple way to think about the whole complex issue. Something in Bradley liked that simplicity.

The mechs still had not arrived but Bradley could see them well enough through the binoculars now to know why. They were riding on self-powered inventions of their own, modified forms of the getarounds mechs sometimes used on streets. These were three-wheeled and made of shiny brass.

They were going slowly, probably running out of energy. As he watched one deployed a solar panel on its back to catch the rising sun and then the others did but this did not speed them up any. They did not look like the elegant social mechs he usually saw zipping on the bike paths, bound on some errand. They were just N- or P-class mechs who had rigged up some wheels.

They came pedaling into the crossroads, using their arms. The one in front saw the hauler on its side and knew something was wrong right away and started pumping hard. Nelson shot at him then even though Dexter had said nothing. He hit the lead mech and it went end over end, arms caught up in its own drive chain. Angel could not resist and she took out the next three with a burst. Then the others came in with a chorus of rattling shots and loud bangs, no weapon sounding like the other, and in the noise Bradley squeezed and felt the butt of the rifle kick him.

He had been aiming at one of the mechs at the rear of the little column and when he looked next the mech was down, sliding across the road with sparks jetting behind it, metal ripping across asphalt.

"Stop! Stop shooting!" Dexter called, and in the sudden silence Bradley could hear the mechs clattering to a halt, clanging and squealing and thumping into the ditch.

"Get them off the road—quick!" Dexter called. He waved Bradley down the hill and the boy ran to see the damage. As he dashed toward them the mechs seemed to be undamaged except for some dents but then up close each showed a few holes. He had time to glance at Paul, who was red-faced, breathing hard, his eyes veiled. There was no time to talk.

The men and women from across the road got most of the mechs started up again on override keys but one had suffered some sort of internal explosion and the back was blown off. Bradley helped three men tilt it up enough to roll off the gentle rounded asphalt, and once they got it going it rolled and slid into a copse of eucalyptus. They threw branches over it. Bradley looked for the one he had shot at but it was impossible to tell which that was now.

He felt a prickly anticipation, a thickening of the air. The fragrances of trees and grass cut into his nostrils, vivid and sharp. They ran back up the slope. Bradley found the rifle he now thought of as his and sprawled down with it in the grass, getting down behind a hummock near Dexter.

Bradley lay there just breathing and looking at the rifle, which seemed to be made of a lot of complicated parts. Dexter tossed him three clips and a box of copper-sheathed ammunition. The box promised that they were armor-piercing. Bradley fumbled a little learning how to load the clips but then moved quickly, sliding the rounds in with a secure click as he heard the distant growl of a tracked vehicle.

It was coming closer along the other road. The crossroads looked pretty clear, no obvious signs of the ambush.

The Mercer team had laid two mines in the road. They had a chameleon surface and within a minute were indistinguishable from the asphalt. Bradley could tell where they were because they were lined up with the white marker stones and from up here were smoother than the asphalt.

He wondered if the mechs could sense that. Their sensorium was better than human in some ways, worse in others. He realized that he had never thought very much about the interior life of a mech, any more than he could truly delve into the inner world of animals. But in principle mechs *were* knowable. Their entire perspective could be digitized and examined minutely.

The clatter and roar of the approach blotted this from his mind. "Activate!" Dexter shouted, his tight voice giving away some of his own excitement.

A big tracked vehicle came flitting through the trees that lined the black road, flickering like a video-game target. There were mechs perched all over it, hitching rides, and many more of them packed its rear platform. When Bradley looked back at the road nearby the mines jumped out at him like a spider on a lace tablecloth. The entire valley vibrated and sparkled with intense, sensory light. Smells coiled up his nostrils, the cool sheen of the rifle spoke to him through his hands.

The mech driver would surely see the mines, stop, and back away, he thought. And the mechs aboard would jump off and some of them would attack the humans, rolling down the road and shooting the lasers they had adapted from industrial purposes. Bradley had heard about mechs that could override their safety commands and fight.

He tightened his grip on his rifle. He was dimly aware of Dexter sighting along his tube-shaped weapon and of Angel muttering to herself as she waited.

"If they were like us they'd stop, first sign of trouble they see," Dexter muttered, probably to himself, but Bradley could hear. "Then they'd deploy fighter mechs on both sides of the road and they'd sweep us, outflank."

"Think they will?" Bradley asked wonderingly.

"Naw. They don't have what we do."

"What . . . what's that?" Bradley knew the wide range of special abilities mechs possessed.

"Balls."

The mechs perched atop the tracked vehicle were looking forward down the road and holding on tight against the rough swerves as they rounded curves.

Then one of them saw the mines and jerked a servo arm toward them. Some mechs sitting near the front began sending warning wails, and the track car slammed on its brakes and slewed across the road. It stopped at the lip of the ditch and made a heavy, grinding noise and began backing up.

Three mechs jumped off its front. Bradley brought his sights down onto one of them and the air splintered with a huge rolling blast that made him flinch and forget about everything else.

The gunmetal hood of the transport seemed to dissolve into a blue cloud. The tailgate of the tracker flew backward with a sharp *whap*.

The air became a fine array of tumbling dots as debris spewed up like a dark fountain and then showered down all across the hillside. Thunks and whacks told of big mech parts hitting nearby. Bradley tucked his head into the grass. He yelped as something nicked his knee and something else tumbled over him and was gone. Pebbles thumped his back.

When Bradley looked up he expected to see nothing but small scraps left on the road. His ears roared with the memory of the sound and he wondered if he would be deaf. But through the smoke he saw several mechs lurching away from the disemboweled transport. There were five of them bunched closely together.

He brought his rifle up and shot very swiftly at the lead mech. It went down and he shot the next object and the next, seeing only the moving forms and the swirling blur of action.

Angel was firing and Nelson too, sharp bangs so regular and fast Bradley thought of the clack of a stick held by a boy as he ran by a picket fence — and in a few seconds there were no more mechs standing on the road.

But there were two in the ditch. Gray smoke billowed everywhere.

Bradley saw a mech moving just as a quick rod of light leaped from it, cutting through the smoke. He heard Angel yelp and swear. She held up her hand and it was bloody.

Another instantaneous rod of light stood for a second in the air and missed her and then a third struck her weapon. It flew to pieces with a loud bang. Bradley aimed at the mech and kept firing until he saw it and the second one sprawl across the ditch and stop moving.

A compressed silence returned to the valley. The transport was burning but beyond its snaps and pops he could see nothing moving on the road.

Angel was moaning with her wound and Nelson took care of her, pulling out a first-aid kit as he ran over. When they saw that her wound was manageable, Dexter and Bradley walked slowly down to the road. Dexter said, "Bet that's the last big party. We'll get strays now, no problems."

Bradley's legs felt like logs thudding into the earth as he walked. He waved to Paul, who was already on the road, but he did not feel like talking to anybody. The air was crisp and layered with so many scents, he felt them sliding in and out of his lungs like separate flavors in an ice cream sundae.

"Hey!" Mercer called from the transport cab. "They got food in here!"

Everyone riveted attention on the cab. Mercer pitched out cartons of dry food, some cans, a case of soft drinks.

"Somethin', huh? — mechs carryin' food," Angel said wonderingly. For several minutes they ate and drank and then Paul called, "There's a boy here."

They found Paul standing over a boy who was half-concealed by a fallen mech. Bradley saw that the group of mechs had been shielding this boy when they were cut down. "Still alive," Paul said, "barely."

"The food was for him," Mercer said.

Bradley bent down. Paul cradled the boy but it was clear from the drawn, white face and masses of blood down the front, some fresh red and most brown, drying, that there was not much hope. They had no way to get him to cryopreservation. Thin lips opened, trembled, and the boy said, "Bad . . . Mommy . . . hurt . . ."

Dexter said, "This ID says he's under mech care."

"How come?" Angel asked.

"Says he's mentally deficient. These're medical care mechs." Dexter pushed one of the mech carcasses and it rolled, showing H-caste insignia.

"Damn, how'd they get mixed in with these reb mechs?" Nelson asked irritably, the way people do when they are looking for something or someone to blame.

"Accident," Dexter said simply. "Confusion. Prob'ly thought they were doing the best thing, getting their charge away from the fighting."

"Damn," Nelson said again. Then his lips moved but nothing came out.

Bradley knelt down and brushed some flies away from the boy's face. He gave the boy some water but the eyes were far away and the lips just spit the water out. Angel was trying to find the wound and stop the bleeding but she had a drawn, waxy look.

"Damn war," Nelson said. "Mechs, they're to blame for this."

Bradley took a self-heating cup of broth from Paul and gave a little to the boy. The face was no more than fifteen and the eyes gazed abstractedly up into a cloudless sky. Bradley watched a butterfly land on the boy's arm. It fluttered its wings in the slanting yellow-gold sunlight and tasted the drying brown blood. Bradley wondered distantly if butterflies ate blood. Then the boy choked and the butterfly flapped away on a breeze, and when Bradley looked back the boy was dead.

They stood for a long moment around the body. The road was a chaos of ripped mech carapaces and tangled innards and the wreck of the exploded transport. Nobody was going to run into an ambush here anymore today and nobody made a move to clear the road.

"Y'know, these med-care mechs, they're pretty smart," Paul said. "They just made the wrong decision."

"Smarter than the boy, probably," Bradley said. The boy was not much younger than Bradley, but in the eyes there had been just an emptiness. "He was human, though."

The grand opening elation he had felt all morning slowly began to seep out of Bradley. "Hell of a note, huh?" he said to no one in particular. Others were doing that, just saying things to the breeze as they slowly dispersed and started to make order out of the shambles.

The snap and sparkle of the air were still with him, though. He had never felt so alive in his life. Suddenly he saw the soft, encased, abstract world he had inhabited since birth as an enclave, a preserve—a trap. The whole of human society had been in a cocoon, a velvet wrapping tended by mechs.

They had found an alternative to war: wealth. And simple human kindness. *Human* kindness.

Maybe that was all gone now.

And it was no tragedy, either. Not if it gave them back the world as it could be, a life of tangs and zests and the gritty rub of real things. He had dwelled in the crystal spaces of the mind while beneath such cool antiseptic entertainments his body yearned for the hot raw earth and its moist mysteries.

Nelson and Mercer were collecting mech insignia. "Want an AB? We found one over here. Musta got caught up and brought along by these worker mechs?" Nelson asked Bradley.

"I'll just take down the serial numbers," Bradley said automatically, not wanting to talk to Nelson more than necessary. Or to anyone. There had been so much talk.

He spent time getting the numbers logged into his comm and then shoving mech carcasses off the road.

Dexter came over to him and said, "Sure you don't want one of these?" It was a laser one of the reb mechs had used. Black, ribbed, with a glossy sheen. "Angel's keeping one. She'll be telling the story of her wound and showing the laser that maybe did it, prob'ly for the rest of her life."

Bradley looked at the sleek, sensuous thing. It gleamed in the raw sunlight like a promise. "No."

"Sure?"

"Take the damned stuff away."

Dexter looked at him funny and walked off. Bradley stared at the mechs he was shoving off the road and tried to think how they were different from the boy, who probably was indeed less intelligent than they were, but it was all clouded over with the memory of how much he liked the rifle and the sweet grass and shooting at the targets when they came up to the crossfire point in the sharp sun. It was hard to think at all as the day got its full heat and after a while he did not try. It was easier that way.

Jack L. Chalker

Jack Chalker began publishing fiction in 1976, after earning notoriety as editor of the small press fantasy magazine Mirage *and as publisher at Mirage Press. His first novel,* A Jungle of Stars, *is a science-fiction tale of alien entities in conflict who fight through human surrogates. With his second novel,* Midnight at the Well of Souls, *the first novel in the Well World quintet, he began his well-known blending of science fiction and otherworld fantasy. The novels in many of his multivolume series—*Soul Rider *(Spirits of Flux and Anchor, Empires of Flux and Anchor, Master of Flux and Anchor, The Birth of Flux and Anchor, Children of Flux and Anchor)* and Rings of the Master *(Lords of the Middle Dark, Pirates of the Thunder, Warriors of the Storm, Masks of the Martyrs)—are renowned for their adventures of human characters on quests in worlds under the control of capricious and unpredictable forces. He is the author of the alternate world fantasy* And the Devil Will Drag You Under, *the short-fiction collection* Dance Band on the *Titanic, and the monumental reference guide* The Science-Fantasy Publishers: A Critical and Bibliographic History.

DANCE BAND ON THE <u>TITANIC</u>

Jack L. Chalker

THE GIRL WAS committing suicide again on the lower afterdeck. They'd told me I'd get used to it, but after four times I could still only pretend to ignore it, pretend that I didn't hear the body go over, hear the splash, and the scream as she was sucked into the screws. It was all too brief and becoming all too familiar.

When the scream was cut short, as it always was, I continued walking forward, toward the bow. I would be needed there to guide the spotlight with which the Captain would have to spot the buoys to get us all safely into Southport harbor.

It was a clear night; once at the bow I could see the stars in all their glory, too numerous to count, or spot familiar constellations. It's a sight that's known and loved by all those who follow the sea, and it had a special meaning for we, who manned the *Orcas*, for the stars were immutable, the one unchanging part of our universe.

I checked the lines, the winch, and ties in the chained-off portion of the bow, then notified the Captain by walkie-talkie that all was ready. He gave me "Very well," and told me that we'd be on the mark in five minutes. This gave me a few moments to relax, adjust my vision to the darkness, and look around.

The bow is an eerie place at night for all its beauty; there is an unreality about a large ferryboat in the dark. Between where I stood on station and the bridge superstructure towering above me there was a broad area always crowded with people in warm weather. The bridge— dominating the aft field of vision, a ghostly, unlit gray-white monolith, reflecting the moonlight with an almost unreal cast and glow. A silent, spinning radar mast on top, and the funnel, end-on, in back of the bridge, with its wing supports and mast giving it a futuristic cast, only made the scene more alien, more awesome.

I glanced around at the people on the deck. Not as many as usual, but then it was very late, and there was a chill in the air. I saw a few familiar faces, and there was some lateral shift in focus on a number of them, indicating that I was seeing at least three levels of reality that night.

Now, that last is kind of hard to explain. I'm not sure whether I understand it, either, but I well remember when I applied for this job, and the explanations I got then.

Working deck on a ferryboat is a funny place for a former English teacher, anyway. But, while I'd been, I like to think, a good teacher, I was in constant fights with the administration over their lax discipline, stuffed-shirt attitudes toward teaching and teachers, and their general incompetence. The educational system isn't made for mavericks; it's designed to make everyone conform to bureaucratic ideals which the teacher is supposed to exemplify. One argument too many, I guess, and there I was, an unemployed teacher in a time when there are too many teachers. So I drifted. I'd lost my parents years before and there were no other close relatives, so I had no responsibilities. I'd always loved ferryboats—raised on them, loved them with the same passion some folks like trains and trolley cars and such—and when I discovered an unskilled job opening on the old Delaware ferry I took it. The fact that I was an ex-teacher actually helped; ferry companies like to hire people who relate well to the general public. After all, deck duty is hectic when the ferry's docking or docked, but for the rest of the time you just sort of stand there, and every tourist and traveler in the world wants to talk. If you aren't willing to talk back and enjoy it, forget ferryboats.

And I met Joanna. I'm not sure if we were in love—maybe *I* was, but I'm pretty sure Joanna wasn't capable of loving anyone. Like all the other men in her life, I was just convenient. For a while things went smoothly—I had a job I liked, and we shared the rent. She had a little daughter she doted on, father unknown, and little Harmony and I hit it off, too. We all gave each other what each needed.

It lasted a little more than a year.

In the space of three weeks my neat, comfortable, complacent world came apart: First she threw that damned party while I was working, and a cigarette or something was left, and the apartment burned. The fire department managed to get Joanna out—but little Harmony had been asleep in a far room and they never got to her through the smoke.

I tried to comfort her, tried to console her, but I guess I was too full of my own life, my own self-importance in her reality, that I just didn't see the signs. A couple of weeks after the fire she'd seemed to brighten up, act more like her normal self.

And, one evening, while I worked on the boat, she hanged herself.

Just a week later that damned bridge-tunnel put the ferry out of business, too. I'd known it was coming, of course, but I'd made few plans beyond the closing—I'd figured I could live off Joanna for a while and we'd make our decisions together.

Now here I was alone, friendless, jobless, and feeling guilty as hell. I seriously thought about ending it all myself about then, maybe going down to the old ferryboat and blowing it and me to hell in one symbolic act of togetherness. But, then, just when I'd sunk to such depths, I got this nice, official-looking envelope in the mail from something called the Bluewater Corporation, Southport, Maine. Just a funny logo, some blue water with an odd, misty-looking shape of a ship in it.

"Dear Mr. Dalton," the letter read. "We have just learned of the closing of the Delaware service, and we are in need of some experienced ferry people. After reviewing your qualifications, we believe that you might fit nicely into our operation, which, we guarantee, will not be put out of business by bridge or tunnel. If this prospect interests you, please come to Southport terminal at your earliest convenience for a final interview. Looking forward to seeing you soon, I remain, sincerely yours, Herbert V. Penobscot, Personnel Manager, Bluewater Corp."

I just stood there staring at the thing for I don't know how long. A ferry job! That alone should have excited me, yet I wondered about it, particularly that line about "reviewing my qualifications" and "final interview." Funny terms. I could see why they'd look for experienced people, and all ferry folk knew when a line was closed and would naturally look for their own replacements there, but—why me? I hadn't applied to them, hadn't even heard of them or their line—or, for that matter, of Southport, Maine, either. Obviously they had some way of preselecting their people—very odd for this kind of a business.

I scrounged up an old atlas and tried to find it. The letterhead said "Southport—St. Michael—The Island," but I could find nothing about any such place in the atlas or almanac. If the letterhead hadn't looked so convincing, I'd have sworn somebody was putting me on. As it was, I had nothing else to do, and it beat drinking myself to death, so I hitch-hiked up.

It wasn't easy finding Southport, I'll tell you. Even people in nearby towns had never heard of it. The whole town was about a dozen houses, a seedy ten-unit motel, a hot dog stand, and a very small ferry terminal with standard but surprisingly large ferry ramp and parking area.

I couldn't believe the place warranted a ferry when I saw it; you had to go about sixty miles into the middle of nowhere on a road the high-way department had deliberately engineered to miss some of the world's prettiest scenery, and had last paved sometime before World War II, just to get there.

There was a light on in the terminal, so I went in. A grayhaired man, about fifty, was in the ticket office, and I went over and introduced my-self. He looked me over carefully, and I knew I didn't present a very good appearance.

"Sit down, Mr. Dalton," he offered in a tone that was friendly but businesslike. "My name's McNeil. I've been expecting you. This really won't take long, but the final interview includes a couple of strange questions. If you don't want to answer any of them, feel free, but I must ask them nonetheless. Will you go along with me?"

I nodded and he fired away. It was the damndest job interview I'd ever had. He barely touched on my knowledge of ferries except to ask whether it mattered to me that the *Orcas* was a single-bridge, twin-screw affair, not a double-ender like I'd been used to. It still loaded on one end and unloaded on the other, though, through a raisable bow, and a ferry was a ferry to me and I told him so.

Most of the questions were of a personal nature, my family and friends, my attitudes, and some were downright *too* personal.

"Have you ever contemplated or attempted suicide?" he asked me in the same tone he'd use to ask if you brushed your teeth in the morning.

I jumped. "What's *that* have to do with anything?" I snapped. After all this I was beginning to see why the job was still open.

"Just answer the question," he responded, sounding almost embar-rassed. "I told you I had to ask them all."

Well, I couldn't figure out what this was all about, but I finally de-cided, what the hell, I had nothing to lose and it was a beautiful spot to work.

"Yes," I told him. "Thought about it, anyway." And I told him why.

He just nodded thoughtfully, jotted something on a preprinted form, and continued. His next question was worse.

"Do you now believe in ghosts, devils, and/or demonic forces?" he asked in that same routine tone.

I couldn't suppress a chuckle. "You mean the ship's haunted?"

He didn't smile back. "Just answer the question, please."

"No," I responded. "I'm not very religious."

Now there was a wisp of a smile there. "And suppose, with your hard-nosed rationalism, you ran into one? Or a whole bunch of them?" He leaned forward, smile gone. "Even an entire shipload of them?"

It was impossible to take this seriously. "What kind of ghosts?" I asked him. "Chain rattlers? White sheets? Foul fiends spouting hateful gibberish?"

He shook his head negatively. "No, ordinary people, for the most part. Dressed a little odd, perhaps; talking a little odd, perhaps, but not really very odd at all. Nice folks, typical passengers."

Cars were coming in now, and I glanced out the window at them. Ordinary-looking cars, ordinary-looking people—campers, a couple of tractor-trailer rigs, like that. Lining up. A U.S. customs man came from the direction of the motel and started talking to some of them.

"They don't look like ghosts to me," I told McNeil.

He sighed. "Look, Mr. Dalton, I know you're an educated man. I have to go out and start selling fares now. She'll be in in about forty minutes, and we've only got a twenty-minute layover. When she's in and loading, go aboard. Look her over. You'll have free rein of the ship. Take the complete round trip, all stops. It's about four hours over, twenty minutes in, and a little slower back. Don't get off the ship, though. Keep an open mind. If you're the one for the *Orcas*, and I think you are, we'll finish our talk when you get back." He got up, took out a cash drawer and receipt load, and went to the door, then turned back to me. "I *hope* you're the one," he said wearily. "I've interviewed over three hundred people and I'm getting sick of it."

We shook hands on that cryptic remark and I wandered around while he manned his little booth and processed the cars, campers, and trucks. A young woman came over from one of the houses and handled the few people who didn't have cars, although how they ever got to Southport I was at a loss to know.

The amount of business was nothing short of incredible. St. Michael was in Nova Scotia, it seemed, and there were the big runs by CN from a couple of places and the Swedish one out of Portland to compete for any business. The fares were reasonable but not cheap enough to drive this far out of the way for—and to get to Southport you *had* to drive far out of your way.

I found a general marine atlas of the Fundy region in McNeil's office and looked at it. Southport made it, but just barely. No designation of it as a ferry terminal, though, and no funny broken line showing a route.

For the life of me I couldn't find a St. Michael, Nova Scotia—nor a St. Clement's Island, either—the midstop that the schedule said it made.

There were an *awful* lot of cars and trucks out there now—it looked like rush hour in Manhattan. Where *had* all those people come from?

And then there was the blast of a great air horn and I rushed out for my first view of the *Orcas*—and I was stunned.

That ship, I remembered thinking, *has no right to be here. Not here, not on this run.*

It was *huge*—all gleaming white, looking brand-new, more like a cruise ship than a ferryboat. I counted three upper decks, and, as I watched, a loud clanging bell sounded electrically on her and her enormous bow lifted, revealing a grooved raising ramp, something like the bow of an old LST. It docked with very little trouble, revealing space for well over a hundred cars and trucks, with small side ramps for a second level available if needed. I learned later that it was 396 feet long—longer than a football field by a third!—and could take over two hundred major vehicles and twelve hundred passengers.

It was close to sundown on a weekday, but they loaded more than fifty vehicles, including a dozen campers, and eight big trucks. Where had they all come from, I wondered again. And why?

I walked on with the passengers, still in something of a daze, and went up top. The lounges were spacious and comfortable, the seats all padded and reclining. There was a large cafeteria, a newsstand, and a very nice bar at the stern of passenger deck 2. The next deck had another lounge section and a number of staterooms up front, while the top level had the bridge, crew's quarters, and a solarium.

It was fancy; and, after it backed out, lowered its bow, and started pouring it on after clearing the harbor lights, the fastest damned thing I could remember, too. Except for the slight swaying and the rhythmic thrumming of the twin diesels you hardly knew you were moving. It was obviously using enormous stabilizers.

The sun was setting and I walked through the ship, just looking and relaxing. As darkness fell and the shoreline receded into nothingness, I started noticing some very odd things, as I'd been warned.

First of all, there seemed to be a whole lot more people on board than I'd remembered loading, and there certainly hadn't been any number staying on from the last run. They all looked real and solid enough, and very ordinary, but there was something decidedly weird about them, too.

Many seemed to be totally unaware of each other's existence, for one thing. Some seemed to shimmer occasionally, others were a little blurred or indistinct to my eyes no matter how I rubbed them.

And, once in a while, they'd walk through each other.

Yes, I'm serious. One big fellow in a flowered aloha shirt and brown pants carrying a tray of soft drinks from the cafeteria to his wife and three kids in the lounge didn't seem to notice this woman in a white tee shirt and jeans walking right into him, nor did she seem aware of him, either.

And they met, and I braced for the collision and spilled drinks—and it didn't happen. They walked right *through* each other, just as if they didn't exist, and continued obliviously on. Not one drop of soda was spilled, not one spot of mustard was splotched.

There were other things, too. Most of the people were dressed normally for summer, but occasionally I'd see people in fairly heavy coats and jackets. Some of the fashions were different, too—some people were overdressed in old-fashioned styles, others wildly underdressed, a couple of the women frankly wearing nothing but the bottoms of string bikinis and a see-through short cape of some kind.

I know I couldn't take my eyes off them for a while, until I got the message that they knew they were being stared at and didn't particularly like it. But they were generally ignored by the others.

There were strange accents, too. Not just the expected Maine twang and Canadian accents, or even just the French Canadian accents—those were normal. But there were some really odd ones, ones where I picked out only a few words, which sounded like English, French, Spanish, and Nordic languages all intermixed and often with weird results.

And men with pigtails and long, braided hair, and women with shaved heads or, occasionally, beards.

It was weird.

Frankly, it scared me a little, and I found the purser and introduced myself.

The officer, a good-looking young man named Gifford Hanley, a

Canadian from his speech, seemed delighted that I'd seen all this and not the least bit disturbed.

"Well, well, well!" he almost beamed. "Maybe we've found our new man at last, eh? Not bloody soon enough, either! We've been working short-handed for too long and it's getting to the others."

He took me up to the bridge—one of the most modern I'd ever seen—and introduced me to the captain and helmsman. They all asked me what I thought of the *Orcas* and how I liked the sea, and none of them would answer my questions on the unusual passengers.

Well, there *was* a St. Clement's Island. A big one, too, from the looks of it, and a fair amount of traffic getting off and wanting on. Some of the vehicles that got on were odd, too; many of the cars looked unfamiliar in design, the trucks also odd, and there were even several horse-drawn wagons!

The island had that same quality as some of the passengers, too. It never seemed to be quite in focus just beyond the ferry terminal, and lights seemed to shift, so that where I thought there were houses or a motel suddenly they were somewhere else, of a different intensity. I was willing to swear that the motel had two stories; later it seemed over on the left, and four stories high, then further back, still later, with a single story.

Even the lighthouse as we sped out of the harbor changed; one time it looked very tall with a house at its base; then, suddenly, it was short and tubby, then an automated light that seemed to be out in the water with no sign of an island.

This continued for most of the trip. St. Michael looked like a carbon copy of Southport, the passengers and vehicles as bizarre—and numerous—and there seemed to be a lot of customs men in different uniforms dashing about, totally ignoring some vehicles while processing others.

The trip back was equally strange. The newsstand contained some books and magazines that were odd to say the least, and papers with strange names and stranger headlines.

This time there were even Indians aboard, speaking odd tongues. Some looked straight out of *The Last of the Mohicans*, complete with wild haircut, others dressed from little to heavy, despite the fact that it was July and very warm and humid.

And, just before we were to make the red and green channel markers and turn into Southport, I saw the girl die for the first time.

She was dressed in red tee shirt, yellow shorts, and sandals; she had long brown hair, was rather short and stocky, and wore oversized granny glasses.

I wasn't paying much attention, really, just watching her looking over the side at the wake, when, before I could even cry out, she suddenly climbed up on the rail and plunged in, very near the stern.

I screamed, and heard her body hit the water and then heard her howl of terror as she dropped close enough so that the propwash caught her, sucked her under, and cut her to pieces.

Several people on the afterdeck looked at me quizzically, but only one or two seemed to realize that a woman had just died.

There was little I could do, but I ran back to Hanley, breathless.

He just nodded sadly.

"Take it easy, man," he said gently. "She's dead, and there's no use going back for the body. Believe me, we *know*. It won't be there."

I was shocked, badly upset. "How do you know that?" I snapped.

"Because we did it every time the last four times she killed herself and we never found the body then, either," he replied sadly.

I had my mouth open, ready to retort, to say *something*, but he got up, put on his officer's hat and coat, and said, "Excuse me. I have to supervise the unloading," and walked out.

As soon as I got off the ship it was like some sort of dreamy fog had lifted from me. Everything looked suddenly bright and clear, and the people and vehicles looked normal. I made my way to the small ferry terminal building.

When they'd loaded and the ship was gone again, I waited for McNeil to return to his office. It looked much the same really, but a few things seemed different. I couldn't quite put my finger on it, but there *was* something odd—like the paneling had been rosewood before, and was now walnut. Small things, but nagging ones.

McNeil came back after seeing the ship clear. It ran almost constantly, according to the schedule.

I glanced out the window as he approached and noticed uniformed customs men checking out the debarked vehicles. They seemed to have different uniforms than I'd remembered.

Then the ticket agent entered the office and I got another shock. He had a beard.

No, it was the same man, all right. No question about it. But the man I'd talked to less than nine hours before had been clean-shaven.

I turned to where the navigation atlas lay, just where I'd put it, still open to the Southport page.

It showed a ferry line from Southport to a rather substantial St. Clement's Island now. But nothing to Nova Scotia.

I turned to the bearded McNeil, who was watching me with mild amusement in his eyes.

"What the *hell* is going on here?" I demanded.

He went over and sat down in his swivel chair. "Want the job?" he asked. "It's yours if you do."

I couldn't believe his attitude. "I want an explanation, damn it!" I fumed.

He chuckled. "I told you I'd give you one if you wanted. Now, you'll have to bear with me, since I'm only repeating what the Company tells me, and I'm not sure I have it all clear myself."

I sat down in the other chair. "Go ahead," I told him.

He sighed. "Well, let's start off by saying that there's been a Bluewater corporation ferry on this run since the mid-1800s—steam packet at first, of course. The *Orcas* is the eleventh ship in the service, put on a year and a half ago."

He reached over, grabbed a cigarette, lit it, and continued.

"Well, anyway, it was a normal operation until about 1910 or so. That's when they started noticing that their counts were off, that there seemed to be more passengers than the manifests called for, different freight, and all that. As it continued, the crews started noticing more and more of the kind of stuff you saw, and things got crazy for them, too. Southport was a big fishing and lobstering town then—nobody does that any more, the whole economy's the ferry.

"Well, anyway, one time this crewman goes crazy, says the woman in his house isn't his wife. A few days later another comes home to find that he has four kids—and he was only married a week before. And so on."

I felt my skin starting to crawl slightly.

"So, they send some big shots up. The men are absolutely nuts, but *they* believe what they claim. Soon everybody who works the ship is spooked, and this can't be dismissed. The experts go for a ride and can't find anything wrong, but now two of the crewmen claim that it *is* their wife, or their kid, or somesuch. Got to be a pain, though, getting crewmen. We finally had to center on loners—people without family, friends, or close personal ties. It kept getting worse each trip. Had a hell of a time keeping men for a while, and that's why it's so hard to recruit new ones."

"You mean the trip drives them crazy?" I asked unbelievingly.

He chuckled. "Oh, no. *You're* sane. It's the rest of 'em. That's the problem. And it gets worse and worse each season. But the trip's *extremely* profitable. So we try to match the crew to the ship and hope they'll accept it. If they do it's one of the best damned ferry jobs there is."

"But what causes it?" I managed. "I mean—I saw people dressed outlandishly. I saw other people walk *through* each other! I even saw a girl commit suicide, and nobody seemed to notice!"

McNeil's face turned grim. "So that's happened again. Too bad. Maybe someday there'll be some chance to save her."

"Look," I said, exasperated. "There must be some explanation for all this. There *has* to be!"

The ticket agent shrugged and stubbed out his cigarette.

"Well, some of the company experts studied it. They say nobody can tell for sure, but the best explanation is that there are a lot of different worlds—different Earths, you might say—all existing one on top of the other, but you can't see any one except the one you're in. Don't ask me how that's possible or how they came up with it, it just *is*, that's all. Well, they say that in some worlds folks don't exist at all, and in others they are different places or doing different things—like getting married to somebody else or somesuch. In some, Canada's still British, in some she's a republic, in others she's a fragmented batch of countries, and in one or two she's part of the U.S. Each one of these places has a different history."

"And this one boat serves them all?" I responded, not accepting a word of that cazy story. "How is that possible?"

McNeil shrugged again. "Who knows? Hell, I don't even understand why that little light goes on in here when I flip the switch. Do most people? I just sell tickets and lower the ramp. I'll tell you the Company's version, that's all. They say that there's a crack—maybe one of many, maybe the only one. The ship's route just happens to parallel that crack, and this allows you to go between the worlds. Not one ship, of course—twenty or more, one for each world. But, as long as they keep the same schedule, they overlap—and can cross into one or more of the others. If you're on the ship in all those worlds, then you cross, too. Anyone coexisting with the ship in multiple worlds can see and hear not only the one he's in but the ones nearest him, too. People perception's a little harder the farther removed the world you're in is from theirs."

"And you believe this?" I asked him, still disbelieving.

"Who knows? Got to believe *something* or you'll go nuts," he replied pragmatically. "Look, did you get to St. Michael this trip?"

I nodded. "Yeah. Looked pretty much like this place."

He pointed to the navigation atlas. "Try and find it. You won't. Take a drive up through New Brunswick and around to the other side. It doesn't exist. In this world, the *Orcas* goes from here to St. Clement's Island and back again. I understand from some of the crew that sometimes Southport doesn't exist, sometimes the Island doesn't, and so forth. And there are so many countries involved I don't even count."

I shook my head, refusing to accept all this. And yet, it made a crazy kind of sense. These people didn't see each other because they were in different worlds. The girl committed suicide five times because she did it in five different worlds — or was it five different girls? It also explained the outlandish dress, the strange mixture of vehicles, people, accents.

"But how come the crew sees people from many worlds and the passengers don't?" I asked him.

McNeil sighed. "That's the other problem. We have to find people who would be up here, working on the *Orcas*, in every world we service. More people's lives parallel than you'd think. The passengers — well, they generally don't exist on a particular run except once. The very few who do still don't take the trip in every world we service. I guess once or twice it's happened that we've had a passenger cross over, but, if so, we've never heard of it."

"And how come I'm here in so many worlds?" I asked him.

McNeil smiled. "You were recruited, of course. The Corporation has a tremendous, intensive recruiting effort involving ferry lines and crewmembers. When they spot one, like you, in just the right circumstance in all worlds, they recruit you — all of you. An even worse job than you'd think, since every season one or two new Bluewater Corporations put identical ferries on this run, or shift routes and overlap with ours. Then we have to make sure the present crew can serve them, too, by recruiting your twin on those worlds."

Suddenly I reached over, grabbed his beard, and yanked.

"*Ouch!* Damn it!" he cried and shoved my hand away.

"I — I'm sorry — I —" I stammered.

He shook his head and grinned. "That's all right, son. You're about the seventh person to do that to me in the last five years. I guess there are a lot of varieties of *me*, too."

I thought about all that traffic. "Do others know of this?" I asked him. "I mean, is there some sort of hidden commerce between the worlds on this ferry?"

He grinned. "I'm not supposed to answer that one," he said carefully.

"But, what the hell. Yes, I think—no, I *know* there is. After all, the shift of people and ships is constant. You move one notch each trip if all of you take the voyage. Sometimes up, sometimes down. If that's true, and if they can recruit a crew that fits the requirements, why not truck drivers? A hell of a lot of truck traffic through here year 'round, you know. No reduced winter service. And some of the rigs are really kinda strange-looking." He sighed. "I only know this—in a couple of hours I'll start selling fares again, and I'll sell a half dozen or so to St. Michael— and *there is no St. Michael*. It isn't even listed on my schedule or maps. I doubt if the Corporation's actually the trader, more the middleman in the deal. But they sure as hell don't make their millions off fares alone."

It was odd the way I was accepting it. Somehow, it seemed to make sense, crazy as it was.

"What's to keep me from using this knowledge somehow?" I asked him. "Maybe bring my own team of experts up?"

"Feel free," McNeil answered. "Unless they overlap they'll get a nice, normal ferry ride. And if you can make a profit, go ahead, as long as it doesn't interfere with Bluewater's cash flow. The *Orcas* cost the company over twenty-four million *reals* and they want it back."

"Twenty-four million *what*?" I shot back.

"*Reals*," he replied, taking a bill from his wallet. I looked at it. It was printed in red, and had a picture of someone very ugly labeled "Prince Juan XVI" and an official seal from the "Bank of New Lisboa." I handed it back.

"What country are we in?" I asked uneasily.

"Portugal," he replied casually. "Portuguese America, actually, al- though only nominally. So many of us Yankees have come in you don't even have to speak Portuguese any more. They even print the local bills in Anglish, now."

Yes, that's what he said. Anglish.

"It's the best ferryboat job in the world, though," McNeil continued. "For someone without ties, that is. You'll meet more different kinds of people from more cultures than you can ever imagine. Three runs on, three off—in as many as twenty-four different variations of these towns, all unique. And a month off in winter to see a little of a different world each time. Never mind whether you buy the explanation—you've seen the results, you know what I say is true. Want the job?"

"I'll give it a try," I told him, fascinated. I wasn't sure if I *did* buy the explanation, but I certainly had something strange and fascinating here.

"Okay, there's twenty *reals* advance," McNeil said, handing me a purple bill from the cash box. "Get some dinner if you didn't eat on the ship and get a good night's sleep at the motel—the Company owns it so there's no charge—and be ready to go aboard at four tomorrow afternoon."

I got up to leave.

"Oh, and Mr. Dalton," he added, and I turned to face him.

"Yes?"

"If, while on shore, you fall for a pretty lass, decide to settle down, then do it—*but don't go back on that ship again!* Quit. If you don't she's going to be greeted by a stranger, and you might never find her again."

"I'll remember," I assured him.

THE JOB WAS EVERYTHING McNeil promised and more. The scenery was spectacular, the people an ever-changing, fascinating group. Even the crew changed slightly—a little shorter sometimes, a little fatter or thinner, beards and mustaches came and went with astonishing rapidity, and accents varied enormously. It didn't matter; you soon adjusted to it as a matter of course, and all shipboard experiences were in common, anyway.

It was like a tight family after a while, really. And there were women in the crew, too, ranging from their twenties to their early fifties, not only in food and bar service but as deckhands and the like as well. Occasionally this was a little unsettling, since, in two or three cases out of 116, they were men in one world, women in another. You got used to even that. It was probably more unsettling for them; they were distinct people, and *they* didn't change sex. The personalities and personal histories tended to parallel, regardless, though, with only a few minor differences.

And the passengers! Some were really amazing. Even seasons were different for some of them, which explained the clothing variations. Certainly what constituted fashion and moral behavior was wildly different, as different as what they ate and the places they came from.

And yet, oddly, people were people. They laughed, and cried, and ate and drank and told jokes—some rather strange, I'll admit—and snapped pictures and all the other things people did. They came from places where the Vikings settled Nova Scotia (called Vinland, naturally), where Nova Scotia was French, or Spanish, or Portuguese, or very, very English. Even one in which Nova Scotia had been settled by Lord Baltimore and called Avalon.

Maine was as wild or wilder. There were two Indian nations running it, the U.S., Canada, Britain, France, Portugal, and lots of variations, some of which I never have gotten straight. There was also a temporal difference sometimes—some people were rather futuristic, with gadgets I couldn't even understand. One truck I loaded was powered by some sort of solar power and carried a cargo of food service robots. Some others were behind—still mainly horses, or oldtime cars and trucks. I am not certain even now if they were running at different speeds from us or whether some inventions had simply been made in some worlds and not in others.

And, McNeil was right. Every new summer season added at least one more. The boat was occasionally so crowded to our crew eyes that we had trouble making our way from one end of the ship to the other. Watching staterooms unload was also wild—it looked occasionally like the circus clown act, where 50 clowns get out of a Volkswagen.

And there *was* some sort of trade between the worlds. It was quickly clear that Bluewater Corporation was behind most of it, and that this was what made the line so profitable.

And, just once, there was a horrible, searing pain that hit the entire crew, and a modern world we didn't meet any more after that, and a particular variation of the crew we never saw again. And the last news-papers from that world had told of a coming war.

There was also a small crew turnover, of course. Some went on vaca-tion and never returned, some returned but would not reboard the ship. The Company was understanding, and it usually meant some extra work for a few weeks until they found someone new and could arrange for them to come on.

THE STARS WERE FADING a little now, and I shined the spot over to the red marker for the Captain. He acknowledged seeing it, and made his turn in, the lights of Southport coming into view and masking the stars a bit.

I went through the motions mechanically, raising the bow when the Captain hit the mark, letting go the bow lines, checking the clearances, and the like. I was thinking about the girl.

We knew that people's lives in the main did parallel from world to world. Seven times now she'd come aboard, seven times she'd looked at the white wake, and seven times she'd jumped to her death.

Maybe it was the temporal dislocation, maybe she just reached the same point at different stages, but she was always there and she always jumped.

I'd been working the *Orcas* three years, had some strange experiences, and generally pleasurable ones. For the first time I had a job I liked, a family of sorts in the crew, and an ever-changing assortment of people and places for a threepoint ferry run. In that time we'd lost one world and gained by our figures three others. That was 26 variants.

Did that girl exist in all 26? I wondered. Would we be subjected to that sadness 19 more times? Or more, as we picked up new worlds?

Oh, I'd tried to find her before she jumped in the past, yes. But she hadn't been consistent, except for the place she chose. We did three runs a day, two crews, so it was six a day more or less. She did it at different seasons, in different years, dressed differently.

You couldn't cover them all.

Not even all the realities of the crew of all worlds, although I knew that we were essentially the same people on all of them and that I—the other me's—were also looking.

I don't even know why I was so fixated, except that I'd been to that point once myself, and I'd discovered that you *could* go on, living with emotional scars, and find a new life.

I didn't even know what I'd say and do if I *did* see her early. I only knew that, if I did, she damned well wasn't going to go over the stern that trip.

In the meantime, my search for her when I could paid other dividends. I prevented a couple of children from going over through childish play, as well as a drunk, and spotted several health problems as I surveyed the people. One turned out to be a woman in advanced labor, and the first mate and I delivered our first child—our first, but the *Orcas'* nineteenth. We helped a lot of people, really, with a lot of different matters.

They were all just spectres, of course; they got on the boat often without us seeing them, and they disembarked for all time the same way. There were some regulars, but they were few. And, for them, we were a ghost crew, there to help and to serve.

But, then, isn't that the way you think of anybody in a service occupation? Firemen are firemen, not individuals; so are waiters, cops, street sweepers, and all the rest. Categories, not people.

We sailed from Point A to Point C stopping at B, and it was our whole life.

And then, one day in July of last year, I spotted her.

She was just coming on board at St. Clement's—that's possibly why I hadn't noticed her before. We backed into St. Clement's, and I was on the bow lines. But we were short, having just lost a deckhand to a nice-looking fellow in the English colony of Annapolis Royal, and it was my turn to do some double duty. So, there I was, routing traffic on the ship when I saw this little rounded station wagon go by and saw *her* in it.

I still almost missed her; I hadn't expected her to be with another person, another woman, and we were loading the Vinland existence, so in July they were more accurately in a state of undress than anything else, but I spotted her all the same. Jackie Carliner, one of the barmaids and a pretty good artist, had sketched her from the one time she'd seen the girl and we'd made copies for everyone.

Even so, I had my loading duties to finish first—there was no one else. But, as soon as we were underway and I'd raised the stern ramp, I made my way topside and to the lower stern deck. I took my walkie-talkie off the belt clip and called the Captain.

"Sir, this is Dalton," I called. "I've seen our suicide girl."

"So what else is new?" grumbled the Captain. "You know policy on that by now."

"But, sir!" I protested. "I mean still alive. Still on board. It's barely sundown, and we're a good half hour from the point yet."

He saw what I meant. "Very well," he said crisply. "But you know we're short-handed. I'll put Caldwell on the bow station this time, but you better get some results or I'll give you so much detail you won't have time to meddle in other people's affairs."

I sighed. Running a ship like this one hardened most people. I wondered if the Captain, with twenty years on the run, ever understood why I cared enough to try and stop this girl I didn't know from going in.

Did *I* know, for that matter?

As I looked around at the people going by, I thought about it. I'd thought about it a great deal before.

Why *did* I care about these faceless people? People from so many different worlds and cultures that they might as well have been from another planet. People who cared not at all about me, who saw me as an object, a cipher, a service, like those robots I mentioned. They didn't care about me. If *I* were perched on that rail and a crowd was around, most of them would probably yell "Jump!"

Most of the crew, too, cared only about each other, to a degree, and about the *Orcas*, our rock of sanity. I thought of that world gone in some atomic fire. What was the measure of an anonymous human being's worth?

I thought of Joanna and Harmony. With pity, yes, but I realized now that Joanna, at least, had been a vampire. She'd needed me, needed a rock to steady herself, to unburden herself to, to brag to. Someone steady and understanding, someone whose manner and character suggested that solidity. She'd never really even considered that I might have my own problems, that her promiscuity and lifestyle might be hurting me. Not that she was trying to hurt me—she just never *considered* me.

Like those people going by now. If they stub their toe, or have a question, or slip, or the boat sinks, they need me. Until then, I'm just a faceless automaton to them.

Ready to serve them, to care about them, if *they* needed somebody.

And that was why I was out here in the surprising chill, out on the stern with my neck stuck out a mile, trying to prevent a suicide I *knew* would happen, knew because I'd seen it three times before.

I was needed.

That was the measure of a human being's true worth, I felt sure. Not how many people ministered to *your* needs, but how many people *you* could help.

That girl—she had been brutalized, somehow, by society. Now I was to provide some counterbalance.

It was the surety of this duty that had kept me from blowing myself up with the old Delaware ferry, or jumping off that stern rail myself.

I glanced uneasily around and looked ahead. There was Shipshead light, tall and proud this time in the darkness, the way I liked it. I thought I could almost make out the marker buoys already. I started to get nervous.

I was certain that she'd jump. It'd happened every time before that we'd known. Maybe, just maybe, I thought, in this existence she won't.

I had no more than gotten the thought through my head when she came around the corner of the deck housing and stood in the starboard corner, looking down.

She certainly looked different this time. Her long hair was blond, not dark, and braided in large pigtails that drooped almost to her waist. She wore only the string bikini and transparent cape the Vinlanders liked in summer, and she had several gold rings on each arm, welded loosely there, I knew, and a marriage ring around her neck.

That was interesting, I thought. She looked so young, so despairing, that I'd never once thought of her as married.

Her friend, as thin and underdeveloped as she was stout, was with her. The friend had darker hair and had it twisted high atop her head. She wore no marriage ring.

I eased slowly over, but not sneakily. Like I said, nobody notices the crewman of a vessel; he's just a part of it.

"Luok, are yo sooure yu don' vant to halve a drink or zumpin?" the friend asked in that curious accent the Vinlanders had developed through cultural pollution by the dominant English and French.

"Naye, I yust vant to smell da zee-zpray," the girl replied. "Go on. I vill be alonk before ze zhip iz docking."

The friend was hesitant; I could see it in her manner. But I could also see she would go, partly because she was chilly, partly because she felt she had to show some trust to her friend.

She walked off. I looked busy checking the stairway supports to the second deck, and she paid me no mind whatsoever.

There were a few others on deck, but most had gone forward to see us come in, and the couple dressed completely in black sitting there on the bench was invisible to the girl as she was to them. She peered down at the black water and started to edge more to the starboard side engine wake, then a little past, almost to the center. Her upper torso didn't move, but I saw a bare, dirty foot go up on the lower rail.

I walked casually over. She heard me, and turned slightly to see if it was anyone she needed to be bothered with.

I went up to her and stood beside her, looking out at the water.

"Don't do it," I said softly, not looking directly at her. "It's too damned selfish a way to go."

She gave a small gasp and turned to look at me in wonder.

"How—how didt yu—?" she managed.

"I'm an old hand at suicides," I told her, that was no lie. Joanna, then almost me, then this woman seven other times.

"I vouldn't really haff—" she began, but I cut her off.

"Yes, you would. You know it and I know it. The only thing you know and I don't is why."

We were inside Shipshead light now. If I could keep her talking just a few more minutes we'd clear the channel markers and slow for the turn and docking. The turn and the slowdown would make it impossible for her to be caught in the propwash, and, I felt, the cycle would be broken, at least for her.

"Vy du yu care?" she asked, turning again to look at the dark sea, only slightly illuminated by the rapidly receding light.

"Well, partly because it's my ship, and I don't like things like that to happen on my ship," I told her. "Partly because I've been there myself, and I know how brutal a suicide is."

She looked at me strangely. "Dat's a fonny t'ing tu zay," she responded. "Jost vun qvick jomp and *pszzt!* All ofer."

"You're wrong," I said. "Besides, why would anyone so young want to end it?"

She had a dreamy quality to her face and voice. She was starting to blur, and I was worried that I might somehow translate into a different world-level as we neared shore.

"My 'usbahnd," she responded. "Goldier vas hiss name." She fingered the marriage ring around her neck. "Zo yong, so 'andzum." She turned her head quickly and looked up at me. "Do yu know vat it iz to be fat and ugly und 'alf bloind and haff ze best uv all men zuddenly pay attenzion to yu, vant to *marry* yu?"

I admitted I didn't, but didn't mention my own experiences.

"What happened? He leave you?" I asked.

There were tears in her eyes. "Ya, in a vay, ya. Goldier he jomped out a tventy-story building, he did. Und itz my own fault, yu know. I shud haff been dere. Or, maybe I didn't giff him vat he needed. I dunno."

"Then you of all people know how brutal suicide really is," I retorted. "Look at what it did to you. You have friends, like your friend here. They care. It will hurt them as your husband's hurt you. This woman with you—she'll carry guilt for leaving you alone the whole rest of her life." She was shaking now, not really from the chill, and I put my arm around her. Where the hell were those marker lights?

"Do you see how cruel it is? What suicide does to others? It leaves a legacy of guilt, much of it false guilt but no less real for that. And you might be needed by somebody else, sometime, to help them. Somebody else might die because you weren't there."

She looked up at me, then seemed to dissolve, collapse into a crescendo of tears, and sat down on the deck. I looked up and saw the red and green markers astern, felt the engines slow, felt the *Orcas* turn.

"*Ghetta!*" The voice was a piercing scream in the night. I looked around and saw her friend running to us after coming down the stairway. Anxiety and concern were on her stricken face, and there were tears in her eyes. She bent down to the still sobbing girl. "I shuld neffer haff left yu!" she sobbed, and hugged the girl tightly.

I sighed. The *Orcas* was making its dock approach now, the ringing of bells said that Caldwell had managed to raise the bow without crashing us into the dock.

"My Gott!" the friend swore, then looked up at me. "Yu stopped her? How can I effer? . . ."

But they both already had that ethereal, unnatural double image about them, both fading into a world different from mine.

"Just remember that there's a million Ghettas out there," I told them both softly. "And you can make them or break them."

I turned and walked away as I heard the satisfying thump and felt the slight jerk of the ferry fitting into the slip. I stopped and glanced back at the stern but I could see no one. Nobody was there.

Who were the ghosts? I mused. Those women, or the crew of the *Orcas*? How many times did hundreds of people from different worlds coexist on this ship without ever knowing it?

How many times did people in the *same* world coexist without noticing each other, or caring about each other, for that matter?

"Mr. Dalton!" snapped a voice in my walkie-talkie.

"Sir?" I responded.

"Well?" the Captain asked expectantly.

"No screams this time, Captain," I told him, satisfaction in my voice. "One young woman will live."

There was a long pause and, for a moment, I thought he might actually be human. Then he snapped, "There's eighty-six assorted vehicles still waiting to be off-loaded, and might I remind you we're short-handed and on a strict schedule?"

I sighed and broke into a trot. Business was business, and I had a whole world to throw out of the car deck so I could run another one in.

Ward Moore

Ward Moore's "Bring the Jubilee," a blend of time travel and alternate history in which a Confederate triumph at the Battle of Gettysburg leads to a Southern victory in the American Civil War, is a landmark in alternate-world science fiction. Moore also wrote the satirical Greener Than You Think, a highly regarded ecodisaster novel, and collaborated with Robert Bradford on Caduceus Wild and Avram Davidson on Joyleg. He published nearly two dozen science-fiction short stories between 1946 and his death in 1978 in The Magazine of Fantasy and Science Fiction, Amazing, The Saturday Evening Post, and Galaxy. His oft-reprinted stories "Lot" and "Lot's Daughter," collected in 1996, are considered high-water marks of nuclear disaster fiction, and were the uncredited basis for the 1962 film Panic in the Year Zero.

BRING THE JUBILEE

Ward Moore

I

ALTHOUGH I AM WRITING this in the year 1877, I was not born until 1921. Neither the dates nor the tenses are error—let me explain:

I was born, as I say, in 1921, but it was not until the early 1930s, when I was about ten, that I began to understand what a peculiarly frustrated and disinherited world was about me. Perhaps my approach to realization was through the crayon portrait of Granpa Hodgins which hung, very solemnly, over the mantel.

Granpa Hodgins, after whom I was named, perhaps a little grandiloquently, Hodgins McCormick Backmaker, had been a veteran of the War of Southron Independence. Like so many young men he had put on a shapeless blue uniform in response to the call of the ill-advised and headstrong—or martyred—Mr. Lincoln. Depending on which of my lives' viewpoint you take.

Granpa lost an arm on the Great Retreat to Philadelphia after the fall of Washington to General Lee's victorious Army of Northern Virginia, so his war ended some six months before the capitulation at Reading and the acknowledgement of the independence of the Confederate States on July 4, 1864. One-armed and embittered, Granpa came home to Wappinger Falls and, like his fellow veterans, tried to remake his life in a different and increasingly hopeless world.

On its face the Peace of Richmond was a just and even generous disposition of a defeated foe by the victor. (Both sides—for different reasons—remembered the mutiny of the Unreconstructed Federals of the Armies of the Cumberland and the Tennessee who, despite defeat at Chattanooga, could not forget Vicksburg and Port Hudson and fought bloodily against the order to surrender.) The South could easily have carved the country up to suit its most fiery patriots, even to the point of detaching the West as a satellite protectorate. Instead the chivalrous Southrons contented themselves with drawing the new boundary along more or less traditional lines. The Mason-Dixon gave them Delaware and Maryland, but they generously returned the panhandle of western Virginia jutting above it. Missouri was naturally included in the Confederacy, but of the disputed territory Colorado and Deseret were conceded to the old Union; only Kansas and California as well as—for obvious defensive reasons—Nevada's tip went to the South.

But the Peace of Richmond had also laid the cost of the war on the beaten North and this was what crippled Granpa Hodgins more than the loss of his arm. The postwar inflation entered the galloping stage during the Vallandigham Administration, became dizzying in the time of President Seymour and precipitated the food riots of 1873 and '74. It was only after the election of President Butler by the Whigs in 1876 and the reorganization and drastic deflation following that money and property became stable, but by this time all normal values were destroyed. Meanwhile the indemnities had to be paid regularly in gold. Granpa and hundreds of thousands like him just never seemed to get back on their feet.

How well I remember, as a small boy in the 1920s and '30s, my mother and father talking bitterly of how the War had ruined everything. They were not speaking of the then fairly recent Emperor's War of 1914–16, but of the War of Southron Independence which still, nearly 70 years later, blighted what was left of the United States. I heard of the strange, bright era when we and our neighbors had owned our own farms outright and had not had to pay rent for them to the banks or half the crop to a landlord. I learned of the bygone time when a man could nearly always get a job for wages which would support himself and a family, before the system of indenture became so common that practically the only alternative to pauperism was to sell oneself to a company. In those days men and women married young and had large families; there might have been five generations between Granpa Hodgins and myself instead of three. And many uncles, aunts, cousins, brothers and sisters. Now late marriages with a single child were the rule.

If it hadn't been for the War—was the basic theme stated with variations suited to the particular circumstance. If it hadn't been for the War the most energetic young men and women would not turn to emigration; foreigners would not visit the United States with condescending contempt; the great powers would think twice before sending troops to "restore order" every time one of their citizens was molested and our own inadequate police forces were unable to protect him. If it hadn't been for the War it would be possible to live like a self-respecting human being, to work reasonable hours for wages that would buy decent food and clothing instead of shoddy.

Perhaps because of the ever increasing hostility to immigrants which culminated in the virtual barring of the country to all, little mention was ever made of Grandfather Backmaker. No enlarged crayon portrait of him hung anywhere, much less over the mantel. Somehow I got the impression my father's father had been not only a foreigner by birth, but a shady character in his own right, a man who actually believed in the things for which Granpa Hodgins had fought. I don't know how I learned that Grandfather Backmaker had made speeches advocating equal rights for Negroes or protesting the mass lynchings so popular in the North, in contrast to the humane treatment accorded these noncitizens in the Confederacy. Nor did I remember how I found out he had been run out of several places before finally settling in Wappinger Falls or that all his life people had muttered darkly at his back, "Dirty Abolitionist!"—a very deep imprecation indeed. I only know that as a consequence of this taint my father, a meek, hardworking, worried little man, was completely dominated by my mother who never let him forget that a Hodgins or a McCormick was worth dozens of Backmakers.

I must have been a great trial to her for I showed no signs of proper Hodgins gumption, such as she had a right to expect in her only child. For one thing I was remarkably unhandy and awkward; of little use in the hundred necessary chores around our dilapidated house. I could not pick up a hammer at her command to do something about fixing the loose weatherboards on the east side without mashing my thumb or splitting the aged, unpainted wood. I could not hoe the kitchen garden without damaging precious vegetables and leaving weeds intact. I could shovel snow in the winter at a tremendous rate for I was strong and had endurance, but work requiring manual dexterity baffled me. I fumbled in harnessing Bessie, our mare, or hitching her to the cart for my father's trips to Poughkeepsie, and as for helping him on the farm or in his smithy—from which most of our meager cash income came—I'm afraid my efforts drove that mild man nearest to a temper he ever experienced. He would lay the reins on the plowhorse's back or his hammer down on the anvil and say mournfully, "Better see if you can help your mother, Hodge. You're only in my way here."

I REMEMBER THE TIME a trackless locomotive—minibiles, they were called—broke down not a quarter of a mile from Father's smithy. This was a golden, unparalleled, unbelievable opportunity. Minibiles, like any other luxury, were rare in the United States though they were common enough in prosperous countries like the German Union or the Confederacy. We had to rely for our transportation on the never-failing horse or on the railroads, wornout and broken down as they were. For decades the great issue in Congress was the never completed Pacific transcontinental line, though Canada had one and the Confederate States seven. (Though sailing balloons were in frequent use they were still looked upon as somehow "impractical.") Only a rare millionaire with the connections in Berlin, Washington-Baltimore or Leesburg could afford the indulgence of the costly and complicated minibile which required a trained driver in order to bounce over the rutted and chuckholed roads. Only one of an extraordinarily adventurous spirit would leave the tar-surfaced streets of New York or its sister city of Brooklyn, where the solid rubber tires of the minibiles could at worst find traction on the horse or cable-car rails, for the morasses or washboard roads which were the only highways north of the Harlem River.

When such a one did it was inevitable that the jolting, jouncing and shaking it received would break or disconnect one of the delicate parts in its complex mechanism. Then the only recourse—apart from telegraphing back to the city if the traveler were fortunate enough to break down near an instrument—was to the closest blacksmith. Smiths rarely knew much of the principles of the minibiles, but with the broken part before them they could fabricate a passable duplicate and, unless the machine had suffered serious damage, put it back in place. It was customary for such a craftsman to compensate himself for the time taken away from horseshoeing or spring-fitting (or just absently chewing on an oatstraw) by demanding exorbitant remuneration, amounting to perhaps 25 or 30 cents an hour, thus revenging his rural poverty and self-sufficiency upon the effete wealth and helplessness of the urban excursionist.

Such a golden opportunity befell my father, as I said, during the fall of 1933 when I was twelve years old. The driver had made his way to the smithy, leaving the owner of the minibile marooned and fuming in the enclosed passenger seat. A hasty visit convinced Father—who could re-pair a clock or broken rake with equal dexterity—that his only course was to bring the machine to the forge since a part, not easy to disassem-ble, had been bent and needed heating and straightening. (The driver, the owner, and Father all repeated the name of the part often enough, but so inept have I been with "practical" things all my life that I couldn't recall it ten minutes later, much less after more than 30 years.)

"Hodge," he said, "run and get the mare and ride over to Jones's. Don't try to saddle her—go bareback. Ask Mr. Jones to kindly lend me his team."

"I'll give the boy a quarter dollar for himself if he's back with the team within twenty minutes," added the owner of the minibile, sticking his head out of the window.

I won't say I was off like the wind, for my life's work has given me a distaste for exaggeration or hyperbole, but I moved faster than I ever had before. A quarter, a whole shining silver quarter, a day's full wage for a boy, half the day's pay of a grown man—all for myself, to spend as I wished.

I ran all the way to the barn, led Bessie out by her halter and jumped on her broad back, my enthralling daydream growing and deepening each moment. With my quarter safely got I could perhaps persuade my father to take me along on his next trip to Poughkeepsie; in the shops there I could find some yards of figured cotton for Mother, or a box of cigars to which Father was partial but rarely bought for himself, or an unimagined something for Mary McCutcheon, temporarily the acme of feminine charm to me.

Or I could take the entire quarter into Newman's Book and Sta-tionery Store. Here I could not afford to buy one of the latest English or Confederate books—even the novels I disdained cost 50 cents in their original and 30 in the pirated United States' edition—but what trea-sures there were in the twelve and a half cent reprints and the dime classics!

With Bessie's legs moving steadily beneath me I pored over in my imagination Mr. Newman's entire stock. Now, my quarter would buy

two reprints, but I would read them in as many evenings and be no better off than before until their memory faded and I could read them
again. Better to invest in paperbacked adventure stories giving sharp,
breathless pictures of life in the West or rekindling the glories of the
War. True, they were written almost entirely by Confederate authors
and I was, thanks perhaps to the portrait of Granpa Hodgins and my
mother's hard patriotism, a devout partisan of the lost cause of Sheridan
and Sherman and Thomas. But patriotism could not steel me against
the excitement of the Confederate paperbacks; literature simply disregarded the boundary stretching to the Pacific.

I had finally determined to invest all my 25 cents, not in five paper-
bound volumes but in ten of the same in secondhand or shopworn
condition, when I suddenly became aware I had been riding Bessie for
some considerable time. I looked around, rather dazed by the abrupt
translation from the dark and slightly musty interior of Newman's bookstore to the bright countryside, to find with dismay that Bessie hadn't
taken me to the Jones farm after all but on some private tour of her own
in the opposite direction.

I'm afraid this little anecdote is pointless (it was momentarily pointed
enough for me that particular evening, for in addition to the loss of the
promised quarter I received a thorough whacking with a willow switch
from my mother after my father had, as usual, dolefully refused his
parental duty) except that it shows that in pursuing the dream I could
lose the reality.

My feeling that books were a part of life, and the most important
part, was no passing phase. Other boys in their early teens dreamed of
going to Dakotah, indenting to a company run by a young and beautiful
woman (this was a favorite theme of many of the paperbacks), discovering the loot hidden by a gang, or emigrating to Australia or the South
African Republic. Or else they faced the reality of carrying on the family farm, petty trade, or indenture. I only wanted to be allowed to read.

The school at Wappinger Falls taught as little as possible as quickly
as possible; parents needed the help of their children to survive or to
build up a small reserve in the illusory hope of buying free of their indenture. Both my mother and my teachers looked askance at my desire
to persist in my studies past an age when my contemporaries were making themselves economically useful.

Nor—even supposing I had the fees—could the Academy at Poughkeepsie provide me with what I wanted. There was no money for Yale,
Harvard, or Columbia, those increasingly decayed and provincialized

colleges which contrasted so painfully with the great and flourishing universities of the Confederacy or Europe. Indeed our financial position was very bad and there was often talk of my father selling the smithy and indenting.

I was of no help; rather I was one who ate three meals a day and occupied a bed. Yet when I spoke of trying to get more learning my mother went into a perfect fury at the very mention of such idleness and self-indulgence. My father merely shrugged resignedly. Only Agnes Jones who had supplanted Mary McCutcheon sympathized and encouraged me. Unhappily, her plans for my future were limited to marrying her and helping her father on his farm, which didn't seem to me any great advance over what I had to look forward to at home.

I was increasingly conscious too of the looks and smiles which followed me. A great lout of seventeen, too lazy to do a stroke of work, always wandering around with his head in the clouds or lying with his nose stuck in a book. Too bad—and the Backmakers such hardworking folks too. Wappinger Falls was intolerable.

A few months before my eighteenth birthday then, I packed my three most cherished books in my good white cotton shirt, and having bade a most romantic goodbye to Agnes (which certainly would have eventuated in the consummation of all her hopes had her father discovered us), I set out on foot for New York.

II

New York, in 1938, had a population of nearly a million, having grown gradually but steadily since the close of the War of Southron Independence. Together with the half million in the city of Brooklyn this represented by far the greatest concentration of people in the United States, though of course it could not compare with the great Confederate centers of Washington (now including Baltimore and Alexandria), St. Louis, or Leesburg (once Mexico City).

The country boy who had never seen anything more metropolitan than Poughkeepsie was tremendously impressed. Cable-cars whizzed northward as far as 59th Street on the west side and all the way to 87th on the east, while horse-cars furnished convenient crosstown transportation with a line every few blocks. Bicycles, rare around Wappinger Falls, were thick as flies, darting ahead and alongside drayhorses pulling wallowing vans, carts and wagons. Prancing trotters drew private carriages, buggies, broughams, victorias, hansoms, dogcarts or sulkies; neither the cyclists, coachmen nor horses seemed overawed or discommoded by occasional minibiles chuffing their way swiftly and implacably over cobblestones or asphalt.

Incredibly intricate traceries of telegraph wires swarmed overhead, crossing and recrossing at all angles, slanting upward into offices and flats or downward into stores, a reminder that no family with pretensions to gentility would be without the clacking instrument in the parlor and every child learned the Morse code before he could read. Thousands of sparrows considered the wires properly their own; they perched and swung, quarrelled and scolded on them, leaving only to satisfy their voracity upon the steaming mounds of horsedung below.

Buildings of eight or ten storeys were common, and there were many of fourteen or fifteen, serviced by pneumatic English lifts, that same marvelous invention which permitted the erection of veritable skyscrapers in Washington and Leesburg. Above them balloons moved gracefully through the air, guided and controlled as skillfully as an old time sailing vessel.

Most exciting of all was simply the number of people who walked, rode, or merely stood around on the streets. It seemed hardly believable that so many humans could crowd themselves so closely. Beggars pleaded, touts wheedled, peddlers hawked, newsboys shouted, bootblacks chanted. Messengers pushed their way, loafers yawned, ladies stared, drunks staggered. For long moments I paused, standing stock still, not thinking of going anywhere, merely watching the spectacle.

I had hardly begun to fondle the sharp edge of wonder when darkness fell and the gas lamps, lit simultaneously by telegraphic sparks, glowed and shone on nearly every corner. Whatever had been drab and dingy in daylight—and even my eyes had not been blind to the signs of dirt and decay—became in an instant magically enchanting, softened and shadowed into mysterious beauty. I breathed the dusty air with a relish I had never felt for that of the country and knew myself for the first time to be spiritually at home.

But spiritual sustenance is not quite enough for an eighteen year old; I began to feel the need for food and rest. The three dollars in my pocket I was resolved to hoard, not having any notion how to go about replenishing it. I could not do without eating, however, so I stopped in at the first gaslit bakery, buying a penny loaf, and walked slowly through the entrancing streets, munching on it.

Now the fronts of the tinugraph lyceums were lit up by porters with long tapers, so that they glowed yellow and inviting, each heralded with a boldly lettered broadside or dashingly drawn cartoon advertising the amusement to be found within. I was sorely tempted to see for myself this magical entertainment of pictures taken so close together they gave the illusion of motion, but the lowest price of admission was five cents. Some of the more garish theaters, which specialized in the incredible phonotos—tinugraphs which were ingeniously combined with a sound-producing machine operated by compressed air, so that the pictures seemed not only to move, but to talk—actually charged ten or even fifteen cents for an hour's spectacle.

By now I ached with tiredness; the insignificant bundle of shirt and books had become a burden. I was pressed by the question of where to sleep, but I didn't connect the glass transparencies behind which gaslight shone through the unpainted letters of BEDS, ROOMS, or HOTEL with my need, for I was looking for the urban version of the inn at Wappinger Falls or the Poughkeepsie Commercial House. I became more and more confused as fatigue blurred impressions of still newer marvels, so that I am not entirely sure whether it was merely one or a succession of enchanting girls who offered delights for a quarter. I know I was solicited by crimps for the Confederate Legion who operated openly in defiance of the laws of the United States and that an incredible number of beggars accosted me.

At last I thought of asking directions from one of the multitude on the wooden or granite sidewalks. But without realizing it I had wandered from thronged, brightly lit avenues into an unpeopled, darkened area where buildings were low and frowning, where the flicker of a candle or the yellow of a kerosene lamp in windows far apart were unrivalled by any streetlights.

My ears had been deafened all day by the clop of hooves, the rattling of iron tires or the puffing of minibiles; now the empty street seemed unnaturally still. The suddenly looming figure of another walker was the luckiest of chances.

"Excuse me, friend," I said. "Can you tell me where's the nearest inn, or anywhere I can get a bed for the night cheap?"

I felt him peering at me. "Rube, huh? Much money you got?"

"Th— Not very much. That's why I want to find cheap lodging."

"OK, Reuben—come along."

"Oh, don't trouble to show me. Just give me an idea how to get there."

He grunted. "No trouble, Reuben. No trouble at all."

Taking my arm just above the elbow in a firm grip he steered me along. For the first time I began to feel alarm. However, before I could even attempt to shrug free, he had shoved me into the mouth of an alley discernible only because its absolute blackness contrasted with the relative darkness of the street.

"Wait—" I began.

"In here, Reuben. Soundest night's sleep you've had in a long time. And cheap—it's free."

I started to break loose and was surprised to find he no longer held me. Before I could even begin to think, however, a terrific blow fell on the right side of my head and I traded the blackness of the alley for the blackness of insensibility.

I WAS RECALLED to consciousness by a smell. More accurately a cacophony of smells. I opened my eyes and shut them against the unbearable pain of light; I groaned at the equally unbearable pain in my skull bones. Feverishly and against my will I tried to identify the walloping odors around me.

The stink of death and rottenness was thick. I knew there was an outhouse—many outhouses—nearby. The ground I lay upon was damp with the water of endless dishwashings and launderings. The noisomeness of offal suggested that the garbage of many families had never been buried, but left to rot in the alley or near it. In addition there was the smell of death—not the sweetish effluvium of blood, such as any country boy who has helped butcher a bull-calf or hog knows—but the unmistakable stench of corrupt, maggotty flesh. Besides all this there was the spoor of humanity.

A new discomfort at last forced my eyes open for the second time. A hard surface was pressing painful knobs into my exposed skin. I looked and felt around me.

The knobs were the cobbles of a fetid alley; not a foot away was the cadaver of a dog, thoroughly putrescent; beyond him a drunk retched and groaned. A trickle of liquid swill wound its way delicately between the stones. My coat, shirt, and shoes were gone; so was the bundle with my books. There was no use searching my pocket for the three dollars—I knew I was lucky the robber left me my pants and my life.

A middleaged man—at least he looked middleaged to my youthful eye—regarded me speculatively over the head of the drunk. "Pretty well cleaned yuh out, huh, boy?"

I nodded—and then was sorry for the motion.

"Reward of virtue. Assuming you was virtuous, which I assume. Come to the same end as me, stinking drunk. Only I still got my shirt. Couldn't hock it no matter how thirsty I got."

I groaned.

"Where yuh from, boy? What rural—see, sober now—precincts miss you?"

"Wappinger Falls, near Poughkeepsie. My name's Hodge Backmaker."

"Well now, that's friendly of you, Hodge. Me, I'm George Pondible. Periodic. Just tapering off."

I hadn't an idea what Pondible was talking about. Trying to understand made my head worse.

"Took everything, I suppose? Haven't a nickel left to help a hangover?"

"My head," I mumbled, quite superfluously.

He staggered to his feet. "Best thing—souse it in the river. Take more to fix mine."

"But . . . can I go through the streets like this?"

"Right," he said. "Quite right."

He stooped down and put one hand beneath the drunk. With the other he removed the jacket, a maneuver betraying practice, for it elicited no protest from the victim. He then performed the still more delicate operation of depriving him of his shirt and shoes, tossing them all to me. They were a loathsome collection of rags not fit to clean a manure-spreader. The jacket was torn and greasy, the pockets hanging like the ears of a dog; the shirt was a filthy tatter, the shoes shapeless fragments of leather with great gapes in the soles.

"It's stealing," I protested.

"Right. Put them on and let's get out of here."

The short walk to the river was through streets lacking the glamour of those of the day before. The tenements were smokestreaked, marked with steps between the parting bricks where mortar had fallen out; great hunks of wall were kept in place only by the support of equally crazy ones abutting. The wretched rags I wore were better suited to this neighborhood than Pondible's though his would have marked him tramp and vagrant in Wappinger Falls.

The Hudson too was soiled, with an oily scum and debris, so that I hesitated even to dip the purloined shirt, much less my aching head. But urged on by Pondible I climbed down the slimy stones between two docks and pushing the flotsam aside, ducked myself in the unappetizing water.

The sun was hot and the shirt dried on my back as we walked away from the river, the jacket over my arm. Yesterday I had entertained vague plans of presenting myself at Columbia College, begging to exchange work of any kind for tuition. In my present state this was manifestly impossible; for a moment I wished I had waded farther into the Hudson and drowned.

"Fixes your head," said Pondible with more assurance than accuracy. "Now for mine."

Now that my mind was clearer my despair grew by the minute. Admitting my plans had been impractical and tenuous, they were yet plans of a kind, something in which I could put—or force—my hopes. Now they were gone, literally knocked out of existence and I had nothing to look forward to, nothing on which to exert my energies and dreams. To go back to Wappinger Falls was out of the question, not simply to dodge the bitterness of admitting defeat so quickly, but because I knew myself to be completely useless to my parents. Yet I had nothing to expect in the city except starvation or a life of petty crime.

Pondible guided me into a saloon, a dark place, gaslit even this early, with a steam piano tinkling away the popular tune "Mormon Girl":

> There's a girl in the State of Deseret
> Whom I love and I'm trying to for-get.
> Forget her for tired feet's sake
> Don't wanna walk miles to Great Salt Lake.
> They ever build that railroad toooo the ocean
> I'd return my darling Mormon girl's devotion.
> But the tracks stop short in Ioway . . .

I couldn't remember the last line.

"Shot," Pondible ordered the bartender, "and buttermilk for my chum."

The bartender kept on polishing the wood in front of him with a wet, dirty rag. "Got any jack?"

"Pay you tomorrow, friend."

The bartender's uninterrupted industry said clearly, then drink tomorrow.

"Listen," argued Pondible, "I'm tapering off. You know me. I've spent plenty of money here."

The bartender shrugged. "Why don't you indent?"

Pondible looked shocked. "At my age? What would a company pay for a wornout old carcass? A hundred dollars maybe. Then a release in a couple of years with a med holdback so I'd have to report every week somewhere. No friend, I've come though this long a free man (in a manner of speaking) and I'll stick it out. Let's have that shot; you can see for yourself I'm tapering off. You'll get your jack tomorrow."

I could see the bartender was weakening; each refusal was less surly and at last, to my astonishment, he set out a glass and bottle for Pondible and an earthenware mug of buttermilk for me. To my astonishment, I say, for credit was rarely extended on either large or small scale. The Inflation, though 60 years in the past, had left indelible impressions; people paid cash or did without. Debt was disgraceful; the notion things could be paid for while, or even after, they were being used was as unthinkable as was the idea of circulation of paper money instead of silver or gold.

I drank my buttermilk slowly, gratefully aware Pondible had ordered the most filling and sustaining liquid in the saloon. For all his unprepossessing appearance and peculiar moral notions, it was evident my new acquaintance had a rude wisdom as well as a rude kindliness.

He swallowed his whiskey in an instant and called upon the bartender for a quart pot of small beer which he now sipped, turning to me and drawing out, not unskillfully, the story not only of my life, but of my hopes, and the despondency I now knew at their shattering.

"Well," he said at last, "you can always take the advice our friend here offered me and indent. A young healthy lad like you could get yourself $1,000 or $1,200 —"

"Yes. And be a slave the rest of my life."

Pondible wiped specks of froth from his beard with the back of his hand. "Oh, indenting ain't slavery—it's better. And worse. For one thing the company that buys you won't hold you after you aren't worth your keep. They cancel your indenture without a cent in payment. Of course they'll take a med holdback so as to get a dollar or two for your corpse, but that's a long time away for you."

"Yes. A long time away. So I wouldn't be a slave for life; just 30 or 40 years. Till I wasn't any good to anyone, including myself."

He seemed to be enjoying himself as he drank his beer. "You're a gloomy gus, Hodge. Tain't as bad as that. Indenting's pretty strictly regulated. That's the idea, anyway. You can't be made to work over 60 hours a week—ten hours a day. With $1,000 or $1,200 you could get all the education you want in your spare time and then turn your learning to account by making enough money to buy yourself free."

I tried to think about it dispassionately, though goodness knows I'd been over the ground often enough. It was true that the amount, a not inconceivable one for a boy willing to indenture himself, would see me comfortably through college. But Pondible's notion that I could turn my "learning to account" I knew to be a fantasy despite its currency. Perhaps in the Confederate States or the German Union knowledge was rewarded with wealth, or at least a comfortable living, but any study I pursued—I knew my own "impracticality" well enough by now—was bound to yield few material benefits in the poor, exploited, backward United States, which existed as a nation at all only on the sufferance and unresolved rivalries of the great powers. I would be lucky to struggle through school and eke out some kind of living as a freeman; I could never hope to earn enough to buy back my indenture on what was left of my time after subtracting 60 hours a week.

Pondible listened as I explained all this, nodding and sipping alternately. "Well then," he said, "there's the gangs."

I looked my horror.

He laughed. "Forget your country rearing. If you leave the parsons' sermons out of it there's no difference joining the gangs than joining the army—if we had one—or the Confederate Legion. Most of the gangsters never even get shot at. They all live high, high as anybody in the 26 states, and every once in a while there's a dividend that's more than a workingman earns in a lifetime."

I began to be sure my benefactor was a gangster. And yet . . . if this were so why had he wheedled credit from the barkeep? Was it simply an elaborate blind to recruit me? It seemed hardly worth it. "A fat dividend maybe. Or a rope."

"Most of the gangsters die of old age. Or competition. Ain't one been hung I can think of in the last five years. But I can see you've no stomach for it. Tell me, Hodge—you a Whig or Populist?"

The sudden change of subject bewildered me. "Why . . . Populist, I guess. Anyway I don't think much of the Whigs' 'Property, Protection, Permanent Population.' The anxiety to build up a prosperous employing class artificially ever since the original industrialists were wiped out by the reparations and inflation is one of the things which has kept the country so poor. The rest is nonsense; they've never attempted to try protection when they were in power for the very good reason that the Confederacy and the German Union won't allow any small nation to put up a tariff wall against their exports. As for 'permanent population,' it's unaffected by elections. Those who can't make a living will continue to emigrate to more prosperous countries where they can—"

My voice trailed off. Pondible cocked an eyebrow over his beer mug, put it down and chewed on a soggy corner of his mustache, still regarding me quizzically.

"I don't feel like leaving the United States," I muttered defensively.

"You heard of the Grand Army?" he asked with apparent irrelevance.

"Who hasn't? Not much difference between them and the regular gangs."

"I dunno, Hodge. Seems to me they got much the same ideas you have. They're Populists. They don't like the United States being a fifth-rate country; they're against indenting; they think prosperity's got to come from the poor upward, not from the rich downward. Maybe they get a little rough with Whigs or Confederate agents once in a while, but you can't make bacon out of a live hog."

Was it the thought of Grandfather Backmaker that made me ask, "And do they want to give Negroes equality?"

He drew back sharply. "Touch of the tarbrush in you, boy? No, I can see you ain't. You just don't understand. We might have won that war if it hadn't been for the Abolitionists. They're better off among their own. Better leave those ideas alone, Hodge; there's enough to be done for our own. Chase the foreigners out; teach their agents a lesson; build up the country again."

"Are you trying to recruit me for the Grand Army?"

Pondible finished his beer. "No. I want to get you somewheres to sleep, three meals a day, and that education you're so anxious for. Come along."

III

He took me to a bookseller's and stationery store on Astor Place with a printshop in the basement and the man to whom he introduced me was the owner, Roger Tyss. I spent almost six years there, and when I left neither the store nor its contents nor Tyss himself seemed to have changed or aged. I know books were sold and others bought to take their places on the shelves or be piled towerwise on the floor; I helped cart in many rolls of sulphide paper and bottles of printers' ink, and delivered many bundles of damp pamphlets, broadsides, letterheads and envelopes. Inked ribbons for typewriting machines, penpoints, ledgers and daybooks; rulers, paperclips, legal forms and cubes of indiarubber came and went. Yet the identical disorder, the same dogeared volumes, the indistinguishable stock, the unaltered cases of type remained fixed for six years, all covered by the same film of dust which responded to vigorous sweeping only by rising into the air, filling it with the sneezes of the sweeper or any customers happening to be present and immediately settling back on the precise spots.

Roger Tyss grew six years older and I can only charge it to the heedless eye of youth that I discerned no signs of that aging or that I was never able to guess his years to my satisfaction. Like Pondible and—as I learned—so many members of the Grand Army, he wore a beard. His was closely trimmed, wiry and grizzled. Above the beard and across his forehead were many fine lines which always held some of the grime of the store or printing press. One did not dwell long on either beard or wrinkles, however; what held you were his eyes: large, dark, fierce and compassionate. Anyone might have dismissed him at first glance as simply an undersized, stoopshouldered, slovenly printer had one not been fixed by those compelling eyes.

For six years that store was home and school, and Roger Tyss was employer, teacher and father to me. I was not indentured to him, nor did he pay me any wages. Our agreement—if so simple and unilateral a statement can be called an agreement—was made ten minutes after he met me for the first time.

"Hodgins," he said, staring piercingly up at me (he never then nor later condescended to the familiar "Hodge" nor did I ever address or even think of him but as Mr. Tyss), "I'll feed you and lodge you, teach you to set type and give you the run of the books. I'll pay you no money; you can steal from me if you have the conscience. You can learn as much here in four months as in a college in four years—or you can learn nothing. I'll expect you to do the work I think needs doing; any time you don't like it you're free to go."

He was my father and teacher, but he was never my friend. Rather he was my adversary. I respected him and the longer I knew him the deeper became my respect, but it was an ambivalent feeling and at-tached only to his zealotry. I detested his ideas, his philosophy and some of his actions; and this detestation grew until I was no longer able to live near him. But I am getting ahead of my story.

Tyss knew books, not only as a bookman knows them—binding, size, edition, value—but as a scholar. He seemed to have read enormously and on every conceivable subject, many of them quite useless in practi-cal application. As a printer he followed the same pattern; he was not concerned solely with setting up a neat page; he wrote much on his own account: poetry, essays, manifestoes, composing directly from the font, running off a proof which he read and immediately destroyed before pieing the type.

I slept on a mattress kept under one of the counters during the day; Tyss had a couch, hardly more luxurious, downstairs by the flatbed press. Each morning before it was time to open, Tyss sent me across town on the horse-cars to the Washington Market to buy six pounds of beef—twelve on Saturdays, for the market, unlike the bookstore, was closed Sundays. It was always the same cut, heart of ox or cow, dressed by the butcher in thin strips. Several times, after I had been with him long enough to tire of the fare, but not long enough to realize the obsti-nacy of his nature, I begged him to let me substitute pork or mutton, or at least some other part of the beef, like brains or tripe which were even cheaper. But he always answered, "The heart, Hodgins; purchase the heart. It is the vital food."

While I was on my errand he would buy three loaves of yesterday's bread, still tolerably fresh; when I returned he took a long two-pronged fork, our only utensil, for the establishment was innocent of other cut-lery or dishes, and spearing a strip of heart held it over the gas flame un-til it was sooted and toasted rather than broiled. We tore the loaves with our fingers and with a hunk of bread in one hand and a piece of meat in the other we each ate a pound of beef and half a loaf of bread for break-fast, dinner, and supper.

Tyss expected me to work but he was not a hard nor inconsiderate master. In 1938–44, when the country was being ground deeper into colonialism by the Confederate States and the German Union, there were few employers so lenient. I read much, practically when I pleased, and he encouraged me; even going to the length, when a particular book was not to be found in his considerable stock, of letting me get it from one of his competitors, to be written up against his account.

Nor was he too scrupulous about the time I took on his errands; if I spent some of it with a girl—and there were many girls in New York who didn't look too unkindly on a tall youth even though he still carried some of the rustic air of Wappinger Falls—he never mentioned that a walk of half a mile had taken me a couple of hours.

It was true he kept rigidly to his original promise never to pay me wages but he often handed me coins for pocket money—evidently satisfied I wasn't stealing—and he replaced my makeshift wardrobe with worn but decent clothing.

He hadn't exaggerated the possibilities of the books which now surrounded me. His brief warning, "—or you can learn nothing," was lost on me. I suppose someone of different temperament might have been surfeited with paper and print; I can only say I wasn't. I nibbled, tasted, gobbled books. After the store was shut I hooked a student lamp to the nearest gas jet by means of a long tube, and lying on my pallet, with a dozen volumes handy, I read till I was no longer able to keep my eyes open or understand the words. Often I woke in the morning to find the light still burning and my fingers holding the pages open.

It seemed to me Tyss must have read everything, mastered every subject, acquired all languages; even now I believe his knowledge to have been incredibly wide. When he came upon me with an open book he would glance at the running title over my shoulder and begin talking, either of the particular work or its topic. What he had to say often gave me an insight I would otherwise have missed, and turned me to other writers, other aspects. He respected no authority simply because it was acclaimed or established; he prodded me to examine every statement, every hypothesis no matter how commonly accepted.

Early in my employment I was attracted to a large framed parchment he kept hanging over his typecase. It was simply but beautifully printed; I knew without being told that he had set it himself:

THE BODY OF

BENJAMIN FRANKLIN

PRINTER

LIKE THE COVER OF AN OLD BOOK

STRIPPED OF ITS LETTERING AND GILDING

LIES HERE

FOOD FOR WORMS.

BUT THE WORK SHALL NOT BE LOST

FOR IT WILL, AS HE BELIEVED,

COME FORTH AGAIN

IN A NEW AND BETTER EDITION

REVISED & CORRRECTED

BY

THE AUTHOR.

When he caught me admiring it Tyss laughed. "Elegant, isn't it, Hodgins? But a lie, a perverse and probably hypocritical lie. There is no Author; the book of life is simply a mess of pied type—a tale told by an idiot, full of sound and fury, signifying nothing. There is no plan, no synopsis to be filled in with pious hopes or hypocritical actions. There is nothing but a vast emptiness in the universe."

I had been reading an obscure Irish theologian—a Protestant curate of some forsaken parish, so ill-esteemed that he had been forced to publish his sermons himself—named George B. Shaw, and I had been impressed by his forceful style if not his philosophy. I quoted him to Tyss, perhaps as much to show erudition as to counter his argument.

"Nonsense," said my employer, "I've seen the good parson's book, and it's a waste of good ink and paper. Man does not think; he only thinks he thinks. An automaton, he responds to external stimuli; he cannot order his thought."

"You mean then that there is no free will—not even a marginal minimum of choice?"

"Exactly. The whole thing is an illusion. We do what we do because someone else has done what he did; he did it because still another someone did what he did. Every action is the rigid result of another action."

"But there must have been a beginning," I objected. "And if there was a beginning, choice existed if only for that split second. And if choice exists once it can exist again."

"You have the makings of a metaphysician, Hodgins," he said contemptuously, for metaphysics was one of the most despised words in his vocabulary. "The objection is childish. Answering you and the Reverend Shaw on your own level, I could say that time is an illusion and that all events occur simultaneously. Or if I grant its existence I can ask, What makes you think time is a simple straight line running flatly through eternity? Why do you assume that time isn't curved? Can you conceive of its end? Can you really assume its beginning? Of course not—then why aren't both the same? The serpent with its tail in its mouth?"

"You mean we not only play a prepared script but repeat the identical lines over and over and over for infinity? There's no heaven in your cosmos, only an unimaginable, never ending hell."

He shrugged his shoulders. "That you should spout emotional theology at me is part of what you call the script, Hodgins. You didn't select the words nor speak them voluntarily. They were called into existence by what I said, which in turn was mere response to what went before."

Weakly I was forced back to a more elementary attack. "You don't act in accordance with your own conviction."

He snorted.

"A thoughtless remark, excusable only because automatic. How could I act differently? Like you, I am a prisoner of stimuli."

"How pointless to risk ruin and imprisonment as a member of the Grand Army when you can't change what's predestined."

"I can no more help engaging myself in the underground than I can help breathing, or my heart beating, or dying when the time comes. Nothing, they say, is certain but death and taxes; actually everything is certain. Everything. . . ."

Tyss never tried to conceal the extent of his activity in the Grand Army any more than he attempted to indoctrinate me with its principles. One illegal paper, the *True American*, came from his press and I often saw crumpled proofs of large-type warnings to "Get Out of Town you Conf. TRAITOR or the GA will HANG YOU!"

I knew that Pondible and the others who bore an indefinable resemblance whether bearded or not came to the store on Grand Army business, and I knew that many of the errands I was sent on advanced, or were supposed to advance, the Grand Army's cause. Unwilling to face the moral issue of being, no matter how remotely, accessory to mayhem, kidnaping and murder, or the connected economic one of being unemployed, I simply refused to acknowledge I was aiding the underground organization, but looked upon my duties solely as concerned with the bookstore.

My distaste for the Grand Army bred in me no sympathy for the Whigs or for those who were generally considered to be their masters, the Confederates. My reading taught me conclusively that, contrary to the accepted view in the United States, the victors in the War of Southron Independence had been men of the highest probity, and the noblest among them was their second president. But I also knew that immediately after the Peace of Richmond, less dedicated individuals became increasingly powerful in the new nation. As Sir John Dahlberg remarked, "Power tends to corrupt."

From his first election in 1865 until his death ten years later, President Lee had been the prisoner of an increasingly headstrong and imperialistic congress. He had opposed the invasion and conquest of Mexico by the Confederacy which had been undertaken on the pretext of restoring order during the conflict between the emperor and the republicans. However, he had too profound a respect for the constitutional processes to continue this opposition in the face of joint resolutions by the Confederate Congress.

Lee remained a symbol, but as the generation which had fought for independence died, the ideals he symbolized faded. Negro emancipation, enacted largely because of the pressure of men like Lee, soon revealed itself as a device for obtaining the benefits of slavery without its obligations. The freedmen on both sides of the new border were without franchise, and indeed for all practical purpose, without civil rights. Yet while the old Union first restricted and then abolished immigration, the Confederacy encouraged it, making the immigrants subjects, like the Latin-Americans who made up so much of the Southron population after the Confederacy expanded southward, limiting full citizenship to posterity of residents in the Confederate States on July Fourth 1864.

My reading of history—and by this time I had found there was no other study holding the same steady attraction for me—together with my strong revulsion to Tyss's philosophy convinced me there had been a radical alteration in the direction of the world's progress during the past century. It seemed to me humanity had been heading for longer and longer stretches of peace, greater intelligence in dealing with its problems, more of the necessities and luxuries of life more evenly distributed. But with the War of Southron Independence the trend changed, not into immediate and obvious retrogression perhaps, but certainly away from the bright future which had seemed so assured in 1850.

Take the pervasive fear of imminent war which hung over the world, a fear which was interrupted only by the outbreak of the conflicts themselves—which ranged from skirmishes between civilized powers equipped with modern weapons of extermination and barbarians with nothing more lethal than a bow or a blowgun, to global belligerency. This fear hung, ever more lowering and insistent as it became increasingly predictable that the antagonists in the great clash would be the Confederacy and the German Union.

Both could date their impetus from 1864 when the North German Confederation beat the Danes. From then on the expansion of the two countries was parallel; while the Confederacy worked its way methodically toward Cape Horn and westward through the Pacific, the German Union absorbed the Balkans and made a close alliance with the suddenly rejuvenated Spanish Empire. In the Emperors' War of 1914–16 the Confederacy had the opportunity of stepping in and giving its rival a mortal blow, and the action would have been popular, for the majority of Southrons, like the inhabitants of the United States, were sympathetic to the cause of England, France and Russia. But for a variety of reasons the Confederacy stayed neutral, allowing the German Union to absorb Ukrainia, Poland and the Baltic States, northern Italy, western France and the Low Countries. The Confederacy took the reward of this course by annexing Alaska from Russia and attaching the crippled British Empire to its orbit in close alliance, so that the two great powers were fairly balanced. The attraction of even so minor a country as the United States not only meant much to either side, but almost surely meant the war itself would be fought on the territory of this new satellite.

Because of all this I realized the Grand Army was in a position to play a much more important part than any similar illegal organization in another country.

Just how it was using its opportunity was something of which I became only gradually aware.

IV

Among customers to whom I frequently delivered parcels of books there was a Monsieur René Enfandin who lived on Eighth Street, not far from Fifth Avenue. M. Enfandin was Consul for the Republic of Haiti; the house he occupied was distinguished from its otherwise equally drab neighbors by a large red and blue escutcheon over the doorway. He did not, however, use the entire dwelling himself, reserving only the parlor floor for the office of the consulate and living quarters; the rest was let to other tenants.

He had an arrangement with Tyss whereby he turned back most of the books he bought for credit on others. I soon saw that if he hadn't, his library would shortly have dispossessed him; as it was, books covered all the space not taken by the essential paraphernalia of his office and bed-room with the exception of a bit of bare wall on which hung a large cru-cifix. He seemed always to have a volume in his large, dark brown hand, politely closed over his thumb, or open for eager sampling.

Enfandin was tall and strong-featured, notable in any company. In the United States, where a black man was an irritating reminder of a di-sastrously lost war and Mr. Lincoln's ill-advised proclamation of eman-cipation, he was the permanent target of rowdy boys and adult hoodlums. Even the diplomatic immunity of his post was poor protec-tion, for it was believed—not without justification—that Haiti, the only American republic south of the Mason-Dixon line to preserve its inde-pendence, was disrupting the official if sporadically executed United States policy of deporting Negroes to Africa by encouraging their emi-gration to its shores or—what was more annoying—assisting persecuted blacks to flee westward to the hospitality of the unconquered Indians of Dakotah and Montana.

Although I was somewhat shy of him at the first, I was drawn to him more and more. Nor was this entirely because he was as avid for reading as myself or because his excursions into learning were more systematic and disciplined. He had a quick and penetrating sympathy that was at times almost telepathic. Beginning with perfunctory interchanges when I delivered his books, our conversations grew longer and more friendly; soon he was advising me and I was learning from him with an eagerness I had never felt for Tyss's proffered erudition.

"History, but certainly, Hodge," he had no discernible accent but sometimes his English was uncolloquial, "it is a noble study. But what is history? How is it written? How is it read? Is it a dispassionate chronicle of events scientifically determined and set down? Or is it the transmuta-tion of the ordinary to the celebrated?"

"It seems to me that the facts are primary and the interpretations sec-ondary," I answered. "If we can find out the facts we can form our own opinions on them."

"Perhaps. Perhaps. But take what is for me the central fact of all his-tory." He pointed sweepingly at the crucifix. "As a Catholic the facts are plain to me; I believe what is written in the Gospels to be literally true: that the Son of Man died for me on that cross. But what are the facts for a contemporary Roman statesman? That an obscure local agitator

threatened the stability of an uneasy province and was promptly executed in the approved Roman fashion, as a warning to others. And for a
contemporary fellow countryman? That no such person existed. You
think these facts are mutually exclusive? Yet you know that no two people see exactly the same thing, too many honest witnesses have contra-
dicted each other. Even the Gospels must be reconciled."

"You are saying that truth is relative."

"Am I? Then I shall have my tongue examined, or my head. Because
I mean to say no such thing. Truth is absolute and for all time. But one
man cannot envisage all of truth; the best he can do is see one aspect of
it whole. That is why I say to you, be a skeptic, Hodge. Always be the
skeptic."

"Ay?" I was finding the admonition a little difficult to harmonize with
his previous confession of faith.

"For the believer skepticism is essential. How else is he to know false
gods from true except by doubting both? One of the most pernicious of
folk-sayings is, 'I cannot believe my eyes!' Why particularly should you
believe your eyes? You were given eyes to see with, not to believe with.
Believe your mind, your intuition, your reason, your emotion if you
like—but not your eyes unaided by any of these interpreters. Your eyes
can see the mirage, the hallucination, as easily as the actual scenery.
Your eyes will tell you nothing exists but matter—"

"Not only my eyes but my boss." I told him of Tyss's mechanistic
creed.

"God have mercy on his soul," muttered Enfandin. "Poor creature.
He has liberated himself from the superstitions of religion in order to
fall into superstition so abject no Christian can conceive it. Imagine it
to yourself"—he began to pace the floor—"time is circular, man is automaton, we are doomed to repeat the identical gestures over and over,
forever. Oh, I say to you, Hodge, this is monstrous."

I nodded. "Yes. But what is the answer? Limitless space, limitless
time? They are almost as horrifying, because they are inconceivable."

"And why should the inconceivable be horrible? But you are right.
This is not the answer. The answer is that all—time, space, matter—all
is illusion. All but the good God. Nothing exists but Him. We are creatures of His fancy, figments of His imagination . . ."

"Then where does free will come in?"

"As a gift, of course—how else? The greatest gift and the greatest
responsibility."

I can't say I was entirely satisfied with Enfandin's exposition, though it was more to my taste than Tyss's. I returned to the conversation at intervals, both in my thoughts and when I saw him, but in the end all I really accepted was his original adjuration to be skeptical, which I doubt I always applied in the way he meant me to.

Frequently he became so interested in our talk, which ranged widely, for he thought it no frivolity to touch on any subject engaging either of us whether it might be considered trivial or not, that he walked back to the bookstore with me, leaving a note on the door of the consulate to say he would be back in ten minutes—a promise I'm afraid seldom fulfilled.

More and more as I came to know him better I felt I ought to tell him of Tyss's connection with the Grand Army, an organization strongly prejudiced against Negroes. Timidity and selfishness combined to keep me quiet; I feared he might buy his books elsewhere and I should lose the benefit of his companionship.

I suppose I had known Enfandin for perhaps a year when I became better acquainted with some of the activities of the Grand Army. It began the day a customer called himself to my attention with a self-conscious clearing of his throat.

"Yes sir—can I help you?"

He was a fat little man with palpably false teeth, and hair that hung down behind over his collar. However, the sum of his appearance was in no way ludicrous; rather he gave the impression of ease and authority, and an assurance so strong there was no necessity to buttress it.

"Why, I was looking for . . ." he began, and then looked at me sharply. "Say, ain't you the young fella I saw walking with a Nigra? Big black buck?"

I felt myself reddening. "There's no law against it, is there?"

He laughed. "I wouldn't know about your damyankee laws, boy. For myself I'd say there's no harm in it, no harm in it at all. Always did like to be around Nigras myself—but then, I was rared among um. Most damyankees seem to think Nigras ain't fitten company. Only goes to show how narrerminded and bigoted you folks can be. Present company excepted."

"M'sieu Enfandin is consul of the Republic of Haiti," I said; "he's a scholar and a gentleman." As soon as the words were out I was bitterly sorry for their condescension and patronage. I felt ashamed, as if I had betrayed him by offering credentials to justify my friendship with him and implying that it took special qualities to overcome the handicap of his color.

"A mussoo, huh? Furrin and educated Nigra? Well, guess they're all right." His tone, still hearty, was slightly dubious. "Ben working here long?"

"Over three years."

"Kind of dull work, ain't it?"

"Oh no—I like to read, and there are plenty of books around here."

Without apparent effort or management he drew from me the story of my ambitions and misadventures since leaving Wappinger Falls.

"Going to be a professional historian, hay? Little out of my line, but I don't suppose they's many of um up north here."

"Not unless you count a handful of college instructors who dabble at it."

He shook his head. "A young fella with your aims could do a lot better down South, I'd think."

"Oh yes. Why, some of the most interesting research is going on right now in Leesburg, Washington-Baltimore and the University of Lima. You are a Confederate yourself, sir?"

"Southron, yes sir, I am that, and mighty proud of it. Now look a-here, boy: I'll lay all my cards on the table, face up. You're a free man, not indented, you said, and you ain't getting any pay here. Now, how'd you like to do a little job for me? They's good money in it—and I imagine I'd be able to fix up one of those deals—what do they call them? scholarships—at the University of Leesburg, after."

A scholarship at Leesburg! Where the Department of History was engaged on a monumental project—nothing less than a compilation of all known source material on the War of Southron Independence! It was only with the strongest effort that I refrained from agreeing blindly.

"It sounds fine, Mr.—?"

"Colonel Tolliburr. Jest call me cunnel."

There wasn't anything remotely military in his bearing. "It sounds good to me, Colonel. What is the job?"

He clicked his too regular teeth thoughtfully. "Hardly anything at all, m'boy. I just want you to keep a list for me. List of the people that come in here regular. Especially the ones that don't seem to buy anything, but want to talk to your boss. Their names if you know um—but that ain't real important—and a sort of rough description, like five foot nine, blue eyes, dark hair, busted nose, scar on right eyebrow. And so on. Nothing real detailed. And a list of deliveries."

Was I tempted? I don't really know. "I'm sorry, Colonel. I'm afraid I can't help you."

"Not even for that scholarship and say, $100 in real money?"

I shook my head.

"They's no harm in it, boy. Likely nothing'll come of it."

"I'm sorry."

"Two hundred?"

"It's not a matter of money, Colonel Tolliburr."

He looked at me shrewdly. "Think it over, boy—no use being hasty. Any time you change your mind, come and see me or send me a telegram." He handed me a card.

"Suppose," I asked Enfandin, "one were placed in position of being an involuntary assistant in a—to a . . ." I was at loss for words which would describe the situation without being too specific. I could not tell Enfandin about Tolliburr and my problem of whether to tell Tyss of the colonel's espionage without revealing Tyss's connection with the Grand Army, and were I to say anything about the Grand Army he would be quite right in condemning my deceit in not warning him earlier. Whatever I said or failed to say, I was somehow culpable.

Enfandin waited patiently while I groped, trying to formulate a question which was no longer a question. "You can't do evil that good may come of it," I burst out at last.

He nodded. "Quite so. But are you not perhaps putting the problem too abstractly? Is it not maybe that your situation—your hypothetical situation—is one of being accessory to wrong rather than face an alternative which means personal misery?"

Again I struggled for words. He had formulated one aspect of my dilemma regarding the Grand Army, but . . . "Yes," I said at last.

"It would be very nice if there were no drawbacks ever attached to the virtuous choice. Then the only ones who would elect to do wrong would be those of twisted minds, the perverse, the insane. No normal man would prefer the devious course if the straight one were just as easy. No, no, my dear Hodge, one cannot escape the responsibility for his choice simply because the other way means inconvenience or hardship or unhappiness."

I said nothing. Was it pettiness which made me contrast his position as an official of a small yet fairly secure power, well enough paid to live comfortably, with mine where a break with Tyss would mean destitution and no further chance of fulfilling the ambition every day more important to me? *Did* circumstances alter cases, and was it easy for Enfandin to talk as he did, unconfronted with harsh alternatives?

"You know, Hodge," he said, as though changing the subject, "I am what is called a career man, which merely means I have no money except my salary. This might seem much to you, but it is really little, especially since protocol insists I spend more than necessary. For the honor of my country. At home I have an establishment to keep up where my wife and children live—"

I had wondered about his apparent bachelorhood.

"—because, to be rudely frank, I do not think, on account of their color, they would be happy or safe in the United States. Besides these expenses I make personal contributions for the assistance of black men who are—how shall we say it?—unhappily circumstanced in your country, because I have found the official allotment is never enough. (Now I have been indiscreet—you know government secrets.) Why do I tell you this? Because, my friend, I should like to help you. Alas, I cannot offer you money. But this I can do, if it will not offend your pride: I suggest you live here—it will be no more uncomfortable than the arrangements you have described in the store—and go to one of the colleges in the city. A medal or an order from the Haitian government judiciously conferred on an eminent educator will undoubtedly get you free tuition. What do you say?"

What could I say? Tell him I had not been open with him? That his generosity deserved a more worthy recipient? I protested, I muttered my thanks, not too coherently, I lapsed again into brooding silence. But the newly opened prospect was too exciting for moodiness; in a moment we were both rapidly sketching plans and supplementing each other's designs with revisions of our own.

After some discussion we decided I was to give Tyss two weeks' notice despite our original agreement making such nicety superfluous. Enfandin meanwhile took it upon himself to discuss my matriculation with several professors whom he knew.

My employer raised a quizzical eyebrow at my information as we were eating our breakfast of bread and half raw meat near the printing press. "Ah, Hodgins, you see how neatly the script works out. Nothing left to chance or choice. If you hadn't been relieved of your trifling capital by a man of enterprise whose methods were more successful than subtle, you might have fumbled at the edge of the academic world for four years and then, having substituted a wad of unrelated facts for common sense and whatever ability to think you might have possessed, fumbled for the rest of your life at the edge of the economic world. You wouldn't have met George Pondible or gotten here where you could discover your own mind without adjustment to a professorial iron maiden."

"I thought it was all arbitrary."

He gave me a reproachful look. "Arbitrary and predetermined are not synonyms, Hodgins, nor does either rule out artistry. And how artistic this development is! You will go on to become a professor yourself and construct iron maidens for promising students who might become your competitors. You will write learned histories, for you are obviously the spectator type. The part written for you does not call for you to be a participant, an instrument for—apparently—influencing events. Hence it is proper that you report them so future generations may imbibe the illusion they are not puppets."

He grinned at me. Instead of pointing out his inconsistencies, I again suffered the pangs for deceitfulness, this time wishing I'd told him of the Confederate agent, Colonel Tolliburr, and warned him that he was evidently under surveillance and suspicion. It almost seemed as though his mechanistic notions were valid and I was destined always to be the ungrateful recipient of kindness.

"Now," he said, swallowing the last of his breakfast, "we've work to do. Those boxes over there go upstairs. Pondible's bringing a van around for them this afternoon."

I suppose there are people who imagine employment in a bookstore is light work, not realizing the heaviness of paper. Many times during the years I was with Roger Tyss I had reason to be thankful for my farm training and muscular constitution. The boxes were deceptively small but they seemed to be packed solid with paper. Even with Tyss carrying up box for box with me I was vastly relieved when I had to quit to run an errand.

When I got back Tyss left to make an offer on someone's library. "There are only four left, and the last two are wrapped in paper. I didn't have enough boxes."

Appreciative of his having left the lighter packages for the last, I almost ran up the stairs with the first box. Returning, I tripped on the lowest step and sprawled forward. Reflexively I threw out my hands and landed on one of the paper-wrapped packages whose covering split under the impact. Its contents—neatly tied rectangular bundles—spilled out between the limp twine.

I had learned enough of the printing trade to recognize the brightly colored oblongs as lithographs, and I wondered as I stooped over to gather them up that such a job should have been given Tyss rather than to a shop specializing in such work. Even under the gaslight the colors were hard and vigorous.

And then I really looked at the bundle I was holding. "ESPANA" was enscrolled across the top; below it was the picture of a man with long nose and jutting underlip, flanked by two ornate figure fives, and beneath them the legend, "CINCO PESETAS." Spanish Empire banknotes. Bundles and bundles of them.

I needed neither expert knowledge nor minute scrutiny to tell me there was a fortune here in counterfeit money. The purpose in forging Spanish paper I could not see; that it was no private undertaking of Tyss's but an activity of the Grand Army, I was certain. Puzzled and apprehensive, I rewrapped the bundles of notes into as neat an imitation of the original package as I could contrive.

For the rest of the day I cast uneasy glances at the mound of boxes. Death was the penalty for counterfeiting United States coins; I had no idea of the punishment for doing the same with foreign paper but I was sure even so minor an accessory as myself would be in a sad way if some officious customer should stumble against one of the packages.

Tyss in no way acted like a man with a guilty conscience or even one with an important secret. He seemed completely unconcerned with any peril; doubtless he was daily in similar situations, only chance and my own lack of observation had prevented my discovering this earlier.

Nor did he show anxiety when Pondible didn't arrive. Darkness came and the gaslamps went on in the streets. The heavy press of traffic outside dwindled, but the incriminating boxes remained undisturbed near the door. At last there was the sound of uncertain wheels slowing up outside and Pondible's voice admonishing, "Wh-whoa!"

When he entered the store in slow dignity it was immediately manifest that he was extremely drunk. His, "Dri-driving wagon. Fell off. Fell off wagon, I mean. See?" was superfluous.

Tyss took him by the arm. "Start loading up, Hodgins. I'll get him to lie down. You'll have to do the delivering."

Rebellious refusal formed in my mind. Why should I be involved? Then I remembered how much I owed to him, and that two more weeks would see me free, and I said nothing.

He gave me an address on 26th Street. "Sprovis is the name. Let them do the unloading. I see there's a full feedbag in the van; that'll be a good time to give it to the horse. They'll load another consignment and drive with you to the destination. Take the van back to the livery stable. Here's money for your supper and carfare back here."

Driving slackly through the almost empty streets, I was less nervous of being stopped by a police officer than resentful of the casual course of events. I continued to be perplexed as to why the Grand Army should counterfeit Spanish pesetas on a wholesale scale.

The address, which I had trouble finding on the poorly lit thoroughfare, was one of those four-storey stuccos a hundred years old, showing few signs of recent repair. Mr. Sprovis, who occupied the basement, had one ear distinctly larger than the other, an anomaly I could not help attributing to a trick of constantly pulling on the lobe. He, like the others who came out with him to unload the van, wore the Grand Army beard.

I began to explain Pondible's absence but he shut me up quickly. "No names! Hear? No names."

I slipped the strap of the feedbag over the horse's ears and started toward 8th Avenue.

"Hey there—where you going?"

"To get something to eat. Anything wrong with that?"

I felt him looking suspiciously at me in the darkness. "All right. But don't keep us waiting. We'll be ready to go in twenty minutes."

"That's right," added one of the others. "Don't want to keep the horse waiting. We're kind to animals, ain't we, Chuck?"

I found a lunchroom where I gorged on fish and potatoes, happy to get away from the unvarying bread and heart. My enjoyment was tarnished though by the knowledge that I was not through with the night's adventure. What freight Sprovis and his companions were loading in the van now, I had no idea—except that it was nothing innocent.

When I turned the corner into 26th Street again, the shadowy mass of the horse and van was gone from its place by the curb. Alarmed, I broke into a run and discovered it turning in the middle of the street. I jumped and caught hold of the dash, pulling myself aboard. "What's the idea?"

A fist caught me in the shoulder, almost knocking me back into the street. Zigzags of shock ran down my arm, terminating in a numbing pain. Desperately, I clung to the dash.

"Hold it," someone growled, "it's the punk who came with. Let him in."

Another voice, evidently belonging to the man who'd hit me, admonished, "Want to watch yourself, chum. Not go jumping up like that without warning. I mighta stuck a shiv in your ribs insteada my hand."

I could only repeat, "What's the idea of trying to run off with the van? I'm responsible for it."

"He's responsible for it, Chuck, see," mocked another voice from the body of the van. "It ain't polite not to wait for him."

I was wedged between the driver and my assailant; my shoulder ached and I was beginning to be frightened now my first anger had passed. These were "action" members of the Grand Army; men who committed battery, mayhem, arson, robbery and murder. I had been both foolhardy and lucky; realizing this, it seemed diplomatic not to try for possession of the reins.

We turned north on 6th Avenue; the street lights showed Sprovis driving. He was one of those who thought a horse was a mechanical contrivance for getting somewhere quickly, regardless of the weight he was pulling or whether he was tired or not. On several counts our speed was stupid; if nothing else it called attention to the van at a time when most commercial vehicles had been stabled for the night and the traffic was almost entirely carriages, buggies, hacks and minibiles.

It was the monotonous chuffing of a minibile coming slowly close behind us that formed the subconscious pattern of my thought; when we turned eastward in the Forties I exclaimed, "There's a minibile following us!"

Even as I spoke the trackless locomotive pulled alongside and then darted ahead to pocket us by nosing diagonally toward the curb. The horse must have been too exhausted to shy; he simply stopped short and I heard the curses of the felled passengers behind me.

"Only half a block from—"

"Quick! Break the guns out—"

"No guns, you fool! Hands or knives. Get them all!"

It was not believable that this could be happening in one of New York's best residential districts in the year 1942. Nor was the speed of the whole incident normal. The tempo was so swift that if there were any spectators in the bordering windows or on the sidewalks they didn't have time to realize what was happening before it was all over.

Four men from the minibile were met by five from the van. The odds were not too unequal, for the attackers had a discipline which Sprovis and his companions lacked. An uneven, distorting light made the action seem jumpy, as though the participants were caught at static moments, changing their attitudes in flashes of invisibility between.

Their leader attempted to parley during one of these seconds of apparent inaction. "Hey, you men—we got nothing against you. They's a thousand dollars apiece in it for you—"

A fist smacked into his mouth. The light caught his face as he was jolted back, but I hardly needed its revelation to confirm my recognition of his voice. It was Colonel Tolliburr all right.

The Confederate agents had brass knuckles and blackjacks; the Grand Army men had knives. Both sides were intent on keeping the struggle as quiet and inconspicuous as possible; no one shouted with anger or screamed with pain. This muffled intensity made the struggle the more gruesome. I heard the impact of blows, the grunts of effort, the choked-back expressions of pain, the scraping of shoes on the pavement and the thud of falls. One of the defenders fell, and two of the attackers, before the two remaining Southrons gave up the battle and attempted to escape.

They started for the minibile, evidently realized they would not have time to get away in it, and began running down the street. Their indecision did for them. As the Grand Army men closed in around them I saw them raise their arms in the traditional gesture of surrender. Then they were struck down.

V

For the next days my reading was pretense. I used the opened book before me to mask my privacy from Tyss while I pondered the meaning and extent of that night's events. From scraps of conversation on which I eavesdropped, from the newspapers, from deduction and remembered fragments I reconstructed the picture which made the background. Its borders reached a long way from Astor Place.

I have explained how the world had waited for years, half in dread,

half in resignation, for war between the German Union and the Confederate States. Everyone expected the point of explosion would be the
Confederacy's ally, the British Empire, and that at least part of the war
would be fought in the United States. Apparently we were helpless to
prevent this.

The Grand Army's scheme was evidently a far-fetched and fantastic
attempt to circumvent the probable course of history. The counterfeiting of Spanish money on a large scale represented an aspect of this attempt, which was nothing less than trying to force the war to start, not
through the Confederacy's ally, but through the German Union's—the
Spanish Empire. With enormous amounts of the spurious currency, the
Grand Army was planning to circulate it by means of emissaries passing
as Confederate agents and thus embroil the Confederacy with Spain in
the hope the war would commence and be fought in the Spanish Empire. It was an ingenuous idea, I see now, evolved by men without
knowledge of the actual mechanics of world politics.

The second delivery had represented the less extravagant and romantic side of the Grand Army. Embarking, as they had years before, on activities of violence, the fine distinction between crimes undertaken to
advance a cause and allied crimes undertaken to supply the organization with funds had become obscured. Relations of increasing intimacy were established with ordinary gangsters. The association was
convenient to both, for the Grand Army often supplied weapons and information in return for more immediately political favors.

Thus, Sprovis had been engaged in comparatively innocent gun-
running to a gang which probably had no other connection with the
Grand Army, when Tolliburr and his friends waylaid us in the minibile.
Undoubtedly what they wanted was proof of the counterfeiting scheme,
but they had overlooked or somehow missed the rendezvous on 26th
Street—disastrously for them.

Any lingering sentimental notions I might have entertained about
the nature of the Grand Army disappeared with the certainty Sprovis
had killed his prisoners. At the first opportunity I used the card Tolliburr
had given me, but the suspicion and lack of information with which I
was received at the address confirmed my idea. No bodies were found
and there was no mention in the newspapers of the disappearance of
any Southrons. Naturally the Confederate government would call no
attention to their fate, but I had no doubts.

Even as I reproached myself for the weakness and moral cowardice which had prevented me from refusing to be an accomplice to these crimes, I looked forward to my release. I had not seen Enfandin since his offer; in a week I should leave the bookstore for his sanctuary, and I resolved my first act should be to tell him everything. And then that dream was exploded just as it was about to be realized.

I do not know who broke into the consulate and was surprised in the act, who shot and wounded Enfandin so seriously he was unable to speak for weeks before he was finally returned to Haiti to recuperate or die. He could not get in touch with me and I was not permitted to see him; the police guard was doubly zealous to keep him from all contact since he was an accredited diplomat and a black man.

I did not know who shot him. It was quite probably no one connected either with the Grand Army or the gang to whom the guns were delivered. But I did not know. I could not know. He *might* have been shot with one of the revolvers which had been in the van that night, or by Sprovis or George Pondible. Since the ultimate chain could have led back to me, it did lead back to me.

The loss of my chance to escape from the bookstore was the least of my despair. It seemed to me I was caught by the inexorable, choiceless circumstance in which Tyss so firmly believed and Enfandin denied. I could escape neither my guilt nor the surroundings conducive to further guilt. I could not change destiny.

Was this all merely the self-torture of an introverted young man? Possibly. I only know that for a long time—long as one in his early twenties measures time—I lost all interest in life, even dallying at intervals with thoughts of suicide. I put books aside with distaste, or indifference—which was worse.

I cannot say precisely when it was my despair began to lift. I know that one day—it was cold and the snow was deep on the ground—I saw a girl walking briskly, red-cheeked, breathing in quick, visible puffs, and for the first time in months my glance was not one of indifference. When I returned to the bookstore I picked up Field Marshal Liddell-Hart's *Life of General Pickett* and opened it to the place where I had abandoned it. In a moment I was fully absorbed.

Paradoxically, once I was myself again I was no longer the same Hodge Backmaker. For the first time I was determined to do what I wanted instead of waiting and hoping events would somehow turn out right for me. Somehow I was going to free myself from the dead end of the bookstore—and I wasn't going to escape into indenture, either.

All this was pointed by my discovery that I was exhausting the possibilities of the volumes around me. The ones I now sought were rare and it became more difficult for me to find them. With the innocence of one who has not been part of academic life I imagined them ready to hand in a dozen college libraries.

Nor, to tell the truth, was I any longer completely satisfied with the second hand, the printed word. My friendship with Enfandin had shown me how a personal, face-to-face relationship between teacher and student could be so much more fruitful and it seemed to me such relationships could develop into ones between fellow scholars—a mutual pursuit of knowledge which was not competitive.

Additionally I wanted to search the real, the original sources, the unpublished manuscripts of participants or scholars, the old diaries and letters which might shade a meaning or subtly change the interpretation of some old, forgotten action.

Ideally my problems could be solved by a fellowship or an instructorship at some college. But how was this to be obtained without the patronage of a Tolliburr or an Enfandin? I had no credentials worth a second's consideration. Even though the immigration bars kept out graduates of British, Confederate or German universities, no college in the United States would accept a self-taught young man who had not only little Latin and less Greek, but no mathematics, languages, or sciences at all.

For a long time I considered possible ways and means, an exercise rarely more practical than spinning daydreams without contriving any steps to attain their consummation. I knew I was waiting to be acted upon, rather than attempting to initiate action on my own account, but it seemed to me impossible to exercise that free will of which Enfandin had spoken.

At last, more in a spirit of whimsical absurdity than in sober hope, I wrote out a letter of application, setting forth the qualifications I imagined myself to possess, assaying the extent of my learning with a conceit which only ingenuousness could palliate, and outlining the work I had projected for my future. With much care and many revisions I set this composition in type. It was undoubtedly a foolish gesture, but not having access to so costly a machine as a typewriter, and not wanting to reveal this by penning the letters by hand, I used this transparent device.

Tyss read one of the copies I struck off. His expression was critical. "Is it very bad?" I asked hopelessly.

"Should have used more leading. And you could have lined it up better and eliminated the hyphens. It's things like that—the details—which make a machine to set type, that inventors have been failing to invent for so long, impractical. I'm afraid you'll never make a first-class printer, Hodgins."

He was concerned only with the typesetting, uninterested in the outcome.

The government mails being one of the favorite victims of holdup men, and pneumatic post limited to local areas, I dispatched the letters by way of Wells, Fargo to a comprehensive list of colleges. I can't say I then waited for the replies to flow in, for though I knew the company's system of heavily armed guards would insure delivery of my applications, I had no anticipation that any of the recipients would bother to answer. As a matter of fact I put it pretty well out of my mind and divided my attention between my work for Tyss, my reading, and a fruitless endeavor to devise some new scheme.

It was several months later, toward the end of September, that the telegram came signed Thomas K. Haggerwells. It read, ACCEPT NO OFFER TILL OUR REPRESENTATIVE EXPLAINS HAGGERSHAVEN.

I had sent no copy of my letter to York, Pennsylvania—where the telegram had originated—nor anywhere near it. I knew of no colleges in that vicinity. And I had never heard of Mr. (or Doctor, or Professor) Haggerwells. I might have thought the message a mean joke, except that Tyss's nature didn't run to this type of humor and no one else knew of the letters except those to whom they were addressed.

I found no reference to Haggershaven in any of the directories I consulted, which was not too surprising, considering the slovenly way such things were put together. I decided that if such a place existed I could only wait patiently till the "representative"—if there really was one—arrived.

Tyss having left for the day, I swept a little, dusted some, straightened a few of the books (any serious attempt to arrange the stock would have been futile) and took up a new emendation of Creasy's *Fifteen Decisive Battles* by one Captain Eisenhower.

I was so deep in the good captain's analysis (what a strategist he would have made himself, given the opportunity!) that I heard no customer enter, sensed no impatient presence. I was only recalled from my book by a rather sharp, "Is the proprietor in?"

"No, ma'am," I answered, reluctantly abandoning the page. "He's out for the moment. Can I help you?"

My eyes, accustomed to the store's poor light, had the advantage over hers, still adjusting from the sunlit street. Secure in my boldness, I measured her vital femininity, a quality which seemed—if such a thing is possible—impersonal. I recognized an insistent sensuality (I think I have indicated my susceptibility to women; such a susceptibility I'm sure acts as an intuitive, a telepathic device) as I recognized the fact she was bareheaded, and almost as tall as I, and rather large-boned. There was nothing immediate or related to myself about it.

Nor was it connected with surface attributes; she was not beautiful, certainly not pretty, though she might have been called handsome in a way. Her hair, ginger-colored and clubbed low on her neck, waved crisply; her eyes seemed slate gray. (Later I learned they could vary from paleness to blue-green.) The fleshly greediness was betrayed, if at all, only by the width and set of her lips and the boldness of her expression.

She smiled, and I decided I had been wrong in thinking her tone peremptory. "I'm Barbara Haggerwells. I'm looking for a Mr. Backmaker"— she glanced at a slip of paper—"a Hodgins M. Backmaker who evidently uses this as an accommodation address."

"I'm Hodge Backmaker," I muttered in despair. "I—I work here."

I suppose I expected her to say nastily, So I see! or the usual inane, It must be fascinating! Instead she said, "I wonder if you've run across a book called *The Properties of* X by Whitehead?"

"Uh—I . . . is it a mystery story?"

"I'm afraid not. It's a book on mathematics by a mathematician very much out of favor. It's quite scarce; I've been trying to get a copy for a long time."

So naturally and easily she led me away from my embarrassment and into talking of books, relieving me of self-consciousness and some of the mortification in being exposed at my humble job by the "representative" of the telegram. I admitted deficient knowledge of mathematics and ignorance of Mr. Whitehead, though stoutly maintaining—truthfully— that the book was not in stock, while she assured me only a specialist would have heard of so obscure a theoretician. This made me ask, with the awe one feels for an expert in an alien field, if she were a mathematician, to which she replied, "Heavens, no—I'm a physicist. But mathematics is my tool."

I looked at her with respect. Anyone, I thought, can read a few books and set himself up as an historian; to be a physicist means genuine learning. And I doubted she was much older than I.

She said abruptly, "My father is interested in knowing something about you."

I acknowledged this with a gesture somewhere between a nod and a bow. What could I say? She had been examining and gauging me for the last half hour. "Your father is Thomas Haggerwells?"

"Haggerwells of Haggershaven," she confirmed, as though explaining everything. There was pride in her voice, and a hint of arrogance.

"I'm dreadfully sorry, Miss Haggerwells, but I'm afraid I'm as ignorant of Haggershaven as of mathematics."

"I thought you said you'd been reading history. It's odd you've come upon no reference to the haven in the records of the past 75 years."

I shook my head helplessly. "I suppose my reading has been scattered. Haggershaven is a college?"

"No. Haggershaven is—Haggershaven." She resumed her equanimity, her air of smiling tolerance. "It's hardly a college since it has neither student body nor faculty—rather, both are one at the haven. Anyone admitted is a scholar or potential scholar anxious to devote himself to learning. Not many are acceptable."

She need hardly have added that; it was obvious I could never be one of the elect, even if I hadn't offended her by never having heard of the haven. I knew I couldn't pass the most lenient of entrance examinations to an ordinary college, much less the dedicated place she represented.

"There are no formal requirements for fellowship," she went on, "beyond the undertaking to work to full capacity, to pool all knowledge and hold back none from scholars anywhere, to contribute economically to the haven in accordance with decisions of the majority of fellows, and to vote on questions without consideration of personal gain. There! That certainly sounds like the stuffiest manifesto delivered this year."

"It sounds too good to be true."

"Oh, it's true enough. But there's another side, not so theoretical. The haven is neither wealthy nor endowed—we have to earn our living. The fellows draw no stipend; they have food, clothes, shelter, whatever books and materials they need—no luxuries. We often have to leave our work to do manual labor to bring in food or money for all."

"I've read admiringly of such communities," I said enthusiastically, "but I thought they'd all disappeared 50 or 60 years ago."

"Have you and did you?" she asked contemptuously. "You'll be surprised that Haggershaven is neither Owenite nor Fourierist. We don't live in phalansteries, practice group marriage or vegetarianism; our organization is expedient, subject to revision, not doctrinaire; contribution to the common stock is voluntary and we are not concerned with each other's private lives."

"I beg your pardon, Miss Haggerwells. I didn't mean to annoy you."

"It's all right. Perhaps I'm touchy; all my life I've seen the suspiciousness of the farmers around—sure that we're up to something immoral, or at least illegal. And the parallel distrust of the conventional schools. Detachedly, the haven may indeed be a refuge for misfits, but is it necessarily wrong not to fit into the civilization around us?"

"I'm prejudiced because I certainly haven't fitted in myself. Do you . . . do you think there's any chance Haggershaven would accept me?" Whatever reserve I'd tried to maintain deserted me; I knew my voice expressed only childish longing.

"I couldn't say," she answered primly. "Acceptance or rejection depends entirely on the vote of the entire fellowship. All I'm here to do is offer you transportation to and from York. Neither you nor the haven is bound."

"I'm perfectly willing to be bound," I said fervently.

"You may not be so rash after a few weeks at the haven."

I was about to reply when Little Aggie—so called to distinguish her from Fat Aggie who was in much the same trade—came in. Little Aggie supplemented her nocturnal earning around Astor Place by begging in the same neighborhood during the day.

"Sorry, Aggie," I said, "Mr. Tyss didn't leave anything for you."

"Maybe the lady would help a poor working girl down on her luck," she suggested, coming very close. "My, that's a pretty outfit you have—looks like real silk, too."

Barbara Haggerwells drew away with anger and loathing on her face. "No," she said sharply. "No, nothing!" She turned to me. "I must be going—I'll leave you to entertain your friend."

"Oh, I'll go," said Little Aggie cheerfully, "no need to get in an uproar. Bye-bye."

I was frankly puzzled; the puritanical reaction didn't seem consistent with Miss Haggerwells' character as I read it. Had I been mistaken? "I'm sorry Little Aggie bothered you. She's really not a bad sort, and she does have a hard time getting along."

"I'm sure you must enjoy her company immensely. I'm sorry we can't offer similar attractions at the haven."

Apparently she thought my relations with Aggie were professional. Even so, her attitude was peculiar. I could not flatter myself she was interested in me as a man, yet her flare-up indicated a strange kind of jealousy—impersonal, like the sensuality I attributed, rightly or wrongly, to her—as though the presence of another woman was an affront. I might have been amused if this were not one more obstacle to Haggershaven.

"Please don't go yet. For one thing"—I cast around for something to hold her till I could restore a more favorable impression "—for one thing you've never told me how Haggershaven happened to get my application."

She gave me a cold, angry look. "Even though we're cranks, educators often turn such letters over to us. After all, they may want to apply themselves some day."

I slowly coaxed her back into her previous mood, and again we talked of books. And now I thought I felt a new warmth in her voice and glance—as though she had won some kind of victory. When she left I hoped she was not too prejudiced against me. As for myself I admitted it would be easy enough to find her desirable—if one were not afraid of the humiliations I felt it was in her nature to inflict.

VI

This time I didn't offer Tyss two weeks' notice. "Well Hodgins, I made all the appropriate valedictory remarks on a previous occasion, so I'll not repeat them, except to say the precision of the script is extraordinary."

It seemed to me Tyss was saying in a roundabout way that everything was for the best. For the first time I saw him as slightly pathetic rather than sinister; extreme pessimism and vulgar optimism evidently met, like his circular time. I smiled indulgently and thanked him sincerely for all his kindness.

In 1944 almost 100 years had passed since New York and eastern Pennsylvania were linked in a railroad network, yet I don't suppose my journey differed much in speed or comfort from one taken by Granpa Hodgins' father. The stream ferry carried me across the Hudson to Jersey. I had heard there were only financial, not technical obstacles to a bridge or tunnel. These had never even been suggested except by impractical dreamers who believed its cost could be saved in a few years by running trains directly to Manhattan.

Nor was the ferry the only antique survival on the trip. The cars were all ancient, obvious discards from Confederate or Canadian lines. Flat wheels were common; the worn out locomotives dragged them protestingly over the wobbly rails and uneven roadbed. First class passengers sat on straw or napless plush seats; second class ones stood in the aisles or on the platforms; the third class rode the roofs—safe enough at the low speed except for sudden jerks or jolts.

There were so many different lines, each jealous of exclusive rights of way, that the traveler hardly got used to his particular car when he had to snatch up his baggage and hustle for the connecting train, which might be on the same track or at the same sooty depot, but was more likely to be a mile away. Even the adjective "connecting" was often ironical for it was not unusual to find timetables arranged so its departure preceded our arrival by minutes, necessitating a stopover of anywhere from one hour to twelve.

If anything could have quieted my excitement on the trip it was the view through the dirt-sprayed windows. "Fruitless" and "unfilled" were the words coming oftenest to my mind. I had forgotten during the past six years just how desolate villages and towns could look when their jerrybuilt structures were sunk in apathetic age without even the false rejuvenation of newer jerrybuilding. I had forgotten the mildewed appearance of tenant farmhouses, the unconvincing attempt to appear businesslike of false-fronted stores with clutters of hopeless merchandise in their dim windows, or the inadequate bluff of factories too small for any adequate production.

We crossed the Susquehanna on an old, old stone bridge that made me think of Meade's valiant men, bloodily bandaged many of them, somnambulistically marching northward, helpless and hopeless after the Confederate triumph at Gettysburg, their only thought to escape Jeb Stuart's pursuing cavalry. Indeed, every square mile now carried on its surface an almost visible weight of historical memories.

York was old, gray and crabbed in the afternoon, but when I got off the train there I was too agitated with the prospect of being soon at Haggershaven to take any strong impression of the town. I inquired the way, and the surly response confirmed Barbara Haggerwells' statement of local animosity. The distance—if my information was accurate—was a matter of some ten miles.

I started off down the highway, building and demolishing daydreams, thinking of Tyss and Enfandin and Miss Haggerwells, trying to picture her father and the fellows of the haven and for the thousandth time marshaling arguments for my acceptance in the face of scornful scrutiny. The early October sun was setting on the rich red and yellow leaves of the maples and oaks; I knew the air would become chilly before long, but exertion kept me warm. I counted on arriving at the haven in plenty of time to introduce myself before bedtime.

Less than a mile out of town the highway assumed the familiar aspect of the roads around Wappinger Falls and Poughkeepsie: rutted, wavering, and with deep, unexpected holes. The rail or stone fences on either side enclosed harvested cornfields, the broken stalks a dull brass, smutted from rain, with copper colored pumpkins scattered through them. But the rich countryside showed paradoxical signs of poverty: the fences were in poor repair and the covered wooden bridges over the creeks all had signs: DANGEROUS, TRAVEL AT YOUR OWN RISK.

There were few to share the highway with me: a farmer with an empty wagon, urging his team on and giving me a churlish glance instead of an invitation to ride; a horseman on an elegant chestnut picking his course carefully between the chuckholes, and a few tramps, each bent on his solitary way, at once defensive and aggressive. The condition of the bridges accounted for the absence of minibiles. However, just about twilight a closed carriage, complete with coachman and footman on the box, rolled haughtily by, stood for a moment outlined atop the slope up which I was trudging and then disappeared down the other side.

I paid little attention except—remembering my boyhood and my father's smithy—to visualize automatically the coachman pulling back on the reins and the footman thrusting forward with the brake as they eased the horses downward. So when I heard first a shout and then feminine screams my instant conclusion was that the carriage had overturned on the treacherous downgrade, broken an axle, or otherwise suffered calamity.

My responsive burst of speed had almost carried me to the top when I heard the shots. First one, like the barking of an uncertain dog, followed by a volley, as though a pack were unleashed.

I ran to the side of the road, close to the field, where I could see with less chance of being seen. Already the twilight was playing tricks, distorting the shape of some objects and momentarily hiding others. It could not, however, falsify the scene in the gully below. Four men on horseback covered the carriage with drawn revolvers; a fifth, also pistol in hand, had dismounted. His horse, reins hanging down, was peacefully investigating the roadside weeds.

None of them attempted to stop the terrified rearing of the carriage team. Only their position, strung across the road, prevented a runaway. I could not see the footman, but the coachman, one hand still clutching the reins, was sprawled backward with his foot caught against the dashboard and his head hanging downward over the wheel.

The door on the far side of the carriage was swung open. I thought for a moment the passengers had managed to escape. However, as the unmounted highwayman advanced, waving his pistol, the other door opened and a man and two women descended into the roadway. After slowly edging forward I could now plainly hear the gang's obscene whistles at sight of the women.

"Well, boys, here's something to keep us warm these cold nights. Hang on to them while I see what the mister has in his pockets."

The gentleman stepped in front, and with a slight accent said, "Take the girl by all means. She is but a peasant, a servant, and may afford you amusement. But the lady is my wife; I will pay you a good ransom for her and myself. I am Don Jaime Escobar y Gallegos, attached to the Spanish legation."

One of those on horseback said, "Well now, that's real kind of you, Don High-me. We might have taken you up at that, was you an American. But we can't afford no company of Spanish Marines coming looking for us, so I guess we'll have to pass up the ransom and settle for whatever you've got handy. And Missus Don and the hired girl. Don't worry about her being a peasant—we'll treat her and the madam exactly the same."

"Madre de Dios," screamed the lady. "Mercy!"

"It will be a good ransom," said the Spaniard, "and I give you my word my government will not bother you."

"Sorry, chum," returned the gangster. "You foreigners have a nasty habit of hanging men who make a living this way. Just can't trust you."

The man on foot took a step forward. The nearest rider swung the maid up before him and another horseman reached for her mistress. Again she screamed; her husband brushed the hand aside and put his wife behind him. At that the gangster raised his pistol and shot twice. The man and woman dropped to the ground. The maid screamed till her captor put his hand over her mouth.

"Now what did you want to do that for? Cutting our woman supply in half that way?"

"Sorry. Mighty damn' sorry. These things always seem to happen to me."

Meanwhile another of the gang slid off his horse and the two went through the dead, stripping them of jewelry and whatever articles of clothing caught their fancy before searching the luggage and the coach itself for valuables. By the time they had finished it was fully dark and I had crept to within a few feet of them, crouching reasonably secure and practically invisible while they debated what to do with the horses. One faction was in favor of taking them along for spare mounts, the other—arguing that they were easily identifiable—for cutting them out and turning them loose. The second group prevailing, they at last galloped away.

Though I'd seen dead men on New York streets, this was in some way different from the sight of a casual corpse or the episode between Sprovis and Tolliburr. It would be too simple to say I was horrified by their ruthlessness, for I still remembered the ruthlessness of Sprovis and the ruthlessness of Don Jaime Escobar in offering the servant girl was equally shocking. The opposing sides had been united in their inhumanity; I couldn't point to either and say, Good, or Bad. The mechanism of Tyss appeared—at least momentarily—as a satisfying moral refuge. If all action were but response to stimuli there was no necessity for making judgments.

I was thus meditating when a thrashing in the cornstalks just beyond the fence startled me into rigidity. Something that might have been a person stumbled toward the carriage, snuffling and moaning, to throw itself down by the prostrate bodies, its anguished noises growing more high-pitched and piercing.

By now I was sure this was a passenger who had jumped from the carriage at the start of the holdup, but whether man or woman it was impossible to tell. I moved forward gingerly, but somehow I must have betrayed my presence, for the creature, with a terrified groan, slumped inertly.

My hands told me it was a woman I raised from the ground and I sensed somehow that she was quite young. "Don't be afraid, Miss," I tried to reassure her. "I'm a friend."

I could hardly leave the girl lying in the road, nor did I feel equal to carrying her to Haggershaven—which I reckoned must be about six miles further. I tried shaking her, rubbing her hands, murmuring encouragement, all the while wishing the moon would come out, feeling somehow it would be easier to revive her in the moonlight.

At last she stirred and began whimpering again. Repeating that I was not one of the gang, I urged her to get up and come with me. I couldn't tell whether she understood or not for she merely moaned at intervals. I managed to get her arm over my shoulder and, supporting her around the waist, began walking again, impeded by my valise on one side and the girl on the other.

I could only guess how much time had been taken by the holdup and how slow my progress to Haggershaven would be. It did not seem I could arrive before midnight unless, which was unlikely, I could leave the girl at a hospitable farmhouse. And I could not imagine a more awkward hour to explain the company of a strange female.

We had made perhaps a mile—a slow and arduous one—when the moon at last came up. The light showed my companion even younger than I had thought, and extraordinarily beautiful. Her eyes were closed in a sort of troubled sleep, and she continued to moan, though at less frequent intervals.

I had just decided to stop for a moment's rest when we came upon one of the horses. He had trailed one of the clumsily cut traces and caught it on the stump of a broken sapling. Though still trembling he was over the worst of his fright; after patting and soothing him I got us onto his back and we proceeded in more comfortable fashion.

It wasn't hard to find Haggershaven; the sideroad to it was well kept and far smoother than the highway. We passed between what looked to be freshly plowed fields and came to a fair sized group of buildings, in some of which I was relieved to see lighted windows. The girl had still not spoken; her eyes remained closed and she moaned occasionally.

Dogs warned of our approach. From a dark doorway a figure came forward with a rifle under his arm. "Who is it?"

"Hodge Backmaker—I've got a girl here who was in a holdup. She's had a bad shock."

He hitched the horse to a post. I lifted the girl down. "I'm Asa Dorn," he said. "Let's go into the main kitchen—it's warm there. Here, take my arm."

She made no response and I half-carried her, with Dorn trying helpfully to share her weight. The building through which we led her was obviously an old farmhouse, having been enlarged and remodelled a number of times. Gas lights revealed Asa Dorn as perhaps 30, with very broad shoulders and very long arms, and a dark, rather melancholy face.

"There's been a gang operating around here," he informed me, "that's why I was on guard with the gun. Must be the same one."

We bustled the girl into a chair before a great fieldstone fireplace which gave the big room its look of welcome, though the even heat came from sets of steampipes under the windows. "Should we give her some soup? Or tea? Or should I get Barbara, or one of the others?"

His fluttering brushed the outside of my mind. My attention was concentrated on the girl, who looked no more than sixteen or seventeen, perhaps because she was severely dressed in some school uniform. Long, thick black hair hung softly in loose curls around her shoulders. Her face, which seemed made to reflect emotions—full, mobile lips, faintly slanted eyes, high nostrils—was instead impassive, devoid of vitality and this unnatural passivity was heightened by the dark eyes, now wide open and expressionless. Her mouth moved slowly, as though to form words, but nothing came forth except the faintest of guttural sounds.

"Why," exclaimed Dorn, "she's . . . dumb!"

She looked agonizedly toward him. I patted her arm helplessly.

"I'll go get—" he began.

A door opened and Barbara Haggerwells blinked at us. "I thought I heard . . ." Then she caught sight of the girl. Her face set in those lines of strange anger I had seen in the bookstore. "Really, Mr. Backmaker, I thought I'd explained there were no facilities here for this sort of thing."

Dorn broke in. "But Barbara, she's been in a holdup. She's dumb—"

Fury made her ugly. "Is that an additional attraction? Dumb or not, get the slut out of here! Get her out right now, I say!"

"Barbara, you're not listening. You don't understand."

She turned her back on him and faced me. "I should have remembered you were a ladies' man, Mr. Self-taught Backmaker. No doubt you imagined Haggershaven as some obscene liberty hall. Well, it isn't! You'll be wasting any further time you spend here. Get out!"

I SUPPOSE—RECALLING the scene with Little Aggie—I was less astonished by her frenzy than I might have been. Besides, her rage and misunderstanding were anti-climactic after the succession of excitements I had been through that day. Instead of amazement or outrage I felt only vague puzzlement and tired annoyance.

Dorn, after getting Barbara out of the room, offered stumbling explanations ("Overwork, overwork") which jolted between the patent loyalty prodding him to cover her defects and a painful desire to distract my mind from the episode. Only when we were relieved of our responsibilities by the arrival of several women who effectually sealed the girl away from all further masculine contact and he took me to Mr. Haggerwells' study, did his nervousness somewhat abate.

Thomas Haggerwells, large-boned like his daughter, with the ginger hair faded, and a florid, handsome complexion, made me welcome, but he seemed to have something else on his mind. Finally he stopped abruptly in the middle of a sentence and turned to Dorn. "Ace, Barbara is quite upset."

I thought this extreme understatement, but Dorn merely nodded. "Misunderstanding, Mr. H," and he explained the situation.

Mr. Haggerwells began pacing the flowered carpet. "Of course, of course. Naturally we can't turn the poor girl out. But how can I explain to Barbara? She . . . she came to me," he said half proudly, half apprehensively. "I don't know quite—" He pulled himself together. "Excuse me, Mr. Backmaker. My daughter is high-strung. I'm afraid I'm allowing concern to interfere with our conversation. . . ."

"Not at all, sir," I said. "I'm very tired, if you'll excuse me . . . ?"

"Of course, of course," he answered with evident relief. "Ace will show you your room. Sleep well—we will talk more tomorrow. And Ace—come back here afterward, will you?"

Barbara Haggerwells certainly seemed to have both Ace Dorn and her father pretty well cowed, I thought, as I lay awake. But it was neither Barbara nor overstimulation from all I'd been through that day which caused my insomnia. A torment, successfully suppressed for some hours, invaded me. The chance the hold-up gang could have been supplied with Sprovis' firearms was remote far beyond probability; connecting the trip of the Escobars with the counterfeiting of Spanish pesetas was fantasy. But what is logic? I could not quench my feeling of responsibility with ridicule, nor charge myself merely with perverse arrogance in magnifying my trivial errands into accountability for all that flowed from the Grand Army. Guilty men cannot sleep because they feel guilty. It is the feeling, not the abstract guilt, which keeps them awake.

At last however, I slept, only to dream Barbara Haggerwells was a great fish pursuing me over endless roads on which my feet bogged in clinging, tenacious mud. But in the clear autumn morning my notions of the night before dwindled, even if they failed to disappear entirely.

How shall I write of Haggershaven as my eyes first saw it twenty-two years ago? Of the rolling acres of rich plowed land, interrupted here and there by stone outcroppings worn smooth and round by time, and trees in woodlots or standing alone, strong and unperturbed? Or the main building, grown from the original farmhouse into a great, rambling eccentricity stopping short of monstrosity only because of its complete innocence of pretence? Shall I describe the two dormitories, severely functional, escaping harshness only because they had not been built by carpenters, and though sturdy enough, betrayed the amateur touch? Or the cottages and apartments—two, four, at most six rooms—for the married fellows and their families? These were scattered all over, some so avid for privacy that one could pass unknowing within feet of the concealing woods, others bold in the sunshine on knolls or on the level.

I could tell of the small shops, the miniature laboratories, the inadequate observatory, the dozens of outbuildings. But these things were not the haven. They were merely the least of its possessions. For Haggershaven was not a material place at all, but a spiritual freedom. Its limits were only the limits of what its fellows could do and think and inquire. It was circumscribed only by the outside world, not by internal rules and taboos, competition or curriculum.

Its history was not only a link with the past, but a possible hint of what might have been if the War of Southron Independence had not interrupted the American pattern. Barbara's great-great-grandfather, Herbert Haggerwells, had been a Confederate major from North Carolina who had fallen in love with the then fat Pennsylvania countryside. After the war he had put everything—not much by Southron standards, but a fortune in depreciated, soon to be repudiated, United States greenbacks—into the farm which became the nucleus of Haggershaven. Then he married a local girl and became completely a Northerner.

Until it became imperceptible with daily custom, I used to stare at his portrait in the library, picturing in idle fancy a possible meeting on the battlefield with this aristocratic gentleman with his curling mustache and daggerlike imperial, and my own plebeian Granpa Hodgins. But the likelihood they had ever come face to face was infinitely remote; I, who had studied both their likenesses, was the only link between them.

Major Haggerwells had patronized several writers and artists, but it was his son who, seeing the deterioration of Northern colleges, had invited a few restive scholars to make their home with him. They were free to pursue their studies under an elastic arrangement which permitted them to be self-supporting through work on the farm.

Thomas Haggerwells' father had organized the scheme further, attracting a larger number of schoolmen who contributed greatly to the material progress of the haven. They patented inventions, marketless at home, which brought regular royalties from more industrialized countries. Agronomists improved the haven's crops and took in a steady income from seed. Chemists found ways of utilizing otherwise wasted by-products; proceeds from scholarly works—and one more popular than scholarly—added to the funds. In his will, Volney Haggerwells left the property to the fellowship.

Except for the scene after my arrival, I didn't see Barbara again for some ten days. Even then it was but a glimpse, caught as she was hurrying in one direction and I sauntering in another. She threw me a single frigid glance and went on. Later, I was talking with Mr. Haggerwells—who had proved to be not quite an amateur of history, but more than a dabbler—when, without knocking, she burst into the room.

"Father, I—" Then she caught sight of me. "Sorry. I didn't know you were entertaining."

His tone was that of one caught in a guilty act. "Come in, come in, Barbara. Hodgins is, after all, something of a protege of yours."

"Really, Father!" She was regal. Wounded, scornful, but majestic. "I'm sure I don't know enough about self-taught pundits to sponsor them. It seems too bad they have to waste your time—"

He flushed. "Please, Barbara. You really . . . really must control . . ."

Her aloof scorn became open anger. "Must I? Must I? And stand by while every pretentious swindler usurps your attention? Oh, I don't ask for any special favors as your daughter—I know too well I have none coming. But I should think at least the consideration due a fellow of the haven would prompt ordinary courtesy even when no natural affection is forthcoming!"

"Barbara, please! Oh, my dear girl, how can you . . . ?"

But she was gone, leaving him obviously distressed and me puzzled. Not at her lack of control so much as her accusation that he lacked a father's love for her. Nothing was clearer than his pride in her achievements or his protective, baffled tenderness. It did not seem possible that so wilful a misunderstanding could be maintained.

From Ace I learned this tortured jealousy was a fixture of her character. Barbara had created feuds, slandered and reviled fellows who had been guilty of nothing but trying to interest her father in some project in which she herself was not concerned. I learned much more also—much he had no desire to convey. But he was a poor hand at concealing anything, and it was clear he was helplessly subject to her, but without the usual kindly anesthetic of illusion. I guessed he had enjoyed her favors, but she evidently didn't bother to hide the fact that the privilege was not exclusive; perhaps, indeed, she insisted on his knowing. I gathered she was a fiercely moral polyandrist, demanding absolute fidelity without offering the slightest hope of reciprocal single-mindedness.

VII

Among those at the haven was an Oliver Midbin, a student of what he chose to call the new and revolutionary science of Emotional Pathology. Tall and thin, with an incongruous little potbelly like an enlarged and far-slipped Adam's-apple, he pounced on me as a readymade and captive audience for his theories.

"Now this case of pseudo-aphonia—"

"He means the dumb girl," explained Ace, aside.

"Nonsense," said Midbin. "Pseudo-aphonia. Purely of an emotional nature. Of course, if you take her to some medical quack he'll convince himself and you and certainly her that there's some impairment of the vocal cords—"

"I'm not the girl's guardian, Mr. Midbin—"

"Doctor. Philosophiae, Gottingen. Trivial matter."

"Excuse me, Dr. Midbin. Anyway, I'm not her guardian so I'm not taking her anywhere. But—just as a theoretical question—suppose examination did reveal a physical impairment?"

He appeared delighted, and rubbed his hands together. "Oh, it would. I assure you it would. These fellows always find what they're looking for. If your disposition is sour they'll find warts on your duodenum—in a post-mortem. Whereas Emotional Pathology deals with the sour disposition and lets the warts, if any, take care of themselves. Matter is a function of the mind. People are dumb or blind or deaf for a purpose. Now what purpose can the girl have in being dumb?"

"No conversation?" I suggested. I didn't doubt Midbin was an authority, but his manner made flippancy almost irresistible.

"I shall find out," he said firmly. "This is bound to be a simpler mal-adjustment than Barbara's—"

"Aw, come on," protested Ace.

"Nonsense, Dorn. Nonsense. Reticence is part of those medical ethics by which the quacks conceal incompetence. Mumbo jumbo to keep the layman from asking annoying questions. Priestly, not scientific approach. Art and mystery of phlebotomy. Don't hold back knowledge—publish it to the world."

"I just think Barbara wouldn't want her private thoughts published to the world."

"Of course not, of course not. Why? Because she's unhappy with her hatred for her dead mother. Exaggerated possessiveness for her father makes her miserable. Her fantasy—"

"Midbin!"

"Her fantasy of going back to childhood in order to injure her mother is a sick notion she cherishes the way a dog licks a wound. Ventilate it. Ventilate it. Now, this girl's case is bound to be simpler. Bring her around tomorrow and we'll begin."

"Me?" I asked.

"Who else? You're the only one she doesn't seem to distrust."

It was annoying to have the girl's puppylike devotion observed. I realized she saw me as the only link with a normal past, but I assumed that after a few days she would turn naturally to the women who took such obvious pleasure in fussing over her affliction. Yet she merely suffered their attentions; no matter how I tried to avoid her she sought me out, running to me with muted, voiceless cries which should have been touching but were only painful.

Mr. Haggerwells had reported her presence to the sheriff's office at York where complete lack of interest was evinced. He had also telegraphed the Spanish legation who replied they knew no other Escobars than Don Jaime and his wife. The girl might be a servant or a stranger; it was no concern of His Most Catholic Majesty.

The school uniform made it unlikely she was a servant but beyond this, little was deducible. She did not respond to questions in either Spanish or English, giving no indication of understanding their meaning. When offered pencil and paper she handled them curiously, then let them slide to the floor.

Midbin's method of treatment was bizarre as any I'd heard of. His subjects were supposed to relax on a couch and say whatever came into their minds. This was the technique he had used with Barbara, as he informed me at length and in detail, and it had produced the story of her matricidal fantasy—which I found so shocking, but which he regarded with true scientific detachment—but little else.

Since this couldn't work with the dumb girl, he had to experiment with modifications. Reclining on a couch seemed to be basic however, so with my reluctant assistance, which consisted only in being present, she was persuaded to comply. But there was no question of relaxation; she lay there warily, tense and stiff, even with her eyes closed.

Again, looking at her lying there so rigidly, I could not but admit she was beautiful. But the admission was made quite dispassionately; the lovely young lines evoked no lust. I felt only vexation because her plight kept me from the wonders of Haggershaven.

It seemed to me I had to cram everything into short days, for I was sure the fellows would never accept me. I realized that these autumn weeks, spent in casual conversation or joining the familiar preparations for rural winter, were a period of thorough and critical examination of my fitness. There was nothing I could do to sway the decision; I could only say, when the opportunity offered, that Haggershaven was literally a revelation to me, an island of civilization in the midst of a chaotic and brutal sea. My dream was to make a landfall there.

Certainly my meager background and scraps of reading would not persuade the men and women of the haven; I could only hope they might see some promise in me. Against this I put Barbara's enmity, a hostility now exacerbated by rage at Oliver Midbin for daring to devote to another the attention which had been her due. Already I had learned something of her persistence and I was sure she could move enough of the fellows to vote against me to insure my rejection.

THE GANG WHICH had been operating in the vicinity—presumably the same one I had encountered—moved on. At least no further crimes were attributed to it. Deputy Sheriff Beasley, who had evidently visited Haggershaven before without attaining much respect, came to question the girl and me.

I think he doubted her dumbness. At any rate he barked his questions so loudly and abruptly they would have terrified a far more securely poised individual. She promptly went into dry hysterics, whereupon he turned his attention to me.

He was clearly dissatisfied with my account of the holdup and left grumbling that it would be more to the point if bookworms learned to identify a man properly instead of logarithms or trigonometry. I didn't see exactly how this applied to me; I certainly was laudably ignorant of both subjects.

But if Officer Beasley was disappointed, Midbin was enchanted by the whole performance. Of course he had heard my narrative before but as he explained it, this was the first time he'd savored its possible impact on the girl. "You see, Backmaker, her pseudo-aphonia is neither congenital nor of long standing. All logic leads to the conclusion that it's the result of her terror during the experience. She must have wanted to scream, but she dared not—she had to remain dumb while she watched the murders."

For the first time it seemed possible to me there was more to Midbin than his garrulity.

"She crushed back that natural, overwhelming impulse," he went on. "She had to—her life depended on it. It was an enormous effort and the effect on her was in proportion; she achieved her object too well, so when it was safe for her to speak again she couldn't."

It all sounded so reasonable that it was some time before I thought to ask him why she didn't understand what we said, or why she didn't write anything down when she was handed pencil and paper.

"Communication," he answered. "She had to cut off communication, and once cut off it's not easy to restore. At least, that's one aspect of it. Another one is a little more tricky. The holdup took place more than a month ago—but do you suppose the affected mind reckons so precisely? Is a precise reckoning possible? Duration may, for all we know, be an entirely subjective thing. Yesterday for you may be today for me. We recognize this to some extent when we speak of hours passing slowly or quickly. The girl may be still undergoing the agony of repressing her screams; the holdup, the murders, are not in the past for her, but in the present. And if she is, is it any wonder she is cut off from the relaxation which would enable her to realize the present?"

He pressed his middle thoughtfully. "Now, if it is possible to recreate in her mind the conditions leading up to and through the crisis, she would have the chance to vent the emotions she was forced to swallow. She might—I don't say she would—she might speak again."

I understood such a process would be lengthy, but I saw no signs he was reaching her at all, much less that he was having an effect. One of the Spanish-speaking fellows translated my account of our meeting and read parts of it to the recumbent girl, following Midbin's excited stage directions and interpolations. Nothing happened.

Gradually I passed from the stage when I wanted the decision of the haven on my application to be postponed as long as possible, to the one in which the suspense became wearing. And now I learned that there was no specific date set; my candidacy would be considered along with other business next time the fellows were called on to make an appropriation, or discuss a new project. This might be next day, or not for months.

When it did come, it was anticlimactic. Several of the fellows recommended me, and Barbara simply ignored my existence. I was a full fellow of Haggershaven, securely at home for the first time since I left Wappinger Falls more than six years before. I knew that in all its history few fellows had ever voluntarily left the haven, still fewer had ever been asked to resign.

Fall became winter. Surplus timber was hauled in from the woodlots and the lignon extracted by compressed air, a method invented by one of the fellows. Lignon was the fuel which kept our hot water furnaces going and provided the gas for lighting. Everyone took part in this work, but my ineptness with things mechanical soon caused me to be set to more congenial tasks in the stables.

I was one afternoon currying a dappled mare when Barbara, her breath still cloudy from the cold outside, came in and stood behind me. I made an artificial cowlick on the mare's flank, then brushed it glossy smooth again.

"Hello," she said.

"Uh . . . hello, Miss Haggerwells."

"Must you, Hodge?"

I roughed up the mare's flank again. "Must I what? I'm afraid I don't understand."

"I think you do. Why do you avoid me? And call me 'Miss Haggerwells' in that prim tone? Do I look so old and ugly and forbidding?"

This, I thought, is going to hurt Ace. Poor Ace, befuddled by a Jezebel; why can't he attach himself to a nice quiet girl who won't tear him in pieces every time she follows her inclinations?

I finished with the mare, put down the currycomb and dusted off my hands. "I think you are the most exciting woman I've ever met, Barbara," I said.

IT IS SAID the attainment of a cherished wish always brings disappointment, but this wasn't true of my life at Haggershaven. My brightest daydreams were fulfilled and more than fulfilled. At first it seemed the years at the bookstore were wasted, but I soon realized the value of that catholic and serendipitous reading for more schematic study. I began to understand what thorough exploration of a subject meant and I threw myself into my chosen work with furious zest.

I also began to understand the central mystery of historical theory. Not chronology, but relationship is ultimately what the historian deals in. The element of time, so vital at first glance, assumes a constantly more subordinate character. That the past is past becomes increasingly less important. Except for perspective it might as well be the present or the future, or—if one can conceive it—a parallel time. I was not exploring a petrification, but a fluid.

During that winter I read philosophy, psychology, archaeology, anthropology. My energy and appetite were prodigious. Even so I found time for Barbara. The "even so" is misleading, however, for this was no diversion, no dalliance. People talk lightly of gusts of passion, but it was nothing less than irresistible force which impelled me to her, day after day. The only thing saving me from enslavement like poor Ace was the belief—correct or incorrect, I am to this day not certain—that to yield the last vestige of detachment and objectivity would make me helpless, not only before her, but to accomplish all my ambitions, now more urgent than ever.

And yet I know I denied much I could have given freely and without harm. I know, too, that my fancied advantage over Ace, based on the fact that I had always had an easy—perhaps too easy—way with women, was no advantage at all. I thought myself the master of the situation because her infidelities—if such a word can be used where the thought of faithfulness is explicitly ruled out—did not bother me. I was wrong; my sophistication was a lack and not an achievement.

Make no mistake. She was no superficial wanton, moved by light and fickle desires. She was driven by deeper and darker than sensual urges; her mad jealousies were provoked by an unappeasable need for constant reassurance. She had to be dominant, she had to be courted by more than one man; at the same time she had to be told constantly what she could never really believe—that she was uniquely desired.

I wondered how she did not burn herself out, not only with conflicting passions, but with her fury of work. Sleep was a weakness she despised, yet she craved much more of it than she allowed herself; she rationed her hours of unconsciousness and drove herself relentlessly.

Ace's panegyrics of her importance as a physicist I discounted, but older and more learned colleagues spoke of her mathematical concepts, not merely with respect, but with awe.

She did not discuss her work with me, for our relationship was not intellectually intimate. I got the impression she was seeking the principle of heavier than air flight, a chimera which had long intrigued inventors. It seemed a pointless pursuit, for it was manifest such levitation could not hope to replace our safe, comfortable guided balloons. Later I learned she was doing nothing of the kind, but not speaking the technical jargon of her science, that was what I made of Ace's vague hints.

In the spring all of us at Haggershaven became single-minded farmers until the fields were plowed and sown. No one grudged these days taken from study; not only were we aware of the haven's dependence on economic self-sufficiency, but we were happy in the work itself. Not until the first, most feverish competition with time was over could we return, even for a moment, to our regular pursuits.

Midbin had for some while been showing the dumb girl drawings of successive stages of the holdup, again nagging and pumping me for details to sharpen their accuracy. Her reactions pleased him immensely, for she responded to the first ones with nods and the throaty noises we recognized as signs of agreement. The scenes of the assault itself, of the shooting of the coachman, the flight of the footman, and her own concealment in the cornfield evoked whimpers, while the brutal depiction of the Escobars' murder made her cower and cover her eyes.

I cannot here omit mentioning that Barbara constantly taunted me with what she called my "devotion" to the girl; when I protested that Midbin had drafted me for the duty she accused me of hypocrisy, lying, faithlessness, sycophancy and various assorted vices and failings. Midbin, of course, explained and excused her outbursts by his "emotional pathology," Ace accepted and suffered them as inescapable, but I saw no necessity of being subject to her tantrums. Once I told her so not, I think, too heatedly, adding, "Maybe we shouldn't see each other alone after this."

"All right," she said, "yes . . . yes. All right, don't."

Her apparent calm deceived me completely; I smiled with relief.

"That's right; laugh—why shouldn't you? You have no feelings, no more than you have an intelligence. You are an oaf, a clod, a real bumpkin. Standing there with a silly grin on your face. Oh, I hate you! How I hate you!"

She wept, she screamed, she rushed at me and then turned away, crying that she hadn't meant it, not a word of it. She coaxed, begging forgiveness for all she'd said, tearfully promising to control herself after this, moaning that she needed me, and finally, when I didn't repulse her, exclaiming that it was her love for me which tormented her so and drove her to such scenes.

Perhaps this storm changed our relationship somewhat for the better, or at least eased the tension between us. At any rate it was after this she began speaking to me of her work, putting us on a friendlier, less passionate plane. I learned now how completely garbled was my notion of what she was doing.

"Heavier than air flying-machines!" she cried. "How utterly absurd!"

"All right. I didn't know."

"My work is theoretical. I'm not a vulgar mechanic."

"All right, all right."

"I'm going to show that time and space are aspects of the same entity."

"All right," I said, thinking of something else.

"What is time?"

"Uh? Dear Barbara, since I don't know anything I can slide gracefully out of that one. I couldn't even begin to define time."

"Oh, you could probably define it all right—in terms of itself. I'm not dealing with definitions but concepts."

"All right, conceive."

"Hodge, like all stuffy people your levity is vulgar."

"Excuse me. Go ahead."

"Time is an aspect."

"So you mentioned. I once knew a man who said it was an illusion. And another who said it was a serpent with its tail in its mouth."

"Mysticism. Time, matter, space and energy are all aspects of the cosmic entity. Interchangeable aspects. Theoretically it should be possible to translate matter into terms of energy and space into terms of time; matter-energy into space-time."

"It sounds so simple I'm ashamed of myself."

"To put it so crudely that the explanation is misleading: suppose matter is resolved into its component—"

"Atoms?" I suggested, since she seemed at loss for a word.

"Something more fundamental than atoms. We have no word because we can't quite grasp the concept yet. Essence, perhaps, or the theological 'spirit.' If matter—"

"A man?"

"Man, machine or chemical compound," she answered impatiently. "Is resolved into its essence it can presumably be reassembled at another point of the time-space aspect."

"You mean . . . like yesterday?"

"No—and yes. What is 'yesterday'? A thing—or an aspect? Oh, words are useless. Even with mathematical symbols you can hardly. . . . But someday I'll establish it. Or lay the groundwork for my successors. Or the successors of my successors."

I nodded. Midbin was at least half right; Barbara was emotionally sick. For what was this "theory" of hers but the rationalization of a daydream, the daydream of discovering a process of going back through time to injure her dead mother and so steal all of her father's affections?

AT THE NEXT MEETING of the fellows Midbin asked an appropriation for experimental work and the help of haven members in the project. Since both requests were modest, their granting would ordinarily have been a formality. But Barbara asked politely if Dr. Midbin wouldn't like to elaborate a little on the purpose of his experiment.

I knew her manner was a danger signal. However Midbin merely answered good-humoredly that he proposed to test a theory of whether an emotionally induced physical handicap could be cured by recreating in the subject's mind the shock which had caused—if he might use a loose and inaccurate term—the impediment.

"I thought so. He wants to waste the haven's money and time on a little tart with whom he's having an affair while important work is held up for lack of funds."

One of the women called out, "Oh, Barbara, no," and there were exclamations of disapproval. Mr. Haggerwells, after trying unsuccessfully to hold Barbara's eye, said, "I must apologize for my daughter—"

"It's all right," interrupted Midbin. "I understand Barbara's notions. I'm sure no one here really thinks there is anything improper between the girl and me. Outside of this, Barbara's original question seems quite in order to me. Briefly, as most of you know, I've been trying to restore speech to a subject who lost it—again I use an inaccurate term for con-venience—during an afflicting experience. Preliminary experiments in-dicate the likelihood of satisfactory response to my proposed method, which is simply to employ a kinematic camera like those used in mak-ing entertainment photinugraphs—"

"He wants to turn the haven into a tinugraph mill with the fellows as mummers!"

"Only this once, Barbara. Not regularly; not as routine."

At this point her father insisted the request be voted on without any more discussion. I was tempted to vote with Barbara, the only dissident, for I foresaw Midbin's photinugraph relying pretty heavily on me, but I didn't have the courage. Instead, I merely abstained, like Midbin him-self, and Ace.

The tinugraph did indeed demand much of my time. I had to set the exact scene where the holdup had taken place and approximate as nearly identical conditions as possible. (Here Midbin was partially foiled by the limitations of his medium, being forced to use the cam-era in full sunlight rather than dusk.) I dressed and instructed the actors in their parts, rehearsing and directing them throughout. The only immunity I got was Midbin's concession that I needn't play the part of myself, since in my early role of spectator I would be invisi-bly concealed, and the succor was omitted as irrelevant to the thera-peutic purpose. Midbin himself, of course, did nothing but tend his camera.

Any tinugraph mill would have snorted at our final product and cer-tainly no tinugraph lyceum would have condescended to show it. After much wavering Midbin had finally decided against making a phonoto of it, feeling that the use of sound would add no value but considerable expense, so that the film did not even have this feature to recommend it. Fortunately, for whatever involuntary professional pride involved, no one was present at the first showing but the girl and I, Ace to work the magic-lantern, and Midbin.

In the darkened room the pictures on the screen gave—after the first few minutes—such an astonishing illusion of reality that when one of the horsemen rode toward the camera we all reflexively shrank back a little. In spite of its amateurishness the tinugraph seemed to us an artis-tic success, but no triumph in satisfying the reason for its existence. The girl reacted no differently than she had toward the drawings: her inar-ticulate noises ran the same scale from pleasure to terror; nothing new was added. But Midbin slapped Ace and me on the back, predicting he'd have her talking like a politician before the year was out.

I suppose the process was imperceptible; certainly there was no discernible difference between one session and the next. Yet the boring routine was continued day after day, and so absolute was Midbin's confidence that we were not too astonished after some weeks when, at the moment "Don Jaime" folded in simulated death, she fainted and remained unconscious for some time.

After this we expected—at least Ace and I did, Midbin only rubbed his palms together—that she would begin talking at a great rate. She didn't, but a few showings later, at the same crucial point, she screamed. It was a genuine scream, high-pitched and piercing, bearing small resemblance to the strangled noises we were accustomed to. There was no doubt Midbin had been vindicated; no mute could have voiced that full, shrill cry.

Pursuing another of his theories, Midbin soon gave up the idea of helping her express the words in her mind in Spanish, but concentrated on teaching her English. It was soon clear she must have had some grounding in this language, and it seemed an amazingly short time before she pointed to me and said clearly, "Hodge . . . Hodge . . ."

A month of common nouns followed, interspersed with a few easy verbs, before she touched her own breast and said, shyly, "Catalina."

Her name was Catalina García; she was the much younger sister of Doña María Escobar, with whom she had lived after the death of her parents. So far as she knew she had no other relatives. Please—we would not send her away from Haggershaven, would we?

Again Mr. Haggerwells communicated with the Spanish diplomats, recalling his original telegram and mentioning their aloof reply. He was answered in person by an official who acted as though he himself had composed the disclaiming response—perhaps he had. Nevertheless he confirmed the existence of one Catalina García and at last satisfied himself that she and our Catalina were the same person. Further, the Señorita García was heiress to a moderate estate. According to embassy records the señorita was not yet eighteen; as an orphan living in foreign lands she was a ward of the Spanish Crown. The señorita would return with him to Philadelphia where she would be suitably accommodated until repatriation could be arranged. The—ah—institution could submit a bill for board and lodging during her stay.

But Catalina protested so earnestly, appealing alternately to me and to Mr. Haggerwells, that Midbin, who was hovering solicitously, insisted he could not guarantee against a relapse. The official shrugged, managing to intimate in that gesture his opinion that the haven was of a very shady character indeed and had possibly engineered the holdup itself. However, if the señorita wished to remain, he had no authority at the moment either to inquire into what influences had persuaded her nor to remove her by—ah—nor to remove her. Of course the—ah—institution understood it could hope for no further compensation, that the señorita would be visited without notification from time to time by an official, that she might be removed whenever His Most Catholic Majesty saw fit, that none of her estate would be released before her eighteenth birthday, and that the whole affair was entirely irregular.

After he left, Catalina put her head against my collarbone, sobbing with relief, and I must admit, now she was able to talk I no longer found her devotion so tiresome—even though I was somewhat uneasy lest Barbara discover us in this situation.

VIII

And now I come to the period of my life which stands in such sharp contrast to all the rest. Was it really eight years I spent at Haggershaven? The arithmetic is indisputable: I arrived in 1944 at the age of 23; I left in 1952 at the age of 31. Indisputable, but not quite believable; like the happy countries which are supposed to have no history I find it hard to go over those eight years and divide them by remarkable events. They blended too smoothly, too contentedly into one another.

There was no question about success in my chosen profession—not even the expected alternation of achievement and disappointment. Once started on the road I kept on going at an even, steady pace. For what would have been my doctoral thesis I wrote a paper on *The Timing of General Stuart's Maneuvers During August 1863 in Pennsylvania*. This received flattering comment from scholars as far away as the Universities of Lima and Cambridge; because of it I was offered instructorships at highly respectable schools.

But I could not think of leaving the haven. The world into which I had been born had never been revealed for what it was until I had escaped from it.

The idea of returning to enter into daily competition with other underpaid, overdriven drudges striving fruitlessly to apply a dilute coating of culture to the unresponsive surface of unwilling students was abhorrent. Life at Haggershaven suited me perfectly.

In those eight years, as I broadened my knowledge I narrowed my field. Perhaps it was presumptuous to take the War of Southron Independence as my specialty when there were already so many comprehensive books on the subject and so many celebrated historians engaged with this epochal event. However, my choice was not made out of arrogance but of fascination, and the readiness of the scene and materials influenced the selection of my goal, which was to be a definitive work on the last thirteen months of the war, from General Lee's invasion of Pennsylvania to the capitulation at Reading.

My monographs were published in learned Confederate, British, and German journals—there were none in the United States—and I was rejoiced when they brought attention, not so much to me as to Haggershaven. I could contribute only this notice and my physical labor; on the other hand I asked little beyond food, clothing and shelter—just books. My field trips I took on foot, often earning my keep by casual labor for farmers, paying for access to private collections of letters or documents by indexing and arranging them.

But it was not the time devoted to scholarship which alone distinguished these eight years. The absence of the shadows of anxiety and violence, the freedom from constant harassment and fear, as well as the positive aspects of life at the haven—the companionship of like-minded people, labor to achieve ends rather than just to stay alive—the surety of acceptance and unselfish praise for achievement, all set this time apart, so I think of it as a golden period, a time of perpetual warm sunshine.

Though sometimes I was inclined to wonder if Barbara Haggerwells' neurosis was not precarious—on the edge of sanity, and there were moments when I found her morality distasteful, it was impossible to deny her attraction. Often we were lovers for as long as a month before the inevitable quarrel came, followed by varying periods of coolness between us. But during those weeks of distance I remembered how she could be tender and gracious, just as during our intimacy I remembered her ruthlessness and dominance.

It was not only her temperamental outbreaks nor even her unappeasable hunger for love and affection which thrust us apart. It was increasingly hard for her to leave her work behind even for moments. She was never allowed to forget either by her own insatiable drive nor by outside acknowledgement that she was already one of the foremost physicists in the country. She had been granted so many honorary de-

grees she no longer traveled to receive them; offers from foreign governments of well-paid jobs connected with their munitions industries were
frequent. Articles were written about her equation of matter, energy,
space and time, acclaiming her as a revolutionary thinker; though she
dismissed them contemptuously as evaluations of elementary work they
nevertheless added to her isolation and curtailed her freedom.

Midbin was, in his way, as much under her spell as Ace or myself.
His triumph over Catalina's dumbness he took lightly now it was accomplished; stabilizing Barbara's emotions was the victory he wanted.
Patiently, whenever she would grant the time—and this was increasingly less often—he tried with her new techniques, but to no apparent
effect. Indeed, it seemed he was, if anything, retrogressing; she no
longer paid him the respect of even partial co-operation; instead she
made fun of his efforts.

There was a great unlikeness between Barbara and Catalina. That
the Spanish girl had in her own way as strong a will was demonstrated
in her determination to become part of Haggershaven. She had gone
resolutely to Thomas Haggerwells. She knew quite well, she told him,
she had neither the aptitudes nor qualifications for admission to fellowship, nor did she ask it. All she wanted was to live in what she now regarded as her only home. She would gladly do any work from washing
dishes to running errands. When she came of age she would turn over
whatever money she inherited to the haven without qualification.

Long after this and similar conversations I heard how he had patiently pointed out that a Spanish subject was a citizen of a wealthier
and more powerful nation than the United States; as an heiress she
could enjoy the luxury and distractions of Madrid and eventually make
a suitable marriage. How silly it would be to give up all these advantages to become an unnoticed, penniless drudge for a group of cranks
near York, Pennsylvania.

Catty—as we soon called Catalina—was adamant. What Mr. Haggerwells said might be true, but she was simply not interested. Evidently
he realized the quality of her determination for eventually he proposed
to the fellows that she be allowed to stay and the offer of her money be
rejected; the motion was carried, with only Barbara—who spoke long
and bitterly against it—voting "no."

Catty, she of enchanting voice, so expressive, so controlled, was a
very different creature from the nameless dumb girl. Even her beauty,
always undeniable, was now heightened and sharpened by the fact

of her speech. I suppose it is a confession of weakness or obtuseness to say that where I had been inclined to impatience or even annoyance at her former all too open devotion, I now felt deprived and even pettish at its lack.

I don't mean by this that Catty was either disingenuous or coquettish. But with the return of speech came a certain maturity and an undeniable dignity. She was self-possessed, self-contained and just a trifle amusedly aloof. Having made it clear she had interest in no other man, she withdrew from all competition. When I wished to seek her out she was there, but she made no attempt to call me to her.

Perhaps I sensed from the beginning what was to happen. Perhaps I was polygamous as Barbara was polyandrous or Catty monogamous. It would be inaccurate to say I wavered between the two; every break with Barbara drew me closer to Catty and there was never any counter-force to reverse the process. What was adventurous and juvenile in me reached out to Barbara; whatever was stable and mature pulled me toward Catty.

The final decision (was it final? I don't know. I shall never know now) hardened when I had been nearly six years at Haggershaven. It had been "on" between Barbara and me for the longest stretch I could recall and I had even begun to wonder if some paradoxical equilibrium had not somehow finally been established in our volatile relationship.

As always, when the mutual hostility which complemented our mutual attraction was eased, Barbara spoke of her work. In spite of such occasional confidences, it was still not her habit to talk of it with me. That intimacy was obviously reserved for Ace, and I didn't begrudge it him, for after all he understood it and I didn't. But now I suppose she was so full of the subject she could hardly hold back, even from one who could hardly distinguish between thermodynamics and kinesthetics.

"Hodge," she said, gray eyes greenish with excitement, "I'm not going to write a book."

This hardly seemed startling. "That's nice," I answered idly. "New, too. Saves time, paper, ink. Sets a different standard; from now on scholars will be known as 'Jones, who didn't write *The Theory of Tidal Waves*,' 'Smith, un-author of *Gas and Its Properties*,' or 'Backmaker, non-recorder of *Gettysburg and After*.'"

"Silly. I only meant it's become customary to spend a lifetime formulating principles—then someone else comes along and puts your principles into practice. It seems more sensible for me to demonstrate my own conclusions instead of writing about them."

I still didn't grasp the import. "You're going to demonstrate— uh . . . ?"

"Cosmic entity."

"You mean you're going to turn matter into space or something like that?"

"Something like that. I intend to attempt translating matter-energy into terms of space-time."

I started up. "You're going to—" I groped for words. "Build an engine which will move through time?"

"That's putting it crudely. But it's close enough for a layman."

"You once told me your work was theoretical. That you were no vulgar mechanic."

"I'll become one."

"Barbara, you're crazy! As a philosophical abstraction this theory of yours is interesting—"

"Thank you!"

"Barbara, listen to me. Midbin—"

"I haven't the faintest interest in Midbin's stodgy fantasies."

"He has in yours, though, and so have I. Don't you see, this decision is based on the fantasy of going back through time to—uh—injure your mother—"

"Midbin is a coarse, stupid, insensate lout. He has taught the dumb to speak, but he's too much of a fool to understand anyone of normal intelligence. He had a set of idiotic theories about diseased emotions and he fits all facts into them even if it means chopping them up to do it or inventing new ones to piece them out. 'Injure my mother' indeed! I have no more interest in her than she ever had in me."

"Ah, Barbara—"

" 'Ah, Barbara,' " she mimicked. "Run along to your pompous windbag of a Midbin, or your cow-eyed Spanish strumpet—"

"Barbara, I'm talking as a friend. Leave Midbin and Catty and personalities out of it and just look at it this way. Don't you see the difference between promulgating a theory and trying a practical demonstration which will certainly appear to the world as going over the borderline into charlatanism? Like a spiritualist medium or—"

"That's enough! 'Charlatan.' You unspeakable guttersnipe. What do you know about anything beyond the seduction of cretins? Go back to your trade, you errand boy!"

"Barbara—"

Her hand caught me across my mouth. Then she strode away.

THE FELLOWS OF HAGGERSHAVEN were not enthusiastic for her project. Nineteen fifty was a bad year; the war was coming closer. At the least, what was left of United States' independence would likely be extinguished. Our energies at the haven had to be directed toward survival rather than new and expensive ventures. Still, Barbara Haggerwells was a famous figure commanding great respect; reluctantly the fellows voted an appropriation.

We had not spoken since the day of the quarrel, nor was there inclination on either side toward reconciliation. She and Ace with a group of the fellows attacked the preliminary job of remodelling an old barn furiously, sawing and hammering, bolting iron beams together, piping in gas for reflected lights which allowed them to work into the night. As for me, I had little interest. I did not believe Barbara Haggerwells would play a further part in my life.

For I finally saw Catty as she really was: loyal, steadfast, sustaining. Suddenly, I was utterly unable to understand how I had hesitated so long. Barbara now seemed brittle and masculine beside Catty. It was Catty with whom I wanted to spend the rest of my life and I regretted wasted time.

Something of this I told her and begged forgiveness.

"Dear Hodge," she answered, "there is nothing to forgive. Love is not a business transaction, nor a case at law in which justice is sought, nor a reward for having good qualities. I understand you, Hodge, better, I think, than you understand yourself. You are not satisfied with what is readily obtained; otherwise you would have been content back in— what is the name?—Wappinger Falls. I have known this for a long time and I could, I think (you must excuse my feminine vanity), have enticed you at any moment by pretending fickleness. Besides, I think you will make a better husband for realizing your incapacity to deal with Barbara."

I can't say I enjoyed this speech. I felt, in fact, rather humiliated, or at least healthily humbled. Which was no doubt what she intended, and as it should be. It also revealed that Catty bore no animosity toward her former rival. This didn't surprise me, but Barbara's attitude did, for as soon as Catty's engagement to me was known the two girls became very friendly. I almost wrote, "became fast friends," but this would overlook their lack of common interests on which to build genuine friendship. However, Catty now spent hours with Barbara and Ace in the workshop (as they called the converted barn) and her real admiration for Barbara grew. Her conversation frequently turned to Barbara's genius, courage and imagination.

Naturally this didn't please me too well, but I could hardly ask Catty to forego society I had so recently found enchanting, nor establish a taboo against mention of a name I had lately whispered with ardor. Besides, I was exhilarated by my own plans. I had completed my notes for *Chancellorsville to the End*, and Catty and I were to be married as soon as volume one was published—shortly after my thirtieth and Catty's twenty-fourth birthday. Although there was no doubt the book would bring an offer from one of the great Confederate universities, Catty was firm for one of the miniature cottages or even smaller apartments the haven provided for married fellows.

From Catty's talk I knew Barbara was running into increasing difficulties now the workshop was complete and actual construction of what was referred to—with unnecessary crypticism, I thought—as HX-1 had begun. The impending war created scarcities, particularly of such materials as steel and copper, of which latter metal HX-1 seemed inordinately greedy. I was not surprised when the fellows apologetically refused Barbara a new appropriation.

The next day Catty said, "Hodge, you know the haven wouldn't take my money."

"And quite right too. Let the rest of us put in everything we get. We owe it to the haven anyway. But you should keep your independence."

"Hodge, I'm going to give it all to Barbara for her HX-1."

"What? Oh, nonsense!"

"Is it any more nonsensical for me to put in money I didn't do anything to get than for her and Ace to put in time and knowledge and labor?"

"Yes, because she's got a crazy idea and Ace has never been quite sane as far as Barbara's concerned. If you go ahead and do this you'll be crazy as they are."

When Catty laughed I remembered with a pang the long months when that lovely sound had been strangled by terror inside her so that these priceless instants were irrevocably lost. I also thought with shame of my own failure and contumely. Had I appreciated her when her need was greatest I might have changed the long and painful process which restored her voice in Midbin's way, or at least eased and quickened it.

"Perhaps I'm crazy—do you think they would admit me to fellowship on that basis? Anyway, I believe in Barbara, even if the fellows don't. Not that I'm criticizing the haven. You were right to be cautious, you have a great deal to consider. I haven't. I believe in her—or perhaps I feel I owe her something. Anyway, with my money she can finish her project. I only tell you this because you may not want to marry me under the circumstances."

"You think I'm marrying you for your money?"

She smiled. "Dear Hodge. You are in some ways so young. No, I know very well you aren't marrying me for money. That would be too practical, too grown up. I think you might not want to marry a woman who'd give all her money away. Especially to Barbara Haggerwells."

"Catty, are you doing this absurd thing to get rid of me? Or to test me?"

This time she again laughed aloud. "Now I'm sure you will marry me after all and turn out to be a puzzled but amenable husband. You are my true Hodge, who studies a war because he can't understand anything simpler or subtler."

She wasn't to be dissuaded from the quixotic gesture. I might not understand subtleties but I was sure I understood Barbara well enough. Foreseeing her request for more funds would be turned down, she had deliberately cultivated Catty in order to use her. Now she'd gotten what she wanted she'd undoubtedly drop Catty or revert to her accustomed virulent abuse.

She did neither. If anything, the amity grew. Catty's vocabulary added words like "magnet," "coil," "induction," "particle," "light-year," "continuum" and many others either incomprehensible or uninteresting to me. Breathlessly she described the strange, asymmetric structure taking shape in the workshop, while my mind was busy with Ewell's Corps and Parrott guns and the weather chart of southern Pennsylvania for July 1863.

The great publishing firm of Ticknor, Harcourt & Knopf contracted for my book—there was no publisher in the United States equipped to handle it—and sent me a sizable advance in Confederate dollars which became even more sizable converted into United States' money. I read the proofs of volume one in a state of semi-consciousness, sent the inevitable telegram changing a footnote on page 99, and waited for the infuriating mails to bring me my complimentary copies. The day after they arrived (with a horrifying typographical error right in the middle of page 12), Catty and I were married.

Perhaps reticence in this narrative has given less than a picture of my wife. I can only say that no man could ask for one more beautiful, finer or more desirable. With the approval of the fellows, I used part of the publisher's advance for a honeymoon. We spent it going over some of the battlefields of the War of Southron Independence.

We settled down in the autumn of 1951, I to work on volume two, Catty to help me and keep house. Somewhat, I admit, to my disappointment, she resumed her daily visit to Barbara's workshop and again regaled me with accounts of my ex-sweetheart's progress.

HX-1 was to be completed in the late spring or early summer. I was not surprised that Barbara's faith survived actual construction of the thing, but that such otherwise level-headed people as Ace and Catty could envisage breathlessly the miracles about to happen was beyond me. Ace, even after all these years, was still bemused—but Catty . . . ?

Just before the turn of the year I got the following letter:

LEE & WASHINGTON UNIVERSITY

Department of History
Leesburg, District of Calhounia, CSA.
December 19, 1951

Mr. Hodgins M. Backmaker
"Haggershaven"
York, Pennsylvania, USA.

Sir:

On page 407 of *Chancellorsville to the End*, volume I, *Turning Tides*, you write, "Chronology and topography—timing and the use of space—were to be the decisive factors, rather than population and industry. Stuart's detachment, which might have proved disastrous, turned out extraordinarily fortunate for Lee, as we shall see in the next volume. Of course the absence of cavalry might have been decisive if the Round Tops had not been occupied by the Southrons on July 1. . . ."

Now, sir, evidently in your forthcoming analysis of Gettysburg you hold (as I presume most Yankees do) to the theory of fortuitousness. We Southrons naturally ascribe the victory to the supreme genius of General Lee, regarding the factors of time and space not as forces in themselves but as opportunities for the display of his talents.

Needless to say, I hardly expect you to change your opinions, rooted as they must be in national pride. I only ask that before you commit them, and the conclusions shaped by them, to print that you satisfy yourself, *as an historian*, of their validity in this particular case. In other words, sir, as one of your readers (and may I add, one who has enjoyed your work), I should like to be assured that you have studied this classic battle as carefully as you have the engagements described in volume I.

> With earnest wishes for your success,
> I remain, sir, cordially yours,
>
> Jefferson Davis Polk

This letter from Dr. Polk, the foremost historian of our day, author of the monumental biography, *The Great Lee*, produced a crisis in my life. Had the Confederate professor pointed out flaws in my work, or even reproached me for undertaking it at all with inadequate equipment, I would, I trust, have acknowledged the reproof and continued to the best of my ability. But this letter was an accolade. Without condescension Dr. Polk admitted me to the ranks of serious historians and besought me as an equal to consider the depth of evaluation.

The truth is I was not without my own increasing doubts. Doubts I had not allowed to rise to the surface of my mind and disturb my plans. Polk's letter brought them into the open.

I had read everything available. I had been over the ground between the Maryland line, South Mountain, Carlisle and the haven so that I could draw a detail map from memory. I had turned up diaries, letters and accounts which had never been published. Yet, with all this, I was not sure I had the whole story, even in the sense of wholeness that historians, knowing they can never achieve a knowledge of every detail, accept. I was not sure that what I thought was the final and just estimate was really either one, or that I had the grand scene in perfectly proper perspective. I admitted to myself the possibility I had perhaps been too rash, too precipitate, in undertaking *Chancellorsville to the End*. I knew the shadowy sign—the one which says in effect, You are ready—had not been given. My confidence was shaken.

What could I do? The entire work was contracted for. The second volume was promised for delivery some eighteen months hence. My notes for it were complete; this was no question of revising, but of wholly re-examining, revaluing and probably discarding them for an entirely new start. It was a job so much bigger than the original, one so discouraging I felt I could not face it—and yet I knew it would be corrupt to produce a work lacking certain conviction.

Catty responded to my awkward recapitulation in a way at once heartening and strange. "Hodge," she said, "you're changing and developing—and for the better, even though I love you as you were. Don't be afraid to put the book aside for a year—ten years if necessary. You must do it to satisfy yourself; never mind what the publishers or the public say. But Hodge, you mustn't, in your anxiety, try any shortcuts. Promise me that."

"I don't know what you're talking about, Catty dear. There are no shortcuts in the writing of history."

She looked at me thoughtfully. "Remember that, Hodge. Oh, remember it well."

IX

I could not bring myself to follow the promptings of my conscience and Catty's advice, nor could I use my notes as though Dr. Polk's letter had never come to shatter my complacency. As a consequence I worked not at all, thus adding to my feelings of guilt and unworthiness. I wandered about the haven, fretful and irritable, interrupting more diligent fellows and generally making myself a nuisance. Inevitably I found my way into Barbara's workshop.

She and Ace had done a thorough job on the old barn. Iron beams held up a catwalk running in a circle about ten feet overhead. On the catwalk there were at intervals what appeared to be batteries of telescopes, all pointed inward and downward at the center of the floor. Just inside the columns was a continuous ring of clear glass, perhaps four inches in diameter, fastened to the beams with glass hooks. On closer inspection the ring proved not to be in one piece, but in sections, ingeniously held together with glass couplings. Back from this circle, around the walls, were various engines, all enclosed except for dial faces and regulators. From the roof was suspended a large, polished reflector.

There was no one in the barn and I wandered about, cautiously avoiding the various pieces of apparatus whose purpose and operation were completely mysterious to me. For a moment I meditated—meanly perhaps—that all this had been paid for by my wife's money. Then I berated myself. Catty owed all she had to the haven, as I did. True, the money might have been put to better use than this one of encouraging a senseless project, but there was no guarantee that it would have been more productive allotted to astronomy or zoology. During eight years at the haven I'd seen many promising schemes come to nothing.

"Like it, Hodge?"

Barbara had come up, unheard, behind me. This was the first time we had been alone together since our break, two years before.

"It looks like a tremendous amount of work," I evaded.

"It was a tremendous amount of work. This construction has been the least of it. Now it's done. Or has begun—depending how you look at it."

"All done?"

She nodded, her face triumphant. "First test today."

"Oh well . . . in that case—"

"Don't go, Hodge—please. I meant to ask you and Catty to the more formal trial, but now you're here for the preliminary I'm glad. Ace, Father and Midbin'll be along in a minute."

"Midbin?"

"I insisted. It'll be nice to show him the mind can produce something besides fantasies and hysterical hallucinations."

I began to speak, then swallowed the words. The dig at Catty was insignificant beside the supreme confidence, the abnormal assurance prompting the invitation to witness a test which could only reveal the impossibility of applying her cherished theories. I felt an overwhelming pity. "Surely," I said at last, seeking to make some preparation for the disillusionment that was bound to come, "surely you don't expect it to work the first time?"

"Why not? There are bound to be minor adjustments to be made, allowances for erratic chronology caused by phenomena like the pull of comets and so forth. It may be some time before Ace can set me down at the exact year, month, day, hour and minute agreed upon. But the fact of space-time-energy-matter correspondence can just as well be established this afternoon as next year."

She was unaccountably at ease for someone whose lifework was about to be weighed. I have shown more nervousness in discussing a disputed date with the honorary secretary of a local historical society.

"Sit down," she invited; "there's nothing to do or see till Ace comes. I've missed you, Hodge."

I felt this was a dangerous remark, and wished I'd stayed far away from the workshop. I hooked my leg over a stool—there were no chairs—and coughed to hide the fact I was afraid to answer, I've missed you too, and afraid not to.

"Tell me about your own work, Hodge. Catty says you're having difficulties."

I was annoyed with Catty, but whether for confiding in Barbara or specifically for revealing something unheroic, I didn't stop to consider. At any rate this annoyance probably diluted the feeling I was somehow disloyal in conversing with Barbara at all. Or it may be the old, long-established bond—I almost wrote, of sympathy, but it was so much more complex than the word indicates—was reawakened by proximity and put me in the mood to tell my troubles. It is even possible I had the altruistic purpose of fortifying Barbara against inevitable disappointment on a misery-loves-company basis. Be that as it may, I found myself pouring out the whole story.

She jumped up and put her hands on my shoulders. I would not be truthful if I said that, looking into her eyes, gray and warm, I did not feel some reciprocation. "Hodge! It's wonderful—don't you see?"

"Oh . . ." I was completely confused. "I . . . uh . . ."

"Look: now you can go back—back to the past in your own person and see everything with your own eyes, instead of relying on second- or third-hand accounts. You can verify every fact, study every move, every actor. You can write history as no one ever did before, for you'll be writing it as a witness, yet with the perspective of a different period. You'll be taking the mind of the present, with its judgment and its knowledge of the patterns, back to receive the impressions of the past. It almost seems HX-1 was devised especially for this."

There was no doubt she believed, that she was really and unselfishly glad her work could aid mine. I was overcome by pity, helpless to soften the blow of disillusionment to fall so soon, and filled with an irrational hatred of the great apparatus she had built and which was about to destroy her.

I was saved from having to mask my emotions by the arrival of her father, Ace and Midbin. Thomas Haggerwells began tensely, "Barbara, Ace says you intend to test this—this thing on yourself. Is that true?"

Midbin didn't wait for her answer. I thought, with something of a shock, Midbin has gotten old; I never noticed it. "Listen to me. There's no point now in saying part of your mind realizes the impossibility of this demonstration and that it's willing for you to annihilate yourself in the attempt and so escape from conflicts which have no resolution—"

Ace Dorn, who looked as strained as they, in contrast to Barbara's ease, growled, "Let's go."

She smiled reassuringly at us. "Please, Father, don't worry. And Oliver . . ."

Her smile was almost mischievous and very unlike the Barbara I had known. "Oliver, HX-1 owes more to you than you will ever know."

She ducked under the transparent ring and walked to the center of the floor, glancing up at the reflector, moving an inch or two to stand directly beneath it. "The controls are already adjusted to minus 52 years and 11 days," she informed us conversationally. "Purely arbitrary. One date is good as another, but January 1, 1900, is an almost automatic choice. I'll be gone 60 seconds. Ready, Ace?"

"Ready." Ace had been slowly circling the engines, checking the dials. He took his place before the largest, holding a watch in his hand. "Three forty-three and ten," he announced.

Barbara was consulting her own watch. "Three forty-three and ten," she confirmed. "Make it at three forty-three and twenty."

"OK. Good luck."

"You might at least try it on an animal first," burst out Midbin, as Ace twirled the valve under his hand. The transparent ring glowed, the metal reflector threw back a dazzling light. I blinked. When I opened my eyes the light was gone and the center of the workshop was empty.

No one moved. Ace frowned over his watch. I stared at the spot where Barbara had stood. I don't think my mind was working; I had the feeling my lungs and heart certainly were not. I was a true spectator, with all faculties save sight and hearing suspended.

". . . on an animal first." Midbin's voice was querulous.

"Oh, God!" muttered Thomas Haggerwells.

Ace said casually—too casually, "The return is automatic. Set before-hand for duration. Thirty more seconds."

Midbin said, "She is . . . this is . . ." He sat down on a stool and bent his head almost to his knees.

Mr. Haggerwells groaned, "Ace, Ace—you should have stopped her."

Still I couldn't think. Barbara had stood there; then she was gone. What . . . ? Midbin must be right; we had let her go to destruction. Certainly much more than a minute had passed now.

The ring glowed and the brilliant light was reflected. "It did, oh, it did!" Barbara cried. "It did!"

She came out of the circle and kissed Ace, who patted her gently on the back. I suddenly noticed the pain of holding my breath and released a tremendous sigh. Barbara kissed her father and Midbin—who was still shaking his head—and, after the faintest hesitation, me. Her lips were ice-cold.

The shock of triumph made her voluble. Striding up and down, she spoke with extraordinary rapidity.

When the light flashed, she too involuntarily closed her eyes. She had felt a strange, terrifying weightlessness, an awful disembodiment, for which she had been unprepared. She thought she had not been actually unconscious, even for an instant, though she had the impression of ceasing to exist as a unique collection of memories, and of being somehow dissolved. Then she had opened her eyes.

At first she was shocked to find the barn as it had been all her life, abandoned and dusty. Then she realized she had indeed moved through time; the disappearance of the engines and reflector showed she had gone back to the unremodelled workshop.

Now she saw the barn was not quite as she had known it, even in her childhood, for while it was unquestionably abandoned, it had evidently not long been so. The thick dust was not so thick as she remembered, the sagging cobwebs not so dense. Straw was still scattered on the floor; it had not yet been entirely carried away by mice or inquisitive nesting birds. Beside the door hung bits of harness beyond repair, some broken bridles, and a faded calendar on which the ink of the numerals 1897 still stood.

The minute she had allotted this first voyage seemed fantastically short and incredibly long. All the paradoxes she had always brushed aside as of no immediate concern now confronted her. Since she had gone back to a time before she was born, she must always have existed as a visitor prior to her own conception; she could presumably be present during her own childhood and growth, and by making a second and third visit, multiply herself as though in facing mirrors, so that an infinite number of Barbara Haggerwells could occupy a single segment of time.

A hundred other parallel speculations raced through her mind without interfering with her rapid and insatiable survey of the commonplace features of the barn, features which could never really be commonplace to her since they proved all her speculations so victoriously right.

Suddenly she shivered with the bitter cold and burst into teeth-chattering laughter. She had made such careful plans to visit the First of January—and had never thought to take along a warm coat.

She looked at her watch; only twenty seconds had passed. The temptation to defy her agreement with Ace not to step outside the tiny circle of HX-1's operating field on the initial experiment was almost irresistible. She longed to touch the fabric of the past, to feel the worn boards of the barn, to handle as well as look. Again her thoughts whirled with speculation; again the petty moment stretched and contracted. She spent eternity and instantaneity at once.

When the moment of return came, she again experienced the feeling of dissolution, followed immediately by the light. When she opened her eyes she was back.

Midbin, who could not deny Barbara's disappearance for a full minute while we all watched, nevertheless insisted she had suffered some kind of hallucination. He could offer no explanation of her vanishing before our eyes, but insisted that this and her alleged traveling in time were two separate phenomena. Her conviction she had been back to 1900 he attributed to her emotional eccentricity.

The logical answer to this obstinate skepticism was to invite him to see for himself. To Ace, of course, belonged the honor of the second journey; he elected to spend three minutes in 1885, returning to report he had found the barn well occupied by both cattle and fowl, and been scared stiff of discovery when dogs set up a furious barking. He brought back with him a new laid egg 67 years old. Or was it? Trips in time are confusing that way.

Barbara was upset—more than I thought warranted. "We daren't be anything but invisible spectators," she scolded. "The faintest indication of our presence, the slightest impingement on the past may change the whole course of events. We have no way of knowing what actions have no consequences—if there can be any. Goodness knows what your idiocy in removing the egg has done. It's absolutely essential not to betray our presence in any way. Remember this in the future."

The next day Midbin spent five minutes in 1820. The barn had not yet been built, and he found himself in a field of wild hay. The faint snick of scythes, and voices not too far off, indicated mowers. Midbin dropped to the ground. His view of the past was restricted to tall grass and some persistent ants who explored his face and hands until the time was up and he returned with broken spears of ripe hay clinging to his clothes.

I was reminded of Enfandin's, "Why should I believe my eyes?" by Midbin's reaction. He did not deny that a phenomenon had taken place, nor that his experience coincided with Barbara's theories. On the other hand he didn't admit he had actually been transported into the past. "The mind can do anything, anything at all. Create boils and cancers—why not ants and grass? I don't know—I don't know. . . ." And he added abruptly, "No one can help her now."

X

For the next two months Barbara and Ace explored HX-1's possibilities. They quickly learned its limited range which was, subject to slight variations, little more than a century. When they tried to operate beyond this range the translation simply didn't take place, though the same feeling of dissolution occurred. When the light faded they were still in the present. Midbin's venture into the hayfield had been a freak, possibly due to peculiar weather conditions at both ends of the journey. They had not known this at the time nor realized that by hazarding this marginal zone the traveler might be lost. They set 1850 as a safe limit.

Nor would HX-1 work in reverse; the future remained closed. Also they discovered that time spent in the past consumed an equal amount of time in the present; they could not return to a point a minute after departure when they had been gone for an hour. As near as I could understand Barbara this was because of the limitations of HX-1: duration was set in the present. In order to come back to a time-point not in correspondence with the period actually spent, another engine—or at least another set of controls—would have to be taken into the past.

Even then radical changes would have to be made since HX-1 didn't work for the future.

Within these limits (and another, more inconvenient one: that they couldn't visit the identical past moment twice; there was no possibility of meeting one's time-traveling self) they roamed almost at will. Ace spent a full week in October 1896, walking as far as Philadelphia, enjoying the enthusiasm and fury of the presidential campaign. Knowing President Bryan was not only going to be elected, but would serve three terms, he found it hard indeed to obey Barbara's stricture and not cover confident Whig bets on Major McKinley.

Though both sampled the war years they brought back nothing useful to me—no information or viewpoint I couldn't have got from any of a score of books. Lacking historians' training or interests, their tidbits were those of limited onlookers, not chroniclers.

I grew increasingly fretful. I held long colloquies with myself which invariably ended inconclusively. *Why not?* I asked myself. *Surely this is the unique opportunity. Never before has it been possible for an historian to check back at will, to go over an event as often as he might please, to write of the past with the detachment of the present and the accuracy of an eye-witness knowing specifically what to look for. Why don't you take advantage of HX-1 and see for yourself?*

Against this reasoning I objected—what? Fear? Uneasiness? The superstition that I was tampering with a taboo, with matters forbidden to human limitations? *"You mustn't try any shortcuts. Promise me that, Hodge."* Well, Catty was a darling. She was my beloved wife, but she was neither scholar nor oracle. Woman's intuition? A respectable phrase, but what did it mean? And didn't Barbara, who first suggested my using HX-1, have womanly intuition also?

A half-dozen times I started to speak to Catty. Each time I repressed the words. What was the use of upsetting her? *Promise me that, Hodge.* But I had not promised. This was something I had to settle for myself.

What was I afraid of? Because I'd never grasped anything to do with the physical sciences did I attribute some anthropomorphism to their manifestations and, like a savage, fear the spirit imprisoned in what I didn't understand? I had never thought of myself as hidebound, but I was acting like a 90-year-old professor asked to use a typewriter instead of a goose quill.

I recalled Tyss's, "You are the spectator type, Hodgins." And once I had called Tyss out of the depths of my memory I couldn't escape his familiar, sardonic, interminable argument. *Why are you fussing yourself, Hodgins? What is the point of all this introspective debate? Don't you know your choice has already been made? And that you have acted according to that decision an infinite number of times and will do so an infinite number of times again? Relax, Hodgins; you have nothing to worry about. Free-will is an illusion; you cannot alter what you are about to decide under the impression that you have decided.*

My reaction to this imagined interjection was frenzied, unreasonable. I cursed Tyss and his damnable philosophy. I cursed the insidiousness of his reasoning which had planted seed in my brain to sprout at a moment like this. Yet in spite of the violence of my rejection of the words I attributed to Tyss, I accepted one of them. I relaxed. The decision had been made. Not by mechanistic forces, not by blind response to stimulus, but by my own desire.

And now to my aid came the image of Tyss's antithesis, Rene Enfandin. *Be a skeptic, Hodge; be always the skeptic. Prove all things; hold fast to that which is true. Joking Pilate, asking,* What is truth? *was blind—but you can see more aspects of the absolute truth than any man has had a chance to see before. Can you use the chance well, Hodge?*

Once I had answered the imaginary question with a wholehearted affirmative and so buttressed my determination to go, I was faced with the problem of telling Catty. I told myself I could not bear the thought of her anxiety; that she would worry despite the fact others had frequently used HX-1. I was sure she would be sick with apprehension while I was gone. No doubt this was all true, but I also remembered her, *Promise me you won't take any shortcuts, Hodge. . . .*

I finally took the weak, the ineffective course. I said I'd decided the only way to face my problem was to spend four or five days going over the actual field of Gettysburg. Here, I explained, unconvincingly, I thought I might at last come to the conclusion whether to scrap all my work and start afresh, or not.

She pretended to believe me and begged me to take her along. After all, we had spent our honeymoon on battlefields. I pleaded that her presence would distract me; my thoughts would go out to her rather than the problem. Her look was tragic with understanding.

I dressed in clothes I often used for walking trips, clothes which bore no mark of any fashion and might pass as current wear among the poorer classes in any era of the past hundred years. I put a packet of dried beef in my pocket and started for the workshop.

As soon as I left the cottage I laughed at my hypersensitivity, at all the to-do I'd made over lying to Catty. This was but the first excursion; I planned many more. There was no reason why she shouldn't accompany me on them. I grew lighthearted as my conscience eased and I even congratulated myself on my skill in not having told a single technical falsehood to Catty. I began to whistle—never a habit of mine—as I made my way along the path to the workshop.

Barbara was alone. Her ginger hair gleamed in the light of a gas globe; her eyes were green as they were when she was exultant. "Well, Hodge?"

"Well, Barbara, I . . ."

"Have you told Catty?"

"Not exactly. How did you know?"

"I knew before you did, Hodge. All right. How long do you want to stay?"

"Four days."

"That's long for a first trip. Don't you think you'd better try a few sample minutes?"

"Why? I've seen you and Ace go often enough and heard your accounts. I'll take care of myself. Have you got it down fine enough yet so you can pick the hour of arrival?"

"Hour and minute," she answered confidently. "What'll it be?"

"About midnight of June 30, 1863," I answered. "I want to come back on the night of July Fourth."

"You'll have to be more exact than that. For the return, I mean. The dials are set on seconds."

"All right, make it midnight going and coming then."

"Have you a watch that keeps perfect time?"

"Well, I don't know about perfect—"

"Take this one. It's synchronized with the master control clock." She handed me a large, rather awkward timepiece, which had two independent faces side by side. "We had two made like this; the two dials were useful before we were able to control HX-1 so exactly. One shows 1952 Haggershaven time."

"Ten thirty-three and fourteen seconds," I said.

"Yes. The other will show 1863 time. You won't be able to reset the first dial—but for goodness sake remember to keep it wound—and set

the second for . . . 11:54, zero. That means in six minutes you'll leave—
to arrive at midnight. Remember to keep that one wound too, for you'll
go by that regardless of variations in local clocks. Whatever else happens, be in the center of the barn at midnight—allow yourself some
leeway—by midnight, July Fourth. I don't want to have to go wandering
around 1863 looking for you."

"You won't have to. I'll be here."

"Five minutes. Now then, food."

"I have some," I answered, slapping my pocket.

"Not enough. Take this concentrated chocolate along. I suppose it
won't hurt to drink the water if you're not observed, but avoid their food.
One never knows what chain might be begun by the casual theft (or
purchase, if you had an old enough coin) of a loaf of bread. The possibilities are limitless. Listen! How can I impress on you the importance
of doing nothing that could possibly change the future—our present?
I'm sure to this day Ace doesn't understand it, and I tremble every moment he spends in the past. The most trivial action may start a series of
disastrous consequences. Don't be seen, don't be heard. Make your trip
as a ghost."

"Barbara, I promise I'll neither assassinate General Lee nor give the
North the idea of a modern six-barreled cannon."

"Four minutes. It's not a joke, Hodge."

"Believe me," I said, "I understand."

She looked at me searchingly. Then she shook her head and began
making her round of the engines, adjusting the dials. I slid under the
glass ring as I'd so often seen her do and stood casually under the reflector. I was not in the least nervous. I don't think I was even particularly
excited.

"Three minutes," said Barbara.

I patted my breast pocket. Notebook, pencils. I nodded.

She ducked under the ring and came toward me. "Hodge . . ."

"Yes?"

She put her arms on my shoulders, leaning forward. I kissed her, a little absently. "Clod!"

I looked at her closely, but there were none of the familiar signs of
anger. "A minute to go, it says here," I told her.

She drew away and went back. "All set. Ready?"

"Ready," I answered cheerfully. "See you midnight, July Fourth,
1863."

"Right. Goodbye, Hodge. Glad you didn't tell Catty."

The expression on her face was the strangest I'd ever seen her wear. I could not, then or now, quite interpret it. Doubt, malice, suffering, vindictiveness, love were all there as her hand moved the switch. I began to answer something—perhaps to bid her wait—then the light made me blink and I too experienced the shattering feeling of transition. My bones seemed to fly from each other; every cell in my body exploded to the ends of space.

The instant of translation was so brief it is hard to believe all the multitude of impressions occurred simultaneously. I was sure my veins were drained of blood, my brain and eyeballs dropped into a bottomless void, my thoughts pressed to the finest powder and blown a universe away. Most of all, I knew the awful sensation of being, for that tiny fragment of time, not Hodgins McCormick Backmaker, but part of an *I* in which the I that was me merged all identity.

Then I opened my eyes. I was emotionally shaken; my knees and wrists were watery points of helplessness, but I was alive and functioning—with my individuality unimpaired. The light had vanished. I was in darkness save for faint moonlight coming through the cracks in the barn. The sweetish smell of cattle was in my nostrils, and the slow, ponderous stamp of hooves in my ears. I had gone back through time.

XI

The barking of the dogs was frenzied, filled with the hoarse note indicating they had been raising the alarm for long without being heeded. I knew they must have been barking at the alien smells of soldiers for the past day, so I was not apprehensive their scent of me would bring investigation. How Barbara and Ace had escaped detection on journeys which didn't coincide with abnormal events was beyond me; with such an unnerving racket in prospect I would either have given up the trips or moved the apparatus.

Strange, I reflected, that the cows and horses were undisturbed. That no hysterical chicken leaped from the roost in panic. Only the dogs scented my unnatural presence. Dogs, who are supposed to sense things beyond the perceptions of man.

Warily I picked my way past the livestock and out of the barn, fervently hoping the dogs were tied for I had no mind to start my adventure by being bitten. Barbara's warnings seemed inadequate indeed; one would think she or Ace would have devised some method of neutralizing the infernal barking.

Once out on the familiar Hanover road every petty feeling of doubt or distress fell away and all the latent excitement took hold of me. I was gloriously in 1863, half a day and some 30 miles from the battle of Gettysburg. If there is a paradise for historians I had achieved it without the annoyance of dying first. I swung along at a good pace, thankful I had trained myself for long tramps, so that 30 miles in less than ten hours was no monstrous feat. The noise of the dogs died away behind me and I breathed the night air joyfully.

I had already decided I dare not attempt to steal a ride on the railroad, even supposing the cars were going through. As I turned off the Hanover road and took the direct one to Gettysburg, I knew I would not be able to keep on it for long. Part of Early's Confederate division was marching along it from recently occupied York; Stuart's cavalry was all around; trifling skirmishes were being fought on or near it; Union troops, regulars as well as the militia called out by Governor Curtin for the emergency, were behind and ahead of me, marching for the Monocacy and Cemetery Ridge.

Leaving the highway would hardly slow me down, for I knew every sideroad, lane, path or shortcut, not only as they existed in my day, but as they had been in the time where I was now. I was going to need this knowledge even more on my return, for on the Fourth of July this road, like every other, would be glutted with beaten Northern troops—supplies and wounded left behind—frantically trying to reorganize as they were harassed by Stuart's cavalry and pressed by the victorious men of Hill, Longstreet, and Ewell. It was with this in mind I had allowed disproportionately longer for coming back.

I saw my first soldier a few miles farther on, a jagged shadow sitting by the roadside with his boots off, massaging his feet. I guessed him Northern from his kepi, but this was not conclusive, for many Southron regiments wore kepis also. I struck off quietly into the field and skirted around him. He never looked up.

At dawn I estimated I was halfway, and except for that single sight of a soldier I might have been taking a nocturnal stroll through a countryside at peace. I was tired but certainly not worn out, and I knew I could count on nervous energy and happy excitement to keep me going long after my muscles began to protest. Progress would be slower from now on—Confederate infantry must be just ahead—but even so, I should be at Gettysburg by six or seven.

The sudden drumming of hooves brushed me off the dusty pike and petrified me into rigidity as a troop dressed in gray and dirty tan galloped by screaming "Eeeeee-yeeee" exultantly. It would be the sideroads from now, I decided.*

But others had the same impulse; the sideroads were well populated. Although I knew the movement of every division and of many regiments, and even had some considerable idea of the civilian dislocation, the picture around me was confused and chaotic. Farmers, merchants, workers in overalls rode or tramped eastward; others, identical in dress and obvious intensity of effort, pushed westward. I passed carriages and carts with women and children traveling at various speeds both ways. Squads and companies of blue-clad troops marched along the roads or through the fields, trampling the crops, a confused sound of singing, swearing, or aimless talk hanging above them like a fog. Spaced by pacific intervals, men in gray or butternut, otherwise indistinguishable, marched in the same direction. I decided I could pass unnoticed in the milling crowds.

It is not easy for the historian, 10, 50, or 500 years away from an event, to put aside for a moment the large concepts of currents and forces, or the mechanical aids of statistics, charts, maps, neat plans and diagrams in which the migration of men, women and children is indicated by an arrow, or a brigade of half-terrified, half-heroic men becomes a neat little rectangle. It is not easy to see behind source material, to visualize state papers, reports, letters, diaries as written by men who spent most of their lives sleeping, eating, yawning, eliminating, squeezing blackheads, lusting, looking out of windows, or talking about nothing in general with no one in particular. We are too impressed with the pattern revealed to us—or which we think has been revealed to us—to remember that for the participants history is a haphazard affair, apparently aimless, produced by human beings whose concern is essentially with the trivial and irrelevent. The historian is always conscious of destiny. The participants rarely—or mistakenly.

So to be set down in the midst of crisis, to be at once involved and apart, is to experience a constant series of shocks against which there is no anesthetic. The soldiers, the stragglers, the refugees, the farm boys shouting at horses, the tophatted gentlemen cursing the teamsters, the teamsters cursing back; the looters, pimps, gamblers, whores, nurses and newspapermen were indisputably what they appeared: vitally important to themselves, of little interest to anyone else. Yet at the same time they were a paragraph, a page, a chapter, a whole series of volumes.

I'm sure I was faithful to the spirit if not the letter of Barbara's warnings, and that none of the hundreds whom I passed or who passed me noted my presence. I, on the other hand, had to repress the constant temptation to peer into every face for signs which could not tell me what fortune or misfortune the decision of the next three days would bring to it.

A few miles from town the crowded confusion became even worse, for the scouts from Ewell's Corps, guarding the Confederate left flank on the York Road, acted like a cork in a bottle. Because I, unlike the other travelers, knew this, I cut sharply south to get back on the circuitous Hanover road I had left shortly after midnight, and crossing the bridge over Rock Creek, stumbled into Gettysburg.

The two and a half storey brick houses with their purplish slate roofs were placid and charming in the hot July sun. A valiant rooster pecked at horsedung in the middle of the street, heedless of the swarming soldiers, any of whom might take a notion for roast chicken. Privates in the black hats of the Army of the Potomac, cavalrymen with wide yellow stripes and cannoneers with red ones on the seams of their pants, swaggered importantly. Lieutenants with hands resting gracefully on sword hilts, captains with arms thrust in unbuttoned tunics, colonels smoking cigars, generals on horseback, all moved back and forth across the street, out of and into houses and stores, each clearly intent on some business which would affect the course of the war. Soldiers spat, leered at an occasional woman, sat dolefully on handy stoops, or marched smartly toward an unknown destination. On the courthouse staff the flag hung doubtfully in the limp summer air. Every so often there was a noise like poorly organized thunder.

Imitating the adaptable infantrymen, I found an unoccupied stoop and sat down, after a curious glance at the house, wondering whether it contained someone whose letters or diaries I had read. Drawing out my packet of dried beef, I munched away without taking any of my attention from the sights and sounds and smells around me. Only I knew how desperately these soldiers would fight this afternoon and all day tomorrow. I alone knew how they would be caught in the inescapable trap on July Third and finally routed, to begin the last act of the war.

That major, I thought, so proud of his new-won golden oak leaves, may have an arm or leg shot off vainly defending Culp's Hill; that sergeant over there may lie faceless under an apple tree before nightfall.

Soon these men would be swept away from the illusory shelter of the houses and out onto the ridges where they would be pounded into defeat and rout. There was nothing for me now in Gettysburg itself— though I could have spent days absorbing the color and feeling. Already I had tempted fate by my casual appearance in the heart of town. At any moment someone might speak to me; an ill considered word or action of mine might change, with ever-widening consequences, the course of the future. I had been foolish enough and long enough; it was time for me to go to the vantage point I had decided upon and observe without peril of being observed.

I rose and stretched, my bones protesting. But a couple of miles more would see me clear of all danger of chance encounter with a too friendly or inquisitive soldier or civilian. I gave a last look, endeavoring to impress every detail on my memory, and turned south on the Emmitsburg Road.

This was no haphazard choice. I knew where and when the crucial, the decisive move upon which all the other moves depended would take place. While thousands of men were struggling and dying on other parts of the field, a Confederate advance force, unnoticed, disregarded, would occupy the position which would eventually dominate the field and win the battle—and the war—for the South. Heavy with knowledge no one else possessed I made my way toward a farm on which there was a field and a peach orchard.

A GREAT BATTLE in its first stages is as tentative, uncertain and indefinite as a courtship just begun. At the beginning the ground was there for either side to take without protest; the other felt no surge of possessive jealousy. I walked unscathed along the Emmitsburg Road; on my left I knew there were Union forces concealed, on my right the Southrons maneuvered. In a few hours, to walk between the lines would mean instant death, but now the declaration had not been made, the vows had not been finally exchanged. It was still possible for either party to withdraw; no furious heat bound the two indissolubly together. I heard the occasional shell and the whine of a minie bullet; mere flirtatious gestures so far.

Despite the hot sun the grass was cool and lush. The shade in the orchard was velvety. From a low branch I picked a near-ripe peach and sucked the wry juice. I sprawled on the ground and waited. For miles around, men from Maine and Wisconsin, from Georgia and North Carolina, assumed the same attitude. But I knew for what I was waiting; they could only guess.

Some acoustical freak dimmed the noises in the air to little more than amplification of the normal summer sounds. Did the ground really tremble faintly, or was I translating my mental picture of the marching armies, the great wagon trains, the heavy cannon, the iron-shod horses into an imagined physical effect? I don't think I dozed, but certainly my attention withdrew from the rows of trees with their runneled and scarred bark, curving branches and graceful leaves, so that I was taken unaware by the unmistakable clump and creak of mounted men.

The blue-uniformed cavalry rode slowly through the peach orchard. They seemed like a group of aimless hunters returning from the futile pursuit of a fox; they chatted, shouted at each other, walked their horses abstractedly. One or two had their sabres out; they cut at the branches overhead and alongside in pure, pointless mischief.

Behind them came the infantrymen, sweating and swearing, more serious. Some few had wounds, others were without their muskets. Their dark blue tunics were carelessly unbuttoned, their lighter pants were stained with mud and dust and grass. They trampled and thrashed around like men long tired out. Quarrels rose among them swiftly and swiftly petered out. No one could mistake them for anything but troops in retreat.

After they had passed, the orchard was still again, but the stillness had a different quality from that which had gone before. The leaves did not rustle, no birds chirped, there were no faint betrayals of the presence of chipmunks or squirrels. Only if one listened very closely was the dry noise of insects perceptible. But I heard the guns now. Clearly, and louder. And more continuously—much more continuously. It was not yet the roar of battle, but death was unmistakable in its low rumble.

Then the Confederates came. Cautiously, but not so cautiously that one could fail to recognize they represented a victorious, invading army. Shabby they certainly were, as they pushed into the orchard, but alert and confident. Only a minority had uniforms which resembled those prescribed by regulation and these were torn, stained and scuffed.

Many of the others wore the semi-official butternut—crudely dyed homespun, streaked and muddy brown. Some had ordinary clothes with military hats and buttons; a few were dressed in federal blue pants with gray or butternut jackets.

Nor were their weapons uniform. There were long rifles, short carbines, muskets of varying age, and I noticed one bearded soldier with a ponderous shotgun. But whatever their dress or arms, their bearing was the bearing of conquerors. If I alone on the field that day knew for sure the outcome of the battle, these Confederate soldiers were close behind in sensing the future.

The straggling Northerners had passed me by with the clouded perception of the retreating. These Southrons, however, were steadfastly attentive to every sight and sound. Too late I realized the difficulty of remaining unnoticed by such sharp, experienced eyes. Even as I berated myself for my stupidity, a great, whiskery fellow in what must once have been a stylish bottle-green coat pointed his gun at me.

"Yank here boys!" Then to me, "What you doing here, fella?"

Three or four came up and surrounded me curiously. "Funniest lookin' damyank I ever did see. Looks like he just fell out of a bathtub."

Since I had walked all night on dusty roads I could only think their standards of cleanliness were not high. And, indeed, this was confirmed by the smell coming from them: the stink of sweat, of clothes long slept in, of unwashed feet and stale tobacco.

"I'm a noncombatant," I said foolishly.

"Whazzat?" asked the beard. "Some kind of Baptist?"

"Let's see your boots, Yank. Mine's sure wore out."

What terrified me now was not the thought of my boots being stolen, or of being treated as a prisoner, or even the remote chance I might be shot as a spy. A greater, more indefinite catastrophe was threatened by my exposure. These men were the advance company of a regiment due to sweep through the orchard and the wheatfield, explore that bit of wild ground known as the Devil's Den and climb up Little Round Top closely followed by an entire Confederate brigade. This was the brigade which held the Round Tops for several hours until artillery was brought up—artillery which dominated the entire field and gave the South its victory at Gettysburg.

There was no allowance for a pause, no matter how trifling, in the peach orchard in any of the accounts I had ever read or heard of. The hazard Barbara had warned so insistently against had happened. I had been discovered, and the mere discovery had altered the course of history.

I tried to shrug it off. The delay of a few minutes could hardly make a significant difference. All historians agreed the capture of the Round Tops was an inevitability; the Confederates would have been foolish to overlook them—in fact, it was hardly possible they could, prominent as they were, both on maps and in physical reality—and they had occupied them hours before the Federals made a belated attempt to take them. I had been unbelievably stupid to expose myself, but I had created no repercussions likely to spread beyond the next few minutes.

"Said let's see them boots. Ain't got all day to wait."

A tall officer with a pointed imperial and a sandy, faintly reddish mustache whose curling ends shone waxily came up, revolver in hand. "What's going on here?"

"Just a Yank, Cap'n. Making a little change of footgear." The tone was surly, almost insolent.

The galloons on the officer's sleeve told me the title was not honorary. "I'm a civilian, Captain," I protested. "I realize I have no business here."

The captain looked at me coldly, with an expression of disdainful contempt. "Local man?" he asked.

"Not exactly. I'm from York."

"Too bad. Thought you could tell me about the Yanks up ahead. Jenks, leave the civilian gentleman in full possession of his boots." There was rage behind that sneer, a hateful anger apparently directed at me for being a civilian, at his men for their obvious lack of respect, at the battle, the world. I suddenly realized his face was intimately familiar. Irritatingly, because I could connect it with no name, place or circumstance.

"How long have you been in this orchard, Mister Civilian-From-York?"

The effort to identify him nagged me, working in the depths of my mind, obtruding even into that top layer which was concerned with what was going on.

What was going on? *Too bad. Thought you could tell me about the Yanks up ahead. How long have you been in this orchard?*

Yanks up ahead? There weren't any.

"I said, 'How long you been in this orchard?' "

Probably an officer later promoted to rank prominent enough to have his picture in one of the minor narratives. Yet I was certain his face was no likeness I'd seen once in a steel engraving and dismissed. These were features often encountered. . . .

"Sure like to have them boots. If we ain't fightin' for Yankee boots, what the hell we fightin' for?"

What could I say? That I'd been in the orchard for half an hour? The next question was bound to be, Had I seen Federal troops? Whichever way I answered I would be betraying my role of spectator.

"Hay Cap'n—this fella knows something. Lookit the silly grin!"

Was I smiling? In what? Terror? Perplexity? In the mere effort of keeping silent, so as to be involved no further?

"Tell yah—he's laughin' cuz he knows somethin'!"

Let them hang me, let them strip me of my boots; from here on I was dumb as dear Catty had been once.

"Out with it, man—you're in a tight spot. Are there Yanks up ahead?"

The confusion in my mind approached chaos. If I knew the captain's eventual rank I could place him. Colonel Soandso. Brigadier-General Blank. What had happened? Why had I let myself be discovered? Why had I spoken at all and made silence so hard now?

"Yanks up ahead—they's Yanks up ahead!"

"Quiet you! I asked him—he didn't say there were Yanks ahead."

"Hay! Damyanks up above. Goin' to mow us down!"

"Fella says the bluebellies are layin' fur us!"

Had the lie been in my mind, to be telepathically plucked by the excited soldier? Was even silence no refuge from participation?

"Man here spotted the whole Fed artillery up above, trained on us!"

"Pull back, boys! Pull back!"

I'd read often enough of the epidemic quality of a perfectly unreasonable notion. A misunderstood word, a baseless rumor, an impossible report, was often enough to set a group of armed men—squad or army— into senseless mob action. Sometimes the infection made for feats of heroism, sometimes for panic. This was certainly less than panic, but my nervous, meaningless smile conveyed a message I had never sent.

"It's a trap. Pull back, boys—let's get away from these trees and out where we can see the Yanks!"

The captain whirled on his men. "Here, damn you," he shouted furiously, "you all gone crazy? The man said nothing. There's no trap!"

The men moved slowly, sullenly away. "I heard him," one of them muttered, looking accusingly toward me.

The captain's shout became a yell. "Come back here! Back here, I say!"

His raging stride overtook the still irresolute men. He grabbed the one called Jenks by the shoulder and whirled him about. Jenks tried to jerk free. There was fear on his face, and hate. "Leave me go, damn you," he screamed. "Leave me go!"

The captain yelled at his men again. Jenks grabbed at the pistol with his left hand; the officer pulled the gun away. Jenks brought his musket upright against the captain's body, the muzzle just under his chin, and pushed—as though the firearm somehow gave him leverage. They wrestled briefly, then the musket went off.

The captain's hat flew upward, and for an instant he stood, bareheaded, in the private's embrace. Then he fell. Jenks wrenched his musket free and disappeared.

When I came out of my shock I walked over to the body. The face had been blown off. Shreds of human meat dribbled bloodily on the gray collar and soiled the fashionably long hair. I had killed a man. Through my interference with the past I had killed a man who had been destined to longer life and even some measure of fame. I was the guilty sorcerer's apprentice.

I stooped down to put my hands inside his coat for papers which would tell me who he was and satisfy the curiosity which still basely persisted. It was not shame which stopped me. Just nausea, and remorse.

I saw the Battle of Gettysburg. I saw it with all the unique advantages of a professional historian thoroughly conversant with the patterns, the movements, the details, who knows where to look for the coming dramatic moment, the recorded decisive stroke. I fulfilled the chronicler's dream.

It was a nightmare.

To begin with, I slept. I slept not far from the captain's body in the peach orchard. This was not callousness, but physical and emotional exhaustion. When I went to sleep the guns were thundering; when I woke they were thundering louder. It was late afternoon. I thought immediately, this is the time for the futile Union charge against the Round Tops.

But the guns were not sounding from there. All the roar was northward, from the town. I knew how the battle went; I had studied it for years. Only now it wasn't happening the way it was written down in the books.

True, the first day was a Confederate victory. But it was not the victory we knew. It was just a little different, just a little short of the triumph recorded. And on the second day, instead of the Confederates getting astride the Taneytown Road and into the position from which they tore Meade's army to bits from three sides, I witnessed a terrible encounter in the peach orchard and the wheatfield—places known to be safely behind the Southron lines.

All my life I'd heard of Pickett's charge on the third day. Of how the disorganized Federals were given the final killing blow in their vitals. Well, I saw Pickett's charge on the third day and it was not the same charge in the historic place. It was a futile attempt to storm superior positions (positions, by established fact, in Lee's hands since July First) ending in slaughter and defeat.

All because the North held the Round Tops.

I cannot tell you how I got back to York. If I walked, it was somnambulistically. Possibly I rode the railroad or in a farmer's cart. Part of my mind—a tiny part that kept coming back to pierce me no matter how often I crushed it out—remembered those who died, those who would have lived, but for me. Another part was concerned only with the longing to get back to my own time, to the haven, to Catty. A much larger part was simply blank, except for the awesome, incredible knowledge that the past could be changed—that the past *had* been changed.

I must have wound my watch—Barbara's watch—for it was 10 o'clock on the night of July Fourth when I got to the barn. Ten o'clock by 1863 time; the other dial showed it to be 8:40—that would be twenty of nine in the morning—1952 time. In two hours I would be home, safe from the nightmare of happenings that never happened, of guilt for the deaths of men not supposed to die, of the awful responsibility of playing destiny. If I could not persuade Barbara to smash her damnable contrivance I would do so myself.

The dogs barked furiously, but I was sure no one heeded. It was the Fourth of July, and a day of victory and rejoicing for all Pennsylvanians. I stole into the barn and settled myself in the exact center, even daring the use of a match—my last one—to be sure I'd be directly under the reflector when it materialized.

I could not sleep, though I longed to blot out the horror and wake in my own time. Detail by detail I went over what I had seen, superimposing it like a palimpsest upon the history I'd always known. Sleep would have kept me from this wretched compulsion and from questioning my sanity, but I could not sleep.

I have heard that in moments of overwhelming shock some irrelevancy, some inconsequential matter persistently forces itself on the attention. The criminal facing execution thinks, not of his imminent fate or of his crime, but of the cigarette stub he left burning in his cell. The bereaved widow dwells, not on her lost husband, but on tomorrow's laundry. So it was with me. Behind that part of my mind reliving the last three days, a more elementary part gnawed at the identification of the slain captain.

I knew that face. Particularly did I know that face set in a sneer, distorted with anger. But I could not remember it in Confederate uniform. I could not remember it with sandy mustaches. And yet the sandy hair, revealed in that terrible moment when his hat flew off, was as familiar as part of the face. Oh, I thought, if I could only place it once and for all and free my mind at least of this trivial thing.

I wished there were some way I could have seen the watch, to concentrate on the creeping progress of the hands and distract myself from the wave after wave of wretched meditations which flowed over me. But the moonlight was not strong enough to make the face distinguishable, much less the figures on the dials. There was no narcotic.

As one always is at such times I was convinced the appointed moment had passed unnoticed. Something had gone wrong. Over and over I had to tell myself that minutes seem hours in the waiting dark; it might feel like 2 or 3 in the morning to me; it was probably barely 11. No use. A minute—or an hour or a second—later I was again positive midnight had passed.

Finally I began to suffer a monstrous illusion. I began to think it was getting lighter. That dawn was coming. Of course, I knew it could not be; what I fancied lifting darkness was only a sick condition of swollen, overtired eyes. Dawn does not come to Pennsylvania at midnight, and it was not yet midnight. At midnight I would be back at Haggershaven, in 1952.

Even when the barn was fully lighted by the rising sun and I could see the cattle peaceful in their stalls I refused to believe what I saw. I took out my watch only to find that something had disturbed the works; the hands registered 5 o'clock. Even when the farmer, milk pails over arm, started in surprise, exclaiming, "Hay, what you doing here?"— even then, I did not believe.

Only when, as I opened my mouth to explain to my involuntary host, did something happen. The puzzle which had pursued me for three days suddenly solved itself. I knew why the face of the Southron captain had been so familiar. Familiar beyond any of the better-known warriors on either side. I had indeed known that face intimately; seen those features enraged or sneering. The nose, the mouth, the eyes, the expression were Barbara Haggerwells'. The man dead in the peach orchard was the man whose portrait hung in the library of Haggershaven, its founder, Herbert Haggerwells. Captain Haggerwells—never to become a major now, or buy this farm. Never to marry a local girl or beget Barbara's great grandfather. Haggershaven had ceased to exist in the future.

XII

I am writing this, as I said, in 1877. I am a healthy man of 45, no doubt with many years ahead of me. I might live to be 100, except for the illogical feeling I must die before 1921. However, 89 should be enough for anyone. So I have time to put my story down. Still, better to have it down and done with; should anything happen to me tomorrow it will be on paper.

For what? As confession and apology? As an inverted substitute for the merciful amnesia which ought to have erased my memory as well as my biography? (I have written to Wappinger Falls; there are no records of any Hodgins family, or of Backmakers. Does this mean that the forces I set in motion destroyed Private Hodgins as well as Captain Haggerwells? Or only that the Hodginses and Backmakers settled elsewhere? In either case I am like Adam—in this world—a special, parentless creation.) There is no one close enough to care, or intimate enough to accept my word in the face of all reason. I have not married in this time, nor shall I. I write only as old men talk to themselves.

The rest of my personal story is simple. The name of the farmer who found me in his barn was Thammis; they had need of a hired hand and I stayed on. I had no desire to go elsewhere. I have continued to stay; their son runs the place now. I shall stay till I die.

Catty. Haggershaven. Are they really gone, irrevocably lost, in a future which never existed, which couldn't exist, once the chain of causation was disturbed? Or do they exist, after all, in a universe in which the

South won the battle of Gettysburg and Major Haggerwells founded Haggershaven? Could another Barbara devise a means to reach that universe? I would give so much to believe this, but I cannot. I simply cannot.

Children know about such things. They close their eyes and pray, "Please God, make it didn't happen." Often they open their eyes to find it happened anyway, but this does not shake their faith that many times the prayer is granted. Adults smile, but can any of them be sure the memories they cherish were the same yesterday? Do they *know* that a past cannot be expunged? Children know it can. And once lost, that particular past can never be regained. Another and another, perhaps, but never the same one. There are no parallel universes—though this one may be sinuous and inconstant.

That this world is a better place than the one into which I was born, and promises to grow still better, seems true. What idealism lay behind the Southron cause triumphed in the reconciliation of men like Lee; what was brutal never got the upper hand as it did in my world. The Negro is free; black legislatures pass advanced laws in South Carolina; black congressmen comport themselves with dignity in Washington.

There are rumors of a deal between northern Republicans and southern Democrats, betraying the victory of the Civil War—how strange it is still, after fourteen years, to use this term instead of the familiar War of Southron Independence—in return for the presidency. If this is true, my brave new world is not so brave.

It may not be so new either. Prussia has beaten France and proclaimed a German Empire; is this the start in a different way of the German Union? Will 1914 see an Emperors' War leaving Germany facing—whom?

Any one of the inventions of my own time would make me a rich man if I could reproduce them—or cared for money. With mounting steel production and the pouring in of immigrants, what a success the minibile would be. Or the tinugraph. Or controllable balloons.

The typewriter I have seen. It has developed along slightly different lines; inevitably, I suppose, given initial divergence. It may mean greater advances; more likely not. The universal use of gaslight must be far in the future if it is to come at all; certainly its advent is delayed by all this talk of inventing electric illumination. If we couldn't put electricity to work it's unlikely my new contemporaries will be able to. Why, they haven't even made the telegraph cheap and convenient.

And something like HX-1? It is inconceivable. Could it be that in destroying the future in which Haggershaven existed, I have also destroyed the only dimension in which time travel was possible?

So strangely easily I can write the words, "I destroyed."

Catty.

But what of Tyss's philosophy? Is it possible I shall be condemned to repeat the destruction throughout eternity? Have I written these lines an infinite number of times before? Or is the mercy envisaged by Enfandin a reality? And what of Barbara's expression as she bade me goodbye? Could she possibly . . .

EDITORIAL NOTE by Frederick Winter Thammis: Quite recently, in the summer of 1953, to be exact, I commissioned the remodelling of my family home near York, Pennsylvania. Among the bundles of old books and papers stored in the attic was a box of personal effects, labelled "H. M. Backmaker." In it was the manuscript concluding with an unfinished sentence, reproduced above.

My father used to tell me that when he was a boy there was an old man living on the farm, nominally as a hired hand, but actually as a pensioner, since he was beyond the age of useful labor. My father said the children considered him not quite right in his mind, but very entertaining, for he often repeated long, disjointed narratives of an impossible world and an impossible society which they found as fascinating as the Oz books. On looking back, he said, Old Hodge talked like an educated man, but this might simply be the impression of young, unaccustomed minds.

Clearly it was in some attempt to give form and unity to his tales that the old man wrote his fable down, and then was too shy to submit it for publication. This is the only reasonable way to account for its existence. Of course he says he wrote it in 1877, when he was far from old, and disconcertingly, analysis of the paper shows it might have been written then.

Two other items should be noted. In the box of Backmaker's belongings there was a watch of unknown manufacture and unique design. Housed in a cheap nickel case, the jeweled movement is of extraordinary precision and delicacy. The face has two dials, independently set and wound.

The second is a quotation. It can be matched by similar quotations in any of half a hundred volumes on the Civil War. I pick this only because it is recent and handy. From W. E. Woodward's *Years of Madness*, p. 202: "... Union troops that night and next morning took a position on Cemetery Hill and Round Top ... The Confederates could have occupied this position but they failed to do so. It was an error with momentous consequences."

Poul Anderson

A multiple winner of the Hugo and Nebula Awards, Poul Anderson has written dozens of novels and hundreds of short stories since his science-fiction debut in 1947. His long-running Technic History saga, a multi-book chronicle of interstellar exploration and empire building, covers fifty centuries of future history and includes the acclaimed novels War of the Wing-Men, The Day of Their Return, *and* The Game of Empire. *Anderson has tackled many of science fiction's classic themes, including human evolution in* Brain Wave *(1954), near-light-speed space travel in* Tau Zero *(1970), and the time travel paradox in his series of Time Patrol stories collected as* Guardians of Time. *He is renowned for his interweaving of science fiction and mythology, notably in his alien-contact novel* The High Crusade. *He also has produced distinguished fantasy fiction, including the heroic sagas* Three Hearts and Three Lions *and* The Broken Sword, *and a novel detailing an alternate history of Earth according to Shakespeare,* A Midsummer Tempest. *He received the Tolkien Memorial Award in 1978. With his wife, Karen, he wrote the* King of Ys *Celtic fantasy quartet. With Gordon Dickson, he has authored the popular comic Hoka series. His short story "Call Me Joe" was chosen for inclusion in the Science Fiction Hall of Fame in 1974, and his short fiction has been collected in several volumes, notably* The Queen of Air and Darkness and Other Stories, All One Universe, *and* The Best of Poul Anderson.

EUTOPIA

Poul Anderson

"GIF THIT NAFN!"

The Danska words barked from the car radio as a jet whine cut across the hum of motor and tires. "Identify yourself!" Iason Philippou cast a look skyward through the bubbletop. He saw a strip of blue between two ragged green walls where pine forest lined the road. Sunlight struck off the flanks of the killer machine up there. It wailed, came about, and made a circle over him.

Sweat started cold from his armpits and ran down his ribs. *I must not panic*, he thought in a corner of his brain. *May the God help me now.* But it was his training he invoked. Psychosomatics: control the symptoms, keep the breath steady, command the pulse to slow, and the fear of death becomes something you can handle. He was young, and thus had much to lose. But the philosophers of Eutopia schooled well the children given into their care. You will be a man, they had told him, and the pride of humanity is that we are not bound by instinct and reflex; we are free because we can master ourselves.

He couldn't pass as an ordinary citizen (no, they said mootman here) of Norland. If nothing else, his Hellenic accent was too strong. But he might fool yonder pilot, for just a few minutes, into believing he was from some other domain of this history. He roughened his tone, as a partial disguise, and assumed the expected arrogance.

"Who are you? What do you want?"

"Runolf Einarsson, captain in the hird of Ottar Thorkelsson, the Lawman of Norland. I pursue one who has brought feud on his own head. Give me your name."

Runolf, Iason thought. *Why, yes, I remember you well, dark and erect with the Tyrker side of your heritage, but you have blue eyes that came long ago from Thule.* In that detached part of him which stood aside watching: *No, here I scramble my histories. I would call the autochthons Erythrai, and you call the country of your European ancestors Danarik.*

"I hight Xipec, a trader from Meyaco," he said. He did not slow down. The border was not many stadia away, so furiously had he driven through the night since he escaped from the Lawman's castle. He had small hope of getting that far, but each turn of the wheels brought him nearer. The forest was blurred with his speed.

"If so be, of course I am sorry to halt you," Runolf's voice crackled. "Call the Lawman and he will send swift gild for the overtreading of your rights. Yet I must have you stop and leave your car, so I may turn the farseer on your face."

"Why?" Another second or two gained.

"There was a visitor from Homeland"—Europe—"who came to Ernvik. Ottar Thorkellson guested him freely. In return, he did a thing that only his death can make clean again. Rather than meet Ottar on the Valfield, he stole a car, the same make as yours, and fled."

"Would it not serve to call him a nithing before the folk?" *I have learned this much of their barbaric customs, anyhow!*

"Now that is a strange thing for a Meyacan to say. Stop at once and get out, or I open fire."

Iason realized his teeth were clenched till they hurt. How in Hades could a man remember the hundreds of little regions, each with its own ways, into which the continent lay divided? Westfall was a more fantastic jumble than all Earth in that history where they called the place America. *Well,* he thought, *now we discover what the odds are of my hearing it named Eutopia again.*

"Very well," he said. "You leave me no choice. But I shall indeed want compensation for this insult."

He braked as slowly as he dared. The road was a hard black ribbon before him, slashed through an immensity of trees. He didn't know if these woods had ever been logged. Perhaps so, when white men first sailed through the Pentalimne (calling them the Five Seas) to found Ernvik where Duluth stood in America and Lykopolis in Eutopia. In those days Norland had spread mightily across the lake country. But then came wars with Dakotas and Magyars, to set a limit; and the development of trade—more recently of synthetics—enabled the people to use their hinterland for the hunting they so savagely loved. Three hundred years could re-establish a climax forest.

Sharply before him stood the vision of this area as he had known it at home: ordered groves and gardens, villages planned for beauty as well as use, lithe brown bodies on the athletic fields, music under moonlight . . . Even America the Dreadful was more human than a wilderness.

They were gone, lost in the multiple dimensions of space-time, he was alone and death walked the sky. *And no self-pity, you idiot! Spend energy for survival.*

The car stopped, hard by the road edge. Iason gathered his thews, opened the door, and sprang.

Perhaps the radio behind him uttered a curse. The jet slewed around and swooped like a hawk. Bullets sleeted at his heels.

Then he was in among the trees. They roofed him with sun-speckled shadow. Their trunks stood in massive masculine strength, their branches breathed fragrance a woman might envy. Fallen needles softened his foot-thud, a thrush warbled, a light wind cooled his cheeks. He threw himself beneath the shelter of one bole and lay in it gasping with a heartbeat which all but drowned the sinister whistle above.

Presently it went away. Runolf must have called back to his lord. Ottar would fly horses and hounds to this place, the only way of pursuit. But Iason had a few hours' grace.

After that— He rallied his training, sat up and thought. If Socrates, feeling the hemlock's chill, could speak wisdom to the young men of Athens, Iason Philippou could assess his own chances. For he wasn't dead yet.

He numbered his assets. A pistol of the local slug-throwing type; a compass; a pocketful of gold and silver coins; a cloak that might double as a blanket, above the tunic-trousers-boots costume of central Westfall. And himself, the ultimate instrument. His body was tall and broad— together with fair hair and short nose, an inheritance from Gallic ancestors—and had been trained by men who won wreaths at the Olympeion. His mind, his entire nervous system, counted for still more. The pedagogues of Eutopia had made logic, semantic consciousness, perspective as natural to him as breathing; his memory was under such control that he had no need of a map; despite one calamitous mistake, he knew he was trained to deal with the most outlandish manifestations of the human spirit.

And, yes, before all else, he had reason to live. It went beyond any blind wish to continue an identity; that was only something the DNA molecule had elaborated in order to make more DNA molecules. He had his beloved to return to. He had his country: Eutopia, the Good Land, which his people had founded two thousand years ago on a new continent, leaving behind the hatreds and horrors of Europe, taking along the work of Aristotle, and writing at last in their Syntagma, "The national purpose is the attainment of universal sanity."

Iason Philippou was bound home.

He rose and started walking south.

THAT WAS ON TETRADE, which his hunters called Onsdag. Some thirty-six hours later, he knew he was not in Pentade but near sunset of Thorsdag. For he lurched through the wood, mouth filled with mummy dust, belly a cavern of emptiness, knees shaking beneath him, flies a thundercloud about the sweat dried on his skin, and heard the distant belling of hounds.

A horn responded, long brazen snarl through the leaf arches. They had gotten his scent, he could not outrun horsemen and he would not see stars again.

One hand dropped to his gun. *I'll take a couple of them with me. . . .* No. He was still a Hellene, who did not kill uselessly, not even barbarians who meant to slay him because he had broken a taboo of theirs. *I will stand under an open sky, take their bullets, and go down into darkness remembering Eutopia and all my friends and Niki whom I love.*

Realization came, dimly, that he had left the pine forest and was in a second growth of beeches. Light gilded their leaves and caressed the slim white trunks. And what was that growl up ahead?

He stopped. A portal might remain. He had driven himself near collapse; but the organism has a reserve which the fully integrated man may call upon. From consciousness he abolished the sound of dogs, every ache and exhaustion. He drew breath after breath of air, noting its calm and purity, visualizing the oxygen atoms that poured through his starved tissues. He made the heartbeat quit racketing, go over to a deep slow pulse; he tensed and relaxed muscles until each functioned smoothly again; pain ceased to feed on itself and died away; despair gave place to calm and calculation. He trod forth.

Plowlands rolled southward before him, their young grain vivid in the light that slanted gold from the west. Not far off stood a cluster of farm buildings, long, low, and peak-roofed. Chimney smoke stained heaven. But his eyes went first to the man closer by. The fellow was cultivating with a tractor. Though the dielectric motor had been invented in this world, its use had not yet spread this far north, and gasoline fumes caught at Iason's nostrils. He had thought that stench one of the worst abominations in America—that hogpen they called Los Angeles!—but now it came to him clean and strong, for it was his hope.

The driver saw him, halted, and unshipped a rifle. Iason approached with palms held forward in token of peace. The driver relaxed. He was a typical Magyar: burly, high in the cheekbones, his beard braided, his tunic colorfully embroidered. *So I did cross the border!* Iason exulted. *I'm out of Norland and into the Voivodate of Dakoty.*

Before they sent him here, the anthropologists of the Parachronic Research Institute had of course given him an electrochemical inculcation in the principal languages of Westfall. (Pity they hadn't been more thorough about teaching him the mores. But then, he had been hastily recruited for the Norland post after Megasthenes' accidental death; and it was assumed that his experience in America gave him special qualifications for this history, which was also non-Alexandrine; and, to be sure, the whole object of missions like his was to learn just how societies on the different Earths did vary.) He formed the Ural-Altaic words with ease:

"Greeting to you. I come as a supplicant."

The farmer sat quiet, tense, looking down on him and listening to the dogs far off in the forest. His rifle stayed ready. "Are you an outlaw?" he asked.

"Not in this realm, freeman." (Still another name and concept for "citizen"!) "I was a peaceful trader from Homeland, visiting Lawman Ottar Thorkelsson in Ernvik. His anger fell upon me, so great that he broke sacred hospitality and sought the life of me, his guest. Now his hunters are on my trail. You hear them yonder."

"Norlanders? But this is Dakoty."

Iason nodded. He let his teeth show, in the grime and stubble of his face. "Right. They've entered your country without so much as a by-your-leave. If you stand idle, they'll ride onto your freehold and slay me, who asks your help."

The farmer hefted his gun. "How do I know you speak truth?"

"Take me to the Voivode," Iason said. "Thus you keep both the law and your honor." Very carefully, he unholstered his pistol and offered it butt foremost. "I am forever your debtor."

Doubt, fear and anger pursued each other across the face of the man of the tractor. He did not take the weapon. Iason waited. *If I've read him correctly, I've gained some hours of life. Perhaps more. That will depend on the Voivode. My whole chance lies in using their own barbarism—their division into petty states, their crazy idea of honor, their fetish of property and privacy—to harness them.*

If I fail, then I shall die like a civilized man. That they cannot take away from me.

"The hounds have winded you. They'll be here before we can escape," said the Magyar uneasily.

Relief made Iason dizzy. He fought down the reaction and said: "We can take care of them for a time. Let me have some gasoline."

"Ah . . . thus!" The other man chuckled and jumped to earth. "Good thinking, stranger. And thanks, by the way. Life has been dull hereabouts for too many years."

He had a spare can of fuel on his machine. They lugged it back along Iason's trail for a considerable distance, dousing soil and trees. If that didn't throw the pack off, nothing would.

"Now, hurry!" The Magyar led the way at a trot.

His farmstead was built around an open courtyard. Sweet scents of hay and livestock came from the barns. Several children ran forth to gape. The wife shooed them back inside, took her husband's rifle, and mounted guard at the door with small change of expression.

Their house was solid, roomy, aesthetically pleasing if you could accept the unrestrained tapestries and painted pillars. Above the fireplace was a niche for a family altar. Though most people in Westfall had left myth long behind them, these peasants still seemed to adore the Triple God Odin-Attila-Manitou. But the man went to a sophisticated radiophone. "I don't have an aircraft myself," he said, "but I can get one."

Iason sat down to wait. A girl neared him shyly with a beaker of beer and a slab of cheese on coarse dark bread. "Be you guest-holy," she said.

"May my blood be yours," Iason answered by rote. He managed to take the refreshment not quite like a wolf.

The farmer came back. "A few more minutes," he said. "I am Arpad, son of Kalman."

"Iason Philippou." It seemed wrong to give a false name. The hand he clasped was hard and warm.

"What made you fall afoul of old Ottar?" Arpad inquired.

"I was lured," Iason said bitterly. "Seeing how free the unwed women were—"

"Ah, indeed. They're a lickerish lot, those Danskar. Nigh as shameless as Tyrkers." Arpad got pipe and tobacco pouch off a shelf. "Smoke?"

"No, thank you." *We don't degrade ourselves with drugs in Eutopia.*

The hounds drew close. Their chant broke into confused yelps. Horns shrilled. Arpad stuffed his pipe as coolly as if this were a show. "How they must be swearing!" he grinned. "I'll give the Danskar credit for being poets, also in their oaths. And brave men, to be sure. I was up that way ten years back, when Voivode Bela sent people to help them after the floods they'd suffered. I saw them laugh as they fought the wild water. And then, their sort gave us a hard time in the old wars."

"Do you think there will ever be wars again?" Iason asked. Mostly he wanted to avoid speaking further of his troubles. He wasn't sure how his host might react.

"Not in Westfall. Too much work to do. If young blood isn't cooled enough by a duel now and then, why, there're wars to hire out for, among the barbarians overseas. Or else the planets. My oldest boy champs to go there."

Iason recalled that several realms further south were pooling their resources for astronautical work. Being approximately at the technological level of the American history, and not required to maintain huge military or social programs, they had put a base on the moon and sent expeditions to Ares. In time, he supposed, they would do what the Hellenes had done a thousand years ago, and make Aphrodite into a new Earth. But would they have a true civilization—be rational men in a rationally planned society—by then? Wearily, he doubted it.

A roar outside brought Arpad to his feet. "There's your wagon," he said. "Best you go. Red Horse will fly you to Varady."

"The Danskar will surely come here soon," Iason worried.

"Let them," Arpad shrugged. "I'll alert the neighborhood, and they're not so stupid that they won't know I have. We'll hold a slanging match, and then I'll order them off my land. Farewell, guest."

"I . . . I wish I could repay your kindness."

"Bah! Was fun. Also, a chance to be a man before my sons."

Iason went out. The aircraft was a helicopter—they hadn't discovered gravitics here—piloted by a taciturn young autochthon. He explained that he was a stock-breeder, and that he was conveying the stranger less as a favor to Arpad than as an answer to the Norlander impudence of entering Dakoty unbidden. Iason was just as happy to be free of conversation.

The machine whirred aloft. As it drove south he saw clustered hamlets, the occasional hall of some magnate, otherwise only rich undulant plains. They kept the population within bounds in Westfall as in

Eutopia. But not because they knew that men need space and clean air, Iason thought. No, they acted from greed on behalf of the reified family. A father did not wish to divide his possessions among many children.

The sun went down and a nearly full moon climbed huge and pumpkin-colored over the eastern rim of the world. Iason sat back, feeling the engine's throb in his bones, almost savoring his fatigue, and watched. No sign of the lunar base was visible. He must return home before he could see the moon glitter with cities.

And home was more than infinitely remote. He could travel to the farthest of those stars which had begun twinkling forth against purple dusk—were it possible to exceed the speed of light—and not find Eutopia. It lay sundered from him by dimensions and destiny. Nothing but the warpfields of a parachronion might take him across the time lines to his own.

He wondered about the why. That was an empty speculation, but his tired brain found relief in childishness. Why had the God willed that time branch and rebranch, enormous, shadowy, bearing universes like the Yggdrasil of Danskar legend? Was it so that man could realize every potentiality there was in him?

Surely not. So many of them were utter horror.

Suppose Alexander the Conqueror had not recovered from the fever that smote him in Babylon. Suppose, instead of being chastened thereby, so that he spent the rest of a long life making firm the foundations of his empire—suppose he had died?

Well, it *did* happen, and probably in more histories than not. There the empire went down in mad-dog wars of succession. Hellas and the Orient broke apart. Nascent science withered away into metaphysics, eventually outright mysticism. A convulsed Mediterranean world was swept up piecemeal by the Romans: cold, cruel, uncreative, claiming to be the heirs of Hellas even as they destroyed Corinth. A heretical Jewish prophet founded a mystery cult which took root everywhere, for men despaired of this life. And that cult knew not the name of tolerance. Its priests denied all but one of the manifold ways in which the God is seen; they cut down the holy groves, took from the house its humble idols, and martyred the last men whose souls were free.

Oh yes, Iason thought, *in time they lost their grip. Science could be born, almost two millennia later than ours. But the poison remained: the idea that men must conform not only in behavior but in belief. Now, in America, they call it totalitarianism. And because of it, the nuclear rockets have had their nightmare hatching.*

I hated that history, its filth, its waste, its ugliness, its restriction, its hypocrisy, its insanity. I will never have a harder task than when I pretended to be an American that I might see from within how they thought they were ordering their lives. But tonight . . . I pity you, poor raped world. I do not know whether to wish you soon dead, as you likeliest will be, or hope that one day your descendants can struggle to what we achieved an age ago.

They were luckier here. I must admit that. Christendom fell before the onslaught of Arab, Viking and Magyar. Afterward the Islamic Empire killed itself in civil wars and the barbarians of Europe could go their own way. When they crossed the Atlantic, a thousand years back, they had not the power to commit genocide on the natives; they must come to terms. They had not the industry, then, to gut the hemisphere; perforce they grew into the land slowly, taking it as a man takes his bride.

But those vast dark forests, mournful plains, unpeopled deserts and mountains where the wild goats run . . . those entered their souls. They will always, inwardly, be savages.

He sighed, settled down, and made himself sleep. Niki haunted his dreams.

Where a waterfall marked the head of navigation on that great river known variously as the Zeus, Mississippi and Longflood, a basically agricultural people who had not developed air transport as far as in Eutopia were sure to build a city. Trade and military power brought with them government, art, science and education. Varady housed a hundred thousand or so—they didn't take censuses in Westfall—whose inward-turning homes surrounded the castle towers of the Voivode. Waking, Iason walked out on his balcony and heard the traffic rumble. Beyond roofs lay the defensive outworks. He wondered if a peace founded on the balance of power between statelets could endure.

But the morning was too cool and bright for such musings. He was here, safe, cleansed and rested. There had been little talk when he arrived. Seeing the condition of the fugitive who sought him, Bela Zsolt's son had given him dinner and sent him to bed.

Soon we'll confer, Iason understood, *and I'll have to be most careful if I'm to live.* But the health which had been restored to him glowed so strong that he felt no need to suppress worry.

A bell chimed within. He re-entered the room, which was spacious and airy however overornamented. Recalling that custom disapproved of nudity, he threw on a robe, not without wincing at its zigzag pattern. "Be welcome," he called in Magyar.

The door opened and a young woman wheeled in his breakfast. "Good luck to you, guest," she said with an accent; she was a Tyrker, and even wore the beaded and fringed dress of her people. "Did you sleep well?"

"Like Coyote after a prank," he laughed.

She smiled back, pleased at his reference, and set a table. She joined him too. Guests did not eat alone. He found venison a rather strong dish this early in the day, but the coffee was delicious and the girl chattered charmingly. She was employed as a maid, she told him, and saving her money for a marriage portion when she returned to Cherokee land.

"Will the Voivode see me?" Iason asked after they had finished.

"He awaits your pleasure." Her lashes fluttered. "But we have no haste." She began to untie her belt.

Hospitality so lavish must be the result of customal superimposition, the easygoing Danskar and still freer Tyrker mores influencing the austere Magyars. Iason felt almost as if he were now home, in a world where individuals found delight in each other as they saw fit. He was tempted, too—that broad smooth brow reminded him of Niki. But no. He had little time. Unless he established his position unbreakably firm before Ottar thought to call Bela, he was trapped.

He leaned across the table and patted one small hand. "I thank you, lovely," he said, "but I am under vow."

She took the answer as naturally as she had posed the question. This world, which had the means to unify, chose as if deliberately to remain in shards of separate culture. Something of his alienation came back to him as he watched her sway out the door. For he had only glimpsed a small liberty. Life in Westfall remained a labyrinth of tradition, manner, law and taboo.

Which had well-nigh cost him his life, he reflected; and might yet. Best hurry!

He tumbled into the clothes laid out for him and made his way down long stone halls. Another servant directed him to the Voivode's seat. Several people waited outside to have complaints heard or disputes adjudicated. But when he announced himself, Iason was passed through immediately.

The room beyond was the most ancient part of the building. Age-cracked timber columns, grotesquely carved with gods and heroes, upheld a low roof. A fire pit in the floor curled smoke toward a hole; enough stayed behind for Iason's eyes to sting. They could easily have given their chief magistrate a modern office, he thought—but no, because his ancestors had judged in this kennel, so must he.

Light filtering through slit windows touched the craggy features of Bela and lost itself in shadow. The Voivode was thickset and gray-haired; his features bespoke a considerable admixture of Tyrker chromosomes. He sat a wooden throne, his body wrapped in a blanket, horns and feathers on his head. His left hand bore a horse-tailed staff and a drawn saber was laid across his lap.

"Greeting, Iason Philippou," he said gravely. He gestured at a stool. "Be seated."

"I thank my lord." The Eutopian remembered how his own people had outgrown titles.

"Are you prepared to speak truth?"

"Yes."

"Good." Abruptly the figure relaxed, crossed legs and extracted a cigar from beneath the blanket. "Smoke? No? Well, I will." A smile meshed the leathery face in wrinkles. "You being a foreigner, I needn't keep up this damned ceremony."

Iason tried to reply in kind. "That's a relief. We haven't much in the Peloponnesian Republic."

"Your home country, eh? I hear things aren't going so well there."

"No. Homeland grows old. We look to Westfall for our tomorrows."

"You said last night that you came to Norland as a trader."

"To negotiate a commercial agreement." Iason was staying as near his cover story as possible. You couldn't tell different histories that the Hellenes had invented the parachronion. Besides changing the very conditions that were being studied, it would be too cruel to let men know that other men lived in perfection. "My country is interested in buying lumber and furs."

"Hm. So Ottar invited you to stay with him. I can grasp why. We don't see many Homelanders. But one day was after your blood. What happened?"

Iason might have claimed privacy, but that wouldn't have sat well. And an outright lie was dangerous; before this throne, one was automatically under oath. "To a degree, no doubt, the fault was mine," he said. "One of his family, almost grown, was attracted to me and—I had been long away from my wife, and everyone had told me the Danskar hold with freedom before marriage, and—well, I meant no harm. I merely encouraged—but Ottar found out, and challenged me."

"Why did you not meet him?"

No use to say that a civilized man did not engage in violence when any alternative existed. "Consider, my lord," Iason said. "If I lost, I'd be dead. If I won, that would be the end of my company's project. The Ottarssons would never have taken weregild, would they? No, at the bare least they'd ban us all from their land. And Peloponnesus needs that timber. I thought I'd do best to escape. Later my associates could disown me before Norland."

"M-m . . . strange reasoning. But you're loyal, anyhow. What do you ask of me?"

"Only safe conduct to—Steinvik." Iason almost said "Neathenai." He checked his eagerness. "We have a factor there, and a ship."

Bela streamed smoke from his mouth and scowled at the glowing cigar end. "I'd like to know why Ottar grew wrathful. Doesn't sound like him. Though I suppose, when a man's daughter is involved, he doesn't feel so lenient." He hunched forward. "For me," he said harshly, "the important thing is that armed Norlanders crossed my border without asking."

"A grievous violation of your rights, true."

Bela uttered a horseman's obscenity. "You don't understand, you. Borders aren't sacred because Attila wills it, whatever the shamans prate. They're sacred because that's the only way to keep the peace. If I don't openly resent this crossing, and punish Ottar for it, some hothead might well someday be tempted; and now everyone has nuclear weapons."

"I don't want war on my account!" Iason exclaimed, appalled. "Send me back to him first!"

"Oh no, no such nonsense. Ottar's punishment shall be that I deny him his revenge, regardless of the rights and wrongs of your case. He'll swallow that."

Bela rose. He put his cigar in an ashtray, lifted the saber, and all at once he was transfigured. A heathen god might have spoken: "Henceforward, Iason Philippou, you are peace-holy in Dakoty. While you remain beneath our shield, ill done you is ill done me, my house and my people. So help me the Three!"

Self-command broke down. Iason went on his knees and gasped his thanks.

"Enough," Bela grunted. "Let's arrange for your transportation as fast as may be. I'll send you by air, with a military squadron. But of course I'll need permission from the realms you'll cross. That will take time. Go back, relax, I'll have you called when everything's ready."

Iason left, still shivering.

He spent a pleasant couple of hours adrift in the castle and its court-yards. The young men of Bela's retinue were eager to show off before a Homelander. He had to grant the picturesqueness of their riding, wres-tling, shooting and riddling contests; something stirred in him as he lis-tened to tales of faring over the plains and into the forests and by river to Unnborg's fabled metropolis; the chant of a bard awakened glories which went deeper than the history told, down to the instincts of man the killer ape.

But these are precisely the bright temptations that we have turned our backs on in Eutopia. For we deny that we are apes. We are men who can reason. In that lies our manhood.

I am going home. I am going home. I am going home.

A servant tapped his arm. "The Voivode wants you." It was a fright-ened voice.

Iason hastened back. What had gone wrong? He was not taken to the room of the high seat. Instead, Bela awaited him on a parapet. Two men-at-arms stood at attention behind, faces blank under the plumed helmets.

The day and the breeze were mocked by Bela's look. He spat on Iason's feet. "Ottar has called me," he said.

"I— Did he say—"

"And I thought you were only trying to bed a girl. Not seeking to de-stroy the house that befriended you!"

"My lord—"

"Have no fears. You sucked my oath out of me. Now I must spend years trying to make amends to Ottar for cheating him."

"But—" *Calm! Calm! You might have expected this.*

"You will not ride in a warcraft. You'll have your escort, yes. But the machine that carries you must be burned afterward. Now go wait by the stables, next to the dung heap, till we're ready."

"I meant no harm," Iason protested. "I did not know."

"Take him away before I kill him," Bela ordered.

Steinvik was old. These narrow cobbled streets, these gaunt houses, had seen dragon ships. But the same wind blew off the Atlantic, salt and fresh, to drive from Iason the last hurt of that sullenness which had rid-den here with him. He pushed whistling through the crowds.

A man of Westfall, or America, would have slunk back. Had he not failed? Must he not be replaced by someone whose cover story bore no hint of Hellas? But they saw with clear eyes in Eutopia. His failure was due to an honest mistake: a mistake he would not have made had they taught him more carefully before sending him out. One learns by error.

The memory of people in Ernvik and Varady—gusty, generous people whose friendship he would have liked to keep—had nagged him awhile. But he put that aside too. There were other worlds, an endlessness of them.

A signboard creaked in the wind. The Brotherhood of Hunyadi and Ivar, Shipfolk. Good camouflage, that, in a town where every second enterprise was bent seaward. He ran to the second floor. The stairs clattered under his boots.

He spread his palm before a chart on the wall. A hidden scanner identified his finger-patterns and a hidden door opened. The room beyond was wainscoted in local fashion. But its clean proportions spoke of home; and a Nike statuette spread wings on a shelf.

Nike . . . Niki . . . I'm coming back to you! The heart leaped in him.

DAIMONAX ARISTIDES LOOKED up from his desk. Iason sometimes wondered if anything could rock the calm of that man. "Rejoice!" the deep voice boomed. "What brings you here?"

"Bad news, I'm afraid."

"So? Your attitude suggests the matter isn't catastrophic." Daimonax's big frame left his chair, went to the wine cabinet, filled a pair of chaste and beautiful goblets, and relaxed on a couch. "Come, tell me."

Iason joined him. "Unknowingly," he said, "I violated what appears to be a prime taboo. I was lucky to get away alive."

"Eh." Daimonax stroked his iron-gray beard. "Not the first such turn, or the last. We fumble our way toward knowledge, but reality will always surprise us. . . . Well, congratulations on your whole skin. I'd have hated to mourn you."

Solemnly, they poured a libation before they drank. The rational man recognizes his own need for ceremony; and why not draw it from otherwise outgrown myth? Besides, the floor was stainproof.

"Do you feel ready to report?" Daimonax asked.

"Yes, I ordered the data in my head on the way here."

Daimonax switched on a recorder, spoke a few cataloguing words and said, "Proceed."

Iason flattered himself that his statement was well arranged: clear, frank and full. But as he spoke, against his will experience came back to him, not in the brain but in the guts. He saw waves sparkle on that greatest of the Pentalimne; he walked the halls of Ernvik castle with eager and wondering young Leif; he faced an Ottar become beast; he stole from the keep and overpowered a guard and by-passed the controls of a car with shaking fingers; he fled down an empty road and stumbled through an empty forest; Bela spat and his triumph was suddenly ashen. At the end, he could not refrain:

"Why wasn't I informed? I'd have taken care. But they said this was a free and healthy folk, before marriage anyway. How could I know?"

"An oversight," Daimonax agreed. "But we haven't been in this business so long that we don't still tend to take too much for granted."

"Why are we here? What have we to learn from these barbarians? With infinity to explore, why are we wasting ourselves on the second most ghastly world we've found?"

Daimonax turned off the recorder. For a time there was silence between the men. Wheels trundled outside, laughter and a snatch of song drifted through the window, the ocean blazed under a low sun.

"You do not know?" Daimonax asked at last, softly.

"Well . . . scientific interest, of course—" Iason swallowed. "I'm sorry. The Institute works for sound reasons. In the American history we're observing ways that man can go wrong. I suppose here also."

Daimonax shook his head. "No."

"What?"

"We are learning something far too precious to give up," Daimonax said. "The lesson is humbling, but our smug Eutopia will be the better for some humility. You weren't aware of it, because to date we haven't sufficient hard facts to publish any conclusions. And then, you are new in the profession, and your first assignment was elsewhen. But you see, we have excellent reason to believe that Westfall is also the Good Land."

"Impossible," Iason whispered.

Daimonax smiled and took a sip of wine. "Think," he said. "What does man require? First, the biological necessities, food, shelter, medicine, sex, a healthful and reasonably safe environment in which to raise his children. Second, the special human need to strive, learn, create. Well, don't they have these things here?"

"One could say the same for any Stone Age tribe. You can't equate contentment with happiness."

"Of course not. And if anything, is not ordered, unified, planned

Eutopia the country of the cows? We have ended every conflict, to the very conflict of man with his own soul; we have mastered the planets; the stars are too distant; were the God not so good as to make possible the parachronion, what would be left for us?"

"Do you mean—" Iason groped after words. He reminded himself that it was not sane to take umbrage at any mere statement, however outrageous. "Without fighting, clannishness, superstition, ritual and taboo . . . man has nothing?"

"More or less that. Society must have structure and meaning. But nature does not dictate what structure or what meaning. Our rationalism is a non-rational choice. Our leashing of the purely animal within us is simply another taboo. We may love as we please, but not hate as we please. So are we more free than men in Westfall?"

"But surely some cultures are better than others!"

"I do not deny that," Daimonax said; "I only point out that each has its price. For what we enjoy at home, we pay dearly. We do not allow ourselves a single unthinking, merely felt impulse. By excluding danger and hardship, by eliminating distinctions between men, we leave no hopes of victory. Worst, perhaps, is this: that we have become pure individuals. We belong to no one. Our sole obligation is negative, not to compel any other individual. The state—an engineered organization, a faceless undemanding mechanism—takes care of each need and each hurt. Where is loyalty unto death? Where is the intimacy of an entire shared lifetime? We play at ceremonies, but because we know they are arbitrary gestures, what is their value? Because we have made our world one, where are color and contrast, where is pride in being peculiarly ourselves?

"Now these Westfall people, with all their faults, do know who they are, what they are, what they belong to and what belongs to them. Tradition is not buried in books but is part of life; and so their dead remain with them in loving memory. Their problems are real; hence their successes are real. They believe in their rites. The family, the kingdom, the race is something to live and die for. They use their brains less, perhaps—though even that I am not certain of—but they use nerves, glands, muscles more. So they know an aspect of being human which our careful world has denied itself.

"If they have kept this while creating science and machine technology, should we not try to learn from them?"

Iason had no answer.

Eventually Daimonax said he might as well return to Eutopia. After a vacation, he could be reassigned to some history he might find more congenial. They parted in friendly wise.

The parachronion hummed. Energies pulsed between the universes. The gate opened and Iason stepped through.

He entered a glazed colonnade. White Neathenai swept in grace and serenity down to the water. The man who received him was a philosopher. Decent tunic and sandals hung ready to be donned. From somewhere resounded a lyre.

Joy trembled in Iason. Leif Ottarsson fell out of memory. He had only been tempted in his loneliness by a chance resemblance to his beloved. Now he was home. And Niki waited for him, Nikias Demostheneou, most beautiful and enchanting of boys.

AFTERWORD

Readers ought to know that writers are not responsible for the opinions and behavior of their characters. But many people don't. In consequence, I, for instance, have been called a fascist to my face. Doubtless the present story will get me accused of worse. And I only wanted to spin a yarn!

Well, perhaps a bit more. That can't be helped. Everybody views the world from his particular philosophical platform. Hence any writer who tries to report what he sees is, inevitably, propagandizing. But as a rule the propaganda lies below the surface. This is twice true of science fiction, which begins by transmuting reality to frank unreality.

So what have I been advocating here? Not any particular form of society. On the contrary, humankind seems to me so splendidly and ironically variable that there can be no perfect social order. I do suspect that few people are biologically adapted to civilization; consider its repeated collapses. This idea could be wrong, of course. Even if true, it may just be another factor which our planning should take into account. But the mutability of man is hardly open to question.

Thus each arrangement he makes will have its flaws, which in the end bring it to ruin; but each will also have its virtues. I myself don't think here-and-now is such a bad place to live. But others might. In fact, others do. At the same time, we cannot deny that *some* ways of life are, on balance, evil. The worst and most dangerous are those which cannot tolerate anything different from themselves.

So in an age of conflict we need a clear understanding of our own values—and the enemy's. Likewise we have to see with equal clarity the drawbacks of both cultures. This is less a moral than a strategic imperative. Only on such a basis can we know what we ought to do and what is possible for us to do.

For we are not caught in a meaningless nightmare. We are inhabiting a real world where events have understandable causes and causes have effects. We were never given any sacred mission, and it would be fatal to believe otherwise. We do, though, have the right of self-preservation. Let us know what it is we want to preserve. Then common sense and old-fashioned guts will probably get us through.

This is rather a heavy sermon to load on a story which was, after all, meant as entertainment. The point was made far better by Robinson Jeffers:

"Long live freedom and damn the ideologies."

William Sanders

William Sanders's *first novel,* Journey to Fusang, *was published in 1988, and garnered acclaim for its irreverent portrait of an alternate world in which the Western Hemisphere was settled by Asians and Arabs. His second novel,* The Wild Blue and the Gray, *proposed with equal imagination a triumphant Confederate States of America coming to the aid of the French and British in World War I. As Will Sundown, he has written the military science-fiction novel* Pockets of Resistance *and its sequel* The Hellbound Train. *His short fiction, which has appeared in* Asimov's, Tomorrow, *and the anthologies* Alternate Generals *and* Wheel of Fortune, *has three times been selected for inclusion in* The Year's Best Science Fiction. *He won the 1998 Sidewise Award for alternate history. In addition to many nonfiction books, he is the author of* Blood Autumn, *a murder mystery set in Oklahoma featuring writer-detective Taggart Roper.*

THE UNDISCOVERED

William Sanders

SO THE WHITE MEN are back! And trying once again to build themselves a town, without so much as asking anyone's permission. I wonder how long they will stay this time. It sounds as if these have no more sense than the ones who came before.

They certainly pick the strangest places to settle. Last time it was that island, where anyone could have told them the weather is bad and the land is no good for corn. Now they have invaded Powhatan's country, and from what you say, they seem to have angered him already. Of course that has never been hard to do.

Oh, yes, we hear about these matters up in the hills. Not many of us actually visit the coastal country—I don't suppose there are ten people in this town, counting myself, who have even seen the sea—but you know how these stories travel. We have heard all about your neighbor Powhatan, and you eastern people are welcome to him. Was there ever a chief so hungry for power? Not in my memory, and I have lived a long time.

But we were speaking of the white men. As you say, they are a strange people indeed. For all their amazing weapons and other possessions, they seem to be ignorant of the simplest things. I think a half-grown boy would know more about how to survive. Or how to behave toward other people in their own country.

And yet they are not the fools they appear. Not all of them, at least. The only one I ever knew was a remarkably wise man in many ways.

Do not make that gesture at me. I tell you that there was a white man who lived right here in our town, for more than ten winters, and I came to know him well.

*   *   *

I REMEMBER THE DAY they brought him in. I was sitting in front of my house, working on a fish spear, when I heard the shouting from the direction of the town gate. Bigkiller and his party, I guessed, returning from their raid on the Tuscaroras. People were running toward the gate, pouring out of the houses, everyone eager for a look.

I stayed where I was. I could tell by the sound that the raid had been successful—no women were screaming, so none of our people had been killed or seriously hurt—and I didn't feel like spending the rest of the day listening to Bigkiller bragging about his latest exploits.

But a young boy came up and said, "They need you, Uncle. Prisoners."

So I put my spear aside and got up and followed him, wondering once again why no one around this place could be bothered to learn to speak Tuscarora. After all, it is not so different from our tongue, not nearly as hard as Catawba or Maskogi or Shawano. Or your own language, which as you see I still speak poorly.

The captives were standing just inside the gate, guarded by a couple of Bigkiller's brothers, who were holding war clubs and looking fierce, as well as pleased with themselves. There was a big crowd of people by now and I had to push my way through before I could see the prisoners. There were a couple of scared-looking Tuscarora women—one young and pretty, the other almost my age and ugly as an alligator—and a small boy with his fist stuck in his mouth. Not much, I thought, to show for all this noise and fuss.

Then I saw the white man.

Do you know, it didn't occur to me at first that that was what he was. After all, white men were very rare creatures in those days, even more so than now. Hardly anyone had actually seen one, and quite a few people refused to believe they existed at all.

Besides, he wasn't really white—not the kind of fish-belly white that I'd always imagined, when people talked about white men—at least where it showed. His face was a strange reddish color, like a boiled crawfish, with little bits of skin peeling from his nose. His arms and legs, where they stuck out from under the single buckskin garment he wore, were so dirty and covered with bruises that it was hard to tell what color the skin was. Of course that was true of all of the captives; Bigkiller and his warriors had not been gentle.

His hair was dark brown rather than black, which I thought was unusual for a Tuscarora, though you do see Leni Lenapes and a few Shawanos with lighter hair. It was pretty thin above his forehead, and the scalp beneath showed through, a nasty bright pink. I looked at that and at the red peeling skin of his face, and thought: well done, Bigkiller, you've brought home a sick man. Some lowland skin disease, and what a job it's going to be purifying everything after he dies. . . .

That was when he turned and looked at me with those blue eyes. Yes, blue. I don't blame you; I didn't believe that story either, until I saw for myself. The white men have eyes the color of a sunny sky. I tell you, it is a weird thing to see when you're not ready for it.

Bigkiller came through the crowd, looking at me and laughing. "Look what we caught, Uncle," he said, and pointed with his spear. "A white man!"

"I knew that," I said, a little crossly. I hated it when he called me "Uncle." I hated it when anyone did it, except children—I was not yet *that* old—but I hated it worse when it came from Bigkiller. Even if he was my nephew.

"He was with the Tuscaroras," one of the warriors, Muskrat by name, told me. "These two women had him carrying firewood—"

"Never mind that." Bigkiller gave Muskrat a bad look. No need to tell the whole town that this brave raid deep into Tuscarora country had amounted to nothing more than the ambush and kidnapping of a small wood-gathering party.

To me Bigkiller said, "Well, Uncle, you're the one who knows all tongues. Can you talk with this white-skin?"

I stepped closer and studied the stranger, who looked back at me with those impossible eyes. He seemed unafraid, but who could read expressions on such an unnatural face?

"Who are you and where do you come from?" I asked in Tuscarora.

He smiled and shook his head, not speaking. The woman beside him, the older one, spoke up suddenly. "He doesn't know our language," she said. "Only a few words, and then you have to talk slow and loud, and kick him a little."

"Nobody in our town could talk with him," the younger woman added. "Our chief speaks a little of your language, and one family has a Catawba slave, and he couldn't understand them either."

By now the crowd was getting noisy, everyone pushing and jostling, trying to get a look at the white man. Everyone was talking, too, saying the silliest things. Old Otter, the elder medicine man, wanted to cut the white man to see what color his blood was. An old woman asked Musk-rat to strip him naked and find out if he was white all over, though I guessed she was really more interested in learning what his male parts looked like.

The young Tuscarora woman said, "Are they going to kill him?"

"I don't know," I told her. "Maybe."

"They shouldn't," she said. "He's a good slave. He's a hard worker, and he can really sing and dance."

I translated this, and to my surprise Muskrat said, "It is true that he is stronger than he looks. He put up a good fight, with no weapon but a stick of firewood. Why do you think I'm holding this club left-handed?" He held up his right arm, which was swollen and dark below the elbow. "He almost broke my arm."

"He did show spirit," Bigkiller agreed. "He could have run away, but he stayed and fought to protect the women. That was well done for a slave."

I looked at the white man again. He didn't look all that impressive, being no more than medium size and pretty thin, but I could see there were real muscles under that strange skin.

"He can do tricks, too," the young Tuscarora woman added. "He walks on his hands, and—"

The older woman grunted loudly. "He's bad luck, that's what he is. We've had nothing but trouble since he came. Look at us now."

I passed all this along to Bigkiller. "I don't know," he said. "I was go-ing to kill him, but maybe I should keep him as a slave. After all, what other chief among the People has a white slave?"

A woman's voice said, "What's going on here?"

I didn't turn around. I didn't have to. There was no one in our town who would not have known that voice. Suddenly everyone got very quiet.

My sister Tsigeyu came through the crowd, everyone moving quickly out of her way, and stopped in front of the white man. She looked him up and down and he looked back at her, still smiling, as if pleased to meet her. That showed real courage. Naturally he had no way of know-ing that she was the Clan Mother of the Wolf Clan—which, if you don't know, means she was by far the most powerful person in our town—but just the sight of her would have made most people uneasy. Tsigeyu was a big woman, not fat but big like a big man, with a face like a limestone cliff. And eyes that went right through you and made your bones go cold. She died a couple of years ago, but at the time I am telling about she was still in the prime of life, and such gray hairs as she had she wore like eagle feathers.

She said, "For me? Why, thank you, Bigkiller."

Bigkiller opened his mouth and shut it. Tsigeyu was the only living creature he feared. He had more reason than most, since she was his mother.

Muskrat muttered something about having the right to kill the prisoner for having injured him.

Tsigeyu looked at Muskrat. Muskrat got a few fingers shorter, or that was how it looked. But after a moment she said, "It is true you are the nearest thing to a wounded warrior among this brave little war party." She gestured at the young Tuscarora woman. "So I think you should get to keep this girl, here."

Muskrat looked a good deal happier.

"The rest of you can decide among yourselves who gets the other woman, and the boy." Tsigeyu turned to me. "My brother, I want you to take charge of this white man for now. Try to teach him to speak properly. You can do it if anyone can."

KNOWE ALL ENGLISH AND OTHER CHRISTIAN MEN:

That I an Englishman and Subjeckt of Her Maiestie Queene *Elizabeth*, did by Misadventure come to this country of *Virginnia* in the Yeere of Our Lord 1591: and after great Hardshipp arriued amongst these *Indians*. Who haue done me no Harme, but rather shewed me most exelent Kindnesse, sans the which I were like to haue dyed in this Wildernesse. Wherefore, good Frend, I coniure you, that you offer these poore Sauages no Offence, nor do them Iniurie: but rather vse them generously and iustly, as they haue me.

Look at this. Did you ever see the like? He made these marks himself on this deerskin, using a sharpened turkey feather and some black paint that he cooked up from burned wood and oak galls. And he told me to keep it safe, and that if other white men came this way I should show it to them, and it would tell them his story.

Yes, I suppose it must be like a wampum belt, in a way. Or those little pictures and secret marks that the wise elders of the Leni Lenapes use to record their tribe's history. So clearly he was some sort of *didahnuwisgi*, a medicine man, even though he did not look old enough to have received such an important teaching.

He was always making these little marks, scratching away on whatever he could get—skins, mostly, or mulberry bark. People thought he was crazy, and I let them, because if they had known the truth not even Tsigeyu could have saved him from being killed for a witch.

But all that came later, during the winter, after he had begun to learn our language and I his. On that first day I was only interested in getting him away from that crowd before there was more trouble. I could see that Otter was working himself up to make one of his speeches, and if nothing else that meant there was a danger of being talked to death.

Inside my house I gave the stranger a gourd of water. When he had eased his thirst I pointed to myself. "Mouse," I said, very slowly and carefully. "*Tsis-de-tsi.*"

He was quick. "*Tsisdetsi,*" he repeated. He got the tones wrong, but it was close enough for a beginning.

I held my hands up under my chin like paws, and pulled my upper lip back to show my front teeth, and crossed my eyes. I waggled one hand behind me to represent a long tail. "*Tsisdetsi,*" I said again.

He laughed out loud. "*Tsisdetsi,*" he said. "*Mus!*"

He raised his hand and stroked his face for a moment, as if thinking of something. Then without warning he turned and grabbed my best war spear off the wall. My bowels went loose, but he made no move to attack me. Instead he began shaking the weapon above his head with one hand, slapping himself on the chest with the other. "*Tsagspa,*" he cried. "*Tsagspa.*"

Crazy as a dog on a hot day, I thought at first. They must have hit him too hard. Then I realized what was happening, and felt almost dizzy. It is no small honor when any man tells you his secret war name—but a stranger, and a prisoner!

"*Digatsisdi atelvhusgo'i,*" I said, when I could finally speak. "Shakes Spear!"

I am him that was call'd William *Shakspere*, of *Stratford-upon-Auon*, late of *London*: a Player, of Lord *Strange* his Company, and thereby hangs a Tale.

Look there, where I am pointing. That is his name! He showed me that, and he even offered to teach me how to make the marks for my own. Naturally I refused—think what an enemy could do with something like that!

When I pointed this out, he laughed and said I might be right. For, he said, many a man of his sort had had bad luck with other people making use of his name.

It hapt that our Company was in *Portsmouth*, hauing beene there engaug'd: but then were forbid to play, the Mayor and Corporation of that towne being of the *Puritann* perswasion. For which cause we were left altogether bankrupt: so that some of our Players did pawne their Cloathing for monny to return Home.

Perhaps someone had cursed him, since he sometimes said that he had never meant to leave his own country. It was the fault of the Puritans, he said. He did not explain what this meant, but once he mentioned that his wife and her family were Puritans. So obviously this is simply the name of his wife's clan. Poor fellow, no wonder he left home. The same thing happened to an uncle of mine. When your wife's clan decides to get rid of you, you don't have a chance.

But I, being made foolish by strong Drinke, did conceive to hyde my selfe on a Ship bownd for *London*. Which did seeme a good Idea at the Time: but when I enquyr'd of some sea-faring men, they shewed me (in rogue Jest, or else mayhap I misconstrew'd their Reply, for I was in sooth most outragiosly drunk) the *Moonlight*, which lay at the Docke. And so by night I stole aboord, and hid my selfe vnder a Boate: wherevpon the Wine did rush to my heade, and I fell asleepe, and wak'd not till the Morrow: to finde the Ship at sea and vnder Sayle, and the morning Sun at her backe.

Naturally it was a long time before we could understand each other well enough to discuss such things. Not as long as you might think, though. To begin with, I discovered that in fact he had picked up quite a bit of Tuscarora—pretending, like any smart captive, to understand less than he did. Besides that, he was a fast learner. You know that languages are my special medicine—I have heard them say that Mouse can talk to a stone, and get it to talk back—but Spearshaker was gifted too. By the time of the first snow, we could get along fairly well, in a mixture of his language and mine. And when words failed, he could express almost any idea, even tell a story, just by the movements of his hands and body and the expression of his face. That in itself was worth seeing.

> When I was discouer'd the Master was most wroth, and commanded that I be put to the hardest Labours, and giuen onely the poorest leauings for food. So it went hard for me on that Voyage: but the Saylors learn'd that I could sing diuers Songs, and new Ballads from *London*, and then I was vsed better. Anon the Captaine, Mr. Edward *Spicer*, ask'd whether I had any skill in Armes. To which I reply'd, that a Player must needs be a Master of Fence, and of all other Artes martiall, forasmuch as we are wont to play Battles, Duelles, Murthers &c. And the Captaine said, that soone I should haue Opportunity to proue my selfe against true Aduersaries and not in play, for we sayl'd for the *Spanish Maine*.

All this time, you understand, there was a great deal of talk concerning the white man. Most of the people came to like him, for he was a friendly fellow and a willing worker. And the Tuscarora girl was certainly right about his singing and dancing. Even Bigkiller had to laugh when Spearshaker went leaping and capering around the fire, and when he walked on his hands and clapped his feet together several women wet themselves—or so I heard.

His songs were strange to the ear, but enjoyable. I remember one we all liked:

> "Wid-a-he
> An-a-ho
> An-a-he-na-ni-no!"

But not everyone was happy about his presence among us. Many of the young men were angry that the women liked him so well, and now and then took him aside to prove it. And old Otter told everyone who would listen that once, long ago, a great band of white men had come up from the south, from the Timucua country, and destroyed the finest towns of the Maskogis, taking many away for slaves and killing the others. And this was true, because when the People moved south they found much of that country empty and ruined.

Spearshaker said that those people were of another tribe, with which his own nation was at war. But not everyone believed him, and Otter kept insisting that white men were simply too dangerous to have around. I began to fear for Spearshaker's life.

At length we came vnto the *Indies*, being there joyn'd by the *Hopewell* and other Ships whose names I knowe not. And we at-tack'd the Spanish Convoy, and took the Galleon *Buen Jesus*, a rich Pryze: and so it came to pass that Will Shakspeare, Actor, did for his greate folly turn Pyrat vpon the salt Sea.

Then, early next spring, the Catawbas came.

This was no mere raid. They came in force and they hit us fast and hard, killing or capturing many of the people working in the fields be-fore they could reach the town palisade. They rushed out of the woods and swarmed over the palisade like ants, and before we knew it we were fighting for our lives in front of our own houses.

That was when Spearshaker astonished us all. Without hesitating, he grabbed a long pole from the meat-drying racks and went after the near-est Catawba with it, jabbing him hard in the guts with the end, exactly as you would use a spear, and then clubbing him over the head. Then he picked up the Catawba's bow and began shooting.

My friend, I have lived long and seen much, but I never was more surprised than that morning. This pale, helpless creature, who could not chip an arrowhead or build a proper fire or even take five steps off a trail without getting lost—he cut those Catawbas down like rotten corn-stalks! He shot one man off the palisade, right over there, from clear down by the council house. I do not think he wasted a single shot. And when he was out of arrows, he picked up a war club from a fallen war-rior and joined the rest of us in fighting off the remaining attackers.

Afterward, he seemed not to think he had done anything remarkable. He said that all the men of his land know stick-fighting and archery, which they learn as boys. "I could have done better," he said, "with a long bow, and some proper arrows, from my own country." And he looked sad, as he always did when he spoke of his home.

From that day there was no more talk against Spearshaker. Not long after, Tsigeyu announced that she was adopting him. Since this also made him Bigkiller's brother, he was safe from anyone in our town. It also made me his uncle, but he was kind enough never to call me *edutsi*. We were friends.

Next we turn'd north for *Virginnia*, Capt. *Spicer* hauing a Commission from Sir Walter *Ralegh* to calle vpon the English that dwelt at *Roanoke*, to discouer their condition. The Gales were cruel all along that Coast, and we were oft in grave Peril: but after much trauail we reached *Hatarask*, where the Captaine sent a party in small Boates, to search out the passage betweene the Islands. And whilst we were thus employ'd, a sudden great Wind arose and scattered the Boates, many being o'erturned and the Mariners drowned. But the Boate I was in was carry'd many Leagues westward, beyond sight of our Fellowes: so we were cast vpon the Shore of the Maine, and sought shelter in the Mouthe of a Riuer. Anon, going ashore, we were attack'd by Sauages: and all the men were slaine, save onely my selfe.

Poor fellow, he was still a long way from home, and small chance of ever seeing his own people again. At least he was better off than he had been with the Tuscaroras. Let alone those people on the coast, if they had caught him. Remember the whites who tried to build a town on that island north of Wococon, and how Powhatan had them all killed?

Yet hauing alone escap'd, and making my way for some dayes along the Riuer, I was surprized by *Indians* of another Nation: who did giue me hard vsage, as a Slaue, for well-nigh a Yeere. Vntil I was taken from them by these mine present sauage Hostes: amongst which, for my Sinnes, I am like to liue out my mortall dayes.

I used to have a big pile of these talking skins of his. Not that I ever expected to have a chance to show them to anyone who could understand them—I can't believe the white men will ever come up into the hill country; they seem to have all they can do just to survive on the coast—but I kept them to remember Spearshaker by.

But the bugs and the mice got into them, and the bark sheets went moldy in the wet season, and now I have only this little bundle. And, as you see, some of these are no more than bits and pieces. Like this worm-eaten scrap:

as concerning these *Indians* (for so men call them: but if this be the Lande of *India* I am an Hebrewe *Iewe*) they are in their owne Tongue clept *Anni-yawia*. Which is, being interpreted, the True or Principall People. By other Tribes they are named *Chelokee*: but the meaning of this word my frend *Mouse* knoweth not, neyther whence deriued. They

I think one reason he spent so much time on his talking marks was that he was afraid he might forget his own language. I have seen this happen, with captives. That Tuscarora woman who was with him still lives here, and by now she can barely speak ten words of Tuscarora. Though Muskrat will tell you that she speaks our language entirely too well—but that is another story.

Spearshaker did teach me quite a lot of his own language—a very difficult one, unlike any I ever encountered—and I tried to speak it with him from time to time, but it can't have been the same as talking with a man of his own kind. What does it sound like? Ah, I remember so little now. Let me see. . . . "*Holt dai tong, dow hor-son nabe!*" That means, "Shut up, you fool!"

He told me many stories about his native land and its marvels. Some I knew to be true, having heard of them from the coast folk: the great floating houses that spread their wings like birds to catch the wind, and the magic weapons that make thunder and lightning. Others were harder to believe, such as his tales about the woman chief of his tribe. Not a clan mother, but a real war chief, like Bigkiller or even Powhatan, and so powerful that any man—even an elder or a leading warrior—can lose his life merely for speaking against her.

He also claimed that the town he came from was so big that it held more people than all of the People's towns put together. That is of course a lie, but you can't blame a man for bragging on his own tribe.

But nothing, I think, was as strange as the *plei*.

Forgive me for using a word you do not know. But as far as I know there is no word in your language for what I am talking about. Nor in ours, and this is because the thing it means has never existed among our peoples. I think the Creator must have given this idea only to the whites, perhaps to compensate them for their poor sense of direction and that skin that burns in the sun.

It all began one evening, at the beginning of his second winter with us, when I came in from a council meeting and found him sitting by the fire, scratching away on a big sheet of mulberry bark. Just to be polite I said, "*Gado hadvhne?* What are you doing?"

Without looking up he said in his own language, "*Raiting a plei.*"

Now I knew what the first part meant; *rai-ting* is what the whites call it when they make those talking marks. But I had never heard the last word before, and I asked what it meant.

Spearshaker laid his turkey feather aside and sat up and looked at me. "Ah, Mouse," he said, "how can I make you understand? This will be hard even for you."

I sat down on the other side of the fire. "Try," I said.

O what a fond and Moone-struck fool am I! Hath the aire of *Virginnia* addl'd my braine? Or did an Enemy smite me on the heade, and I knewe it not? For here in this wilde country, where e'en the Artes of Letters are altogether unknowne, I haue begun the writing of a Play. And sure it is I shall neuer see it acted, neyther shall any other man: wherefore 'tis Lunacy indeede. Yet me thinkes if I do it not, I am the more certain to go mad: for I find my selfe growing more like vnto these *Indians*, and I feare I may forget what manner of man I was. Therefore the Play's the thing, whereby Ile saue my Minde by intentional folly: forsooth, there's Method in my Madnesse.

Well, he was right. He talked far into the night, and the more he talked the less I understood. I asked more questions than a rattlesnake has scales, and the answers only left me more confused. It was a long time before I began to see it.

Didn't you, as a child, pretend you were a warrior or a chief or maybe a medicine man, and make up stories and adventures for yourself? And your sisters had dolls that they gave names to, and talked to, and so on?

Or . . . let me try this another way. Don't your people have dances, like our Bear Dance, in which a man imitates some sort of animal? And don't your warriors sometimes dance around the fire acting out their own deeds, showing how they killed men or sneaked up on an enemy town—and maybe making it a little better than it really happened? Yes, it is the same with us.

Now this *plei* thing is a little like those dances, and a little like the pretending of children. A group of people dress up in fancy clothes and pretend to be other people, and pretend to do various things, and in this way they tell a story.

Yes, grown men. Yes, right up in front of everybody.

But understand, this isn't a dance. Well, there is some singing and dancing, but mostly they just talk. And gesture, and make faces, and now and then pretend to kill each other. They do a lot of that last. I guess it is something like a war dance at that.

You'd be surprised what can be done in this way. A man like Spear-shaker, who really knows how—*ak-ta* is what they are called—can make you see almost anything. He could imitate a man's expression and voice and way of moving—or a woman's—so well you'd swear he had turned into that person. He could make you think he was Bigkiller, standing right there in front of you, grunting and growling and waving his war club. He could do Blackfox's funny walk, or Locust wiggling his eyebrows, or Tsigeyu crossing her arms and staring at somebody she didn't like. He could even be Muskrat and his Tuscarora woman arguing, changing back and forth and doing both voices, till I laughed so hard my ribs hurt.

Now understand this. These *akta* people don't just make up their words and actions as they go along, as children or dancers do. No, the whole story is already known to them, and each *akta* has words that must be said, and things that must be done, at exactly the right times. You may be sure this takes a good memory. They have as much to remember as the Master of the Green Corn Dance.

And so, to help them, one man puts the whole thing down in those little marks. Obviously this is a very important job, and Spearshaker said that it was only in recent times, two or three winters before leaving his native land, that he himself had been accounted worthy of this honor. Well, I had known he was a *didahnvwisgi*, but I hadn't realized he was of such high rank.

> I first purpos'd to compose some pretty conceited Comedy, like vnto my Loue's Labour's Lost: but alas, me seemes my Wit hath dry'd vp from Misfortune. Then I bethought my selfe of the Play of the Prince of Denmark, by Thomas *Kyd*: which I had been employ'd in reuising for our Company not long ere we departed *London*, and had oft said to Richard *Burbage*, that I trow I could write a Better. And so I haue commenced, and praye God I may compleat, my owne Tragedie of Prince *Hamlet*.

I asked what sort of stories his people told in this curious manner. That is something that always interests me—you can learn a lot about any tribe from their stories. Like the ones the Maskogis tell about Rabbit, or our own tale about the Thunder Boys, or—you know.

I don't know what I was thinking. By then I should have known that white people do *everything* differently from everyone else in the world.

First he started to tell me about a dream somebody had on a summer night. That sounded good, but then it turned out to be about the Little People! Naturally I stopped him fast, and I told him that we do not talk about . . . *them*. I felt sorry for the poor man who dreamed about them, but there was no helping him now.

Then Spearshaker told me a couple of stories about famous chiefs of his own tribe. I couldn't really follow this very well, partly because I knew so little about white laws and customs, but also because a lot of their chiefs seemed to have the same name. I never did understand whether there were two different chiefs named *Ritsad*, or just one with a very strange nature.

The oddest thing, though, was that none of these stories seemed to have any *point*. They didn't tell you why the moon changes its face, or how the People were created, or where the mountains came from, or where the raccoon got his tail, or anything. They were just . . . *stories*. Like old women's gossip.

Maybe I missed something.

~~To liue, or not to liue, there lyes the~~
~~To liue, or dye? Shall I~~
~~To dye or~~
~~To be or what? It~~

He certainly worked hard at his task. More often than not, I could hear him grinding his teeth and muttering to himself as he sat hunched over his marks. And now and then he would jump up and throw the sheet to the ground and run outside in the snow and the night wind, and I would hear him shouting in his own language. At least I took it to be his language, though the words were not among those I knew. Part of his medicine, no doubt, so I said nothing.

God's Teethe! Haue I beene so long in this Wildernesse, that I haue forgot all Skill? I that could bombast out a lyne of blank Uerse as readily as a Fishe doth swimm, now fumble for Wordes like a Drunkard who cannot finde his owne Cod-peece with both Handes.

I'm telling you, it was a *long* winter.

> *For who would thus endure the Paines of time:*
> *To-morrow and to-morrow and to-morrow,*
> *That waite in patient and most grim Array,*
> *Each arm'd with Speares and Arrowes of Misfortune,*
> *Like* Indians *ambuscaded in the Forest?*
> *But that the dread of something after Death,*
> *That vndiscouered country, from whose Shores*
> *No Traueller returnes, puzzels the Will,*
> *And makes vs rather beare that which we knowe*
> *Than wantonly embarke for the Vnknowne.*

One evening, soon after the snows began to melt, I noticed that Spearshaker was not at his usual nightly work. He was just sitting there staring into the fire, not even looking at his skins and bark sheets, which were stacked beside him. The turkey feathers and black paint were nowhere in sight.

I said, "Is something wrong?" and then it came to me. "Finished?"

He let out a long sigh. "Yes," he said. "*Mo ful ai,*" he added, which was something he often said, though I never quite got what it meant.

It was easy to see he was feeling bad. So I said, "Tell me the story."

He didn't want to, but finally he told it to me. He got pretty worked up as he went along, sometimes jumping up to act out an exciting part, till I thought he was going to wreck my house. Now and then he picked up a skin or mulberry-bark sheet and spoke the words, so I could hear the sound. I had thought I was learning his language pretty well, but I couldn't understand one word in ten.

But the story itself was clear enough. There were parts I didn't follow, but on the whole it was the best he'd ever told me. At the end I said, "Good story."

He tilted his head to one side, like a bird. "Truly?"

"*Doyu,*" I said. I meant it, too.

He sighed again and picked up his pile of *raiting*. "I am a fool," he said.

I saw that he was about to throw the whole thing into the fire, so I went over and took it from him. "This is a good thing," I told him. "Be proud."

"Why?" He shrugged his shoulders. "Who will ever see it? Only the bugs and the worms. And the mice," he added, giving me his little smile.

I stood there, trying to think of something to make him feel better. Ninekiller's oldest daughter had been making eyes at Spearshaker lately and I wondered if I should go get her. Then I looked down at what I was holding in my hands and it came to me.

"My friend," I said, "I've got an idea. Why don't we put on your *plei* right here?"

> And now is Lunacy compownded vpon Lunacy, *Bedlam* pyled on *Bedlam*: for I am embark'd on an Enterprize, the like of which this Globe hath neuer seene. Yet Ile undertake this Foolery, and flynch not: mayhap it will please these People, who are become my onely Frends. They shall haue of Will his best will.

It sounded simple when I heard myself say it. Doing it was another matter. First, there were people to be spoken with.

We *Aniyuwiya* like to keep everything loose and easy. Our chiefs have far less authority than yours, and even the power of the clan mothers has its limits. Our laws are few, and everyone knows what they are, so things tend to go along without much trouble.

But there were no rules for what we wanted to do, because it had never been done before. Besides, we were going to need the help of many people. So it seemed better to go carefully—but I admit I had no idea that our little proposal would create such a stir. In the end there was a regular meeting at the council house to talk it over.

Naturally it was Otter who made the biggest fuss. "This is white men's medicine," he shouted. "Do you want the People to become as weak and useless as the whites?"

"If it will make all our warriors shoot as straight as Spearshaker," Bigkiller told him, "then it might be worth it."

Otter waved his skinny old arms. He was so angry by now that his face was whiter than Spearshaker's. "Then answer this," he said. "How is it that this dance—"

"It's not a dance," I said. Usually I would not interrupt an elder in council, but if you waited for Otter to finish you might be there all night.

"Whatever you call it," he said, "it's close enough to a dance to be Bird Clan business, right? And you, Mouse, are Wolf Clan—as is your white friend, by adoption. So you have no right to do this thing."

Old Dotsuya spoke up. She was the Bird Clan Mother, and the oldest person present. Maybe the oldest in town, now I think of it.

"The Bird Clan has no objection," she said. "Mouse and Spearshaker have our permission to put on their *plei*. Which I, for one, would like to see. Nothing ever happens around this town."

Tsigeyu spoke next. "*Howa*," she said. "I agree. This sounds interesting."

Of course Otter wasn't willing to let it go so easily; he made quite a speech, going all the way back to the origins of the People and predicting every kind of calamity if this sacrilege was permitted. It didn't do him much good, though. No one liked Otter, who had gotten both meaner and longer-winded with age, and who had never been a very good *didahnvwisgi* anyway. Besides, half the people in the council house were asleep long before he was done.

After the council gave its approval there was no trouble getting people to help. Rather we had more help than we needed. For days there was a crowd hanging around my house, wanting to be part of the *plei*. Bigkiller said if he could get that many people to join a war party, he could take care of the Catawbas for good.

And everyone wanted to be an *akta*. We were going to have to turn some people away, and we would have to be careful how we did it, or there would be trouble. I asked Spearshaker how many *aktas* we needed. "How many men, that is," I added, as he began counting on his fingers. "The women are a different problem."

He stopped counting and stared at me as if I were wearing owl feathers. Then he told me something so shocking you will hardly believe it. In his country, the women in a *plei* are actually *men wearing women's clothes!*

I told him quick enough that the People don't go in for that sort of thing—whatever they may get up to in certain other tribes—and he'd better not even talk about it around here. Do you know, he got so upset that it took me the rest of the day to talk him out of calling the whole thing off. . . .

> Women! Mercifull Jesu! Women, on a Stage, acting in a Play! I shall feele like an Whore-Master!

Men or women, it was hard to know which people to choose. None of them had ever done anything like this before, so there was no way to know whether they would be any good or not. Spearshaker asked me questions about each person, in white language so no one would be offended: Is he quick to learn? Does he dance or sing well? Can he work with other people, and do as he is told? And he had them stand on one side of the stickball field, while he stood on the other, and made them speak their names and clans, to learn how well their voices carried.

I had thought age would come into it, since the *plei* included both older and younger people. But it turned out that Spearshaker knew an art of painting a man's face, and putting white in his hair, till he might be mistaken for his own grandfather.

No doubt he could have done the same with women, but that wasn't necessary. There were only two women's parts in this story, and we gave the younger woman's part to Ninekiller's daughter Cricket—who would have hung upside-down in a tree like a possum if it would please Spearshaker—and the older to a cousin of mine, about my age, who had lost her husband to the Shawanos and wanted something to do.

For those who could not be *aktas*, there was plenty of other work. A big platform had to be built, with space cleared around it, and log benches for the people who would watch. There were torches to be prepared, since we would be doing it at night, and special clothes to be made, as well as things like fake spears so no one would get hurt.

Locust and Blackfox were particularly good workers; Spearshaker said it was as if they had been born for this. They even told him that if he still wanted to follow the custom of his own tribe, with men dressed as women, they would be willing to take those parts. Well, I always had wondered about those two.

But Spearshaker was working harder than anyone else. Besides being in charge of all the other preparations, he had to remake his whole *plei* to suit our needs. No doubt he had made a fine *plei* for white men, but for us, as it was, it would never do.

Many a Play haue I reuis'd and amended: cut short or long at the Company's desyre, or alter'd this or that Speeche to please a Player: e'en carued the very Guttes out of a scene on command of the Office of the Reuels, for some imagin'd Sedition or vnseemely Speeche. But now must I out-do all I euer did before, in the making of my *Hamlet* into a thing comprehensible to the *Anni-yawia*. Scarce is there a line which doth not haue to be rewrit: yea, and much ta'en out intire: as, the Play within the Play, which Mouse saith, that none here will vnderstande. And the Scene must be mov'd from *Denmark* to *Virginnia*, and *Elsinore Castle* transformed into an *Indian* towne. For marry, it were Alchemy enow that I should transmute vnletter'd Sauages into tragick Actors: but to make royal *Danskers* of swart-fac'd *Indians* were beyond all Reason. (Speak'st thou now of Reason, Will Shakespere? Is't not ouerlate for that?)

You should have seen us teaching the *aktas* their parts. First Spearshaker would look at the marks and say the words in his language. Then he would explain to me any parts I hadn't understood—which was most of it, usually—and then I would translate the whole thing for the *akta* in our language. Or as close as I could get; there are some things you cannot really interpret. By now Spearshaker was fluent enough to help me.

Then the *akta* would try to say the words back to us, almost always getting it all wrong and having to start again. And later on all the people in the *plei* had to get together and speak their parts in order, and do all the things they would do in the *plei*, and that was like a bad dream. Not only did they forget their words; they bumped into each other and stepped on each other's feet, and got carried away in the fight parts and nearly killed each other. And Spearshaker would jump up and down and pull his hair—which had already begun to fall out, for some reason—and sometimes weep, and when he had settled down we would try again.

Verily, my lot is harder than that of the *Iewes* of *Moses*. For Scripture saith, that *Pharo* did command that they make Brickes without Strawe, wherefore their trauail was greate: but now I must make my Brickes, euen without Mudd.

Let me tell you the story of Spearshaker's *plei*.

Once there was a great war chief who was killed by his own brother. Not in a fight, but secretly, by poison. The brother took over as chief, and also took his dead brother's woman, who didn't object.

But the dead man had a son, a young warrior named Amaledi. One night the dead chief appeared to Amaledi and told him the whole story. And, of course, demanded that he do something about it.

Poor Amaledi was in a bad fix. Obviously he mustn't go against his mother's wishes, and kill her new man without her permission. On the other hand, no one wants to anger a ghost—and this one was plenty angry already.

So Amaledi couldn't decide what to do. To make things worse, the bad brother had guessed that Amaledi knew something. He and this really nasty, windy old man named Quolonisi—sounds like Otter—began trying to get rid of Amaledi.

To protect himself Amaledi became a Crazy, doing and saying everything backward, or in ways that made no sense. This made his medicine strong enough to protect him from his uncle and Quolonisi, at least for a time.

Quolonisi had a daughter, Tsigalili, who wanted Amaledi for her man. But she didn't want to live with a Crazy—who does?—and she kept coming around and crying and begging him to quit. At the same time his mother was giving him a hard time for being disrespectful toward her new man. And all the while the ghost kept showing up and yelling at Amaledi for taking so long. It got so bad Amaledi thought about killing himself, but then he realized that he would go to the spirit world, where his father would *never* leave him alone.

So Amaledi thought of a plan. There was a big dance one night to honor the new chief, and some visiting singers from another town were going to take part. Amaledi took their lead singer aside and got him to change the song, telling him the new words had been given to him in a dream. And that night, with the dancers going around the fire and the women shaking the turtle shells and the whole town watching, the visiting leader sang:

> "Now he pours it,
> Now he is pouring the poison,
> See, there are two brothers,
> See, now there is one."

That was when it all blew up like a hot rock in a fire. The bad chief jumped up and ran away from the dance grounds, afraid he had just been witched. Amaledi had a big argument with his mother and told her what he thought of the way she was acting. Then he killed Quolonisi. He said it was an accident but I think he was just tired of listening to the old fool.

Tsigalili couldn't stand any more. She jumped into a waterfall and killed herself. There was a fine funeral.

Now Amaledi was determined to kill his uncle. The uncle was just as determined to kill Amaledi, but he was too big a coward to do it himself. So he got Quolonisi's son Panther to call Amaledi out for a fight.

Panther was a good fighter and he was hot to kill Amaledi, because of his father and his sister. But the chief wasn't taking any chances. He put some poison on Panther's spear. He also had a gourd of water, with poison in it, in case nothing else worked.

So Amaledi and Panther painted their faces red and took their spears and faced each other, right in front of the chief's house. Amaledi was just as good as Panther, but finally he got nicked on the arm. Before the poison could act, they got into some hand-to-hand wrestling, and the spears got mixed up. Now Panther took a couple of hits. Yes, with the poisoned spear.

Meanwhile Amaledi's mother got thirsty and went over and took a drink, before anyone could stop her, from the poisoned gourd. Pretty soon she fell down. Amaledi and Panther stopped fighting and rushed over, but she was already dead.

By now they were both feeling the poison themselves. Panther fell down and died. So did Amaledi, but before he went down he got his uncle with the poisoned spear. So in the end *everyone* died.

You do?

Well, I suppose you had to be there.

And so 'tis afoote: to-morrow night we are to perform. Thank God *Burbage* cannot be there to witnesse it: for it were a Question which should come first, that he dye of Laughter, or I of Shame.

It was a warm and pleasant night. Everyone was there, even Otter. By the time it was dark all the seats were full and many people were standing, or sitting on the ground.

The platform had only been finished a few days before—with Bigkiller complaining about the waste of timber and labor, that could have gone into strengthening the town's defenses—and it looked very fine. Locust and Blackfox had hung some reed mats on poles to represent the walls of houses, and also to give us a place to wait out of sight before going on. To keep the crowd from getting restless, Spearshaker had asked Dotsuya to have some Bird Clan men sing and dance while we were lighting the torches and making other last preparations.

Then it was time to begin.

What? Oh, no, I was not an *akta*. By now I knew the words to the whole *plei*, from having translated and repeated them so many times.

So I stood behind a reed screen and called out the words, in a voice too low for the crowd to hear, when anyone forgot what came next.

Spearshaker, yes. He was the ghost. He had put some paint on his face that made it even whiter, and he did something with his voice that made the hair stand up on your neck.

But in fact everyone did very well, much better than I had expected. The only bad moment came when Amaledi—that was Tsigeyu's son Hummingbird—shouted, "Na! Dili, dili!"—"There! A skunk, a skunk!"—and slammed his war club into the wall of the "chief's house," forgetting it was really just a reed mat. And Beartrack, who was being Quolonisi, took such a blow to the head that he was out for the rest of the plei. But it didn't matter, since he had no more words to speak, and he made a very good dead man for Amaledi to drag out.

And the people loved it, all of it. How they laughed and laughed! I never heard so many laugh so hard for so long. At the end, when Amaledi fell dead between his mother and Panther and the platform was covered with corpses, there was so much howling and hooting you would have taken it for a hurricane. I looked out through the mats and saw Tsigeyu and Bigkiller holding on to each other to keep from falling off the bench. Warriors were wiping tears from their eyes and women were clutching themselves between the legs and old Dotsuya was lying on the ground kicking her feet like a baby.

I turned to Spearshaker, who was standing beside me. "See," I said. "And you were afraid they wouldn't understand it!"

AFTER THAT everything got confused for a while. Locust and Blackfox rushed up and dragged Spearshaker away, and the next time I saw him he was down in front of the platform with Tsigeyu embracing him and Bigkiller slapping him on the back. I couldn't see his face, which was hidden by Tsigeyu's very large front.

By then people were making a fuss over all of us. Even me. A Paint Clan woman, not bad-looking for her age, took me away for some attention. She was limber and had a lot of energy, so it was late by the time I finally got home.

Spearshaker was there, sitting by the fire. He didn't look up when I came in. His face was so pale I thought at first he was still wearing his ghost paint.

I said, "*Gusdi nusdi?* Is something wrong?"

"They laughed," he said. He didn't sound happy about it.

"They laughed," I agreed. "They laughed as they have never laughed before, every one of them. Except for Otter, and no one has ever seen him laugh."

I sat down beside him. "You did something fine tonight, Spearshaker. You made the People happy. They have a hard life, and you made them laugh."

He made a snorting sound. "Yes. They laughed to see us making fools of ourselves. Perhaps that is good."

"No, no." I saw it now. "Is that what you think? That they laughed because we did the *plei* so badly?"

I put my hand on his shoulder and turned him to face me. "My friend, no one there tonight ever saw a *plei* before, except for you. How would they know if it was bad? It was certainly the best *plei* they ever saw."

He blinked slowly, like a turtle. I saw his eyes were red.

"Believe me, Spearshaker," I told him, "they were laughing because it was such a funny story. And that was your doing."

His expression was very strange indeed. "They thought it comical?"

"Well, who wouldn't? All those crazy people up there, killing each other—and themselves—and then that part at the end, where *everyone* gets killed!" I had to stop and laugh, myself, remembering. "I tell you," I said when I had my breath back, "even though I knew the whole thing by memory, I nearly lost control of myself a few times there."

I got up. "Come, Spearshaker. You need to go to sleep. You have been working too hard."

But he only put his head down in his hands and made some odd sounds in his throat, and muttered some words I did not know. And so I left him there and went to bed.

If I live until the mountains fall, I will never understand white men.

If I liue vntil our *Saviour's* returne, I shall neuer vnderstande *Indians*. Warre they count as Sport, and bloody Murther an occasion of Merriment: 'tis because they hold Life itselfe but lightly, and think Death no greate matter neyther: and so that which we call Tragick, they take for Comedie. And though I be damned for't, I cannot sweare that they haue not the Right of it.

Whatever happened that night, it changed something in Spearshaker. He lived with us for many more years, but never again did he make a *plei* for us.

That was sad, for we had all enjoyed the Amaledi story so much, and were hoping for more. And many people tried to get Spearshaker to change his mind—Tsigeyu actually begged him; I think it was the only time in her life she ever begged anyone for anything—but it did no good. He would not even talk about it.

And at last we realized that his medicine had gone, and we left him in peace. It is a terrible thing for a *didahnvwisgi* when his power leaves him. Perhaps his ancestors' spirits were somehow offended by our *plei*. I hope not, since it was my idea.

That summer Ninekiller's daughter Cricket became Spearshaker's wife. I gave them my house, and moved in with the Paint Clan woman. I visited my friend often, and we talked of many things, but of one thing we never spoke.

Cricket told me he still made his talking marks, from time to time. If he ever tried to make another *plei*, though, he never told anyone.

I believe it was five winters ago—it was not more—when Cricket came in one day and found him dead. It was a strange thing, for he had not been sick, and was still a fairly young man. As far as anyone knew there was nothing wrong with him, except that his hair had fallen out.

I think his spirit simply decided to go back to his native land.

Cricket grieved for a long time. She still has not taken another husband. Did you happen to see a small boy with pale skin and brown hair, as you came through our town? That is their son Wili.

Look what Cricket gave me. This is the turkey feather that was in Spearshaker's hand when she found him that day. And this is the piece of mulberry bark that was lying beside him. I will always wonder what it says.

We are such stuff as Dreames are made on: and our little Life
Is rounded in a sle ●

NOTES

1. Elizabethan spelling was fabulously irregular; the same person might spell the same word in various ways on a single page. Shakespeare's own spelling is known only from the Quarto and Folio printings

of the plays, and the published poetry; and no one knows how far this may have been altered by the printer. It is not even known how close the published texts are to Shakespeare's original in wording, let alone spelling. All we have in his own hand is his signature, and this indicates that he spelled his own name differently almost every time he wrote it.

I have followed the spelling of the Folio for the most part, but felt free to use my own judgment and even whim, since that was what the original speller did.

I have, however, regularized spelling and punctuation to some extent, and modernized spelling and usage in some instances, so that the text would be readable. I assume this magazine's readership is well-educated, but it seems unrealistic to expect them to be Elizabethan scholars.

2. Cherokee pronunciation is difficult to render in Roman letters. Even our own syllabary system of writing, invented in the nineteenth century by Sequoyah, does not entirely succeed, as there is no way to indicate the tones and glottal stops. I have followed, more or less, the standard system of transliteration, in which "v" is used for the nasal grunting vowel that has no English equivalent.

It hardly matters, since we do not know how sixteenth-century Cherokees pronounced the language. The sounds have changed considerably in the century and a half since the forced march to Oklahoma; what they were like four hundred years ago is highly conjectural. So is the location of the various tribes of Virginia and the Carolinas during this period; and, of course, so is their culture. (The Cherokees may not then have been the warlike tribe they later became—though, given the national penchant for names incorporating the verb "to kill," this is unlikely.) The Catawbas were a very old and hated enemy.

3. Edward Spicer's voyage to America to learn the fate of the Roanoke Colony—or rather his detour to Virginia after a successful privateering operation—did happen, including the bad weather and the loss of a couple of boats, though there is no record that any boat reached the mainland. The disappearance of the Roanoke colonists is a famous event. It is only conjecture—though based on considerable evidence, and accepted by many historians—that Powhatan had the colonists murdered, after they had taken sanctuary with a minor coastal tribe. Disney fantasies to the contrary, Powhatan was not a nice man.

4. I have accepted, for the sake of the story, the view of many scholars that Shakespeare first got the concept of *Hamlet* in the process of revising Thomas Kyd's earlier play on the same subject. Thus he might well

have had the general idea in his head as early as 1591—assuming, as most do, that by this time he was employed with a regular theatrical company—even though the historic *Hamlet* is generally agreed to have been written considerably later.

5. As to those who argue that William Shakespeare was not actually the author of *Hamlet*, but that the plays were written by Francis Bacon or the Earl of Southampton or Elvis Presley, one can only reply: *Hah!* And again, *Hah!*

Bruce Sterling

Bruce Sterling began publishing science fiction in 1976, and his first novel, the picaresque extraplanetary adventure Involution Ocean, *was published the following year. Shortly after, he made his mark with a series of visionary short stories about bioengineering and prosthetic transformation set in his Shaper/Mechanist universe, which culminated in the novel* Schismatrix. *With the publication of* Islands in the Net *in 1988, Sterling came to be regarded as one of the most provocative writers in the cyberpunk medium, and confirmed his role as its leading prophet with his groundbreaking* Mirrorshades *anthology. His novels, which frequently focus on the cultural dislocation and social alienation that has come with the information age and computer revolution, include* Heavy Weather, Holy Fire, *and the satirical* Distraction. *His short fiction has been collected in* Crystal Express, Globalhead, *and* A Good Old-Fashioned Future.

Lewis Shiner

Although Lewis Shiner entered the fiction world with the burgeoning cyberpunk movement of the early 1980s, he prefers not to be bound by the tropes of any one literary genre or movement, instead writing fiction that transcends these limitations. When he does write science fiction or fantasy, as in the novels Frontera, Deserted Cities of the Heart, *and* Glimpses, *he combines realistic extrapolations of the future with sparse prose that acknowledges elements of mystery and literary fiction as well. He is also an accomplished short story writer, with more than thirty-five stories published in all fiction areas, from children's books to fantasy to horror. He has also written several nonfiction articles, including an appreciation of James P. Blaylock and articles for* The New York Review of Science Fiction, *and edited the anthology* When the Music's Over.

MOZART IN MIRRORSHADES

Bruce Sterling and Lewis Shiner

FROM THE HILL north of the city, Rice saw eighteenth-century Salzburg spread out below him like a half-eaten lunch.

Huge cracking towers and swollen, bulbous storage tanks dwarfed the ruins of the St. Rupert Cathedral. Thick white smoke billowed from the refinery's stacks. Rice could taste the familiar petrochemical tang from where he sat, under the leaves of a wilting oak.

The sheer spectacle of it delighted him. You didn't sign up for a time-travel project, he thought, unless you had a taste for incongruity. Like the phallic pumping station lurking in the central square of the convent, or the ruler-straight elevated pipelines ripping through Salzburg's maze of cobbled streets. A bit tough on the city, maybe, but that was hardly Rice's fault. The temporal beam had focused randomly in the bedrock below Salzburg, forming an expandable bubble connecting this world to Rice's own time.

This was the first time he'd seen the complex from outside its high chain-link fences. For two years, he'd been up to his neck getting the refinery operational. He'd directed teams all over the planet, as they caulked up Nantucket whalers to serve as tankers, or trained local pipefitters to lay down line as far away as the Sinai and the Gulf of Mexico.

Now, finally, he was outside. Sutherland, the company's political liaison, had warned him against going into the city. But Rice had no patience with her attitude. The smallest thing seemed to set Sutherland off. She lost sleep over the most trivial local complaints. She spent hours haranguing the "gate people," the locals who waited day and night outside the square-mile complex, begging for radios, nylons, a jab of penicillin.

To hell with her, Rice thought. The plant was up and breaking design records, and Rice was due for a little R and R. The way he saw it, anyone who couldn't find some action in the Year of Our Lord 1775 had to be dead between the ears. He stood up, dusting windblown soot from his hands with a cambric handkerchief.

A moped sputtered up the hill toward him, wobbling crazily. The rider couldn't seem to keep his high-heeled, buckled pumps on the pedals while carrying a huge portable stereo in the crook of his right arm. The moped lurched to a stop at a respectful distance, and Rice recognized the music from the tape player: Symphony No. 40 in G Minor.

The boy turned the volume down as Rice walked toward him. "Good evening, Mr. Plant Manager, sir. I am not interrupting?"

"No, that's okay." Rice glanced at the bristling hedgehog cut that had replaced the boy's outmoded wig. He'd seen the kid around the gates; he was one of the regulars. But the music had made something else fall into place. "You're Mozart, aren't you?"

"Wolfgang Amadeus Mozart, your servant."

"I'll be goddamned. Do you know what that tape is?"

"It has my name on it."

"Yeah. You wrote it. Or would have, I guess I should say. About fifteen years from now."

Mozart nodded. "It is so beautiful. I have not the English to say how it is to hear it."

By this time most of the other gate people would have been well into some kind of pitch. Rice was impressed by the boy's tact, not to mention his command of English. The standard native vocabulary didn't go much beyond *radio, drugs,* and *fuck.* "Are you headed back toward town?" Rice asked.

"Yes, Mr. Plant Manager, sir."

Something about the kid appealed to Rice. The enthusiasm, the gleam in the eyes. And, of course, he did happen to be one of the greatest composers of all time.

"Forget the titles," Rice said. "Where does a guy go for some fun around here?"

*   *   *

AT FIRST Sutherland hadn't wanted Rice at the meeting with Jefferson. But Rice knew a little temporal physics, and Jefferson had been pestering the American personnel with questions about time holes and parallel worlds.

Rice, for his part, was thrilled at the chance to meet Thomas Jefferson, the first President of the United States. He'd never liked George Washington, was glad the man's Masonic connections had made him refuse to join the company's "godless" American government.

Rice squirmed in his Dacron double knits as he and Sutherland waited in the newly air-conditioned boardroom of the Hohensalzburg Castle. "I forgot how greasy these suits feel," he said.

"At least," Sutherland said, "you didn't wear that goddamned hat today." The VTOL jet from America was late, and she kept looking at her watch.

"My tricorne?" Rice said. "You don't like it?"

"It's a Masonista hat, for Christ's sake. It's a symbol of anti-modern reaction." The Freemason Liberation Front was another of Sutherland's nightmares, a local politico-religious group that had made a few pathetic attacks on the pipeline.

"Oh, loosen up, will you, Sutherland? Some groupie of Mozart's gave me the hat. Theresa Maria Angela something-or-other, some broken-down aristocrat. They all hang out together in this music dive downtown. I just liked the way it looked."

"Mozart? You've been fraternizing with him? Don't you think we should just let him be? After everything we've done to him?"

"Bullshit," Rice said. "I'm entitled. I spent two years on start-up while you were playing touch football with Robespierre and Thomas Paine. I make a few night spots with Wolfgang and you're all over me. What about Parker? I don't hear you bitching about him playing rock and roll on his late show every night. You can hear it blasting out of every cheap transistor in town."

"He's propaganda officer. Believe me, if I could stop him I would, but Parker's a special case. He's got connections all over the place back in Realtime." She rubbed her cheek. "Let's drop it, okay? Just try to be polite to President Jefferson. He's had a hard time of it lately."

Sutherland's secretary, a former Hapsburg lady-in-waiting, stepped in to announce the plane's arrival. Jefferson pushed angrily past her. He was tall for a local, with a mane of blazing red hair and the shiftiest eyes

Rice had ever seen. "Sit down, Mr. President." Sutherland waved at the far side of the table. "Would you like some coffee or tea?"

Jefferson scowled. "Perhaps some Madeira," he said. "If you have it."

Sutherland nodded to her secretary, who stared for a moment in incomprehension, then hurried off. "How was the flight?" Sutherland asked.

"Your engines are most impressive," Jefferson said, "as you well know." Rice saw the subtle trembling of the man's hands; he hadn't taken well to jet flight. "I only wish your political sensitivities were as advanced."

"You know I can't speak for my employers," Sutherland said. "For myself, I deeply regret the darker aspects of our operations. Florida will be missed."

Irritated, Rice leaned forward. "You're not really here to discuss sensibilities, are you?"

"Freedom, sir," Jefferson said. "Freedom is the issue." The secretary returned with a dust-caked bottle of sherry and a stack of clear plastic cups. Jefferson, his hands visibly shaking now, poured a glass and tossed it back. Color returned to his face. He said, "You made certain promises when we joined forces. You guaranteed us liberty and equality and the freedom to pursue our own happiness. Instead we find your machinery on all sides, your cheap manufactured goods seducing the people of our great country, our minerals and works of art disappearing into your fortresses, never to reappear!" The last line brought Jefferson to his feet.

Sutherland shrank back into her chair. "The common good requires a certain period of—uh, adjustment—"

"Oh, come on, Tom," Rice broke in. "We didn't 'join forces,' that's a lot of crap. We kicked the Brits out and you in, and you had damn-all to do with it. Second, if we drill for oil and carry off a few paintings, it doesn't have a goddamned thing to do with your liberty. We don't care. Do whatever you like, just stay out of our way. Right? If we wanted a lot of back talk we could have left the damn British in power."

Jefferson sat down. Sutherland meekly poured him another glass, which he drank off at once. "I cannot understand you," he said. "You claim you come from the future, yet you seem bent on destroying your own past."

"But we're not," Rice said. "It's this way. History is like a tree, okay? When you go back and mess with the past, another branch of history splits off from the main trunk. Well, this world is just one of those branches."

"So," Jefferson said. "This world — my world — does not lead to your future."

"Right," Rice said.

"Leaving you free to rape and pillage here at will! While your own world is untouched and secure!" Jefferson was on his feet again. "I find the idea monstrous beyond belief, intolerable! How can you be party to such despotism? Have you no human feelings?"

"Oh, for God's sake," Rice said. "Of course we do. What about the radios and the magazines and the medicine we hand out? Personally I think you've got a lot of nerve, coming in here with your smallpox scars and your unwashed shirt and all those slaves of yours back home, lecturing us on humanity."

"Rice?" Sutherland said.

Rice locked eyes with Jefferson. Slowly, Jefferson sat down. "Look," Rice said, relenting. "We don't mean to be unreasonable. Maybe things aren't working out just the way you pictured them, but hey, that's life, you know? What do you want, *really*? Cars? Movies? Telephones? Birth control? Just say the word and they're yours."

Jefferson pressed his thumbs into the corners of his eyes. "Your words mean nothing to me, sir. I only want . . . I want only to return to my home. To Monticello. And as soon as possible."

"Is it one of your migraines, Mr. President?" Sutherland asked. "I had these made up for you." She pushed a vial of pills across the table toward him.

"What are these?"

Sutherland shrugged. "You'll feel better."

After Jefferson left, Rice half expected a reprimand. Instead, Sutherland said, "You seem to have a tremendous faith in the project."

"Oh, cheer up," Rice said, "You've been spending too much time with these politicals. Believe me, this is a simple time, with simple people. Sure, Jefferson was a little ticked off, but he'll come around. Relax!"

RICE FOUND MOZART clearing tables in the main dining hall of the Hohensalzburg Castle. In his faded jeans, camo jacket, and mirrored sunglasses, he might almost have passed for a teenager from Rice's time.

"Wolfgang!" Rice called to him. "How's the new job?"

Mozart set a stack of dishes aside and ran his hands over his short-cropped hair. "Wolf," he said. "Call me Wolf, okay? Sounds more . . . modern, you know? But yes, I really want to thank you for everything you have done for me. The tapes, the history books, this job—it is so wonderful just to be around here."

His English, Rice noticed, had improved remarkably in the last three weeks. "You still living in the city?"

"Yes, but I have my own place now. You are coming to the gig tonight?"

"Sure," Rice said. "Why don't you finish up around here, I'll go change, and then we can go out for some sachertorte, okay? We'll make a night of it."

Rice dressed carefully, wearing mesh body armor under his velvet coat and knee britches. He crammed his pockets with giveaway consumer goods, then met Mozart by a rear door.

Security had been stepped up around the castle, and floodlights swept the sky. Rice sensed a new tension in the festive abandon of the crowds downtown.

Like everyone else from his time, he towered over the locals; even incognito he felt dangerously conspicuous.

Within the club Rice faded into the darkness and relaxed. The place had been converted from the lower half of some young aristo's town house; protruding bricks still marked the lines of the old walls. The patrons were locals, mostly, dressed in any Realtime garments they could scavenge. Rice even saw one kid wearing a pair of beige silk panties on his head.

Mozart took the stage. Minuetlike guitar arpeggios screamed over sequenced choral motifs. Stacks of amps blasted synthesizer riffs lifted from a tape of K-Tel pop hits. The howling audience showered Mozart with confetti stripped from the club's hand-painted wallpaper.

Afterward Mozart smoked a joint of Turkish hash and asked Rice about the future.

"Mine, you mean?" Rice said. "You wouldn't believe it. Six billion people, and nobody has to work if they don't want to. Five-hundred-channel TV in every house. Cars, helicopters, clothes that would knock your eyes out. Plenty of easy sex. You want music? You could have your own recording studio. It'd make your gear on stage look like a god-damned clavichord."

"Really? I would give anything to see that. I can't understand why you would leave."

Rice shrugged. "So I'm giving up maybe fifteen years. When I get back, it's the best of everything. Anything I want."

"Fifteen years?"

"Yeah. You gotta understand how the portal works. Right now it's as big around as you are tall, just big enough for a phone cable and a pipeline full of oil, maybe the odd bag of mail, heading for Realtime. To make it any bigger, like to move people or equipment through, is expensive as hell. So expensive they only do it twice, at the beginning and the end of the project. So, yeah, I guess we're stuck here."

Rice coughed harshly and drank off his glass. That Ottoman Empire hash had untied his mental shoelaces. Here he was opening up to Mozart, making the kid want to emigrate, and there was no way in hell Rice could get him a Green Card. Not with all the millions that wanted a free ride into the future—billions, if you counted the other projects, like the Roman Empire or New Kingdom Egypt.

"But I'm really *glad* to be here," Rice said. "It's like . . . like shuffling the deck of history. You never know what'll come up next." Rice passed the joint to one of Mozart's groupies, Antonia something-or-other. "This is a great time to be alive. Look at you. You're doing okay, aren't you?" He leaned across the table, in the grip of a sudden sincerity. "I mean, it's okay, right? It's not like you hate all of us for fucking up your world or anything?"

"Are you making a joke? You are looking at the hero of Salzburg. In fact, your Mr. Parker is supposed to make a tape of my last set tonight. Soon all of Europe will know of me!" Someone shouted at Mozart, in German, from across the club. Mozart glanced up and gestured cryptically. "Be cool, man." He turned back to Rice. "You can see that I am doing fine."

"Sutherland, she worries about stuff like all those symphonies you're never going to write."

"Bullshit! I don't want to write symphonies. I can listen to them any time I want! Who is this Sutherland? Is she your girlfriend?"

"No. She goes for the locals. Danton, Robespierre, like that. How about you? You got anybody?"

"Nobody special. Not since I was a kid."

"Oh, yeah?"

"Well, when I was about six I was at Maria Theresa's court. I used to play with her daughter—Maria Antonia. Marie Antoinette she calls herself now. The most beautiful girl of the age. We used to play duets. We made a joke that we would be married, but she went off to France with that swine, Louis."

"Goddamn," Rice said. "This is really amazing. You know, she's practically a legend where I come from. They cut her head off in the French Revolution for throwing too many parties."

"No they didn't . . ."

"That was *our* French Revolution," Rice said. "Yours was a lot less messy."

"You should go see her, if you're that interested. Surely she owes you a favor for saving her life."

Before Rice could answer, Parker arrived at their table, surrounded by ex-ladies-in-waiting in spandex capris and sequined tube tops. "Hey, Rice," Parker shouted, serenely anachronistic in a glitter T-shirt and black leather jeans. "Where did you get those unhip threads? Come on, let's party!"

Rice watched as the girls crowded around the table and gnawed the corks out of a crate of champagne. As short, fat, and repulsive as Parker might be, they would gladly knife one another for a chance to sleep in his clean sheets and raid his medicine cabinet.

"No, thanks," Rice said, untangling himself from the miles of wire connected to Parker's recording gear.

The image of Marie Antoinette had seized him and would not let go.

RICE SAT NAKED on the edge of the canopied bed, shivering a little in the air conditioning. Past the jutting window unit, through clouded panes of eighteenth-century glass, he saw a lush, green landscape sprinkled with tiny waterfalls.

At ground level, a garden crew of former aristos in blue-denim overalls trimmed weeds under the bored supervision of a peasant guard. The guard, clothed head to foot in camouflage except for a tricolor cockade on his fatigue cap, chewed gum and toyed with the strap of his cheap plastic machine gun. The gardens of Petit Trianon, like Versailles itself, were treasures deserving the best of care. They belonged to the Nation, since they were too large to be crammed through a time portal.

Marie Antoinette sprawled across the bed's expanse of pink satin, wearing a scrap of black-lace underwear and leafing through an issue of *Vogue*. The bedroom's walls were crowded with Boucher canvases: acres of pert silky rumps, pink haunches, knowingly pursed lips. Rice looked dazedly from the portrait of Louise O'Morphy, kittenishly sprawled on a divan, to the sleek, creamy expanse of Toinette's back and thighs. He took a deep, exhausted breath. "Man," he said, "that guy could really paint."

Toinette cracked off a square of Hershey's chocolate and pointed to the magazine. "I want the leather bikini," she said. "Always, when I am a girl, my goddamn mother, she keep me in the goddamn corsets. She think my what-you-call, my shoulder blade sticks out too much."

Rice leaned back across her solid thighs and patted her bottom reassuringly. He felt wonderfully stupid; a week and a half of obsessive carnality had reduced him to a euphoric animal. "Forget your mother, baby. You're with *me* now. You want ze goddamn leather bikini, I get it for you."

Toinette licked chocolate from her fingertips. "Tomorrow we go out to the cottage, okay, man? We dress up like the peasants and make love in the hedges like noble savages."

Rice hesitated. His weekend furlough to Paris had stretched into a week and a half; by now security would be looking for him. To hell with them, he thought. "Great," he said. "I'll phone us up a picnic lunch. Foie gras and truffles, maybe some terrapin—"

Toinette pouted. "I want the modern food. The pizza and burritos and the chicken fried." When Rice shrugged, she threw her arms around his neck. "You love me, Rice?"

"Love you? Baby, I love the very *idea* of you." He was drunk on history out of control, careening under him like some great black motorcycle of the imagination. When he thought of Paris, take-out quiche-to-go stores springing up where guillotines might have been, a six-year-old Napoleon munching Dubble Bubble in Corsica, he felt like the archangel Michael on speed.

Megalomania, he knew, was an occupational hazard. But he'd get back to work soon enough, in just a few more days. . . .

The phone rang. Rice burrowed into a plush house robe formerly owned by Louis XVI. Louis wouldn't mind; he was now a happily divorced locksmith in Nice.

Mozart's face appeared on the phone's tiny screen. "Hey, man, where are you?"

"France," Rice said vaguely. "What's up?"

"Trouble, man. Sutherland flipped out, and they've got her sedated. At least six key people have gone over the hill, counting you." Mozart's voice had only the faintest trace of accent left.

"Hey, I'm not over the hill. I'll be back in just a couple days. We've got—what, thirty other people in Northern Europe? If you're worried about the quotas—"

"Fuck the quotas. This is serious. There's uprisings. Comanches raising hell on the rigs in Texas. Labor strikes in London and Vienna. Real-time is pissed. They're talking about pulling us out."

"What?" Now he was alarmed.

"Yeah. Word came down the line today. They say you guys let this whole operation get sloppy. Too much contamination, too much fraternization. Sutherland made a lot of trouble with the locals before she got found out. She was organizing the Masonistas for some kind of passive resistance and God knows what else."

"Shit." The fucking politicals had screwed it up again. It wasn't enough that he'd busted ass getting the plant up and on line; now he had to clean up after Sutherland. He glared at Mozart. "Speaking of fraternization, what's all this *we* stuff? What the hell are you doing calling me?"

Mozart paled. "Just trying to help. I got a job in communications now."

"That takes a Green Card. Where the hell did you get that?"

"Uh, listen, man, I got to go. Get back here, will you? We need you." Mozart's eyes flickered, looking past Rice's shoulder. "You can bring your little time-bunny along if you want. But hurry."

"I . . . oh, shit, okay," Rice said.

RICE'S HOVERCAR huffed along at a steady 80 kph, blasting clouds of dust from the deeply rutted highway. They were near the Bavarian border. Ragged Alps jutted into the sky over radiant green meadows, tiny picturesque farmhouses, and clear, vivid streams of melted snow.

They'd just had their first argument. Toinette had asked for a Green Card, and Rice had told her he couldn't do it. He offered her a Gray Card instead, that would get her from one branch of time to another without letting her visit Realtime. He knew he'd be reassigned if the project pulled out, and he wanted to take her with him. He wanted to do the decent thing, not leave her behind in a world without Hersheys and *Vogues*.

But she wasn't having any of it. After a few kilometers of weighty silence she started to squirm. "I have to pee," she said finally. "Pull over by the goddamn trees."

"Okay," Rice said. "Okay."

He cut the fans and whirred to a stop. A herd of brindled cattle spooked off with a clank of cowbells. The road was deserted.

Rice got out and stretched, watching Toinette climb a wooden stile and walk toward a stand of trees.

"What's the deal?" Rice yelled. "There's nobody around. Get on with it!"

A dozen men burst up from the cover of a ditch and rushed him. In an instant they'd surrounded him, leveling flintlock pistols. They wore tricornes and wigs and lace-cuffed highwayman's coats; black domino masks hid their faces. "What the fuck is this?" Rice asked, amazed. "Mardi Gras?"

The leader ripped off his mask and bowed ironically. His handsome Teutonic features were powdered, his lips rouged. "I am Count Axel Ferson. Servant, sir."

Rice knew the name; Ferson had been Toinette's lover before the Revolution. "Look, Count, maybe you're a little upset about Toinette, but I'm sure we can make a deal. Wouldn't you really rather have a color TV?"

"Spare us your satanic blandishments, sir!" Ferson roared. "I would not soil my hands on the collaborationist cow. We are the Freemason Liberation Front!"

"Christ," Rice said. "You can't possibly be serious. Are you taking on the project with these popguns?"

"We are aware of your advantage in armaments, sir. This is why we have made you our hostage." He spoke to the others in German. They tied Rice's hands and hustled him into the back of a horse-drawn wagon that had clopped out of the woods.

"Can't we at least take the car?" Rice asked. Glancing back, he saw Toinette sitting dejectedly in the road by the hovercraft.

"We reject your machines," Ferson said. "They are one more facet of your godlessness. Soon we will drive you back to hell, from whence you came!"

"With what? Broomsticks?" Rice sat up in the back of the wagon, ignoring the stink of manure and rotting hay. "Don't mistake our kindness for weakness. If they send the Gray Card Army through that portal, there won't be enough left of you to fill an ashtray."

"We are prepared to sacrifice! Each day thousands flock to our worldwide movement, under the banner of the All-Seeing Eye! We shall reclaim our destiny! The destiny you have stolen from us!"

"Your *destiny*?" Rice was aghast. "Listen, Count, you ever hear of guillotines?"

"I wish to hear no more of your machines." Ferson gestured to a subordinate. "Gag him."

THEY HAULED RICE to a farmhouse outside Salzburg. During fifteen bone-jarring hours in the wagon he thought of nothing but Toinette's betrayal. If he'd promised her the Green Card, would she still have led him into the ambush? That card was the only thing she wanted, but how could the Masonistas get her one?

Rice's guards paced restlessly in front of the windows, their boots squeaking on the loosely pegged floorboards. From their constant references to Salzburg he gathered that some kind of siege was in progress.

Nobody had shown up to negotiate Rice's release, and the Masonistas were getting nervous. If he could just gnaw through his gag, Rice was sure he'd be able to talk some sense into them.

He heard a distant drone, building slowly to a roar. Four of the men ran outside, leaving a single guard at the open door. Rice squirmed in his bonds and tried to sit up.

Suddenly the clapboards above his head were blasted to splinters by heavy machine-gun fire. Grenades whumped in front of the house, and the windows exploded in a gush of black smoke. A choking Masonista lifted his flintlock at Rice. Before he could pull the trigger a burst of gunfire threw the terrorist against the wall.

A short, heavyset man in flak jacket and leather pants stalked into the room. He stripped goggles from his smoke-blackened face, revealing Oriental eyes. A pair of greased braids hung down his back. He cradled an assault rifle in the crook of one arm and wore two bandoliers of grenades. "Good," he grunted. "The last of them." He tore the gag from Rice's mouth. He smelled of sweat and smoke and badly cured leather. "You are Rice?"

Rice could only nod and gasp for breath.

His rescuer hauled him to his feet and cut his ropes with a bayonet. "I am Jebe Noyon. Trans-Temporal Army." He forced a leather flask of rancid mare's milk into Rice's hands. The smell made Rice want to vomit. "Drink!" Jebe insisted. "Is koumiss, is good for you! Drink, Jebe Noyon tells you!"

Rice took a sip, which curdled his tongue and brought bile to his throat. "You're the Gray Cards, right?" he said weakly.

"Gray Card Army, yes," Jebe said. "Baddest-ass warriors of all times and places! Only five guards here, I kill them all! I, Jebe Noyon, was chief general to Genghis Khan, terror of the earth, okay, man?" He stared at Rice with great, sad eyes. "You have not heard of me."

"Sorry, Jebe, no."

"The earth turned black in the footprints of my horse."

"I'm sure it did, man."

"You will mount up behind me," he said, dragging Rice toward the door. "You will watch the earth turn black in the tireprints of my Harley, man, okay?"

FROM THE HILLS above Salzburg they looked down on anachronism gone wild.

Local soldiers in waistcoats and gaiters lay in bloody heaps by the gates of the refinery. Another battalion marched forward in formation, muskets at the ready. A handful of Huns and Mongols, deployed at the gates, cut them up with orange tracer fire and watched the survivors scatter.

Jebe Noyon laughed hugely. "Is like siege of Cambaluc! Only no stacking up heads or even taking ears any more, man, now we are civilized, okay? Later maybe we call in, like, grunts, choppers from 'Nam, napalm the son-of-a-bitches, far out, man."

"You can't do that, Jebe," Rice said sternly. "The poor bastards don't have a chance. No point in exterminating them."

Jebe shrugged. "I forget sometimes, okay? Always thinking to conquer the world." He revved the cycle and scowled. Rice grabbed the Mongol's stinking flak jacket as they roared downhill. Jebe took his disappointment out on the enemy, tearing through the streets in high gear, deliberately running down a group of Brunswick grenadiers. Only panic strength saved Rice from falling off as legs and torsos thumped and crunched beneath their tires.

Jebe skidded to a stop inside the gates of the complex. A jabbering horde of Mongols in ammo belts and combat fatigues surrounded them at once. Rice pushed through them, his kidneys aching.

Ionizing radiation smeared the evening sky around the Hohensalz-burg Castle. They were kicking the portal up to the high-energy maximum, running cars full of Gray Cards in and sending the same cars back loaded to the ceiling with art and jewelry.

Over the rattling of gunfire Rice could hear the whine of VTOL jets bringing in the evacuees from the US and Africa. Roman centurions, wrapped in mesh body armor and carrying shoulder-launched rockets, herded Realtime personnel into the tunnels that led to the portal.

Mozart was in the crowd, waving enthusiastically to Rice. "We're pulling out, man! Fantastic, huh? Back to Realtime!"

Rice looked at the clustered towers of pumps, coolers, and catalytic cracking units. "It's a goddamned shame," he said. "All that work, shot to hell."

"We were losing too many people, man. Forget it. There's plenty of eighteenth centuries."

The guards, sniping at the crowds outside, suddenly leaped aside as Rice's hovercar burst through the ages. Half a dozen Masonic fanatics still clung to the doors and pounded on the windscreen. Jebe's Mongols yanked the invaders free and axed them while a Roman flamethrower unit gushed fire across the gates.

Marie Antoinette leaped out of the hovercar. Jebe grabbed for her, but her sleeve came off in his hand. She spotted Mozart and ran for him, Jebe only a few steps behind.

"Wolf, you bastard!" she shouted. "You leave me behind! What about your promises, you merde, you pig-dog!"

Mozart whipped off his mirrorshades. He turned to Rice. "Who is this woman?"

"The Green Card, Wolf! You say I sell Rice to the Masonistas, you get me the card!" She stopped for breath and Jebe caught her by one arm. When she whirled on him, he cracked her across the jaw, and she dropped to the tarmac.

The Mongol focused his smoldering eyes on Mozart. "Was you, eh? You, the traitor?" With the speed of a striking cobra he pulled his machine pistol and jammed the muzzle against Mozart's nose. "I put my gun on rock and roll, there nothing left of you but ears, man."

A single shot echoed across the courtyard. Jebe's head rocked back, and he fell in a heap.

Rice spun to his right. Parker, the DJ, stood in the doorway of an equipment shed. He held a Walther PPK. "Take it easy, Rice," Parker said, walking toward him. "He's just a grunt, expendable."

"You *killed* him!"

"So what?" Parker said, throwing one arm around Mozart's frail shoulders. "This here's my boy! I transmitted a couple of his new tunes up the line a month ago. You know what? The kid's number five on the *Billboard* charts! Number five!" Parker shoved the gun into his belt. "With a bullet!"

"You gave him the Green Card, Parker?"

"No," Mozart said. "It was Sutherland."

"What did you do to her?"

"Nothing! I swear to you, man! Well, maybe I kind of lived up to what she wanted to see. A broken man, you know, his music stolen from him, his very soul?" Mozart rolled his eyes upward. "She gave me the Green Card, but that still wasn't enough. She couldn't handle the guilt. You know the rest."

"And when she got caught, you were afraid we wouldn't pull out. So you decided to drag *me* into it! You got Toinette to turn me over to the Masons. That was *your* doing!"

As if hearing her name, Toinette moaned softly from the tarmac. Rice didn't care about the bruises, the dirt, the rips in her leopard-skin jeans. She was still the most gorgeous creature he'd ever seen.

Mozart shrugged. "I was a Freemason once. Look, man, they're very uncool. I mean, all I did was drop a few hints, and look what happened." He waved casually at the carnage all around them. "I knew you'd get away from them somehow."

"You can't just *use* people like that!"

"Bullshit, Rice! You do it all the time! I *needed* this siege so Realtime would haul us out! For Christ's sake, I can't wait fifteen years to go up the line. History says I'm going to be *dead* in fifteen years! I don't want to die in this dump! I want that car and that recording studio!"

"Forget it, pal," Rice said. "When they hear back in Realtime how you screwed things up here—"

Parker laughed. "Shove off, Rice. We're talking Top of the Pops, here. Not some penny-ante refinery." He took Mozart's arm protectively.

"Listen, Wolf, baby, let's get into those tunnels. I got some papers for you to sign as soon as we hit the future."

The sun had set, but muzzle-loading cannon lit the night, pumping shells into the city. For a moment Rice stood stunned as cannonballs clanged harmlessly off the storage tanks. Then, finally, he shook his head. Salzburg's time had run out.

Hoisting Toinette over one shoulder, he ran toward the safety of the tunnels.

Allen Steele

With the publication of his novel Orbital Decay—about the engineering and political problems that zero-g "beamjacks" overcome to build satellites in outer space—and its sequel Lunar Descent, Allen Steele earned comparisons to Robert Heinlein and established his credentials as a promising new writer of hard science fiction. Since then, Steele has set his novels aboard space stations (Clarke County, Space; A King of Infinite Space), in undersea research facilities (Oceanspace), and in an earthquake-devastated near-future St. Louis (The Jericho Iteration). The Tranquillity Alternative is set at a civilian-manned moon base in an alternate world where manned space flight occurred in 1984 and lunar colonization took place shortly thereafter. A prodigious writer of short fiction, some of which has been collected in All-American Alien Boy and Rude Astronauts, Steele is the author of the Hugo Award–winning stories "The Good Rat," "The Death of Captain Future," and "Where Angels Fear to Tread."

THE DEATH OF CAPTAIN FUTURE

Allen Steele

The name of Captain Future, the supreme foe of all evil and evildoers, was known to every inhabitant of the Solar System.

That tall, cheerful, red-haired young adventurer of ready laugh and flying fists was the implacable Nemesis of all oppressors and exploiters of the System's human and planetary races. Combining a gay audacity with an unswervable purposefulness and an unparalleled mastery of science, he had blazed a brilliant trail across the nine worlds in defense of the right.
—EDMOND HAMILTON,
   Captain Future and the Space Emperor *(1940)*

THIS IS THE TRUE STORY of how Captain Future died.

We were crossing the inner belt, coasting toward our scheduled rendezvous with Ceres, when the message was received by the ship's comlink.

"Rohr . . . ? Rohr, wake up, please."

The voice coming from the ceiling was tall, dark, and handsome, sampled from one of the old Hercules vids in the captain's collection. It penetrated the darkness of my quarters on the mid-deck where I lay asleep after standing an eight-hour watch on the bridge.

I turned my head to squint at the computer terminal next to my bunk. Lines of alphanumeric code scrolled down the screen, displaying the routine systems-checks and updates that, as second officer, I was supposed to be monitoring at all times, even when I was off-duty and dead to the world. No red-bordered emergency messages, though; at first glance, everything looked copacetic.

Except the time. It was 0335 Zulu, the middle of the goddamn night.

"Rohr?" The voice was a little louder now. "*Mister Furland? Please wake up. . . .*"

I groaned and rolled over. "Okay, okay, I'm awake. What'dya want, Brain?"

The Brain. It was bad enough that the ship's AI sounded like Steve Reeves; it also had to have a stupid name like The Brain. On every vessel on which I had served, crewmembers had given their AIs human names—Rudy, Beth, Kim, George, Stan, Lisa, dubbed after friends or family members or deceased shipmates—or nicknames, either clever or overused: Boswell, Isaac, Slim, Flash, Ramrod, plus the usual Hals and Datas from the nostalgia buffs. I once held down a gig on a lunar tug where the AI was called Fughead—as in *Hey, Fughead, gimme the traffic grid for Tycho Station*—but no one but a bonehead would give their AI a silly-ass moniker like The Brain.

No one but Captain Future, that is . . . and I still hadn't decided whether or not my current boss was a bonehead, or just insane.

"*The captain asked me to awaken you,*" The Brain said. "*He wants you on the bridge at once. He says that it's urgent.*"

I checked the screen again. "I don't see anything urgent."

"*Captain's orders, Mr. Furland.*" The ceiling fluorescents began to slowly brighten behind their cracked and dusty panes, causing me to squint and clap my hand over my eyes. "*If you don't report to the bridge in ten minutes, you'll be docked one hour time-lost and a mark will be entered on your union card.*"

Threats like that usually don't faze me—everyone loses a few hours or gains a few marks during a long voyage—but I couldn't afford a bad service report now. In two more days the TBSA *Comet* would reach Ceres, where I was scheduled to join up with the *Jove Commerce*, outbound for Callisto. I had been lucky to get this far, and I didn't want my next CO to ground me just because of a bad report from my previous captain.

"Okay," I muttered. "Tell 'em I'm on my way."

I swung my legs over the side and felt around for where I had dropped my clothes on the deck. I could have used a rinse, a shave, and a nice long meditation in the head, not to mention a mug of coffee and a muffin from the galley, but it was obvious that I wasn't going to get that.

Music began to float from the walls, an orchestral overture that gradually rose in volume. I paused, my calves halfway into the trouser legs, as the strings soared upward, gathering heroic strength. German opera. Wagner. *The Flight of the Valkyries*, for God's sake. . . .

"Cut it out, Brain," I said.

The music stopped in mid-chord. *"The captain thought it would help rouse you."*

"I'm roused." I stood up and pulled my trousers the rest of the way on. In the dim light, I glimpsed a small motion near the corner of my compartment beside the locker; one moment it was there, then it was gone. "There's a cockroach in here," I said. "Wanna do something about it?"

"I'm sorry, Rohr. I have tried to disinfect the vessel, but so far I have been unable to locate all the nests. If you'll leave your cabin door unlocked while you're gone, I'll send a drone inside to . . ."

"Never mind." I zipped up my pants, pulled on a sweatshirt and looked around for my stikshoes. They were kicked under my bunk; I knelt down on the threadbare carpet and pulled them out. "I'll take care of it myself."

The Brain meant nothing by that comment; it was only trying to get rid of another pest which had found its way aboard the *Comet* before the freighter had departed from Lagrange Four. Cockroaches, fleas, ants, even the occasional mouse; they managed to get into any vessel that regularly rendezvoused with near-Earth spaceports, but I had never been on any ship so infested as the *Comet*. Yet I wasn't about to leave my cabin door unlocked. One of a few inviolable union rules I still enjoyed aboard this ship was the ability to seal my cabin, and I didn't want to give the captain a chance to go poking through my stuff. He was convinced that I was carrying contraband with me to Ceres Station, and even though he was right—two fifths of lunar mash whiskey, a traditional coming-aboard present for my next commanding officer—I didn't want him pouring good liquor down the sink because of Association regulations no one else bothered to observe.

I pulled on my shoes, fastened a utility belt around my waist and left the cabin, carefully locking the door behind me with my thumbprint. A short, upward-curving corridor took me past the closed doors of two other crew cabins, marked CAPTAIN and FIRST OFFICER. The captain was already on the bridge, and I assumed that Jeri was with him.

A manhole led to the central access shaft and the carousel. Before I went up to the bridge, though, I stopped by the wardroom to fill a squeezebulb with coffee from the pot. The wardroom was a disaster: a dinner tray had been left on the table, discarded food wrappers lay on the floor, and a small spider-like robot waded in the galley's sink, waging solitary battle against the crusty cookware that had been abandoned there. The captain had been here recently; I was surprised that he hadn't summoned me to clean up after him. At least there was some hot coffee left in the carafe, although judging from its odor and viscosity it was probably at least ten hours old; I toned it down with sugar and half-sour milk from the fridge before I poured it into a squeezebulb.

As always, the pictures on the wardroom walls caught my eye: framed reproductions of covers from ancient pulp magazines well over a hundred years old. The magazines themselves, crumbling and priceless, were bagged and hermetically sealed within a locker in the Captain's quarters. Lurid paintings of fishbowl-helmeted spacemen fighting improbable alien monsters and mad scientists that, in turn, menaced buxom young women in see-thru outfits. The adolescent fantasies of the last century—"Planets In Peril," "Quest Beyond the Stars," "Star Trail to Glory"—and above them all, printed in a bold swath across the top of each cover, a title . . .

CAPTAIN FUTURE

Man of Tomorrow

At that moment, my reverie was broken by a harsh voice coming from the ceiling:

"*Furland! Where are you?*"

"In the wardroom, Captain." I pinched off the lip of the squeezebulb and sealed it with a catheter, then clipped it to my belt. "Just grabbing some coffee. I'll be up there in a minute."

"*You got sixty seconds to find your duty station or I'll dock your pay for your last shift! Now hustle your lazy butt up here!*"

"Coming right now. . . ." I walked out of the wardroom, heading up the corridor toward the shaft. "Toad," I whispered under my breath when I was through the hatch and out of earshot from the ship's comnet. Who's calling who lazy?

Captain Future, Man of Tomorrow. God help us if that were true.

Ten minutes later a small ship shaped like an elongated teardrop rose from an underground hangar on the lunar surface. It was the Comet, the superswift craft of the Futuremen, known far and wide through the System as the swiftest ship in space.
—Hamilton, Calling Captain Future *(1940)*

My name's Rohr Furland. For better or worse, I'm a spacer, just like my father and his mother before him.

Call it family tradition. Grandma was one of the original beamjacks who helped build the first powersat in Earth orbit before she immigrated to the Moon, where she conceived my dad as the result of a one-night stand with some nameless moondog who was killed in a blowout only two days later. Dad grew up as an unwanted child in Descartes Station; he ran away at eighteen and stowed away aboard a Skycorp freighter to Earth, where he lived like a stray dog in Memphis before he got homesick and signed up with a Russian company looking for native-born selenians. Dad got home in time to see Grandma through her last years, fight in the Moon War on the side of the Pax Astra and, not incidentally, meet my mother, who was a geologist at Tycho Station.

I was born in the luxury of a two-room apartment beneath Tycho on the first anniversary of the Pax's independence. I'm told that my dad celebrated my arrival by getting drunk on cheap luna wine and balling the midwife who had delivered me. It's remarkable that my parents stayed together long enough for me to graduate from suit camp. Mom went back to Earth while Dad and I stayed on the Moon to receive the benefits of full citizenship in the Pax: Class A oxygen cards, good for air even if we were unemployed and dead broke. Which was quite often, in Dad's case.

All of which makes me a mutt, a true son of a bastard, suckled on air bottles and moonwalking before I was out of my diapers. On my sixteenth birthday, I was given my union card and told to get a job; two weeks before my eighteenth birthday, the LEO shuttle that had just hired me as a cargo handler touched down on a landing strip in Galveston, and with the aid of an exoskeleton I walked for the first time on Earth. I spent one week there, long enough for me to break my right arm by falling on a Dallas sidewalk, lose my virginity to an El Paso whore, and get one hell of a case of agoraphobia from all that wide-open Texas landscape. Fuck the cradle of humanity and the horse it rode in on; I caught the next boat back to the Moon and turned eighteen with a birthday cake that had no candles.

Twelve years later, I had handled almost every union job someone with my qualifications could hold—dock slob, cargo grunt, navigator, life support chief, even a couple of second-mate assignments—on more vessels than I could count, ranging from orbital tugs and lunar freighters to passenger shuttles and Apollo-class ore haulers. None of these gigs had ever lasted much longer than a year; in order to guarantee equal opportunity for all its members, the union shifted people from ship to ship, allowing only captains and first-mates to remain with their vessels for longer than eighteen months. It was a hell of a system; by the time you became accustomed to one ship and its captain, you were transferred to another ship and had to learn all over again. Or, worse, you went without work for several months at a time, which meant hanging around some spacer bar at Tycho Station or Descartes City, waiting for the local union rep to throw some other guy out of his present assignment and give you his job.

It was a life, but it wasn't much of a living. I was thirty years old and still possessed all my fingers and toes, but had precious little money in the bank. After fifteen years of hard work, the nearest thing I had to a permanent address was the storage locker in Tycho where I kept my few belongings. Between jobs, I lived in union hostels on the Moon or the elfives, usually occupying a bunk barely large enough to swing either a cat or a call-girl. Even the whores lived better than I did; sometimes I'd pay them just to let me sleep in a decent bed for a change, and never mind the sex.

To make matters worse, I was bored out of my wits. Except for one cycleship run out to Mars when I was twenty-five, I had spent my entire career—hell, my entire life—running between LEO and the Moon. It's not a bad existence, but it's not a great one either. There's no shortage of sad old farts hanging around the union halls, telling big lies to anyone who'll listen about their glory days as beamjacks or moondogs while drinking away their pensions. I was damned if I would end up like them, but I knew that if I didn't get off the Moon real soon, I would be schlepping LOX tanks for the rest of my life.

Meanwhile, a new frontier was being opened in the outer system. Deep-space freighters hauled helium-3 from Jupiter to feed the fusion tokamaks on Earth, and although Queen Macedonia had placed Titan off-limits because of the Plague, the Iapetus colony was still operational. There was good money to be made from landing a gig on one of the big ships that cruised between the gas giants and the belt, and union members who found work on the Jupiter and Saturn runs had guaranteed three-year contracts. It wasn't the same thing as making another trip between Moon and LEO every few days. The risks were greater, but so was the payoff.

Competition for jobs on the outer-system ships was tight, but that didn't stop me from applying anyway. My fifteen-year service record, with few complaints from previous captains and one Mars run to my name, helped me put a leg up over most of the other applicants. I held down a job as a cargo grunt for another year while I waited, but the union eventually rotated me out and left me hanging in Sloppy Joe's Bar in Tycho. Six weeks later, just as I was considering signing up as a tractor operator on the Clavius Dome construction project, the word came: the *Jove Commerce* needed a new executive officer, and my name had been drawn from the hat.

There was only one hitch. Since the *Commerce* didn't come further in-system than Ceres, and because the union didn't guarantee passage to the belt as part of the deal, I would have to either travel aboard a clipper—out of the question, since I didn't have money—or find a temporary job on an outbound asteroid freighter.

Okay, I was willing to do that, but now there was another complication: few freighters had available gigs for selenians. Most vessels which operated in the main belt were owned by the Transient Body Shipping Association, and TBSA captains preferred to hire crewmembers from other ships owned by the co-op rather than from my union. Nor did they want to sign up some dude who would only be making a one-way trip, because they'd lose him on Ceres before the trip was half-over.

The predicament was explained to me by my union rep when I met with him in his office in Tycho. Schumacher was an old buddy; he and I had worked together aboard a LEO tugboat before the union had hired him as its Tycho Station representative, so he knew my face and was willing to cut me some slack.

"Look, Rohr," he said, propping his moccasins up on his desk, "here's the scoop. I've checked around for a boat that'll take you on, and I found what you were looking for. An Ares-class ore freighter, outbound for Ceres . . . in fact, she's already docked at Lagrange Four and is ready to launch as soon as her captain finds a new second."

As he spoke, Schumacher punched up a holo of the ship, and it revolved in the tank above his desk. It was a standard rock hauler: eighty-two meters in length, with a gas-core nuclear engine at one end and a drum-shaped crew module at the other, joined at the center by the long narrow spine and open cargo bays. An uprated tugboat, really; nothing about it was either unfamiliar or daunting. I took a slug off the whisky flask he had pulled out of his desk drawer. "Great. What's her name?"

He hesitated. "The TBSA *Comet*," he said reluctantly. "Her captain is Bo McKinnon."

I shrugged and passed the flask back to him. "So what's the catch?"

Schumacher blinked. Instead of taking a hit off the whisky, he re-capped the flask and shoved it back in the drawer. "Let me repeat that," he said. "The *Comet*. Bo McKinnon." He peered at me as if I had come down with Titan Plague. "You're telling me you've never heard of him?"

I didn't keep up with the TBSA freighters or their captains; they re-turned to the Moon only once every few months to drop off their cargo and change crews, so few selenians happened to see them unless they were getting drunk in some bar. "Not a clue," I said.

Schumacher closed his eyes. "Terrific," he murmured. "The one guy who's never heard of Captain Future and it's gotta be you."

"Captain who?"

He looked back at me. "Look, just forget the whole thing, okay? Pre-tend I never mentioned it. There's another rock hauler heading out to Ceres in about six or seven weeks. I'll talk to the Association, try to get you a gig on that one instead. . . ."

I shook my head. "I can't wait another six or seven weeks. If I'm not on Ceres in three months, I'll lose the *Jove Commerce* job. What's wrong with this gig?"

Schumacher sighed as he reached back into the drawer for the flask. "What's wrong," he said, "is the nut who's in command. McKinnon is the worst captain in the Association. No one who's shipped out with him has ever stayed aboard, except maybe the google he's got for a first mate."

I had to bite my tongue when he said that. We were pals, but racism isn't an endearing trait. Sure, Superiors can be weird—their eyes, for starters, which was why some people called them by that name—but if you also use words like nigger, slant, kike or spic to describe people, then you're no friend of mine.

On the other hand, when you're hungry for work, you'll put up with just about anything.

Schumacher read the expression on my face. "It's not just that," he said hastily. "I understand the first officer is okay." *For a google, that is,* although he didn't say it aloud. "It's McKinnon himself. People have jumped ship, faked illness, torn up their union cards . . . anything to get off the *Comet*."

"That bad?"

"That bad." He took a long hit off the flask, gasped, and passed it back across the desk to me. "Oh, the pay's okay . . . minimum wage, but by Association standards that's better than union scale . . . and the *Comet* passes all the safety requirements, or at least so at inspection time. But McKinnon's running a tank short of a full load, if y'know what I mean."

I didn't drink from the flask. "Naw, man, I don't know what you mean. What's with this . . . what did you call him?"

"Captain Future. That's what he calls himself, Christ knows why." He grinned. "Not only that, but he also calls his AI 'The Brain' . . ."

I laughed out loud. "The Brain? Like, what? He's got a brain floating in a jar? I don't get it. . . ."

"I dunno. It's a fetish of some kind." He shook his head. "Anyway, everyone who's worked for him says that he thinks he's some kinda space hero, and he expects everyone to go along with the idea. And he's supposed to be real tough on people . . . you might think he was a perfectionist, if he wasn't such a slob himself."

I had worked for both kinds before, along with a few weirdos. They didn't bother me, so long as the money was right and they minded their own business. "Ever met him?"

Schumacher held out his hand; I passed the flask back to him and he took another swig. Must be the life, sitting on your ass all day, getting drunk and deciding people's futures. I envied him so much, I hoped someone would kindly cut my throat if I was ever in his position.

"Nope," he said. "Not once. He spends all his time on the *Comet*, even when he's back here. Hardly ever leaves the ship, from what I've been told . . . and that's another thing. Guys who've worked for him say that he expects his crew to do everything but wipe his butt after he visits the head. Nobody gets a break on his ship, except maybe his first officer."

"What about him?"

"Her. Nice girl, name of . . ." He thought hard for a moment, then snapped his fingers. "Jeri. Jeri Lee-Bose, that's it." He smiled. "I met her once, not long before she went to work on the *Comet*. She's sweet, for a google."

He winked and dropped his voice a bit. "I hear she's got a thing for us apes," he murmured. "In fact, I've been told she's bunking with her captain. If half of what I've heard about McKinnon is true, that must make him twice as sick as I've heard."

I didn't reply. Schumacher dropped his feet and leaned across the desk, lacing his fingers together as he looked straight at me. "Look, Rohr," he said, as deadly serious as if he were discussing my wanting to

marry his sister, "I know you're working under a time limit and how much the *Jove Commerce* job means to you. But I gotta tell you, the only reason why Captain Future would even consider taking aboard a short-timer is because nobody else will work for him. He's just as des-
. perate as you are, but I don't give a shit about him. If you wanna turn it down, I won't add it to your card and I'll save your place in line. It'll just be between you and me. Okay?"

"And if I turn it down?"

He waved his hand back and forth. "Like I said, I can try to find you another gig. The *Nickel Queen's* due home in another six weeks or so. I've got some pull with her captain, so maybe I can get you a job there . . . but honest to Jesus, I can't promise anything. The *Queen's* a good ship and everyone I know wants to work for her, just as much as nobody wants to get within a klick of the *Comet.*"

"So what do you suggest I do?"

Schumacher just smiled and said nothing. As my union rep, he was legally forbidden against making any decisions for me; as a pal, he had done his best to warn me about the risks. From both points of view, though, he knew I didn't have any real choice. I could spend three months aboard a ship run by a borderline psycho, or the rest of my life jacking off on the Moon.

I thought about it for a few moments, then I asked for the contract.

The three Futuremen who were Curt Newton's faithful, lifelong comrades made a striking contrast to their tall, red-haired young leader.
—HAMILTON, The Comet Kings (1942)

One-sixth gravity disappeared as I crawled through the carousel hatch and entered the bridge.

The *Comet's* command center was located in the non-rotating forward deck of the crew module. The bridge was the largest single compartment in the ship, but even in freefall it was cramped: chairs, consoles, screens, emergency suit lockers, the central navigation table with its holo tank and, at the center of the low ceiling, the hemispherical bulge of the observation blister.

The ceiling lamps were turned down low when I came in—The Brain was mimicking Earth-time night—but I could see Jeri seated at her duty station on the far end of the circular deck. She looked around when she heard the hatch open.

"Morning," she said, smiling at me. "Hey, is that coffee?"

"Something like it," I muttered. She gazed enviously at the squeeze-bulb in my hand. "Sorry I didn't bring you any," I added, "but the Captain . . ."

"Right. I heard Bo yell at you." She feigned a pout which didn't last very long. "That's okay. I can get some later after we make the burn."

Jeri Lee-Bose: six-foot-two, which is short for a Superior, with the oversized dark blue eyes that give bioengineered spacers their unsavory nickname. Thin and flat-chested to the point of emaciation, the fingers of her ambidextrous hands were long and slender, her thumbs almost extending to the tips of her index fingers. Her ash-blond hair was shaved nearly to the skull, except for the long braid that extended from the nape of her neck nearly down to the base of her narrow spine, where her double-jointed legs began.

The pale skin of her face was marked with finely etched tattoos around her eyes, nose, and mouth, forming the wings of a monarch butterfly. She had been given these when she had turned five, and since Superiors customarily add another tattoo on their birthdays and Jeri Lee was twenty-five, pictograms covered most of her arms and her shoulders, constellations and dragons which weaved their way under and around the tank-top she wore. I had no idea of what else lay beneath her clothes, but I imagined that she was well on her way to becoming a living painting.

Jeri was strange, even for a Superior. For one thing, her kind usually segregate themselves from Primaries, as they politely call us baseline humans (or apes, when we're not around). They tend to remain within their family-based clans, operating independent satrapies that deal with the TBSA and the major space companies only out of economic necessity, so it's rare to find a lone Superior working on a vessel owned by a Primary.

For another thing, although I've been around Superiors most of my life and they don't give me the creeps like they do most groundhogs and even many spacers, I've never appreciated the aloof condescension the majority of them display around unenhanced humans. Give one of them a few minutes, and they'll bend your ear about the Superior philosophy of extropic evolution and all that jive. Yet Jeri was the refreshing, and even oddball, exception to the rule. She had a sweet disposition, and from the moment I had come aboard the *Comet*, she had accepted me both as an equal and as a new-found friend. No stuffiness, no harangues about celibacy or the unspirituality of eating meat or using profanity; she was a fellow crewmate, and that was that.

No. That wasn't quite all there was to it.

When one got past the fact that she was a scarecrow with feet that functioned as a second pair of hands and eyes the size of fuel valves, she was sensual as hell. She was a pretty woman, and I had become infatuated with her. Schumacher would have twitched at the thought of sleeping with a google, but in three weeks since The Brain had revived us from the zombie tanks, there had been more than a few times when my desire to see the rest of her body exceeded simple curiosity about her tattoos.

Yet I knew very little about her. As much as I loved looking at her, that was surpassed by my admiration for her innate talent as a spacer. In terms of professional skill, Jeri Lee-Bose was one of the best First Officers I had ever met. Any Royal Navy, TBSA, or free-trader captain would have killed to sign her aboard.

So what the hell was she doing aboard a scow like the *Comet*, serving under a bozo like Bo McKinnon?

I tucked in my knees and did a half-gainer that landed the soles of my stikshoes against the carpet. Feet now firmly planted on the floor, I walked across the circular compartment to the nav table, sucking on the squeezebulb in my left hand. "Where's the captain?" I asked.

"Topside, taking a sextant reading." She nodded toward the observation blister above us. "He'll be down in a minute."

Typical. Part of the reason why Superiors have enhanced eyes is for optical work like sextant sightings. This should be Jeri's job, but McKinnon seemed to regard the blister as his personal throne. I sighed as I settled down in my chair and buckled in. "Should have known," I muttered. "Wakes you up in the middle of the goddamn night, then disappears when you want a straight answer."

Her mouth pursed into sympathetic frown. "Bo will tell you more when he comes down," she said, then she swiveled around in her chair as she returned her attention to her board.

Jeri was the only person aboard who was permitted to call Captain Future by his real name. I didn't have that privilege, and The Brain hadn't been programmed to do otherwise. The fondness I had developed for Jeri over the last three weeks was tempered by the fact that, in almost any disagreement, she usually sided with the captain.

Obviously, there was something else she knew but wasn't telling me, preferring to defer the issue to McKinnon. I had become used to such behavior over the last few months, but it was still irritating. Most first officers act as intermediaries between captain and crew, and in that sense Jeri performed well, yet at times like this I felt as if I had more in common with The Brain than with her.

So be it. I swiveled my chair to face the nav table. "Hey, Brain," I called out. "Gimme a holo of our current position and trajectory, please."

The space within the holo tank coruscated briefly, then an arch-shaped slice of the main belt appeared above the table. Tiny spots of orange light depicting major asteroids slowly moved along blue sidereal tracks, each designated by their catalog numbers. The *Comet* was pinpointed by a small silver replica of the vessel, leading the end of a broken red line which bisected the asteroid orbits.

The *Comet* was near the edge of the third Kirkwood gap, one of the "empty spaces" in the belt where Martian and Jovian gravitational forces caused the number of identified asteroids to diminish per fraction of an astronomical unit. We were now in the ⅓ gap, about two and a half A.U.'s from the Sun. In another couple of days we would enter the main belt and be closing in on Ceres. Once we arrived, the *Comet* would unload the cargo it had carried from the Moon and, in return, take on the raw ore TBSA prospectors had mined from the belt and shipped to Ceres Station. It was also there that I was scheduled to depart the *Comet* and await the arrival of the *Jove Commerce*.

At least, that was the itinerary. Now, as I studied the holo, I noticed a not-so-subtle change. The red line depicting the freighter's trajectory had been altered since the end of my last watch about four hours earlier.

It no longer intercepted Ceres. In fact, it didn't even come close to the asteroid's orbit.

The *Comet* had changed course while I slept.

Without saying anything to Jeri, I unbuckled my harness and pushed over to the table, where I silently stared at the holo for a couple of minutes, using the keypad to manually focus and enlarge the image. Our new bearing took us almost a quarter of a million kilometers from Ceres, on just the other side of the ⅓ Kirkwood gap.

"Brain," I said, "what's our destination?"

"*The asteroid 2046-Barr*," it replied. It displayed a new orange spot in the tank, directly in front of the *Comet's* red line.

The last of my drowsiness dissipated into a pulse of white-hot rage. I could feel Jeri's eyes on my back.

"Rohr . . ." she began.

I didn't care. I stabbed the intercom button on the table. "McKinnon!" I bellowed. "Get down here!"

Long silence. I knew he could hear me.

"Goddammit, get down here! Now!"

Motors whined in the ceiling above me, then the hatch below the observation blister irised open and a wingback chair began to descend into the bridge, carrying the commanding officer of the TBSA *Comet*. It wasn't until the chair reached the deck that the figure seated in it spoke.

"You can call me . . . Captain Future."

In the ancient pulp magazines he so adored, Captain Future was six-and-a-half feet in height, ruggedly handsome, bronze-skinned and red-haired. None of this applied to Bo McKinnon. Squat and obese, he filled the chair like a half-ton of lard. Black curly hair, turning gray at the temples and filthy with dandruff, receded from his forehead and fell around his shoulders, while an oily, unkempt beard dripped down the sides of his fat cheeks, themselves the color of mildewed wax. There were old food stains on the front of his worn-out sweatshirt and dark marks in the crotch of his trousers where he had failed to properly shake himself after the last time he had visited the head. And he smelled like a fart.

If my description seems uncharitable, let there be no mistake: Bo McKinnon was a butt-ugly, foul-looking son of a whore, and I have met plenty of slobs like him to judge by comparison. He had little respect for personal hygiene and fewer social graces, he had no business being anyone's role model, and I was in no mood for his melodramatic bull-shit just now.

"You changed course." I pointed at the holo tank behind me, my voice quavering in anger. "We're supposed to come out of the Kirkwood in another few hours, and while I was asleep you changed course."

McKinnon calmly stared back at me. "Yes, Mister Furland, that I did. I changed the *Comet*'s trajectory while you were in your quarters."

"We're no longer heading for Ceres . . . Christ, we're going to come nowhere *near* Ceres!"

He made no move to rise from his throne. "That's correct," he said, slowly nodding his head. "I ordered The Brain to alter our course so that we'd intercept 2046-Barr. We fired maneuvering thrusters at 0130 shiptime, and in two hours we'll execute another course correction. That should put us within range of the asteroid in about . . ."

"Eight hours, Captain," Jeri said.

"Thank you, Mister Bose," he said, otherwise barely acknowledging her. "Eight hours. At this time the *Comet* will be secured for emergency action."

He folded his hands across his vast stomach and gazed back at me querulously. "Any further questions, Mister Furland?"

Further questions?

My mouth hung agape for a few moments. I was unable to speak, unable to protest, unable to do anything except wonder at the unmitigated gall of this mutant amalgamation of human and frog genes.

"Just one," I finally managed to say. "How do you expect me to make my rendezvous with the *Jove Commerce* if we detour to . . ."

"2046-Barr," Jeri said softly.

McKinnon didn't so much as blink. "We won't," he said. "In fact, I've already sent a message to Ceres Station, stating that the *Comet* will be delayed and that our new ETA is indefinite. With any luck, we'll reach Ceres in about forty-eight hours. You should be able to . . ."

"No, I won't." I grasped the armrest of his chair with both hands and leaned forward until my face was only a few inches from his. "The *Jove* is due to leave Ceres in forty-*two* hours . . . and that's at the latest, if it's going to meet its launch window for Callisto. They'll go, with or without me, and if they go without me, I'm stuck on Ceres."

No. That wasn't entirely true. Ceres Station wasn't like the Moon; it was too small an outpost to allow a shipwrecked spacer to simply hang around until the next outer-system vessel passed through. The TBSA rep on Ceres would demand that I find a new gig, even if it entailed signing aboard a prospector as grunt labor. This was little better than indentured servitude, since my union card didn't mean shit out here in terms of room, board, and guaranteed oxygen supplies; my paychecks would be swallowed up by all the above. Even then, there was no guarantee that I'd swing another job aboard the next Jupiter or Saturn tanker; I was lucky enough to get the *Jove Commerce* job.

That, or I could tuck tail and go back the way I came—and that meant remaining aboard the *Comet* for its return flight to the Moon.

In the latter case, I'd sooner try to walk home.

Try to understand. For the past three weeks, beginning with the moment I had crawled out of the zombie tank, I had been forced to endure almost every indignity possible while serving under Bo McKinnon. His first order, in fact, had been in the hibernation deck, when he had told me to take the catheter off his prick and hold a bag for him to pee in.

That had been only the beginning. Standing double-watches on the bridge because he was too lazy to get out of bed. Repairing decrepit equipment that should have been replaced years ago, only to have it break down again within a few more days after he had abused it past its tolerance levels. Being issued spurious orders on a whim, only to have those same orders countermanded before the task was half-complete because McKinnon had more scut-work he wanted me to do — then being berated because the first assignment had been left unfinished. Meals skipped because the captain decided that now was the time for me to go EVA and inspect the davits in the payload bay. Rest periods interrupted because he wanted a snack fetched from the galley and was too "busy" to get it himself. . . .

But most of all, the sibilant, high-pitched whine of his voice, like that of a spoiled brat who had been given too many toys by an overindulgent parent. Which was, indeed, exactly what he was.

Bo McKinnon hadn't earned his TBSA commission. It had been purchased for him by his stepfather, a wealthy lunar businessman who was one of the Association's principal stockholders. The *Comet* had been an obsolete ore freighter on the verge of being condemned and scuttled when the old man had bought it for the kid as a means of getting his unwanted stepson out of his hair. Before that, McKinnon had been a customs inspector at Descartes, a minor bureaucrat with delusions of grandeur fostered by the cheap space operas in his collection of moldering twentieth century magazines, for which he apparently spent every spare credit he had in the bank. No doubt his stepfather had been as sick of McKinnon as I was. At least this way the pompous geek spent most of his time out in the belt, hauling rock and bellowing orders at whoever was unlucky enough to have been talked into signing aboard the *Comet*.

This much I had learned after I had been aboard for three weeks. By the time I had sent a message to Schumacher, demanding to know what else he hadn't told me about Bo McKinnon, I was almost ready to steal the *Comet*'s skiff and attempt flying it to Mars. When Schumacher sent me his reply, he gave a lame apology for not telling me everything about McKinnon's background; after all, it was his job to muster crewmembers for deep-space craft, and he couldn't play favorites, so sorry, et cetera. . . .

By then I had figured out the rest. Bo McKinnon was a rich kid playing at being a spacecraft commander. He wanted the role, but he didn't want to pay the dues, the hard-won experience that any true commander has to accomplish. Instead, he managed to shanghai washed-up cases like me to do his dirty work for him. No telling what arrangement he had worked out with Jeri; for my part, I was the latest in a long line of flunkies.

I didn't hijack the skiff, if only because doing so would have ruined my career and Mars colonists are notoriously unkind to uninvited guests. Besides, I figured that this was a temporary thing: three weeks of Captain Future, and I'd have a story to tell my shipmates aboard the *Jove Commerce* as we sipped whisky around the wardroom table. You think this captain's a hardass? Hey, let me tell you about my last one. . . .

Now, as much as I still wanted to get the hell off the *Comet*, I did not wish to be marooned on Ceres, where I would be at the tender mercies of the station chief.

Time to try a different tack with Captain Future.

I released the armrests and backed off, taking a deep breath as I forced myself to calm down. "Look, Captain," I said, "what's so important about this asteroid? I mean, if you've located a possible lode, you can always stake a claim with the Association and come back for it later. What's the rush?"

McKinnon raised an imperious eyebrow. "Mr. Furland, I am not a prospector," he huffed. "If I were, I wouldn't be commanding the *Comet*, would I?"

No, I silently responded, you wouldn't. No self-respecting rock-hounds would have you aboard their ship. "Then what's so important?"

Without a word, McKinnon unbuckled his seat harness and pushed out his chair. Microgravity is the great equalizer for overweight men; he floated across the narrow compartment with the grace of a lunar trapeze artist, somersaulting in mid-air and catching a ceiling rung above the navigation table, where he swung upside-down and typed a command into the keyboard.

The holo expanded until 2046-Barr filled the tank. Now I could see that it was a potato-shaped rock, about three klicks in length and seven hundred meters in diameter. An octopus-like machine clung to one end of the asteroid, with a narrow, elongated pistol thrust out into space.

I recognized it immediately. A General Astronautics Class-B Mass Driver, the type used by the Association to push large carbonaceous-chrondite asteroids into the inner belt. In effect, a mobile mining rig.

Long bores sunk into the asteroid extracted raw material from its core, which in turn were fed into the machine's barrel-shaped refinery, where heavy metals and volatiles were separated from the ancient stone. The remaining till was then shot through an electromagnetic railgun as reaction mass that propelled both asteroid and mass driver in whatever direction was desired.

By the time the asteroid reached lunar orbit, the rig would have refined enough nickel, copper, titanium, carbon, and hydrogen to make the effort worthwhile. The hollowed out remains of the asteroid could then be sold to one of the companies, who would then begin the process of transforming it into another LaGrange colony.

"That's the TBSA *Fool's Gold*," McKinnon said, pointing at the computer-generated image. "It's supposed to reach lunar orbit in four months. Twelve persons are aboard, including its captain, first officer, executive officer, physician, two metallurgists, three engineers . . ."

"Yeah, okay. Twelve guys who are going to get rich when the shares are divvied up." I couldn't keep the envy out of my voice. Only one or two main-belt asteroids made their way in-system every few years, mainly because prospectors didn't find enough such rocks to make them worth the time, money, and attention. The smaller ones were usually broken up by nukes, and anything much larger was claimed and mined by prospectors. On the other hand, if just the right asteroid was located and claimed, the bonanza was enough to make its finders wealthy enough to retire. "So what?"

McKinnon stared at me for a moment, then he cartwheeled until he was no longer upside-down and dug into a pocket. He handed me a wadded-up slip of printout. "Read," he said.

I read:

MESS. 1473 0118 GMT 7/26/73 CODE A1/0947
TRANSMISSION FROM CERES STATION TO ALL SPACECRAFT
PRIORITY REPEATER
MESSAGE BEGINS
MAYDAY RECEIVED 1240 GMT 7/25/46 FROM TBSA MASS DRIVER
"FOOL'S GOLD" BREAK VESSEL EXPERIENCING UNKNOWN—
REPEAT UNKNOWN—PROBLEMS BREAK CASUALTIES AND
POSSIBLE FATALITIES REPORTED DUE TO UNDETERMINED
CAUSES BREAK SHIP STATUS UNKNOWN BREAK NO FURTHER
COMMUNICATION FOLLOWING MAYDAY BREAK VESSEL FAILS TO
RESPOND TO QUERIES BREAK REQUEST URGENT ASSISTANCE

FROM NEAREST VESSEL OF ANY REGISTRY BREAK PLEASE
RESPOND ASAP
MESSAGE ENDS
(TRANSMISSION REPEATS)
0119 GMT 7/26/73 CODE A1/0947

I turned to Jeri. "Are we the nearest vessel?"

She gravely nodded her head. "I checked. The only other ship within range is a prospector near Gaspara, and it's thirty-four hours from Barr. Everything else is closer to Ceres than we are."

Damn.

According to common law, the closest vessel to a spacecraft transmitting a Mayday was obligated to respond, regardless of any other mission or prior obligation in all but the most extreme emergency . . . and my job aboard the *Jove Commerce* didn't qualify as such, as much as I might have liked to think otherwise.

McKinnon held out his hand. I handed the paper back to him. "I guess you've already informed Ceres that we're on our way."

The captain silently reached to another panel and pushed a set of buttons. A flatscreen lit, displaying a playback of the transmission he had sent to Ceres Station. A simulacrum of the fictional Curt Newton appeared on the screen.

"*This is Captain Future, calling from the TBSA Comet, registry Mexico Alpha Foxtrot one-six-seven-five.*" The voice belonged to McKinnon even if the handsome face did not. The Brain had lip-synched them together, and the effect was sadly absurd. *I've received your transmission, and I'm on our way to investigate the situation aboard the* Fool's Gold. *The Futuremen and I will keep you informed. Captain Future, over and out.*"

I groaned as I watched this. The idiot couldn't keep his fantasy life out of anything, even a distress signal. Captain Future and the—yech!—Futuremen to the rescue.

"You have something to say, Mister Furland?"

McKinnon's hairy chin was thrust out at me with what he probably thought was obstinate resolve, but which actually resembled the petulance of an insecure child daring someone to step into his corner of the sandbox. Not for the first time, I realized that his only way of dealing with people was to boss them around with what little authority he could muster—and since this was his ship, no one could either object or walk out on him. Least of all me.

"Nothing, Captain." I pushed off from the nav table and floated back to my duty station. Like it or not, we were committed; he had both law and his commission on his side, and I wasn't about to commit mutiny because I had refused my commander's orders to respond to a distress signal.

"Very good." McKinnon shoved himself in the direction of the carousel hatch. "The sextant confirms we're on course for Barr. I'll be in my cabin if you need me."

He stopped, then looked over his shoulder. "You'll need to arm the weapons pod. There may be . . . trouble."

Then he was gone, undoubtedly to claim the sleep I had lost.

"Trouble, my ass," I murmured under my breath.

I glanced over at Jeri. If I expected a sly wink or an understanding smile, I received nothing of the kind. Her face was stoical behind the butterfly mask she wore; she touched her jaw, speaking into the microphone implanted beneath her skin at childhood. "TBSA *Fool's Gold*, this is TBSA *Comet*, Mexico Alpha Foxtrot one-six-seven-five. Do you copy? Over."

I was trapped aboard a ship commanded by a lunatic.

Or so I thought. The real insanity was yet to come.

Space pirates were no new thing, to the System. There were always some corsairs infesting the outlaw asteroids or the wilder moons of the outer planets.
—Hamilton, Outlaw World (1945)

One good thing could be said about standing a second consecutive watch on the bridge: I finally learned a little more about Jeri Lee-Bose.

Does it seem surprising that I could have spent three weeks of active duty aboard a spacecraft without hearing a shipmate's entire life story? If so, understand that there's a certain code of conduct among spacers; since many of us have unsavory pasts that we'd rather not discuss, it's not considered proper etiquette to bug someone about private matters unless they themselves bring it up first. Of course, some shipmates will bore you to death, blabbing about everything they've ever said or done until you want to push them into the nearest airlock. On the other hand I've known several people for many years without ever learning where they were born or who their parents were.

Jeri fell into the latter category. After we were revived from biostasis, I had learned many little things about her, but not very many big things. It wasn't as if she was consciously hiding her past; it was simply that the subject had never really come up, during the few times that we had been alone together without Captain Future's presence looming over us. Indeed, she might have completed the voyage as a near-stranger, had I not made an offhand comment.

"I bet the selfish son-of-a-bitch has never thought of anyone else in his life," I said.

I had just returned from the galley, where I had fetched two fresh squeezebulbs of coffee for us. I was still fuming from the argument I had lost, and since McKinnon wasn't in earshot I gave Jeri an earful.

She passively sipped her coffee as I pissed and moaned about my misfortunes, listening patiently as I paced back and forth in my stikshoes, ranting about the commanding officer's dubious mental balance, his unflattering physiognomy, his questionable taste in literature, his body odor and anything else that came to mind, and when I paused for breath she finally put in her quarter-credit.

"He saved my life," she said.

That caught me literally off-balance. My shoes came unstuck from the carpet, and I had to grab hold of a ceiling handrail.

"Say what?" I asked.

Not looking up at me, Jeri Lee absently played with the squeezebulb in her left hand, her right foot holding open the pages of her personal logbook. "You said that he's never thought of anyone else in his life," she replied. "Whatever else you might say about him, you're wrong there, because he saved my life."

I shifted hands so I could sip my coffee. "Anything you want to talk about?"

She shrugged. "Nothing that probably hasn't occurred to you already. I mean, you've probably wondered why a google is serving as first officer aboard this ship, haven't you?" When my mouth gaped open, she smiled a little. "Don't look so surprised. We're not telepathic, rumors to the contrary . . . it's just that I've heard the same thing over the last several years we've been together."

Jeri gazed pensively through the forward windows. Although we were out of the Kirkwood gap, no asteroids could be seen. The belt is much less dense than many people think, so all we saw was limitless starscape, with Mars a distant ruddy orb off to the port side.

"You know how Superiors mate, don't you?" she asked at last, still not looking at me.

I felt my face grow warm. Actually, I didn't know, although I had frequently fantasized about Jeri helping me find out. Then I realized that she was speaking literally. "Prearranged marriages, right?"

She nodded. "All very carefully planned, in order to avoid inbreeding while expanding the gene pool as far as possible. It allows for some selection, of course . . . no one tells us exactly *whom* we should marry, just as long as it's outside of our own clans and it's not to Primaries."

She paused to finish her coffee, then she crumpled the squeezebulb and batted it aside with her right foot. It floated in midair, finding its own miniature orbit within the compartment. "Well, sometimes it doesn't work out that way. When I was twenty, I fell in love with a boy at Descartes Station . . . a Primary, as luck would have it. At least I thought I was in love. . . ."

She grimaced, brushing her long braid away from her delicate shoulders. "In hindsight, I guess we were just good in bed. In the long run it didn't matter, because as soon as he discovered that he had knocked me up, he got the union to ship him off to Mars. They were only too glad to do so, in order to avoid . . ."

"A messy situation. I see." I took a deep breath. "Leaving you stuck with his child."

She shook her head. "No. No child. I tried to keep it, but the miscarriage . . . anyway, the less said about that, the better."

"I'm sorry." What else could I have said? She should have known better, since there had never been a successful crossbreeding between Superiors and Primaries? She had been young and stupid; both are forgivable sins, especially when they usually occur in tandem.

Jeri heaved a sigh. "It didn't matter. By then, my family had disowned me, mainly because I had violated the partnership that had already been made for me with another clan. Both clans were scandalized, and as a result neither one wanted me." She looked askance at me. "Bigotry works both ways, you know. You call us googles, we call you apes, and I had slept with an ape. An insult against the extropic ideal."

She closed the logbook, tossed it from her left foot to her right hand, and tucked it into a web beneath the console. "So I was grounded at Descartes. A small pension, just enough to pay the rent, but nothing really to live for. I suppose they expected me to become a prostitute . . . which I did, for a short time . . . or commit ritual suicide and save everyone the sweat."

"That's cold." But not unheard of. There were a few grounded Superiors to be found in the inner system, poor sad cases working at menial tasks in Lagranges or on the Moon. I remembered an alcoholic google who hung out at Sloppy Joe's; he had eagle wings tattooed across his back, and he cadged drinks off tourists in return for performing cartwheels across the bar. An eagle with clipped tailfeathers. Every so often, one would hear of a Superior who checked out by walking into an airlock and pushing the void button. No one knew why, but now I had an answer. It was the Superior way.

"That's extropy for you." She laughed bitterly, then was quiet for a moment. "I was considering taking the long walk," she said at last, "but Bo found me first, when I . . . well, propositioned him. He bought me a couple of drinks and listened to my story, and when I was done crying he told me he needed a new first officer. No one else would work for him, so he offered me the job, for as long as I cared to keep it."

"And you've kept it."

"And I've kept it," she finished. "For the record, Mr. Furland, he has always treated me with the greatest of respect, despite what anyone else might have told you. I've never slept with him, nor has he ever demanded that I do so . . ."

"I didn't . . . !"

"No, of course you haven't, but you've probably wondered, haven't you?" When I turned red, she laughed again. "Everyone who has worked the *Comet* has, and sometimes they like to tell stories about the google and the fat slob, fucking in his cabin between shifts."

She smiled, slowly shaking her head. "It isn't so . . . but, to tell the truth, if he ever asked, I'd do so without a second thought. I owe him that little."

I didn't say anything for a couple of minutes. It isn't often when a shipmate unburdens his or her soul, and Jeri had given me much to consider. Not the least of which was the slow realization that, now more than before, I was becoming quite fond of her.

Before he had gone below, McKinnon had told me to activate the external missile pod, so I pushed myself over to his station and used that minor task to cover for my embarrassment.

Strapping on EMP to an Ares-class freighter was another example of McKinnon's overheated imagination. When I had once asked why, he'd told me that he'd purchased it as war surplus from the Pax Astra Royal Navy back in '71, after the hijacking of the TBSA *Olympia*. No one had ever discovered who had taken the *Olympia*—indeed, the hijack wasn't discovered until five months later, when the uncrewed solar-sail vessel arrived at Ceres Station with its cargo holds empty—but it was widely believed to be the work of indie prospectors desperate for food and various supplies.

I had to cover my smile when McKinnon told me that he was worried about "pirates" trying to waylay the *Comet*. Having four 10k nukes tucked behind the *Comet*'s cargo section was like arming a gig with heatseekers. Not that McKinnon wouldn't have loved it if someone *did* try to steal his ship—Captain Future meets the Asteroid Pirates and all that—but I was worried that he might open fire on some off-course prospector ship that was unlucky enough to cross his path.

Another thought occurred to me. "When he picked you . . . um, when you signed on as First Officer . . . were you aware that he doesn't have a firm grip on reality?"

Jeri didn't answer immediately. I was about to repeat myself when I felt a gentle nudge against my arm. Looking down, I saw her left foot slide past me, its thumb-sized toes toggling the MISSILE STANDBY switch I had neglected to throw.

"Sure," she said. "In fact, he used to call me Joan . . . as in Joan Randall, Curt Newton's girlfriend . . . until I got him to cut it out."

"Really?"

"Um-hmm." She rested her right leg against the back of my chair. "Consider yourself lucky he doesn't call you Otho or Grag. He used to do that to other crewmen until I told him that no one got the joke." She grinned. "You ought to try reading some of those stories sometime. He's loaded them into The Brain's library annex. Not great literature, to be sure . . . in fact, they're rather silly . . . but for early twentieth century science fiction, they're . . ."

"Science what?"

"Science fiction. What they used to call fantasy back . . . well, never mind." She pulled her leg back and folded it beneath her bottom as she gazed again out the window. "Look, I know Bo can be weird most of the time, but you have to realize that he's a romantic stuck in an age where most people don't even know what the word means anymore. He wants derring-do, swashbuckling, great adventure . . . he wants to be a hero."

"Uh-huh. Bo McKinnon, space hero." I tried to transpose him on the magazine covers he had framed in the galley: wielding a ray gun in each hand, defending Jeri from ravaging monsters. It didn't work, except to make me stifle a chuckle.

"That isn't too much to ask for, is it?" There was sadness in her eyes when she glanced my way. Before I could get the grin off my face, she returned her gaze to the windows. "Perhaps so. This isn't an age of heroes. We move rock back and forth across the system, put money in the bank, and congratulate ourselves for our ingenuity. A hundred years ago, what we're doing now was the stuff of dreams, and the people who did it were larger than life. That's what he finds so attractive in those stories. But now . . ."

She let out her breath. "Who can blame Bo for wanting something he can't have? He's stuck on a second-hand freighter with an ex-whore for a first officer and a second officer who openly despises him, and he's the butt of every joke from Earth to Iapetus. No wonder he drops everything to answer a Mayday. This may be the only chance he gets."

I was about to retort that my only chance to get a job on a decent ship was slipping through my fingers when her console double-beeped. A moment later, The Brain's voice came through the ceiling speaker.

"Pardon me, but we're scheduled for course correction maneuvers. Do you wish for me to execute?"

Jeri swiveled her chair around. "That's okay, Brain. We'll handle it by manual control. Give me the coordinates."

The AI responded by displaying a three-dimensional grid on her flatscreens. "Want me to do anything?" I asked, although it was obvious that she had matters well in hand.

"I've got everything covered," she said, her long fingers typing in the coordinates. "Get some sleep, if you want." She cast a quick grin over her shoulder. "Don't worry. I won't tell Bo you dozed off in his chair."

End of conversation. Besides, she had a good idea. I cranked back the chair, buckled the seat belt and tucked my hands in my pockets so they wouldn't drift around in freefall. It might be a while before I got another chance; once we reached 2046-Barr, Captain Future would be back on deck, bellowing orders and otherwise making my life painful.

She had told me a lot about Bo McKinnon, but nothing I had heard gave me much affection for the man. So far as I was concerned, he was still the biggest dork I had ever met . . . and if there was anyone aboard the TBSA *Comet* who deserved my sympathy, it was Jeri Lee-Bose, who was meant for better things than this.

As I shut my eyes, it occurred to me that the captain's chair fitted me a lot better than it did McKinnon. One day, perhaps I'd have enough money in the bank to buy him out. It would be interesting to see if he took orders as well as he gave them.

It was a warm and comforting thought, and I snuggled against it like a pillow as I fell asleep.

"Look, Arraj—it is a meteor!" cried the younger Martian excitedly. "And there's a ship guiding it!"

The two stared for a moment at the incredible spectacle. The expanding black spot was clearly a giant meteor, rushing now at tremendous speed toward Mars. And close beside the booming meteor rushed a dark spaceship, playing rays upon the great mass. The ship was propelling the meteor toward Mars.
—HAMILTON, Captain Future's Challenge (1940)

Several hours later, the *Comet* rendezvoused with 2046-Barr.

The asteroid looked much the same as the holo tank had depicted it—an enormous rock the color of charcoal—but the *Fool's Gold* itself was the largest spacecraft I had ever seen short of a Lagrange colony. It dwarfed the *Comet* like a yacht parked alongside an ocean liner, a humongous machine attached to one end of the asteroid's mass.

A humongous machine, and apparently lifeless. We approached the mass-driver with great caution, being careful to avoid its stern lest we get nailed by the stream of debris being constantly ejected by its railgun. That was the only apparent sign of activity; although light gleamed from the portals of the rotating command sphere, we could detect no motion within the windows, and the radio remained as silent as it had been for the last eighteen hours.

"Look yonder." I pointed through the window at the hangar bay, a wide berth within the barrel-shaped main hull just forward of the railgun. Its doors were open, and as the *Comet* slowly cruised past we could see the gig and service pods parked in their cradles. "Everything's there. Even the lifeboats are still in place."

Jeri angled the camera on the outrigger telemetry boom until it peered into the bay. Her wide eyes narrowed as she studied a close-up view on a flatscreen. "That's weird," she murmured. "Why would they depressurize the bay and open the doors if they didn't . . . ?"

"Knock it off, you two!"

McKinnon was strapped in his chair, on the other side of Jeri Lee's duty station from mine. "It doesn't matter why they did it. Just keep your eyes peeled for pirates . . . they could be lurking somewhere nearby."

I chose to remain silent as I piloted the *Comet* past the mass-driver's massive anchor-arms and over the top of the asteroid. Ever since

McKinnon had returned to the bridge an hour ago—following the shower and leisurely breakfast I myself had been denied—he had been riding his favorite hobby horse: asteroid pirates had seized control of the *Fool's Gold* and taken its crew hostage.

This despite the fact that we had not spotted any other spacecraft during our long journey and that none could now be seen in the vicinity of the asteroid. It could also be logically argued that the four-person crew of a prospector ship would have a hard time overcoming the twelve-person crew of a mass-driver, but logic meant little to Captain Future. His left hand rested on the console near the EMP controls, itching to launch a nuke at the pirate ship he was certain to find lurking in the asteroid's shadow.

Yet, when we completed a fly-by of 2046-Barr, none were to be found. In fact, nothing moved at all, save for the asteroid itself. . . .

A thought occurred to me. "Hey, Brain," I said aloud, "have you got a fix on the mass-driver's position and bearing?"

"*Affirmative, Mr. Furland. It is X-ray one-seven-six, Yankee two . . .*"

"Mr. Furland!" McKinnon snapped. "I didn't give orders for you to . . ."

I ignored him. "Skip the numbers, Brain. Just tell me if it's still on course for cislunar rendezvous."

A momentary pause, then: "*Negative, Mr. Furland. The* Fool's Gold *has altered its trajectory. According to my calculations, there is a seventy-two-point-one probability that it is now on collision course with the planet Mars.*"

Jeri went pale as she sucked in her breath, and even McKinnon managed to shut up. "Show it to me on the tank," I said as I turned my chair around to face the nav table.

The tank lit, displaying a holographic diagram of the *Fool's Gold's* present position in relationship with the Martian sidereal-hour. Mars still lay half an A.U. away, but as The Brain traced a shallow-curving orange line through the belt, we saw that it neatly intercepted the red planet as it advanced on its orbit around the Sun.

The Brain translated the math it had displayed in a box next to the three-dimensional grid. "*Assuming that its present delta-vee remains unchecked, in two hundred and thirty-six hours, twelve minutes, and twenty-four seconds, 2046-Barr will collide with Mars.*"

I did some arithmetic in my head. "That's about ten days from now."

"*Nine-point-eight-three Earth standard days, to be exact.*" The Brain expanded the image of Mars until it filled the tank; a bull's-eye appeared at a point just above the equator. *"Estimated point of impact will be approximately twelve degrees North by sixty-three degrees West, near the edge of the Lunae Planum."*

"Just north of Valles Marineris," Jeri said. "Oh God, Rohr, that's near . . ."

"I know." I didn't need a refresher course in planetary geography. The impact point was in the low plains above Mariner Valley, only a few hundred klicks northeast of Arsia Station, not to mention closer to the smaller settlements scattered around the vast canyon system. For all I knew, there could now be a small mining town on the Lunae Planum itself; Mars was being colonized so quickly these days, it was hard to keep track of where a bunch of its one and a half million inhabitants decided to pitch claims and call themselves New Chattanooga or whatever.

"Sabotage!" McKinnon yelled. He unbuckled his harness and pushed himself closer to the nav table, where he stared at the holo. "Someone has sabotaged the mass-driver so that it'll collide with Mars! Do you realize . . . ?"

"Shut up, Captain." I didn't need his histrionics to tell me what would occur if . . . *when* . . . 2046-Barr came down in the middle of the Lunae Planum.

The Martian ecosystem wasn't as fragile as Earth's. Indeed, it was much more volatile, as the attempt in the '50s to terraform the planet and make the climate more stable had ultimately proved. However, the Mars colonists who still remained after the boondoggle had come to depend upon its seasonal patterns in order to grow crops, maintain solar farms, continue mining operations and other activities which insured their basic survival.

It was a very tenuous sort of existence that relied upon conservative prediction of climatic changes. The impact of a three-kilometer asteroid in the equatorial region would throw all that straight into the compost toilet. Localized quakes and duststorms would only be the beginning; two or three hundred people might be killed outright, but the worst would be yet to come. The amount of dust that would be raised into the atmosphere by the collision would blot out the sky for months on end, causing global temperatures to drop from Olympus Mons to the Hellas Plantia. As a result, everything from agriculture to power supplies would be affected, to put it mildly, with starvation in the cold and dark awaiting most of the survivors.

It wasn't quite doomsday. A few isolated settlements might get by with the aid of emergency relief efforts from Earth. But as the major colony world of humankind, Mars would cease to exist.

McKinnon was still transfixed upon the holo tank, jabbing his finger at Mars while raving about saboteurs and space pirates and God knows what else, when I turned back to Jeri. She had taken the helm in my absence, and as the *Comet* came up on the *Fool's Gold* again, I closely studied the mass-driver on the flatscreens.

"Okay," I said quietly. "The hangar bay is out . . . we can't send the skiff in there while it's depressurized and the cradles are full. Maybe if we . . ."

She was way ahead of me. "There's an auxiliary docking collar here," she said, pointing to a port on the spar leading to the command sphere. "It'll be tight, but I think we can squeeze us in there."

I looked at the screen. Tight indeed. Despite the fact that the *Comet* had a universal docking adapter, the freighter wasn't designed for mating with a craft as large as *Fool's Gold*. "That's cutting it close," I said. "If we can collapse the telemetry boom, though, we might be able to make it."

She nodded. "We can do that, no problem . . . except it means losing contact with Ceres."

"But if we don't hard-dock," I replied, "then someone's got to go EVA and try entering a service airlock."

Knowing that this someone would probably be me, I didn't much relish the idea. An untethered spacewalk between two vessels under acceleration is an iffy business at best. On the other hand, cutting off our radio link with Ceres under these circumstances was probably not a good idea. If we fucked up in some major way, then no one at Ceres Station would be informed of the situation, and early warning from Ceres to Arsia Station might save a few lives, if evacuation of settlements near Lunae Planum was started soon enough.

I made up my mind. "We'll hard-dock," I said, turning in my seat toward the communications console, "but first we send a squib to Ceres, let them know what's . . ."

"Hey! What are you two doing?"

Captain Future had finally decided to see what the Futuremen were doing behind his back. He kicked off the nav table and pushed over to us, grabbing the backs of our chairs with one hand each to hover over us. "I haven't issued any orders, and nothing is done on my ship without my . . ."

"Bo, have you been listening to what we've been saying?" Jeri's expression was carefully neutral as she stared up at him. "Have you heard a word either Rohr or I have said?"

"Of course I . . . !"

"Then you know that this is the only recourse," she said, still speaking calmly. "If we don't hard-dock with the *Gold*, then we won't have a chance of shutting down the railgun or averting its course."

"But the pirates. They might . . . !"

I sighed. "Look, get it through your head. There's no . . ."

"Rohr," she interrupted, casting me a stern look that shut me up. When I dummied up once more, she transfixed McKinnon again with her wide blue eyes. "If there are pirates aboard the *Gold*," she said patiently, "we'll find them. But right now, this isn't something we can solve by firing missiles. Rohr's right. First, we send a squib to Ceres, let them know what's going on. Then . . ."

"I know that!"

"Then, we have to dock with . . ."

"I know that! I know that!" His greasy hair scattered in all directions as he shook his head in frustration. "But I didn't . . . I didn't give the orders and . . ."

He stopped, sullenly glaring at me with inchoate rage, and I suddenly realized the true reason for his anger. McKinnon's subordinate second officer, whom he had harassed and chastised constantly for three weeks, had become uppity by reaching a solution that had evaded him. Worse yet, the second officer had done it with the cooperation of the Captain's first officer, who had tacitly agreed with him on all previous occasions.

Yet this wasn't a trifling matter such as checking the primary fuel pump or cleaning the galley. Countless lives were at stake, time was running out, and while he was spewing obvious nonsense about space pirates, Mister Furland was trying to take command of his ship.

Had I a taser conveniently tucked in my belt, I would have settled the argument by giving him a few volts and strapping his dead ass in his precious chair, thereby allowing Jeri Lee and me to continue our work unfettered. But since outright mutiny runs against my grain, compromise was my only weapon now.

"Begging your pardon, Captain," I said. "You're quite right. You haven't issued orders, and I apologize."

Then I turned around in my chair, folded my hands in my lap, and waited.

McKinnon sucked in his breath. He stared through the windows at the *Fool's Gold*, looked over his shoulder once more at the holo tank, weighing the few options available against the mass of his ego. After too many wasted seconds, he finally reached a decision.

"Very well," he said. He let go of our chairs and shoved himself back to his accustomed seat. "Ms. Bose, prepare to dock with the *Fool's Gold*. Mr. Furland, ready the main airlock hatch and prepare to go EVA."

"Aye, sir," Jeri said.

"Um, yeah . . . aye, sir."

"Meanwhile, I'll send a message to Ceres Station and inform them of the situation before we lose contact." Satisfied that he had reached a proper decision, he laid his hands on the armrest. "Good work, Future-men," he added. "You've done well."

"Thank you, Captain," Jeri said.

"Aye, sir. Thank you." I unbuckled my seat harness and pushed off toward the bridge hatch, trying hard not to smile.

A little victory. Insignificant as it then seemed, I didn't have any idea how much my life depended upon it.

He took the pilot chair and headed the Comet *across the zone toward the computed position of the invisible asteroid.*

"They'll surely see us approaching!" Ezra warned. "The Magician of Mars will be taking no chances, Cap'n Future!"

"We're going to use a stratagem to get onto that asteroid without him suspecting," Curt informed. *"Watch."*

—HAMILTON, The Magician of Mars *(1941)*

I'm a creature of habit, at least when it comes to established safety procedures, and so it was out of habit that I donned an EVA suit before I cycled through the *Comet's* airlock and entered the *Fool's Gold*.

On one hand, wearing the bulky spacesuit within a pressurized spacecraft is stupidly redundant, and the panel within the airlock told me that there was positive pressure on the other side of the hatch. Yet it could be argued the airlock sensors might be out of whack and there was nothing but hard vacuum within the spar; this has been known to happen before, albeit rarely, and people have died as a result. In any case, the *Astronaut's General Handbook* says that an EVA suit should be worn when boarding another craft under uncertain conditions, and so I followed the book.

Doing so saved my life.

I went alone, leaving Jeri and McKinnon behind inside the freighter. The hatch led past the *Gold*'s airlock into the spar's access tunnel, all of which was vacant. Switching on the helmet's external mike, I heard nothing but the customary background hum of the ventilation system, further evidence that the vessel crew compartments were still pressurized.

At that point, I could well have removed my helmet and hung it from a strap on my utility belt. In fact, the only reason I didn't was that I didn't want it banging around as I went through the carrousel, which lay at the end of the tunnel to my right. Besides, the stillness of the tunnel gave me the chills. Surely someone would have noticed the unscheduled docking of an Ares-class freighter, let alone one so far from Ceres. Why wasn't there an officer waiting at the airlock to chew me out for risking collision with his precious ship?

The answer came after I rotated through the carrousel and entered the rotating command sphere. That's when I found the first corpse.

A naked man hung upside down through an open manhole, his limp arms dangling above the wide pool of blood on the deck. It was difficult to see his face, because the blood that had dyed it crimson came from a scimitar-shaped gash in his neck. Looking up through the manhole, I saw that his feet had been neatly lashed together with a bungee cord, which in turn was tied to a conduit in the ceiling of the corridor directly above.

Since there were no bloodstains below his shoulders, it was obvious that his throat had been slit after he had been hung from the conduit. The blood was dry—most of it, anyway—and the body was stiff. He had been here for quite some time.

I reported what I found to Jeri and McKinnon, and then I gingerly pushed the body out of the way and continued down the corridor.

Please understand if everything I tell you sounds coldly methodical, even callous. First, if you've worked in space as long as I have—that is, all my life—then death, no matter how horrible it may be, is no stranger. The first time I saw a man die was when I was nine years old, when a one-in-a-million micrometeorite punched through the helmet faceplate of one of my school teachers while he was leading us on a field trip to the Apollo 17 landing site at Taurus Lithrow. Since then, I've seen the grisly results of explosive decompression, fatal radiation overexposure, freak mining accidents, careless suit-up procedures, hull fires and electrocutions, even someone who choked on his own vomit after consuming too much bathtub vodka during a birthday party. Death comes to us all, eventually; if you're careful and wise, all you can do is make sure that it isn't too painful and no one is stuck with a mess to clean up.

Second: if I attempted now to describe each and every body I discovered as I made my way through the *Fool's Gold*, not only would the result be gratuitous pandering to those who wallow in such details, but I would never be able to complete this testimony.

To put it succinctly, the command sphere of the *Fool's Gold* was a slaughterhouse.

I found ten more bodies, each more gruesome than the last. They were in crew cabins and passageways, in the galley and in the head, in the rec room and the quartermaster's office.

Most were alone, but two of them were together, each apparently dead from wounds they had inflicted upon one another: a man and a woman, who had tried to carve each other up with knives they had taken from the nearby galley.

A couple of the bodies were nude, like the first, but most were fully or partially clothed. For the most part, they had died of stabbing or bludgeon wounds, by means of anything that could be used as a weapon, whether it be a ballpoint pen, a screwdriver, or a pipefitter's wrench.

One woman was lucky. She had committed suicide by hanging herself by a coiled bedsheet she had cast over the top of a door. I hope that she had successfully strangled herself before whoever found her body seared off her right arm with the cutting torch cast nearby.

As I climbed up ladders, poked my helmet through hatches, and stepped over stiffening corpses, I kept up a running monologue, informing the *Comet* of where I exactly was within the vessel and what I had just found. I made no speculation as to why this massacre had taken place, only to note that the bodies seemed reasonably fresh and that most of the bloodstains were dry.

And blood lay everywhere. It was splattered across walls and soaked into carpets and dripping from wall fixtures, until it no longer resembled blood and just looked like spilled red paint. I was glad I had my helmet on, because the visor helped distance me from the carnage, and the rank odor would have made me even more sickened than I was now.

Although I heard an occasional gasp or exclamation from Jeri through my headset, after a while I couldn't detect McKinnon's voice any longer. I assumed that he had gone someplace private to vomit. This was understandable; the violence around me was mind shattering.

There were four decks in the command sphere, one above the other. By the time I reached the top deck, I had counted eleven corpses. Remembering that McKinnon had told me earlier that the crew complement of the *Fool's Gold* was twelve, I had begun to wonder where the last body lay.

The hatch leading to the bridge was sealed shut; I used the laser welding torch from my belt to cut the lock. When I grasped the lock-wheel and prized it open, it made a faint grinding noise, and it was at that moment that I heard a methodical, almost rhythmic thumping, as if something were being beaten against a bulkhead.

I first thought it was another background noise from the vessel itself, but when I pushed the hatch farther open, the noise it made interrupted the rhythm.

I stopped, holding the hatch ajar as I listened intently. I heard a faint giggle, then the thumping sound recommenced.

Someone was alive within the bridge.

The command center was dimly lit, the fluorescents switched off; the only light came from computer displays, flatscreens, and multicolored switches. The deck was in ruins, as if there had been a blowout, although the external pressure gauge told me it was still pressurized: up-ended chairs, ripped logbooks and manuals strewn across the floor, the remains of a bloody shirt.

The thumping continued. Seeking its unseen source, I switched on the helmet lamp and walked within its beam, my eyes darting back and forth as I searched for the sole survivor of the *Fool's Gold*. I was halfway across the bridge when my eye caught something scrawled across a bulkhead. Two words, fingerpainted in blood across the gray surface:

PLAGUE

TITAN

It was then that I knew that wearing an EVA suit had saved my life.

Trembling within its insulated layers, I crossed the deserted bridge, looking for the last remaining crewmember of the *Fool's Gold*.

I found him in the emergency airlock, huddled in a corner next to the hatch, his knees drawn up to his chin. The jumpsuit he wore was streaked with gore, but I could still make out the captain's stars on its epaulets. His wary eyes winced from the glare of my lamp, and he giggled like a small child who had been caught exploring his mother's dresser drawers.

And then he continued to beat at the deck with the severed human arm he grasped in his left hand.

I don't know how long I stared at him. A few seconds, several minutes, perhaps longer. Jeri was saying something I couldn't under-stand; I paid no attention, nor could I respond. It wasn't until I heard another noise—from behind me, the faint sound of the hatch being shoved open—that I tore my eyes away from the mad captain of the *Fool's Gold*.

Bo McKinnon.

He had followed me from the *Comet*.

And, like the idiot he was, he wasn't wearing an EVA suit.

> *The little teardrop ship, the* Comet, *blasted at top speed toward the Earth and its summoning call. Captain Future thought somberly of the many times he had answered that call. Each time, he and the Futuremen had found themselves called on to battle deadly perils. Was it to be the same this time?*
>
> *"We can't always win," he thought grimly. "We've been lucky, but the law of averages eventually has to turn against us."*
> —HAMILTON, The Triumph of Captain Future *(1940)*

Despite the name, no one knows the exact origin of the Titan Plague. It was first contracted by members of the *Herschel Explorer* expedition of 2069, during the Pax's ill-fated attempt to establish a research outpost on Titan. Although it was later theorized that the virus was indigenous to Titan itself, the fact that it thrived in an oxygen-nitrogen environ-ment led many people to speculate that the Plague had originated some-where other than Titan's nitrogen-methane atmosphere. There was even hearsay that the expedition had encountered an extrasolar race on Titan and that the Plague had been passed from Them . . . but, of course, that was just rumor.

Regardless, the indisputable facts are these: by the time the PARN *Herschel Explorer* returned to the inner system, the majority of its crew had been driven insane by an airborne virus. The only reason why the three surviving expedition members, including the ship's commander, were not infected was that they had managed to seal themselves within the command center, where they survived on emergency oxygen sup-plies and carefully rationed food and water. Most of the unquarantined members butchered each other during the long voyage home; those who did not died in agony when the disease rotted their brains in its terminal stages.

Once the *Herschel Explorer* reached the asteroid belt, the survivors parked it in orbit around Vesta, then used a lifeboat to escape. Three months later, the *Herschel Explorer* was scuttled by the PARN *Intrepid*. By then, Queen Macedonia had decreed that no further expeditions would be sent to Titan and that any vessels attempting to land there would be destroyed by Her Majesty's navy.

Despite the precautions, though, there had been a few isolated outbreaks of Titan Plague, albeit rare and confined to colonies in the outer system. No one knew exactly how the disease spread from the *Herschel Explorer*, although it was believed that it had been carried by the survivors themselves despite rigorous decontamination. Even though the first symptoms resembled little more than the once-common cold, the homicidal dementia that quickly followed was unmistakable. When someone came down with the Plague, there was no other option than to isolate them, remove anything that could be used as a weapon, and wait until they died.

No cure had ever been found.

Somehow, in some way we would never know, the Plague had found its way aboard the *Fool's Gold*. In the close confines of the mass-driver, it had swept through the entire vessel, driving its crew insane before they realized what had hit them. Perhaps the captain had figured it out, yet despite his precautions he himself was infected.

I was safe because I had worn a spacesuit while exploring the ship.

But Bo McKinnon . . .

Captain Future, Man of Tomorrow, dauntless hero of the spaceways. In his search for adventure, McKinnon had recklessly entered the vessel without bothering to don a suit.

"Did you shut the airlock?" I snapped.

"What? Huh?" Pale, visibly shaken by the horrors he had seen, McKinnon was staring at the maniac crouched in the airlock behind us. "Airlock? What . . . which . . . ?"

I grabbed his shoulders and shook him so hard his headset fell down around his neck. "The *Comet* airlock! Did you shut it behind you, or did you leave it open?"

Unable to hear me now, he stammered until he realized that his headset was ajar. He fumbled with it until the earphones were back in place. "The airlock? I think so, I . . ."

"I think so? You moron, did you . . . ?"

"Furland, oh my God . . ." He gaped at the wreckage around him. "What happened to these people? Did they . . . watch out!"

I turned around just in time to catch a glimpse of the madman as he lurched to his feet. Howling at the top of his lungs, he charged toward us, flailing the severed arm like a cricket bat.

I threw McKinnon aside. As he sprawled across the deck, I grabbed the airlock hatch and shoved it closed. An instant later the creature hit the opposite side of the hatch. He almost banged it open, but I put my shoulder against it. The hatch held, and a twist of lockwheel sealed it airtight; nonetheless, I could feel dull vibrations as the madman hammered against it with his hideous trophy.

I couldn't keep him locked in there forever. Sooner or later, he would find the lockwheel and remember how it worked. Perhaps then I could overcome him—if I was lucky, considering his berserk rage—but even then, I didn't dare bring him aboard the *Comet*.

There was only one solution. I found the airlock's outer control panel and flipped open its cover. "I'm sorry, sir," I whispered to the lunatic. "May God have mercy on us both."

Then I pushed the switch that jettisoned the outer hatch.

The alarm bells that rang throughout the bridge were the poor man's funeral dirge. There was long silence after I shut off the alarms, finally broken by McKinnon's voice.

"Mr. Furland, you just murdered that man."

I turned back around. McKinnon had managed to struggle to his feet; he clutched the back of a chair for support, and he glared at me with outraged eyes.

Before I could respond, Jeri's voice came to me over the comlink: *"Rohr, he shut the airlock on the way out. The* Comet *hasn't been infected."*

I let out my breath. For once, Bo had managed to do something right ,on his own. "Good deal, kiddo. Keep it shut until I come back aboard."

I stepped away from the airlock, heading for the helm station on the other side of the bridge. McKinnon planted himself in my path. "Did you hear me, Mr. Furland?" he demanded, his adam's apple bobbing beneath his beard. "You just killed a man . . . I saw you do it! You . . ."

"Don't remind me. Now get out of my way." I pushed him aside and marched toward the helm.

One of its flatscreens depicted a schematic chart of the asteroid's position and estimated course. As I suspected, someone aboard the mass-driver had deliberately laid in the new course during a fit of insanity. Probably the captain himself, considering the fact that he had locked himself in here.

"I'm placing you under arrest!" McKinnon yelled. "Under my jurisdiction as an agent of the Planet Police, I . . ."

"There's no such thing." I bent over the keypad and went to work accessing the main computer, my fingers thick and clumsy within the suit gloves. "No Planet Police, no asteroid pirates. Just a ship whose air ducts are crawling with the Plague. You're . . ."

"I'm Captain Future!"

The virus must have already affected him. I could have checked to see if he was displaying any of the flu-like symptoms that were supposed to be the Plague's first signs, but he was the least of my worries just now.

No matter what I did, I couldn't access the program for the central navigation system. Lack of a password that had probably died along with one of the damned souls aboard this ship, and none of the standard overrides or interfaces worked either. I was completely locked out, unable to alter the vessel's velocity or trajectory that had it propelling 2046-Barr straight toward Mars.

"And what are you talking about, not letting anyone aboard the *Comet* until you give the word?" McKinnon was no longer hovering over me; he had found the late captain's chair and had taken it as his own, as if assuming command of a vessel far larger than his measly freighter. "I'm the boss of this ship, not you, and I'm staying in charge until . . ."

Okay. The helm wouldn't obey any new instructions. Maybe it was still possible to scuttle the *Fool's Gold*. I accessed the engineering subsystem and began searching for a way to shut down the primary coolant loop of the gas-core reactor and its redundant safety systems. If I timed it right, perhaps the *Comet* would make a clean getaway before the reactor overloaded . . . and if we were goddamned lucky, the explosion might knock the asteroid sufficiently off-course.

"*Rohr?*" Jeri again. "*What's going on up there?*" I didn't want to tell her, not with McKinnon eavesdropping on our comlink.

At the sound of her voice, he surged to his feet. "Joan! He's working for Ul Quorn, the Magician of Mars! He's going to . . . !"

I heard him coming long before he reached me. I stood up and, pulling back my arm, landed a right hook square against his hairy jaw.

It stopped him, but it wouldn't keep him stopped. McKinnon was a big guy. He staggered back, his eyes unfocused as he groped at the chair for support. "Traitor," he mumbled, feeling at his mouth with his left hand. "You traitor, you . . ."

I didn't have time for this shit, so I punched him again, this time square in the nose. Second shot did the trick; he reeled backward, sagged against the chair, and flopped flat on his back.

"*What are you doing?*" she demanded.

Even within the thick padding of my gloves, my knuckles hurt like hell. "Something that should have been done a long time ago," I murmured.

Cute line. I used up the last of my luck that way. I scrambled at the helm console for several more minutes before I submitted to the inevitable. Like the navigation controls, the engineering subsystem wouldn't obey my commands without the proper passwords. It was possible that they were written down somewhere, but I didn't have the time or inclination to go searching through the operations manuals, especially since most of them were strewn across the bridge like so much garbage.

We weren't out of options yet. There was still a final alternative, one which McKinnon himself had given us.

It was then that I knew that Captain Future had to die.

"*Captain Future is dead!*"

The rumbling voice of the big green Jovian space-sailor rose above the laughter and chatter and clink of goblets, in this crowded Venusopolis spacemen's cafe. He eyed his little knot of companions at the bar, as though challenging them to dispute him.

One of the hard-bitten spacemen, a swarthy little Mercurian, shook his head thoughtfully.

"I'm not so sure. It's true that the Futuremen have been missing for months. But they'd be a hard bunch to kill."

—HAMILTON, *Outlaws of the Moon* (1942)

As I write, I'm back on the Moon, occupying a corner table in Sloppy Joe's. It's almost closing time; the crowds have thinned out and the bartender has rung the bell for last call. He'll let me stay after he shuts the doors, though. Heroes never get booted out with the riffraff, and there's been no shortage of free drinks ever since I returned from Ceres.

After all, I'm the last person to see Captain Future alive.

The news media helped us maintain our alibi. It was a story that had everything. Adventure, romance, blood and guts, countless lives at stake.

Best of all, a noble act of self-sacrifice. It'll make a great vid. I sold the rights yesterday.

Because it's been so widely told, you already know how the story ends. Realizing that he had been fatally infected with Titan Plague, Bo McKinnon—excuse me, Captain Future—issued his final instructions as commanding officer of the TBSA *Comet*.

He told me to return to the ship, and once I was safely aboard, he ordered Jeri to cast off and get the *Comet* as far away as possible.

Realizing what he intended to do, we tried to talk him out of it. Oh, and how we argued and pleaded with him, telling him that we could place him in biostasis until we returned to Earth, where doctors could attempt to save his life.

In the end, though, McKinnon simply cut off his comlink so that he could meet his end with dignity and grace.

Once the *Comet* was gone and safely out of range, Captain Future managed to instruct the mass-driver's main computer to overload the vessel reactors. While he sat alone in the abandoned bridge, waiting for the countdown, there was just enough time for him to transmit one final message of courage. . . .

Don't make me repeat it, please. It's bad enough that the Queen read it aloud during the memorial service, but now I understand that it's going to be inscribed upon the base of the twice-life-size statue of McKinnon that's going to be erected at Arsia Station. Jeri did her best when she wrote it, but between you and me, I still think it's a complete crock.

Anyway, the thermonuclear blast not only obliterated the *Fool's Gold*, but it also sufficiently altered the trajectory of 2046. The asteroid came within five thousand kilometers of Mars; its close passage was recorded by the observatory on Phobos, and the settlements in the Central Meridian reported the largest meteor shower in the history of the colonies.

And now Bo McKinnon is remembered as Captain Future, one of the greatest heroes in the history of humankind.

It was the least Jeri could have done for him.

Considering what a jerk Bo had been all the way to the end, I could have tried to claim the credit, but her strong will persevered. I suppose she's right; it would look bad if it was known that McKinnon had gone out as a raving lunatic who had to be coldcocked by his second officer.

Likewise, no one has to know that four missiles launched from the *Comet* destroyed the mass-driver's main reactor, thus causing the explosion that averted 2046-Barr from its doomsday course. The empty weapon pod was jettisoned before the *Comet* reached Ceres, and the small bribe paid to a minor Pax bureaucrat insured that all records of it ever having been installed on the freighter were completely erased.

It hardly matters. In the end, everyone got what they wanted.

As first officer of the *Comet*, Jeri became its new commander. She offered me her old job, and since the *Jove Commerce* deal was down the tubes, I gratefully accepted. It wasn't long after that before she also offered to show me the rest of her tattoos, an invitation that I also accepted. Her clan still won't speak to her, especially since she now plans to marry a Primary, but at least her fellow Superiors have been forced to claim her as one of their own.

For now, life is good. There's money in the bank, we've shucked our black sheep status, and there's no shortage of companies who want to hire the legendary Futuremen of the TBSA *Comet*. Who knows? Once we get tired of working the belt, maybe we'll settle down and take a shot at beating the odds on this whole cross-breeding thing.

And Bo got what he wanted, even though he didn't live long enough to enjoy it. In doing so, perhaps humankind got what it needed.

There's only one thing that still bothers me.

When McKinnon went nuts aboard the *Fool's Gold* and tried to attack me, I assumed that he had come down with the Plague. This was a correct assumption; he had been infected the moment he had come through the airlock.

However, I later learned that it takes at least six hours for Titan Plague to fully incubate within a human being, and neither of us had been aboard the *Fool's Gold* for nearly half that long.

If McKinnon was crazy at the end, it wasn't because of the Plague. To this day, I have no idea what made him snap . . . unless he believed that I was trying to run off with his ship, his girl, and his goddamn glory.

Hell, maybe I was.

Last night, some nervous kid—a cargo grunt off some LEO freighter, his union card probably still uncreased—sidled up to me at the bar and asked for my autograph. While I was signing the inside cover of his logbook, he told me a strange rumor he had recently heard: Captain Future managed to escape from the *Fool's Gold* just before it blew. According to him, prospectors in the inner belt report spotting a gig on their screens, one whose pilot answers their calls as Curt Newton before transmissions are lost.

I bought the youngster a drink and told him the truth. Naturally, he refused to believe me, nor can I blame him.

Heroes are hard to find. We need to welcome them whenever they appear in our midst. You've just got to be careful to pick the right guy, because it's easy for someone to pretend to be what they're not.

Captain Future is dead.

Long live Captain Future.

Brad Linaweaver

"Moon of Ice," Brad Linaweaver's contribution to this volume, was a
Nebula finalist story in 1982, and was later expanded into the successful
novel of the same name. He has worked almost exclusively in the alternate history subgenre, producing stories such as "Destination: Indies," an
alternate telling of Christopher Columbus's journey across the Atlantic,
and "Unmerited Favor," which takes a more militant approach to the
story of Jesus Christ's life. He is also the author of the novels Clownface,
The Land Beyond Summer, and Sliders: The Novel. Winner of the Prometheus Award in 1989, he lives and works in Los Angeles, California.

MOON OF ICE

Brad Linaweaver

If you gaze long into an abyss, the abyss will gaze back into you.
—NIETZSCHE, *Beyond Good and Evil*

To all doubts and questions, the new man of the first German Empire has only one answer: Nevertheless, I will!
—ALFRED ROSENBERG, *The Myth of the Twentieth Century*

I have seen the man of the future; he is cruel; I am frightened by him.
—ADOLF HITLER TO HERMANN RAUSCHNING

ENTRIES FROM THE DIARY
OF DR. JOSEPH GOEBBELS, NEW BERLIN
—Translated into English by HILDA GOEBBELS

APRIL 1965

TODAY I ATTENDED the state funeral for Adolf Hitler. They asked me to give the eulogy. It wouldn't have been so bothersome except that Himmler pulled himself out of his thankful retirement to advise me on all the things I mustn't say. The old fool still believes that we are laying the foundation for a religion. Acquainted as he is with my natural skepticism, he never ceases to worry that I will say something in public not meant for the consumption of the masses. It is a pointless worry on his part; not even early senility should enable him to forget that I am the propaganda expert. Still, I do not question his insistence that he is in rapport with what the masses feel most deeply. I leave such matters to one who is uniquely qualified for the task.

I suppose that I was the last member of the entourage to see Hitler alive. Speer had just left, openly anxious to get back to his work with the Von Braun team. In his declining years he has taken to involving himself full-time with the space program. This question of whether the Americans or we will reach the moon first seems to me a negligible concern. I am convinced by our military experts that the space program that really matters is in terms of orbiting platforms for the purpose of global intimidation. Such a measure seems entirely justified if we are to give the *Führer* his thousand-year Reich (or something even close).

The *Führer* and I talked of Himmler's plans to make him an SS saint. "How many centuries will it be," he asked in a surprisingly firm voice, "before they forget I was a man of flesh and blood?"

"Can an Aryan be any other?" I responded dryly, and he smiled as he is wont to do at my more jestful moments.

"The spirit of Aryanism is another matter," he said. "The same as destiny or any other workable myth."

"Himmler would ritualize these myths into a new reality," I pointed out.

"Of course," agreed Hitler. "That has always been *his* purpose. You and I are realists. We make use of what is available." He reflected for a moment and then continued: "The war was a cultural one. If you ask the man in the street what I really stood for, he would not come near the truth. Nor should he!"

I smiled. I'm sure he took that as a sign of assent. This duality of Hitler, with its concern for exact hierarchies to replace the old social order—and what is true for the *Volk* is not always what is true for us— seemed to me just another workable myth, often contrary to our stated purposes. I would never admit that to him. In his own way Hitler was quite the bone-headed philosopher.

"*Mein Führer,*" I began, entirely a formality in such a situation but I could tell that he was pleased I had used the address, "the Americans love to make fun of your most famous statement about the Reich that will last one thousand years, as though what we have accomplished now is an immutable status quo."

He laughed. "I love those Americans. I really do. They believe their own democratic propaganda . . . so obviously what we tell our people must be what we believe! American credulity is downright refreshing at times, especially after dealing with Russians."

On the subject of Russians Hitler and I did not always agree, so there was no point in continuing that line of dialogue at this late date. Before he died I desperately wished to ask him some questions that had been haunting me. I could see that his condition was deteriorating. This would be my last opportunity.

The conversation rambled on for a bit, and we again amused ourselves over how Franklin Delano Roosevelt had plagiarized National Socialism's Twenty-five Points when he issued his own list of economic rights. How fortunate for us that when FDR borrowed other of our policies, he fell flat on his face. War will always be the most effective method for disposing of surplus production, although infinitely more hazardous in a nuclear age. We never thought that FDR could push America into using our approach for armaments production.

Hitler summed up: "Roosevelt fell under the influence of the madman Churchill; that's what happened!"

"Fortunately our greatest enemy in America was impeached," I said. The last thing we'd needed was a competing empire-builder with the resources of the North American continent. I still fondly recalled the afternoon the American Congress was presented with evidence that FDR was a traitor on the Pearl Harbor question.

"I've never understood why President Dewey didn't follow FDR's lead, *domestically*," Hitler went on. "They remained in the war, after all. My God, the man even released American-Japanese from those concentration camps and insisted on restitution payments! And this during the worst fighting in the Pacific!"

"That was largely the influence of Vice President Taft," I reminded Hitler. His remarkable memory had suffered these last years.

"Crazy Americans," he said, shaking his head. "They are the most unpredictable people on earth. They pay for their soft hearts in racial pollution."

We moved on into small talk, gossiping about various wives, when that old perceptiveness of the *Führer* touched me once again. He could tell that I wasn't speaking my mind. "Joseph, you and I were brothers in Munich," he said. "I am on my deathbed. Surely you can't be hesitant to ask me *anything*. Speak, man. I would talk in my remaining hours."

And how he could talk. I remember one dinner party for which an invitation was extended to my two eldest daughters, Helga and Hilda. Hitler entertained us with a brilliant monologue on why he hated modern architecture anywhere but factories. He illustrated many of his points about the dehumanizing aspect of giant cities with references to the film *Metropolis*. Yet despite her great love for the cinema Hilda would not be brought out by his entreaties. Everyone else enjoyed the evening immensely.

On this solemn occasion I asked if he had believed his last speech of encouragement in the final days of the war when it seemed certain that we would be annihilated. Despite his words of stern optimism there was quite literally no way of his knowing that our scientists had at that moment solved the shape-charge problem. Thanks to Otto Hahn and Werner Heisenberg working together, we had developed the atomic bomb first. Different departments had been stupidly fighting over limited supplies of uranium and heavy water. Speer took care of that, and then everything began moving in our direction. After the first plutonium came from a German atomic pile it was a certain principle that we would win.

I still viewed that period as miraculous. If Speer and I had not convinced the army and air force to cease their rivalry for funds, we never would have developed the V-3 in time to deliver those lovely new bombs.

In the small hours of the morning one cannot help but wonder how things might have been different. We'd been granted one advantage when the cross-Channel invasion was delayed in 1943. But 1944 was the real turning point of the war. Hitler hesitated to use the nuclear devices, deeply fearful of the radiation hazards to our side as well as the enemy. If it had not been for the assassination attempt of July 20th, he might not have found the resolve to issue the all-important order: destroy Patton and his Third Army before they become operational, before they invade Europe like a cancer. What a glorious time that was for all of us, as well as my own career. For the Russians there were to be many bombs, and many German deaths among them. It was a small price to stop Marxism cold. Even our concentration camps in the East received a final termination order in the form of the by-now familiar mushroom clouds.

If the damned Allies had agreed to negotiate, all that misery could have been avoided. Killing was dictated by history. Hitler fulfilled Destiny. He never forgave the West for forcing him into a two-front war, when he, the chosen one, was their best protection against the Slavic hordes.

How he'd wanted the British Empire on our side. How he'd punished them for their folly. A remaining V-3 had delivered The Bomb on London, fulfilling a political prophecy of the *Führer*. He had regretted that;

but the premier war criminal of our time, Winston Churchill, had left him no alternative. They started unrestricted bombing of civilians; well, we finished it. Besides, it made up for the failure of Operation Sea Lion.

Right doesn't guarantee might. The last years of the war taught us that. How had Hitler found the strength to fill us all with hope when there was no reason for anything but despair? Could he really foretell the future?

"Of course not," he answered. "I had reached the point where I said we would recover at the last second with a secret weapon of invincible might . . . *without believing it at all*! It was pure rhetoric. I had lost hope long ago. The timing on that last speech could not have been better. Fate *was* on our side."

So at last I knew. Hitler had bluffed us all again. As he had begun, so did he end: the living embodiment of *will*.

I remembered his exaltation at the films of nuclear destruction. He hadn't been that excited, I'm told, since he was convinced of the claim for Von Braun's rockets—and it took a film for that, as well.

At each report of radiation dangers, he had the more feverishly buried himself in the *Führerbunker*, despite assurances of every expert that Berlin was safe from fallout. Never in my life have I known a man more concerned for his health, more worried about the least bit of a sore throat after a grueling harangue of a speech. And the absurd lengths he went to for his diet, limited even by vegetarian standards. Yet his precautions had brought him to this date, to see himself master of all Europe. Who was in a position to criticize *him*?

He had a way of making me feel like a giant. "I should have listened to you so much earlier," he now told me, "when you called for Totalization of War on the homefront. I was too soft on Germany's womanhood. Why didn't I listen to you?" Once he complimented a subordinate, he was prone to continue. "It was an inspiration, the way you pushed that morale-boosting joke: 'If you think the war is bad, wait until you see the peace, should we lose.'" He kept on, remembering to include my handling of the foreign press during *Kristalnacht*, and finally concluding with his favorite of all my propaganda symbols: "Your idea to use the same railway carriage from the shameful surrender of 1918, to receive France's surrender in 1940, was the greatest pleasure of my life." His pleasure was contagious.

He propped himself up slightly in bed, a gleam of joy in his eyes. He looked like a little boy again. "I'll tell you something about my thousand years. Himmler invests it with the mysticism you'd expect. Ever notice how Jews, Muslims, Christians, and our very own pagans have a predilection for millennia? The number works a magic spell on them."

"Pundits in America observe that also. They say the number is merely good psychology, and point to the longevity of the ancient empires of China, Rome, and Egypt for similar numerical records. They say that Germany will never hold out that long."

"It won't," said Hitler, matter-of-factly.

"What do you mean?" I asked, suddenly not sure of the direction he was moving. I suspected it had something to do with the cultural theories, but of his grandest dreams for the future Hitler had always been reticent . . . even with me.

"It will take at least that long," he said, "for the New Culture to take root on earth. For the New Europe to be what I have foreseen."

"If Von Braun has his way, we'll be long gone from earth by then! At least he seems to plan passages for many Germans on his spaceships."

"Germans!" spat out Hitler. "What care I for Germans or Von Braun's space armada? Let the technical side of Europe spread out its power in any direction it chooses. Speer will be *their* god. He is the best of that collection. But let the other side determine the values, man. The values, the spiritual essence. Let them move through the galaxy for all I care, so long as they look homeward to me for the guiding cultural principles. And Europe will be the eternal monument to that vision. I speak of a Reich lasting a thousand years? It will take that long to finish the job, to build something that will then last for the rest of eternity."

The old fire was returning. His voice was its old, strong hypnotic self. His body quivered with the glory of his personal vision, externalized for the whole of mankind to touch, to worship . . . or to fear. I bowed my head in the presence of the greatest man in history.

He fell back for a minute, exhausted, lost in the phantasms behind his occluded eyes. Looking at the weary remains of this once-human dynamo, I was sympathetic, almost sentimental. I said: "Remember when we first met through our anti-Semitic activities? It was an immediate bond between us."

He chuckled. "Oh, for the early days of the Party again. At the beginning you thought me too bourgeois."

He was dying in front of me, but his mind was as alert as ever. "Few people understand why we singled out the Jew, even with all the Nazi literature available," I continued.

He took a deep breath. "I was going to turn all of Europe into a canvas on which I'd paint the future of humanity. The Jew would have been my severest and most obstinate critic." The *Führer* always had a gift for the apt metaphor. "Your propaganda helped keep the populace inflamed. That anger was only fuel for the task at hand."

We had discussed on previous occasions the fundamental nature of the Judeo-Christian ethic, and how the Christian was a spiritual Semite (as any pope would observe). The Jew had made an easy scapegoat. There was such a fine old tradition behind it. But once the Jew was for all practical purposes removed from Europe, there remained the vast mass of Christians, many Germans among them. Hitler had promised strong measures in confidential statements to high officials of the SS. Martin Bormann had been the most ardent advocate of the *Kirchenkampf*, the campaign against the churches. In the ensuing years of peace and the nuclear stalemate with the United States little had come of it. I brought up the subject again.

"It will take generations," he answered. "The Jew is only the first step. And please remember that Christianity will by no means be the last obstacle, either. Our ultimate enemy is an idea dominant in the United States in theory, if not in practice. Their love of the individual is more dangerous to us than even mystical egalitarianism. In the end the decadent idea of complete freedom will be more difficult to handle than all the religions and other imperial governments put together." He lapsed back into silence, but only for a moment. "We are the last bastion of true Western civilization. America is always a few steps from anarchy. They would sacrifice the state to the individual! But Soviet communism—despite an ideology—was little better. Its state was all muscles and no brain. It forbade them to get the optimum use out of their best people. Ah, only in the German Empire, and especially here in New Berlin, do we see the ideal at work. The state uses most individuals as the sheep they were meant to be. More important is that the superior individual is allowed to use the state."

"Like most of the *Gauleiters*?" I asked, again in a puckish mood.

He laughed in a loud and healthy voice. "Good God," he said. "Nothing's perfect . . . except the SS, and the work you did in Berlin."

I did not have the heart to tell him that I thought he had been proved soundly mistaken on one of his predictions for the United States. With the nuclear stalemate and the end of the war—America having used its atomic bombs in the Orient, and riveting the world's attention in the same fashion as we—the isolationist forces in that country had had a resurgence. In a few years they had moved the country back to the foreign policy it held before the Spanish-American War. Hitler had predicted grim consequences for that country's economy. The reverse unobligingly came true. This was in part because the new isolationists didn't believe in economic isolation by any means; they freed American corporations to protect their own interests.

The latest reports I had seen demonstrated that the American Republic was thriving, even as our economy was badly suffering from numerous entanglements that go hand-in-gauntlet with an imperial foreign policy. We had quite simply overextended ourselves. New Berlin, after all, was modeled on the old Rome . . . and like the Roman Empire we were having trouble financing the operation and keeping the population amused. There are times I miss our old slogan: Gold or Blood?

I'm as dedicated a National Socialist as ever, but I must admit that America does not have our problems. What it has is a lot of goods, a willingness to do business in gold (our stockpile of which increased markedly after the war), and paper guarantees that we would not interfere in their hemisphere. We keep our part of the bargain fairly well: all adults understand that Latin America is fair game.

There is, of course, no censorship for the upper strata of Nazi Germany. The friends and families of high Reich officialdom can openly read or see anything they want. I still have trouble with this modification in our policy. At least I keep cherished memories of 1933, when I personally gave the order to burn the books at the Franz Joseph Platz outside Berlin University. I have never enjoyed myself more than in the period when I perfected an acid rhetoric as editor of *Der Angriff*, which more often than not inspired the destruction of writings inimical to our point of view. It was a pleasure putting troublesome editors in the camps. Those days seem far away now. Many enjoy *All Quiet on the Western Front*!

Hitler would not have minded a hearty exchange on the subject of censorship. He likes any topic that relates at some point to the arts. He would have certainly preferred such a discussion to arguing about capitalist policy in America. I didn't pursue either. I am satisfied to leave to these diary pages my conclusion that running an empire is a lot more expensive than having a fat republic, sitting back, and collecting profits. The British used to understand. If they hadn't forgotten, we probably wouldn't be where we are today.

Ironically for someone reputed to be a political and military genius,

Hitler has spent the entirety of his retirement (he holds his title for life) ignoring both subjects and concentrating on his cultural theories. He became a correspondent with the woman who chairs the anthropology department of New Berlin University (no hearth and home for her) and behaved almost as though he were jealous of her job. Lucky for her that he didn't stage a *putsch*. Besides, she was a fully accredited Nazi.

I think that Eva took it quite well. *Kinder, Küche, Kirche!*

As I stood in Hitler's sickroom, watching the man to whom I had devoted my life waning before me, I felt an odd ambivalence. On one hand I was sorry to see him go. On the other hand I felt a kind of—I'm not sure how to put it—release. It was as though, when he died, I would at last begin my true retirement. The other years of supposed resignation from public life did not count. Truly Adolf Hitler had been at the very center of my life.

I wish that he had not made his parting comment. *"Herr Dr. Goebbels,"* he said, and the returned formality made me uncharacteristically adopt a military posture, "I want to remind you of one thing. Shortly before his death Goering agreed with me that our greatest coup was the secrecy with which we handled the Jewish policy. The atom-bombing of camps was a bonus. Despite the passage of time I believe this secret should be preserved. In fact, there may come a day when no official in the German government knows of it. Only the hierarchy of the SS will preserve the knowledge in their initiatory rites."

"Allied propaganda continues to speak of it, *mein Führer*. Various Jewish organizations in America and elsewhere continue to mourn the lost millions every year. At least Stalin receives his share of blame."

"Propaganda is one thing. Proof is another. You know this as well as anyone. I'd like to hear you agree that the program should remain a secret. As for Stalin's death camps, talk that up forever."

I was taken aback that he would even speak of it. "Without question, I agree!" I remembered how we had exploited in our propaganda the Russian massacre of the Poles at Katyn. The evidence was solid . . . and there is such a thing as world opinion. I could see his point. At this late date there was little advantage in admitting to our vigorous policy for the Jews. The world situation had changed since the war.

Nevertheless his request seemed peculiar and unnecessary. In the light of later events I cannot help but wonder whether or not Hitler really was psychic. Could he have known of the personal disaster that would soon engulf members of my family?

*   *   *

THE CONVERSATION kept running through my mind on the way to the funeral. As we traveled under Speer's Arch of Triumph, I marveled for—I suppose—the hundredth time at his architectural genius. Germany would be paying for this city for the next fifty years, but it was worth it. Besides, we had to do something with all that Russian gold! What is gold, in the end, but a down payment on the future, be it the greatest city in the world or buying products from America?

The procession moved at a snail's pace, and considering the distance we had to cover I felt it might be the middle of the night by the time we made it to the Great Hall. The day lasted long enough, as it turned out.

The streets were thronged with sobbing people, Hitler's beloved *Volk*. The swastika flew from every window; I thought to conceive a poetic image to describe the thousands of fluttering black shapes, but when all I could think of was a myriad of spiders, I gave up. *Leave poetry to those more qualified*, I thought—*copywriting is never an ode.*

Finally we were moving down the great avenue between Goering's Palace and the Soldier's Hall. The endless vertical lines of these towering structures always remind me of Speer's ice-cathedral lighting effects at Nuremberg. Nothing he has done in concrete has ever matched what he did with pure light.

God, what a lot of white marble! The glare hurts my eyes sometimes. When I think of how we denuded Italy of its marble to accomplish all this, I recognize the Duce's one invaluable contribution to the Greater Reich.

Everywhere you turn in New Berlin there are statues of heroes and horses; horses and heroes. And flags, flags, flags. Sometimes I become just a little bored with our glorious Third Reich. Perhaps success must lead to excess. But it keeps beer and cheese on the table, as my wife, Magda, would say. I am an author of it. I helped to build this gigantic edifice with my ideas as surely as the workmen did with the sweat of their brows and the stones from the quarries. And Hitler, dear, sweet Hitler—he ate up little inferior countries and spat out the mortar of this metropolis. Never has a man been more the father of a city.

The automobiles had to drive slowly to keep pace with the horses in the lead, pulling the funeral caisson of the *Führer*. I was thankful when we reached our destination.

It took a while to seat the officialdom. As I was in the lead group, and seated first, I had to wait interminably while everyone else ponderously filed in. The hall holds thousands upon thousands. Speer saw to that. I had to sit still and watch what seemed like the whole German nation enter and take seats.

Many spoke ahead of me. After all, when I was finished with the official eulogy, there would be nothing left but to take him down and pop him in the vault. When Norway's grand old man, Quisling, rose to say a few words, I was delighted that he only took a minute. Really amazing. He praised Hitler as the destroyer of the Versailles penalties, and that was pretty much it.

The only moment of interest came when a representative of the sovereign nation of Burgundy stood in full SS regalia. A hush fell over the audience. Most Germans have never felt overly secure at the thought of Burgundy, a nation given exclusively to the SS . . . and outside the jurisdiction of German law. It was one of the wartime promises Hitler made that he kept to the letter. The country was carved out of France (which I'm sure never noticed—all they ever cared about was Paris, anyway).

The SS man spoke of blood and iron. He reminded us that the war had not ended all that long ago, although many Germans would like to forget that and merely wallow in the proceeds from the adventure. This feudalist was also the only speaker at the funeral to raise the old specter of the International Zionist Conspiracy, which I thought was a justifiable piece of nostalgia, considering the moment. As he droned on in a somewhat monotonous voice, I thought about Hitler's comment regarding the secret death camps. Of course, there are still Jews in the world, and Jewish organizations in America worth reckoning with, and a group trying to reestablish Israel—so far unsuccessfully—and understandably no group of people would rather see us destroyed. What I think is important to remember is that the Jew is hardly the only enemy of the Nazi.

By the time he was finished the crowd was seething in that old, pleasing, violent way . . . and I noticed that many of them restrained themselves with good Prussian discipline from cheering and applauding the speaker (which would not be entirely proper at a funeral). If they had broken protocol, however, I would have gladly joined in!

It seemed that an eternity had passed by the time I stood at the microphone to make my oration. I was surrounded by television cameras. How things have changed since the relatively simple days of radio. I'm sure that many of my ardent supporters were disappointed that I did not give a more rousing speech. I was the greatest orator of them all, even better than Hitler (if I may say so). My radio speeches are universally acclaimed as having been the instrumental factor in upholding German morale. I was more than just the Minister of Propaganda—I was the soul of National Socialism.

Toward the end of the war I made the greatest speech of my career, and this in the face of total disaster. I had no more believed at the time that we could win than Hitler had when he made his final boast about a mysterious secret weapon still later in the darkest of dark hours. My friends were astonished that after my emotional speech I could sit back and dispassionately evaluate the effect I had had upon my listeners. Such is the nature of a good propagandist.

Alas for the nostalgia buffs, there was no fire or fury in my words that day. I was economical of phrase. I listed his most noteworthy achievements; I made an objective statement about his sure and certain place in history; I told the mourners that they were privileged to have lived in the time of this man. That sort of thing, you know.

I finished on a quiet note. I said: "This man was a symbol. He was an inspiration. He took up a sword against the enemies of a noble idea that had almost vanished. He fought small and mean notions of man's destiny. Adolf Hitler restored the beliefs of our strong ancestors. Adolf Hitler restored the sanctity of our"—and I used the loaded term—"race." (I could feel the stirring in the crowd. It works every time.) "Adolf Hitler is gone. But what he accomplished will never die . . . *if* "—I gave them my best stare—"you work to make sure that his world is your world."

I was finished. The last echoes of my voice died to be replaced by the strains of *Die Walküre* from the Berlin Philharmonic.

On the way to the vault I found myself thinking about numerous things, none of them having to do directly with Hitler. I thought of Speer and the space program; I philosophized that Jewry is an *idea*; I reveled in the undying pleasure that England had become the Reich's "Ireland"; I briefly ran an inventory of my mistress, my children, my wife; I wondered what it would be like to live in America, with a color television and bomb shelter in every home.

The coffin was deposited in the vault, behind a bulletproof sheet of glass. His waxen-skinned image would remain there indefinitely, preserved for the future. I went home, then blissfully to bed and sleep.

OCTOBER 1965

Last night I dreamed that I was eighteen years old again. I remembered a Jewish teacher I had at the time, a pleasant and competent fellow. What I remember best about him was his sardonic sense of humor.

Funny how after all this time I still think about Jews. I have written that they were the inventor of the lie. I used that device to powerful effect in my propaganda. (Hitler claimed to have made this historic "discovery.")

My so-called retirement keeps me busier than ever. The number of books on which I'm currently engaged is monumental. I shudder to think of all the unfinished works I shall leave behind at my death. The publisher called the other day to tell me that the Goebbels war memoirs are going into their ninth printing. That is certainly gratifying. They sell quite well all over the world.

My daughter Hilda, besides being a competent chemist, is serious about becoming a writer as well, and if her letters are any sign I have no doubt but that she will succeed on her own merits. Alas, her political views become more dangerous all the time, and I fear she would be in grave trouble by now were it not for her prominent name. The German Freedom League, of which she is a conspicuous member, is composed of sons and daughters of approved families and so enjoys its immunity from prosecution. At least they are not rabble-rousers (not that I would mind if they had the proper Nazi ideas). They are purely intellectual critics and as such are accommodated. We are embracing a risk.

It was not too many years after our victory before the charter was passed allowing for freedom of thought for the elite of our citizenry. I laugh to think how I initially opposed the move, and remember all too well Hitler's surprising indifference to the measure. After the war he was a tired man, willing to leave administration to party functionaries, and the extension of ideology to the SS in Burgundy. He became frankly indolent in his new lifestyle.

Anyway, it doesn't matter now. "Freedom of thought" for the properly indoctrinated Aryan appears harmless enough. So long as he benefits from the privilege of real personal power at a fairly early age, the zealous desire for reform is quickly sublimated into the necessities of intelligent and disciplined management.

Friday's *New Berlin Post* arrived with my letter in answer to a question frequently raised by the new crop of young Nazis, not the least of whom is my own son Helmuth, currently under apprenticeship in Burgundy. I love him dearly, but what a bother he is sometimes. What a family! Those six kids were more trouble than the French underground. But I digress.

These youngsters are always asking why we didn't launch an A-bomb attack on New York City when we had the bomb before America did. If only they would read more! The explanation is self-evident to anyone acquainted with the facts. Today's youth has grown up surrounded by a phalanx of missiles tipped with H-bomb calling cards. They have no notion of how close we were to defeat. The Allies knew about Peenemünde. The V-3 was only finished in the nick of time. As for the rest, the physicists were not able to provide us with a limitless supply of A-bombs. There wasn't even time to test one. We used all but one against the invading armies; the last we threw at London, praying that some sympathetic Valkyrie would help guide it on its course so it would come somewhere near the target. The result was more than we anticipated.

The letter explained all this and also went into considerable detail on the technical reasons preventing a strike on New York. Admittedly we had developed a long range bomber for the purpose. It was ready within a month of our turning back the invasion. But there were no more A-bombs to be deployed at that moment. Our intelligence reported that America's Manhattan project was about to bear its fiery fruit. That's when the negotiations began. We much preferred the Americans teaching Japan (loyal ally though it had been) a lesson rather than making an atomic deposit on our shores. Besides, the war between us had truly reached a stalemate, our U-boats against their aircraft carriers; and each side's bombers against the other's. One plan was to deliver an atomic rocket from a submarine against America . . . but by then both sides were suing for peace. I still believe we made the best policy under the circumstances.

What would the young critics prefer? Nuclear annihilation? They may not appreciate that we live in an age of detente, but such are the cruel realities. We Nazis never intended to subjugate decadent America anyway. Ours was a European vision. Dominating the world is fine, but actually trying to administer the entire planet would be clearly self-defeating. Nobody could be that crazy . . . except for a Bolshevik, perhaps.

Facts have a tendency to show through the haze of even the best propaganda, no matter how effectively the myth would screen out unpleasantries. So it is that my daughter, the idealist of the German Freedom League, is not critical of our Russian policy. Why should it be otherwise? She worries about freedom for citizens, and gives the idea of freedom for a serf no more thought than the actual Russian serf gives it. Which is to say none at all. Here is one of the few areas where I heartily agree with the late Alfred Rosenberg.

*   *   *

ONCE AGAIN MY *Führer* calls me. And I was so certain all that was over. They want me at the official opening of the Hitler Memoriam at the museum. His paintings will be there, along with his architectural sketches. And his stuffed Shepherd dogs. And his complete collection of Busby Berkeley movies from America. Ah well, I will have to go.

There is just enough time before departing for me to shower, have some tea, and listen to Beethoven's Pastorale.

DECEMBER 1965

I loathe Christmas. It is not that I mind being with my family, but the rest of it is so commercialized, or else syrupy with contemptible Christian sentiments. Now if they could restore the vigor of the original Roman holiday. Perhaps I should speak to Himmler. . . . What am I saying? Never Himmler! Too bad Rosenberg isn't around.

Helga, my eldest daughter, visited us for a week. She is a geneticist. Currently she is working on a paper to show the limitations of our eugenic policies, and to demonstrate the possibilities opened up by genetic engineering. All this is over my head. DNA, RNA, microbiology, and *literal* supermen in the end? When Hitler said to let the technical side move in any direction it chooses, he was not saying much. There seems no way to stop them.

There is an old man in the neighborhood who belongs to the Nordic cult, body and soul. He and I spoke last week, all the time watching youngsters ice skating under a startlingly blue afternoon sky. There was almost a fairy-tale-like quality about the scene, as this old fellow told me in no uncertain terms that this science business is so much fertilizer. "The only great scientist I've ever seen was Horbiger," he announced proudly. "And he was more than a scientist. He was of the true blood, and held the true historical vision."

I didn't have the heart to tell him that the way in which Horbiger was more than a scientist was in his mysticism. Horbiger was useful to us in his day, and one of Himmler's prophets. But the man's cosmogony was utterly discredited by our scientists. Speer's technical Germany has a low tolerance for hoaxes.

This old man would hear none of it at any rate. He still believed every sacred pronouncement. "When I look up at the moon," he told me in a confidential whisper, "I know what I am seeing." *Green cheese*, I thought to myself, but I was aware of what was coming next.

"You still believe that the moon is made of ice?" I asked him.

"It is the truth," he announced gravely, suddenly affronted as though my tone had given me away. "Horbiger proved it," he said with finality.

Horbiger said it, I thought to myself. So that's all you need for "proof." I left the eccentric to his idle speculations on the meaning of the universe. I had to get back to one of my books. It had been languishing in the typewriter too long.

Frau Goebbels was in a sufficiently charitable mood come Christmas to invite the entire neighborhood over. I felt that I was about to live through another endless procession of representatives of the German nation—all the pomp of a funeral without any fun. The old eccentric was invited as well. I was just as happy that he did not come. Arguing about Horbiger is not my favorite pastime.

Speer and his wife dropped by. Mostly he wanted to talk about Von Braun and the moon project. Since we had put up the first satellite, the Americans were working around the clock to beat us to Luna and restore their international prestige. As far as I was concerned, propaganda would play the deciding role on world opinion (as always). This was an area in which America had always struck me as deficient.

I listened politely to Speer's worries, and finally pointed out that the United States wouldn't be in the position it currently held if so many of our rocketry people hadn't defected at the end of the war. "It seems to be a race between their German scientists and ours," I said with a hearty chuckle.

Speer did not seem amused. He replied with surprising coldness that Germany would be better off if we hadn't lost so many of our Jewish geniuses when Hitler came to power. I swallowed hard on my bourbon, and perhaps Speer saw consternation on my face, because he was immediately trying to smooth things over with me. Speer is no idealist, but one hell of an expert in his field. I look upon him as I would a well-kept piece of machinery. I hope no harm ever comes to it.

Speer always seems to have up-to-date information on all sorts of interesting subjects. He had just learned that an investigation of many years had been dropped with regard to a missing German geneticist, Richard Dietrich. Since this famous scientist had vanished only a few years after the conclusion of the war, the authorities supposed he had either defected to the Americans in secret or had been kidnapped. After two decades of fruitless inquiry, a department decides to cut off funds for the search. I'm sure that a few detectives had made a lucrative career out of the job. Too bad for them.

Magda and I spent part of the holidays returning to my birthplace on the Rhineland. I like to see the old homestead from time to time. I'm happy it hasn't been turned into a damned shrine as happened with Hitler's childhood home. Looking at reminders of the past in a dry, flaky snowfall—brittle, yet seemingly endless, the same as time itself—I couldn't help but wonder what the future holds. Space travel. Genetic engineering. Ah, I am an old man. I feel it in my bones.

MAY 1966

I have been invited to Burgundy. My son Helmuth has passed his initiation and is now a fully accredited student of the SS, on his way to joining the inner circle. Naturally he is in a celebratory mood and wants his father to witness the victory. I am proud, of course, but just a little wary of what his future holds in store. I remain the convinced ideologue, and critical of the bourgeois frame of mind. (Our revolution was against that sort of sentimentality.) But I don't mind some bourgeois comforts. My son will live a hard and austere life that I hope will not prove too much for him.

No sooner had I been sent the invitation than I also received a telegram from my daughter Hilda, whom I had not seen since Yuletide, when she stopped by for Christmas dinner. Somehow she had learned of the invitation from Helmuth and insisted that I must see her before leaving on the trip. She told me that I was in danger! The message was clouded in mystery because she did not even offer a hint of a reason. Nevertheless I agreed to meet her at the proposed rendezvous because it was conveniently on the way. And I am always worried that Hilda will find herself in jail for going too far with her unrealistic views.

The same evening I was cleaning out a desk when I came across a letter Hilda had written when she was seventeen years old—from the summer of 1952. I had the urge to read it again:

Dear Father:
I appreciate your last letter and its frankness, although I don't understand the point you made. Why have you not been able to think of anything to say to me for nearly a year? I know that you and Mother have found me to be your most difficult daughter. An

example comes to mind: Helga, Holly, and Hedda never gave Mother trouble about their clothes. I didn't object to the dresses she put on me, but could I help it if they were torn when I played? It simply seemed to me that more casual attire suited climbing trees and hiking and playing soccer.

From the earliest age I can remember, I've always thought boys had more fun than girls because they get to play all those wonderful games. I didn't want to be left out! Why did that make Mother so upset that she cried?

Ever since Heide died in that automobile accident, Mother has become very protective of her daughters. Only Helmuth escaped that sort of overwhelming protectiveness, and that's just because he's a boy.

At first I wasn't sure that I wanted to be sent to this private school, but a few weeks here convinced me that you had made the right decision. The mountains give you room to stretch your legs. The horses they let us have are magnificent. Wolfgang is mine and he is absolutely the fastest. I'm sure of it.

Soon I will be ready to take my examinations for the university. Your concern that I do well runs through your entire letter. Now we have something to talk about again. At this point it is too late to worry. I'm sure I'll do fine. I've been studying chemistry every chance I get and love it.

My only complaint is that the library is much too small. My favorite book is the unexpurgated Nietzsche, where he talks about the things the Party forbade as subjects of public discussion. At first I was surprised to discover how pro-Jewish he was, not to mention pro-freedom. The more I read of him, the more I understand his point of view.

One lucky development was a box of new books that had been confiscated from unauthorized people (what you would call the wrong type for intellectual endeavor, Father). Suddenly I had in front of me an orgy of exciting reading material. I especially enjoyed the Kafka . . . but I'm not sure why.

Some other students here want to form a club. They are in correspondence with others of our peer group who are allowed to read the old forbidden books. We have not decided on what we would call the organization. We are playing with the idea of the German Reading League. Other titles may occur to us later.

Another reason I like it better in the country than in the city is that there are not as many rules out here. Oh, the school has its curfews and other nonsense but they don't really pay much attention and we can do as we please most of the time. Only one of the teachers doesn't like me and she called me a little reprobate. I suspect she might make trouble for me except that everyone knows that you're my Father. That has always helped.

I was becoming interested in a boy named Franz but it came to the dean's attention and she told me that he was not from a good enough family for me to pursue the friendship. I ignored the advice but within a month Franz had left without saying a word. I know that you are against the old class boundaries, Father, but believe me when I say that they are still around. The people must not know that Hitler socialized them.

Now that I think about it, there are more rules out here than I first realized. Why must there be so many rules?

Why can't I just be me without causing so much trouble?

Well, I don't want to end this letter with a question. I hope you and Mother are happy. You should probably take that vacation you keep telling everyone will be any year now! I want to get those postcards from Hong Kong!

Love,
Hilda

I sat at the desk and thought about my daughter. I had to admit that she was my favorite and always had been. Where had I gone wrong with her? How had her healthy radicalism become channeled in such an unproductive direction? There was more to it than just the books. It was something in her. I was looking forward to seeing her again.

On a Wednesday morning I boarded a luxury train; the power of the rocket engines is deliberately held down so that passengers may enjoy the scenery instead of merely rushing through. I would be meeting Hilda in a small French hamlet directly in line with my final destination. I took along a manuscript—work, always work—this diary, and, for relaxation, a mystery novel by an Englishman. What is it about the British that makes this genre uniquely their own?

Speaking of books, I noticed a rotund gentleman—very much the Goering type—reading a copy of my prewar novel, *Michael*. I congratulated him on his excellent taste and he recognized me immediately. As I was autographing his copy, he asked if I were doing any new novels. I explained that I found plays and movie scripts a more comfortable form with which to work and suggested he see my filmed sequel to *The Wanderer* the next time he was in New Berlin. The director was no less than Leni Riefenstahl! I've never had any trouble living with the fact that my name is a household word. It makes of me a toastmaster much in demand. My most requested lecture topic remains the film, *Kolberg*.

I contemplated the numerous ways in which my wife's social calendar would keep her occupied in my absence. Since the children have grown up and left home, she seems more active than before! It's amazing the number of things she can find to do in a day. I would have liked to attend the Richard Strauss concert with her but duty calls.

The food on the train was quite good. The wine was only adequate, however. I had high hopes that that French hamlet would live up to its reputation for prime vintages.

The porter on the train looked Jewish to me. Probably is. There are people of Jewish ancestry living in Europe. It doesn't matter, so long as the practicing Jew is forever removed. God, we made the blood flow to cleanse this soil. Of course, I'm speaking figuratively. But what could one *do* with Jews, Gypsies, Partisans, homosexuals, the feebleminded, race-mixers, and all the rest?

We reached the station at dusk and my daughter was waiting for me. She is such a lovely child, except that she is no child any longer! I can see why she has so many admirers. Her political activities (if they even deserve such a label) have not made her any the less attractive. She has the classic features. On her thirtieth birthday I once again brought up the subject of why she had never married. Oh, I am aware that she has many lovers. Not as many as her father, but still a respectable number. The question is: Can that be enough? That she may never reproduce vexes me greatly. As always her deep-throated laugh mocks my concern.

A few seconds after I disembarked she was pulling at my sleeve and rushing me to a cab. I had never seen her looking so agitated. We virtually ran through the lobby of my hotel, and I felt as though I were under some type of house arrest as she bustled me up to my room and bolted the door behind us.

"Father," she said almost breathlessly. "I have terrible news." I found the melodramatic derring-do a trifle annoying. After all, I had put those days firmly behind me (or so I thought). Leave intrigues to the young, I always say . . . suddenly remembering in that case my daughter still qualifies for numerous adventures. If only she would leave me out of it!

"My darling," I said, "I am tired from my trip and in want of a bath.

Surely your message can wait until after I am changed? Over dinner we may . . ."

"No," she announced sternly. "It can't wait."

"Very well," I said, recognizing that my ploy had failed miserably and surrendering to her—shall we say—blitzkrieg. "Tell me," I said as I sat in a chair.

"You must not go to Burgundy," she began, and then paused as though anticipating an outburst from me. I am a master at that game. I told her to get on with it.

"Father, you may think me mad when I am finished, but I must tell you!" A *chip off the old block*, I thought. I nodded assent, if only to get it over with.

She was pacing as she spoke: "First of all, the German Freedom League has learned something that could have the worst consequences for the future of our country." I did not attempt to mask my expression of disgust but she plowed on regardless. "Think whatever you will of the League, but facts are facts. And we have uncovered the most diabolical secret."

"Which is?" I prompted her, expecting something anticlimactic.

"I am sure that you have not the slightest inkling of this, but during the war millions of Jews were put to death in horrible ways. What we thought were concentration camps suffering from typhus infections and lacking supplies, were in reality death camps at which was carried out a systematic program of *genocide*." I could not believe she'd used Raphael Lemkin's smear word!

The stunned expression on my face was no act. My daughter interpreted it as befitted her love for me—she took it, if you will, at face value.

"I can see that you're shocked," she said. "Even though you staged those public demonstrations against the Jews, I realize that was to force the Nazi Party's emigration policy through. I detest that policy, but it wasn't murder."

"Dear," I said, trying to keep my voice even, "what you are telling me is nothing more than thoroughly discredited Allied propaganda. We shot Jewish Partisans, but there's no evidence of systematic—"

"There is now," she said, and I believe that my jaw dropped at the revelation. She went on, oblivious to my horror: "The records that were kept for those camps are all forgeries. A separate set of records, detailing the genocide, has been uncovered by the League."

What a damnably stupid German thing to do. To keep records of *everything*. I knew it had to be true. It was as if my daughter disappeared from the room at that second. I could still see her, but only in a fuzzy way. A far more solid form stood between us, the image of the man who had been my life. It was as if the ghost of Adolf Hitler stood before me then, in our common distress, in our common deed. I could hear his voice and remember my promise to him. Oh God, it was my own daughter who was to provide the test. I really had not the least desire to see her eliminated. I liked her.

What I said next was not entirely in keeping with my feigned ignorance, and if she had been less upset she might have noticed the implications of my remark as I asked her: "Hilda, how many people have you told?"

She answered without hesitation. "Only members of the League and now you." I heaved a sigh of relief.

"Don't you think it would be a good idea to keep this extreme theory to yourself?" I asked.

"It's no theory. It's a fact. And I have no intention of advertising this. It would make me a target for those lunatics in the SS."

So that was the Burgundy connection! I still didn't see why I should be in any danger during my trip to Burgundy. Even if I were innocent of the truth—which every SS official knew to be absurd, since I was an architect of our policy—my sheer prominence in the Nazi Party would keep me safe from harm in Burgundy.

I asked my daughter what this fancy of hers had to do with my impending trip. "Only everything," she answered.

"Are you afraid that they will suspect I've learned of this so-called secret, which is nothing more than patent nonsense to begin with?"

She surprised me by answering, "No." There was an executioner's silence.

"What then?" I asked.

"It is not this crime of the past that endangers you," came the sound of her voice in portentous tones. "It is a crime of the future."

"You should have been the poet of the family."

"If you go to Burgundy, you risk your life. They are planning a new crime against humanity that will make World War II and the concentration camps, on both the Allied and Axis sides, seem like nothing but a prelude. And you will be one of the first victims!"

Never have I felt more acutely the pain of a father for his offspring. I could not help but conclude that my youngest daughter's mind had only a tenuous connection to reality. Her political activities must be to blame! On the other hand I regarded Hilda with a genuine affection. She seemed concerned for my welfare in a manner I supposed would not apply to a stranger. The decadent creed she had embraced had not led to any disaffection from her father.

I thought back to the grand old days of intrigue within the Party and the period in the war years when I referred most often to that wise advice of Machiavelli: "Cruelties should be committed all at once, as in that way each separate one is less felt, and gives less offense." We had come perilously close to *Götterdämmerung* then, but in the end our policy proved sound. I was beyond all that. The state was secure, Europe was secure . . . and the only conceivable threat to my safety would come from foreign sources. Yet here was Hilda, her face a mixture of concern and anger and—perhaps love? She was telling me to beware the Burgundians. She had as much as accused them of plotting against the Reich itself!

I remember how they had invited me to one of the conferences to decide the formation of the new nation of Burgundy. Those were hectic times in the postwar period. As *Gauleiter* of Berlin (one of the *Führer's* few appointments of that title of which I always approved) I had been primarily concerned with Speer's work to build New Berlin. The film industry was flowering under my personal supervision, I was busy writing my memoirs, and I was involved heavily with diplomatic projects. I hadn't really given Burgundy much thought. I knew that it had been a country in medieval times, and had read a little about the Duchy of Burgundy. I remembered that the historical country had traded in grain, wines, and finished wool.

They announced at the conference that the historical Burgundy would be restored, encompassing the area to the south of Champagne, east of Bourbonais, and north and west of Savoy. There was some debate on whether or not to restore the original place-names or else borrow from Wagner to create a series of new ones. In the end the latter camp won out. The capital was named Tarnhelm, after the magic helmet in the *Nibelungenlied* that could change the wearer into a variety of shapes.

Hitler did not officially single out any of the departments that made up the SS: Waffen, Death's Head, or General SS. We in his entourage realized, however, that the gift was to those members of the inner circle who had been most intimately involved with both the ideological and practical side of the extermination program. The true believers! Given the Reich's policy of secrecy, there was no need to blatantly advertise the reasons for the gift. Himmler, as *Reichsführer* of the SS and Hitler's adviser on racial matters, was naturally instrumental in this transfer of power to the new nation. His rival, Rosenberg, met his death.

The officials who would oversee the creation of Burgundy were carefully selected. Their mission was to make certain that Burgundy became a unique nation in all of Europe, devoted to certain chivalric values of the past, and the formation of pure Aryan specimens. It was nothing more than the logical extension of our propaganda, the secularizing of the myths and legends with which we had kept the people fed during the dark days of lost hope. The final result was a picturesque fairy-tale kingdom that made its money almost entirely out of the tourist trade. America loves to boast of its amusement parks but it has nothing to match this.

Hilda interrupted my reverie by asking me in a voice bordering on sternness: "Well, what are you going to do?"

"Unless you make sense, I will continue on my journey to Tarnhelm to see Helmuth." He was living at the headquarters of the SS leaders, the territory that was closed off to outsiders, even during the tourist season. Yet it was by no means unusual for occasional visitors from New Berlin to be invited there. My daughter's melodramatics had not yet given cause to worry. All I could think of was how I'd like to get my hands around the throat of whoever put these idiotic notions in her pretty head.

She was visibly distressed, but in control. She tossed her hair back and said, "I am not sure that the proof I have to offer will be sufficient to convince you."

"Aren't you getting ahead of yourself?" I asked. "You haven't even made a concrete accusation yet! Drop this pose. Tell me what you think constitutes the danger."

"They think you're a traitor," she said.

"What?" I was astounded to hear such words from anyone for any reason. "To Germany?"

"No," she answered. "To the true Nazi ideal."

I laughed. "That's the craziest thing I've ever heard. I'm one of the key—"

"You don't understand," she interrupted. "I'm talking about the religion."

"Oh, Hilda, is that all? You and your group have stumbled upon some threatening comments from the Thule Society, I take it?"

Now it was her turn to be surprised. She sat upon the bed. "Yes," she answered. "But then you know . . . ?"

"The specifics? Not at all. They change their game every few months. Who has the time to keep up? Let me tell you something. The leaders of the SS have always had ties to an occult group called the Thule Society, but there is nothing surprising about that. It is a purely academic exercise in playing with the occult, the same as the British equivalent—The Golden Dawn. I'm sure you're aware that many prominent Englishmen belonged to that club!

"These people are always harmless eccentrics. Our movement made use of the type without stepping on pet beliefs. It's the same as dealing with any religious person whom you want to be on your side. If you receive cooperation, it won't be through insulting his spiritual beliefs."

"What about the messages we intercepted?" she went on. "The threatening tone, the almost deranged—"

"It's how they entertain themselves!" I insisted. "Listen, you're familiar with Horbiger, aren't you?" She nodded. "Burgundians believe that stuff. Even after the launching of Von Braun's satellite, which in no way disturbed the eternal ice, as that old fool predicted! His followers don't care about facts. Hell, they still believe the moon in our sky is the fourth moon this planet has had, that it is made of ice like the other three, that all of the cosmos is an eternal struggle of fire and ice. Even our *Führer* toyed with those ideas in the old days. The Burgundians no more want to give up their sacred ideas merely because modern science has exploded them than fundamentalist Baptists in America want to listen to Darwin."

"I know," she said. "You are acting as though they aren't dangerous."

"They're not."

"Soon Helmuth will be accepted into the inner circle."

"Why not? He's been working for that ever since he was a teenager."

"But the inner circle," she repeated with added emphasis.

"So he'll be a Hitler Youth for the rest of his life. He'll never grow up."

"You don't understand."

"I'm tired of this conversation," I told her bluntly. "Do you remember several years ago when your brother went on that pilgrimage to Lower Saxony to one of Himmler's shrines? You were terribly upset but you didn't have a shred of reason why he shouldn't have gone. You had nightmares. Your mother and I wondered if it was because as a little girl you were frightened by Wagner."

"Now I have reasons."

"Mysterious threatening messages! The Thule Society! It should be taken with a grain of salt. I saw Adolf Hitler once listen to a harangue from an especially unrealistic believer in the Nordic cult, bow solemnly when the man was finished, enter his private office—where I accompanied him—and break out in laughter that would wake the dead. He didn't want to offend the fellow. The man was a good Nazi, at least."

My daughter was fishing around in her purse as I told her these things. She passed me a piece of paper when I was finished. I unfolded it and read:

JOSEPH GOEBBELS MUST ARRIVE ON SCHEDULE FOR THE RITUAL
HE WILL NEVER TELL ANYONE

"What is this?" I asked her. I was becoming angry.

"A member of the Freedom League intercepted a message from Burgundy to someone in New Berlin. It was coded, but we were able to break it."

"To whom was the message addressed?"

"To Heinrich Himmler."

Suddenly I felt very, very cold. I had never trusted *der treue Heinrich*. Admittedly I didn't trust anything that came from the German Freedom League, with a contradiction built into its very title. Nevertheless something in me was clawing at the pit of my stomach. Something told me that maybe, just maybe, there was danger after all. Crazy as Himmler had been during the war years, he had become much worse in peacetime. At least he was competent regarding his own industrial empire.

"How do I know that this note is genuine?" I asked.

"You don't," she answered. "I had to take a great risk in bringing it to you, if that helps you to believe."

"The Burgundians would have stopped you?"

"If they knew about it. I was referring to the German Freedom League. They hate you as much as the rest of them."

My face flushed with anger and I jumped to my feet so abruptly that it put an insupportable strain on my clubfoot. I had to grab for a nearby lamp to keep from stumbling. "Why," I virtually hissed, "do you belong to that despicable bunch of bums and poseurs?"

She stood also, picking up her purse as she did so. "Father, I am going. You may do with this information as you wish. I will offer one last suggestion. Why don't you take another comfortable passenger train back to New Berlin, and call Tarnhelm to say that you will be one day late? See what their reaction is? You didn't manage to attend my college graduation and I'm none the worse for it. Would it matter so much to my brother were you to help him celebrate after the ceremony?"

She turned to go. "Wait," I said. "I'm sorry I spoke so harshly. You mean well."

"We've been through this before," she answered, her back still to me.

"I don't see any harm in doing what you suggest. If it will make you happy, I'll delay the trip."

"Thank you," she said, and walked out. I watched the closed door for several minutes, not moving, not really thinking.

A half-hour later I was back at the railroad station, boarding an even slower passenger train back to New Berlin. I love this sort of travel. The rocket engines were held down to their minimum output. The straining hum they made only accentuated the fact of their great power held in check. Trains are the most human form of mass transportation.

With my state of mind in such turmoil I could not do any serious work. I decided to relax and resumed reading the English mystery novel. I had narrowed it down to three suspects, all members of the aris- tocracy, naturally—all highly offensive people. The servant I had ruled out as much too obvious. As is typical of the form, a few key sentences give up the solution if you know what they are. I had just passed over what I took to be such a phrase, and returned to it. Looking up from my book to contemplate the puzzle, I noticed that the woman sitting across from me was also reading a book, a French title that seemed vaguely fa- miliar: *Le Théosophisme, histoire d'une pseudo-religion,* by René Guenon.

I looked back to my book when I suddenly noticed that the train was slowing down. There was no reason for it, as we were far from our next stop. Looking out the window, I saw nothing but wooded landscape un- der a starry night sky. A tall man up the aisle was addressing the porter. His rather lengthy monologue boiled down to a simple question: Why was there the delay? The poor official was shaking his head with bewil- derment and indicated that he would move forward to inquire. That's when I noticed the gas.

It was yellow. It was seeping in from the air-conditioning system. Like everyone else I started to get up in hopes of finding a means of egress. Already I was coughing. As I turned to the window, with the idea of releasing the emergency lock, I slipped back down into the cushions as consciousness fled. The last thing I remember was seriously regretting that I had not found the time to sample a glass of wine from that hamlet.

I must have dreamed. I was standing alone in the middle of a great lake, frozen over in the dead of winter. I was not dressed for the weather but had on only my Party uniform. I looked down at the icy expanse at my feet and noticed that my boots were freshly shined, the luster already becoming covered by flakes of snow. I heard the sound of hoofbeats echoing hollowly on the ice, and looked up to see a small army on horseback approaching. I recognized them immediately. They were the Teutonic Knights. The dark armor, the stern faces, the great, black horses, the bright lances and swords and shields. They could be nothing else.

They did not appear to be friendly. I started walking away from them. The sound of their approach was a thunder pounding at my brain. I cursed my lameness, cursed my inability to fly, suddenly found myself suspended in the air, and then I had fallen on the ice, skinning my knees. Struggling to turn over, I heard a bloodcurdling yell and they were all around me. There was a whooshing of blades in the still, icy air. I was screaming. Then I was trying to reason with them.

"I helped Germany win the war . . . I believe in the Aryan race . . . I helped destroy the Jews. . . ." But I knew it was to no avail. They were killing me. The swords plunged in deeply.

I AWAKENED aboard a small jet flying in the early dawn. For a moment I thought I was tied to my seat. When I glanced to see what kind of cords had my wrists bound to the arms of the chair, I saw that I was mistaken. The feeling of constriction I attributed to the effects of the gas. Painfully I lifted a hand . . . then with even more anguish I raised my head, noticing that the compartment was empty except for me. The door to the cockpit was closed.

The most difficult task that confronted me was to turn my head to the left so that I could have a better view of our location. A dozen tiny needles pricked at the muscles in my neck but I succeeded. I was placed near the wing and could see a good portion of the countryside unfolding like a map beneath it. We were over a rundown railroad station. One last bit of track snaked on beyond it for about half a mile—we seemed to be flying almost parallel to it—when it suddenly stopped, blocked off by a tremendous oak tree, the size of which was noticeable even from the great height.

I knew where we were immediately. We had just flown over the eastern border of Burgundy.

I leaned back in my seat, attempting to have my muscles relax, but met with little success. They stubbornly insisted on having their way despite my *will* that they be otherwise. I was terribly thirsty. I assumed that if I stood I would have a serious dizzy spell, so I called out instead: "Steward!" No sooner was the word out of my mouth than a young, blonde man in a spotless white jacket came up behind me holding a small, fancy menu.

"What would you like?" he asked.

"An explanation."

"I'm afraid that is not on this menu. I'm sure you will find what you seek when we reach our destination. In the meantime would you care to dine?"

"No," I said, relapsing back into the depths of my seat, terribly tired again.

"Some coffee?" the steward asked, persisting.

I assented to this. It was very good coffee and soon I was feeling better. Looking out the window again, I observed that we were over a lake. There was a long-ship plying the clear, blue water—its dragon's head glared at the horizon. My son had written me about the Viking Club when he first took up residence in Burgundy. This had to be one of their outings.

Thirty minutes and two cups of coffee later the intercom announced that we would be landing at Tarnhelm. From the air the view was excellent: several monasteries—now devoted to SS training as *Ordensbürgen*— were situated near the village that housed the Russian serfs. Beyond that was still another lake and then came the imposing castle in which I knew I would find my son.

There was a narrow landing strip within the castle grounds and the pilot was every bit the professional. We hadn't been down longer than five minutes when who should enter the plane but my son Helmuth! I looked at him. He had blonde hair and blue eyes. The only trouble was that my son did not have blonde hair and blue eyes. Of course, I knew that the hair could be dyed, but somehow it looked quite authentic. As for the eyes, I could think of no explanation but for contact lenses. Helmuth had also lost weight and never appeared more muscular or healthy than he did now.

Here I was, surrounded by mystery—angry, bewildered, unsettled. And yet the first thing that escaped my lips was: "Helmuth, what's happened to you?" He guessed my meaning.

"This is real blonde hair," he said proudly. "And the eye color is real as well. I regret that I am not of the true genotype, any more than you are. I was given a hormone treatment to change the color of my hair. A special radiation treatment took care of the eyes."

As he was saying this, he was helping me to my feet, as I was still groggy. "Why?" I asked him. He would say no more about it.

The sun hurt my eyes as we exited down the ramp from the plane. Two tall, young men—also blonde-haired and blue-eyed—joined my son and helped to usher me inside the castle. They were dressed in Bavarian hunting gear, with large knives strapped on at their waists. Their clothes had the smell of freshest leather.

We had entered from the courtyard of the inner bailey. The hall we traversed was covered in plush red carpets and was illuminated by torches burning in the walls; this cast a weird lighting effect over the numerous suits of armor standing there. I could not help but think of the medieval castles Speer drew for his children every Christmas.

It was a long trek before we reached a stone staircase that we immediately began to ascend. I was not completely recovered from the effects of the gas and wished that we could pause. My clubfoot was giving me considerable difficulty. I did not want to show any weakness to these men, and I knew that my sturdy son was right behind me. I took those steps without slowing down the pace.

We finally came out on a floor that was awash in light from fluorescent tubes. A closed-circuit television console dominated the center of the room, with pictures of all the other floors of the castle, from the keep to the highest tower. There was also a portrait of Meister Eckhart.

"Wait here," Helmuth announced, and before I could make any protestations he and the other two had gone the way we had come, with the door locked behind them. I considered the large window on the right side of the room with a comfortable couch beside it. I gratefully sat there and surveyed my position from the new vantage point. Below me was another courtyard. In one corner was what could be nothing else but an unused funeral pyre. Its height was staggering. There was no body upon it. Along the wall that ran from the pyre to the other end of the compound were letters inscribed of a size easy to read even from such distance. It was a familiar quotation: ANY DESCRIPTION OF ORGANIZATION, MISSION, AND STRUCTURE OF THE SS CANNOT BE UNDERSTOOD UNLESS ONE TRIES TO CONCEIVE IT INWARDLY WITH ONE'S BLOOD AND HEART. IT CANNOT BE EXPLAINED WHY WE CONTAIN SO MUCH STRENGTH THOUGH WE NUMBER SO FEW. Underneath the quote in equally large letters was the name of its author: HEINRICH HIMMLER.

"A statement that you know well," came a low voice behind me and I turned to face Kurt Kaufmann, the most important man in Burgundy. I had met him a few times socially in New Berlin.

Smiling in as engaging a manner as I could (under the circumstances), I said, "Kurt," stressing that I was not addressing him formally, "I have no idea why you have seemingly kidnapped me, but there will be hell to pay!"

He bowed. "What you fail to appreciate, Dr. Goebbels, is that I will receive that payment."

I studied his face—the bushy blonde hair and beard, and of course the bright blue eyes. The monocle he wore over one of them seemed quite superfluous. I knew that he had 20/20 vision.

"I have no idea what you are talking about."

"You lack ideas, it is true," he answered. "Of facts you do not lack. We knew your daughter contacted you . . ."

Even at the time this dialogue struck me as remarkably melodramatic. Nevertheless it was happening *to me*. At the mention of my daughter I failed to mask my feelings. Kaufmann had to notice the expression of consternation on my face. The whole affair was turning into a hideous game that I feared I was losing.

I stood. "My daughter's associations with a subversive political group are well known." There was no reason to mince words with him. "I was attempting to dissuade her from a suicidal course. Why would you be spying on that?"

The ploy failed miserably. "We bugged the room," he said softly.

"You dare to spy on *me*? Have you any idea of the danger?"

"Yes," he said. "You don't."

I made to comment but he raised a hand to silence me. "Do not continue. Soon you will have more answers than you desire. Now I suggest you follow me."

The room had many doors. We left through one at the opposite end from my original point of entry. I was walking down yet another hall. This one, however, was lit by electricity, and at the end of it we entered an elevator. The contrast between modern technology and Burgundian simplicity was becoming more jarring all the time. Like most Germans who had visited the country, I only knew it firsthand as a tourist. The reports I had once received on their training operations were not as detailed as I would have liked but certainly gave no hint of dire conspiracy against the Fatherland. The thought was too fantastic to credit. Even now I hoped for a denouement more in keeping with the known facts. Could the entire thing be an elaborate practical joke? Who would run the risk of such a folly?

The elevator doors opened and we were looking out onto the battlements of the castle. I followed Kaufmann onto the walk, and noticed that the view was utterly magnificent. To the left I saw the imported Russian serfs working in the fields; to the right I saw young Burgundians doing calisthenics in the warm morning air. I was used to observing many blonde heads in the SS. Yet here there was nothing but that suddenly predictable homogeneity.

We looked down at the young bodies. Beyond them other young men were dressed in chain-mail shirts and helmets. They were having at one another with the most intensive swordplay I had ever witnessed.

"Isn't that a bit dangerous?" I asked Kaufmann, gesturing at the fencing.

"What do you mean?" he said, as one of the men ran his sword through the chest of another. The blood spurted out in a fountain as the body slumped to the ground. I was aghast, and Kaufmann's voice seemed to be far away as I dimly heard it say: "Did you notice how the loser did not scream? That is what I call discipline." It occurred to me that the man might have simply died too quickly to express his opinion.

Kaufmann seemed wryly amused by my wan expression. "Dr. Goebbels, do you remember the *Kirchenkampf*?"

I recovered my composure. "The campaign against the churches? What about it?"

"Martin Bormann was disappointed in its failure," he said.

"No more than I. The war years allowed little time for less important matters. You know that the economic policies we established after the war helped to undermine the strength of the churches. They have never been weaker. European cinema constantly makes fun of them."

"They still exist," said Kaufmann evenly. "The gods of the Germanic tribes are not fools—their indignation is as great as ever." I stared at this man with amazement as he continued to preach: "The gods remember how Roman missionaries built early Christian churches on the sacred sites, believing that the common people would still climb the same hills they always had to worship . . . only now they would pay homage to a false god!"

"The masses are not easily cured of the addiction," I pointed out.

"You compare religion to a drug?"

"It was one of the few wise statements of Marx," I said, with a deliberate edge in my voice. Kaufmann's face quickly darkened into a scowl. "Not all religions are the same," I concluded in an ameliorative tone. I had no desire to argue with him about the two faiths of Burgundy, the remnants of Rosenberg's Gnostics, and the majority of Himmler's Pagans.

"You say that, but it is only words. Let me tell you a story about yourself, Herr Goebbels." I did not consider the sudden formality a good sign, not the way he said it. He continued: "You always prided yourself on being the true radical of the Nazi Party. You hammered that home whenever you could. Nobody hated the bourgeoisie more than Goebbels. Nobody was more ardent about burning books than Goebbels. As *Reichspropagandaminister* you brilliantly staged the demonstrations against the Jews."

Now the man was making sense. I volunteered another item to his admirable list: "I overheard some young men humming the Horst Wessel song down there during calisthenics." Manufacturing a martyr to give the party its anthem was still one of my favorites. My influence was still on the Germanic world, including Burgundy.

Kaufmann had been surveying rows of men doing pushups . . . as well as the removal of the corpse from the tourney field. Now his stone face turned in my direction, breaking into an unpleasant smile. I preferred his frown. "You misunderstand the direction of my comments, Herr Doktor. I will clarify it. I was told a story about you once. I was only a simple soldier at the time but the story made an indelible impression. You were at a party, showing off for your friends by making four brief political speeches; the first presented the case for the restoration of the monarchy; the second sung the praises of the Weimar Republic; the third proved how communism could be successfully adopted by the German Reich; the fourth was in favor of National Socialism, at last. How relieved they were. How tempted they had been to agree with each of the other three speeches."

I could not believe what I was hearing. How could this dull oaf be in charge of anything but a petty bureaucratic department? Had he no sense of humor, no irony? "I was demonstrating the power of propaganda," I told him.

"In what do you believe?" he asked.

"This is preposterous," I nearly shouted. "Are you impugning—"

"It is not necessary to answer," he said consolingly. "I'm aware that you have only believed in one thing in your life: a man, not an idea. With Hitler dead, what is left for you to believe?"

"This is insane," I replied, not liking the shrill sound of my own voice in my ears. "When I was made Reich Director for Total War, I demonstrated my genius for understanding and operating the mechanisms of a dictatorship. I was crucial to the war effort then."

He completely ignored my point and continued on his solitary course: "Hitler was more than a man. He was a living part of an idea. He did not always recognize his own importance. He was chosen by the Vril Society, the sacred order of the Luminous Lodge, the purest, finest product of the believers in the Thule. Adolf Hitler was the medium. The Society used him accordingly. He was the focal point. Behind him were powerful magicians. The great work has only begun. Soon it will be time for the second step. Only the true man deserves *Lebensraum*."

Kaufmann was working himself up, I could see that. He stood close to me and said, "You are a political animal, Goebbels. You believe that politics is an end in itself. The truth is that governments are nothing in the face of destiny. We are near the cleansing of the world. You should be proud. Your own son will play an important part. The finest jest is that modern scientific method will also have a role."

He turned to go. I had no recourse but to follow him. There was nowhere else to go but straight down to sudden death.

We reentered the elevator. "Have I been brought here to witness an honor bestowed on my son?" I asked.

"In part. You will also have a role. You saw the telegram!"

That was enough. There could no longer be any doubt. I was trapped amidst madmen. Having made up my mind what to do, I feigned an attack of pain in my clubfoot and crouched at the same time. When Kaufmann made to offer aid, I struck wildly, almost blindly. I tried to knee him in the groin but—failing that—brought my fist down on the back of his neck. The fool went out like a light, falling hard on his face. I congratulated myself on such prowess for an old man.

No sooner had the body slumped to the floor than the elevator came to a stop and the doors opened automatically. I jumped out into the hall. Standing there was a naked seven-foot giant who reached down and lifted me into the air. He was laughing. His voice sounded like a tuba.

"They call me Thor," he said. I struggled. He held.

Then I heard the voice of my son: "That, Father, is what we call a true Aryan."

I was carried like so much baggage down the hall, hearing voices distantly talking about Kaufmann. I was tossed on to the hard floor of a brightly lit room and the door was slammed behind me. A muscle had been pulled in my back and I lay there, gasping in pain like a fish out of water. I could see that I was in some sort of laboratory. In a corner was a humming machine the purpose of which I could not guess. A young woman was standing over me, wearing a white lab smock. I could not help but notice two things about her straightaway: she was a brunette, and she was holding a sword at my throat.

As I LOOK BACK, the entire affair has an air of unreality about it. Events were becoming more fantastic in direct proportion to the speed with which they occurred. It had all the logic of a dream.

As I lay upon the floor, under that sword held by such an unlikely guardian (I had always supported military service for women, but when encountering the real thing I found it a bit difficult to take seriously), I began to take an inventory of my pains. The backache was subsiding so long as I did not move. I was becoming aware, however, that the hand with which I had dispatched Kaufmann felt like a hot balloon of agony, expanding without an upper limit. My vision was blurred and I shook my head trying to clear it. I dimly heard voices in the background, and then a particularly resonant one was near at hand, speaking with complete authority: "Oh, don't be ridiculous. Help him up."

The woman put down the sword, and was suddenly assisted by a young Japanese girl gingerly lifting me off the floor and propelling me in the direction of a nearby chair. Still I did not see the author of that powerful voice.

Then I was sitting down and the females were moving away. He was standing there, his hands on his hips, looking at me with the sort of analytical probing I always respect. At first I didn't recognize him, but had instead the eerie feeling that I was in a movie. The face made me think of something too ridiculous to credit . . . and then I knew who it really was: Professor Dietrich, the missing geneticist. I examined him more closely. My first impression had been more correct than I thought. The man hardly resembled the photographs of his youth. His hair had turned white and he had let it grow. Seeing him in person, I could not help but notice how angular were his features . . . how much like the face of the late actor Rudolf Klein-Rogge in the role of Dr. Mabuse, Fritz Lang's character that had become the symbol of a super-scientific, scheming Germany to the rest of the world. Although the later films were banned for the average German, the American-made series (Mabuse's second life, you could say) had become so popular through-out the world that Reich officials considered it a mark of distinction to own copies of all twenty. We still preferred the original series, where Mabuse was obviously Jewish.

Since the death of Klein-Rogge other actors had taken over the part, but always the producers looked for that same startling visage. This man Dietrich was meant for the role. Thea von Harbou would approve.

"What are you staring at?" he asked. I told him. He laughed. "You chose the right profession," he continued. "You have a cinematic imagi-nation. I am flattered by the comparison."

"What is happening?" I asked.

"Much. Not all of it is necessary. This show they are putting on for your benefit is rather pointless, for instance."

I was becoming comfortable in the chair, and my back had momen-tarily ceased to annoy me. I hoped that I would not have to move for still another guided tour of something I wasn't sure that I wanted to see. To my relief Dietrich pulled up a chair, sat down across from me and started talking:

"I expect that Kaufmann meant to introduce you to Thor when the elevator doors opened and then enjoy your startled expression as you were escorted down the hall to my laboratory. They didn't think you'd improvise on the set! Well, they're only amateurs and you are the expert when it comes to good, silly melodrama."

"Thor . . ." I began lamely, but could think of nothing to say.

"He's not overly intelligent. I'm impressed that he finished the scene with such dispatch. I apologize for my assistant. She had been watching the entire thing on one of our monitors and must have come to the con-clusion that you are a dangerous fellow. In person, I mean. We all know what you are capable of in an official capacity."

As we talked, I took in my surroundings. The size of the laboratory was tremendous. It was like being in a scientific warehouse. Although without technical training myself, I noticed that there seemed to be a lack of systematic arrangement: materials were jumbled together in a downright sloppy fashion, even if there were a good reason for the close proximity of totally different apparatuses. Nevertheless I realized that I was out of my depth and I might be having nothing more than an aesthetic response.

"They closed the file on you," I said. "I thought you had been kidnapped by American agents."

"That was the cover story."

"Then you were kidnapped by the Burgundians?"

"A reasonable deduction, but wrong. I volunteered."

"For what?"

"Dr. Goebbels, I said that you have a cinematic imagination. That is good. It will help you to appreciate this." He snapped his fingers and the Japanese girl was by his side so swiftly that I didn't see where she had come from. She was holding a small plastic box. He opened it and showed me the interior: two cylinders, each with a tiny suction cup on the end. He took one out. "Examine this," he said, passing it to me.

"One of your inventions?" I asked, noticing that it was as light as if it were made out of tissue paper. But I could tell that whatever the material was, it was sturdy.

"A colleague came up with that," he told me. "He's dead now, unfortunately. Politics." He retrieved the cylinder, did something with the untipped end, then stood. "It won't hurt," he said. "If you will cooperate, I promise a cinematic experience unlike anything you've ever sampled."

There was no point in resisting. They had me. Whatever their purpose, I was in no position to oppose it. Nor is there any denying that my curiosity was aroused by this seeming toy.

Dietrich leaned forward, saying, "Allow me to attach this to your head and you will enjoy a unique production of the Burgundian Propaganda Ministry, if you will—the story of my life."

Without further ado he pressed the small suction cup against the center of my forehead. There was a tingling sensation and then my sight began to dim! I knew that my eyes were still open and I had not lost consciousness. For a moment I feared that I was going blind.

There were new images. I began to dream while wide awake, except that they were not my dreams. They were someone else's!

I was someone else!

I was Dietrich . . . as a child.

I was buttoning my collar on a cold day in February before going to school. The face that looked back from the mirror held a cherubic—almost beautiful—aspect. I was happy to be who I was.

As I skipped down cobbled streets, it suddenly struck me with solemn force that I was a Jew.

My German parents had been strict, orthodox, and humorless. An industrial accident had taken them from me. I was not to be alone for long. An uncle in Spain had sent for me and I went to live there. He had become a gentile (not without difficulty) but was able to take a child from a practicing Jewish family into his household.

It did not take more than a few days at school for the beatings to begin, whereupon they increased with ferocity. There was a bubbling fountain in easy distance of the schoolyard where I went to wash away the blood.

One day I watched the water turn crimson over the rippling reflection of my scarred face. I decided that whatever it was a Jew was supposed to be, I surely didn't qualify. I had the same color blood as my classmates, after all. Therefore I could not be a real Jew.

I announced this revelation the next day at school and was nearly killed for my trouble. One particularly stupid lad was so distressed by my logic that he expressed his displeasure with a critique made up of a two-by-four. Yet somehow in all this pain and anguish—as I fled for my life—I did not think to condemn the attackers. My conclusion was that surely the Jew must be a monstrous creature indeed to inspire such a display. Cursing the memory of my parents, I felt certain that through some happy fluke I was not really of their flesh and blood.

Amazing as it seems, I became an anti-Semite. I took a Star of David to the playground and in full view of my classmates destroyed it. A picture of a rabbi I also burned. Some were not impressed by this display, but others restrained them from resuming the beatings. For the first time I knew security in that schoolyard. None of them became any friendlier; they did not seem to know how to take it.

Suddenly the pictures of Dietrich's early life disappeared into a swirling darkness. I was confused, disoriented.

Time had passed. Now I was Dietrich as a young man back in Germany, dedicating myself to a life's work in genetic research. I joined the Nazi Party on the eve of its power, not so much out of vanity as out of a pragmatic reading of the *Zeitgeist*. Naturally I used my Spanish gentile pedigree, and entertained my new "friends" with a little-known quotation from the canon of Karl Marx, circa 1844: "Once society has succeeded in abolishing the empirical essence of Judaism—huckstering and its preconditions—the Jew will have become impossible."

The Nazis were developing their eugenic theories at the time. To say the basis of their programs was at best pseudoscientific would still be to compliment it. At best, the only science involved was terminology borrowed from the field of eugenics.

I was doing real research, however, despite the limitations I faced due to Party funding and propaganda requirements. My work involved negative eugenics, the study of how to eliminate defective genes from the gene pool through selective breeding. Assuming an entire society could be turned into a laboratory, defective genes could be eliminated in one generation, although the problem might still crop up from time to time because of recessive genes (easily handled).

The decision to breed something out of the population having been made, the door opened as to what to breed *for*, or positive eugenics. Now, so long as we were restricting ourselves to a question of a particular genetic disease, we could do something. But even then there were problems. What if some invaluable genius had such a genetic disability? Would you throw out the possibility of his having intelligent offspring just because of one risk?

Add to this valid concern the deranged, mystical ideas of the Nazi with regard to genetics, and the complications really set in. They wanted to breed for qualities that in many cases fell outside the province of real genetics—because they fell outside reality in the first place.

During this period in my life I made another discovery. I was no longer a racist. My anti-Semitism vanished as in a vagrant breeze. I had learned that there was no scientific basis for it. The sincere Nazi belief that the Jew was a creature outside of nature was so much rot. As for the cultural/mystical ideas that revolved around the Jew, the more I learned of how the Nazis perceived this, the more convinced I became that Hitler's party was composed of the insane. (An ironic note was that many European Jews were not even Semitic, but that is beside the point. The Nazis had little concern with, say, Arabs. It was the European Jew they were after, for whatever reasons were handy.)

Although I had come full circle on the question of racism, something else had happened to me in the interim. My hatred for one group of humanity had *not* vanished. My view of the common heritage of *Homo sapiens* led me to despise all of the human race. The implications of this escaped me at the time, but it was the turning point of my life.

Even at the peak of their popularity the world of genetics was only slightly influenced by Nazi thinking. Scientists are scientists first, ideologues second, if at all. To the extent that most scientists have a philosophy it is a general sort of positive humanism: so it was with my teacher in genetics, a brilliant man—who happened to fit the Aryan stereotype coincidentally—and his collaborator, a Jew who was open about his family background, unlike me.

They were the first to discover the structure of DNA. No, they are not in the history books. By then Hitler had come to power. The Nazis destroyed many of their papers when they were judged enemies of the state—for political improprieties having nothing to do with the research. But I was never found guilty of harboring any traitorous notions. Long before the world heard of it, I continued this work with DNA. Publishing this information was the last thing I wanted to do. I had other ideas. By giving the Nazis gobbledygook to make their idiot policies sound good, I remained unmolested. There would be a place for me in the New Order. I remembered when Einstein said that should his theory of relativity prove untrue, the French would declare him a German, and the Germans call him a Jew. At least I knew my place in advance.

Through the haze of Dietrich's memories I could still think; could reflect on what I was assimilating directly from a pattern taken from another's mind. I was impressed that such a man existed, working in secret for decades on what had only recently riveted the world's attention. Only last year had a news story dealt with microbiologists doing gene splicing. Yet he had done the same sort of experimentation decades earlier.

What had been a trickle suddenly turned into a torrent of concepts and formulae beyond my comprehension. I felt the strain. With quivering fingers I reached for the cylinder and . . .

The images stopped; the words stopped; the kaleidoscope exploding inside my head stopped; the pressure stopped . . .

"You have not finished the program, Dr. Goebbels," said Dietrich. "It was at least another ten minutes before the 'reel change.'" He was holding the other cylinder in his hand, tossing it lightly into the air and catching it as though it were of no importance.

"It's too much," I gasped, "to take all at once. Hold on, I've just remembered something: Thor, in the hallway . . . is it possible?" I thought back over what I had experienced. Dietrich had left simple eugenic breeding programs far behind. His search was for the chemical mysteries of life itself, like some sort of mad alchemist seeking the knowledge of a Frankenstein. "Did you—" I paused, hardly knowing how to phrase it. "Did you create Thor?"

He laughed. "Don't I wish!" he said, almost playfully. "Do you have any idea what you are talking about? To find the genetic formula for human beings would require a language I do not possess."

"A language?"

"You'd have to break the code, be able to read the hieroglyphic wonders of not just one, but millions of genes. It's all there, in the chromosomes, but I haven't been able to find it yet. No one has." He put his face near to mine, grinning, eyes wide and staring. "But I will be the first. Nobody can beat me to it, because only I can do it!"

For a moment I thought I was back in the presence of Hitler. This man was certainly a visionary. Moreover he was dangerous in a fashion beyond any politician.

"Why are you here?" I asked.

"They finance me well. Look at these toys," he said, pointing at what he told me was an atmosphere chamber. "The work is expensive. Do you know how to invade the hidden territory of life itself? With radiation and poison to break down the structures and begin anew. To build! I can never live long enough, never receive enough sponsorship. It is the work of many lifetimes. If only I had more subtle tools . . ."

Before I lost him to a scientist's reverie, I changed the subject: "My son's hair and eyes have changed."

"That's nothing but cosmetics," he said disdainfully.

"The SS wants you to do that?"

"It is considered a mark of distinction. My beautician there"—he pointed at the Japanese girl—"provides this minor and unimportant service."

Only a few blonde-haired, blue-eyed people were working in the laboratory. I asked why everyone had not undergone the treatment. The reason was because the few I had just seen were authentic members of that genotype. Dietrich was blunt: "We don't play SS games in here."

He showed me his workshop, treating the technicians as no more than expensive equipment. I wondered how Speer would react to all this. The place was even larger than I had first thought. I wondered what Holly would make of it all, cramped in her small cubbyhole at the university.

The seemingly endless walk activated my pains again. My host noticed this distress and suggested we sit down again. He had not misplaced the other cylinder. Somehow I was not surprised when he suggested that I sample its contents.

"Did I really share in your memories?" I asked him.

"A carefully edited production, but yes."

"Is there more of the same in this other one?"

"I hold in my hand images from a different point of view. I believe that you might find these even more interesting." He put the thing on my palm. "Do you want it?"

"I have a thousand unanswered questions."

"This will help."

Shrugging, I placed it to the same point on my forehead and . . . *I did not know who I was.*

In vain I searched for the identity into which I had been plunged. What there was of me seemed to be a disembodied consciousness floating high above the European continent. It was like seeing in all directions at once. The moon above was very large, very near the earth—it was made of ice.

Horbiger's *Welteislehre!* It was a projection of one of his prophecies, when the moon would fall toward the earth, causing great upheavals in the crust—and working bizarre mutations on the life of the planet.

There was a panorama unfolding like the Worm Ouroboros: ancient epochs and the far future were melded together in an unbreakable circle. The world and civilization I knew were nothing but a passing aberration in the history of the globe.

I saw ancient Atlantis, not the one spoken of by Plato, but from a time when men were not supposed to exist. The first Atlantis, inhabited by great giants who preceded man and taught the human race all its important knowledge: I beheld Prometheus as real.

Then I was shown that the pantheon of Nordic gods also had a basis in this revelation. Fabled Asgard was not a myth, but a legend—a vague memory of the giant cities that once thrived on earth.

Humanity was incredibly older than the best estimates of the scientists. More startling than that was the tapestry flickering in myriad colors to depict a faraway but inevitable future. All of the human race had perished but for a remnant of Aryans. And these last men, these idealized

Viking types, were happily preparing for their own extermination—making way for the *Übermenschen* who had nothing in common with them but for superficial appearances. The human race—as I knew it—was not really "human" at all. The Aryan was shown as that type closest to True Man, but when mutations caused by the descending moon brought back the giants, then the Aryan could join his fellows in welcome oblivion. The masters had returned. They would cherish this world, and perform the rites on the way to the next apocalypse, the *Ragnarök* when the cycle would start again—for the moon of ice would have at last smashed into the earth.

These images burned into my brain: gargantuan cities with spires threatening the stars; science utterly replaced by a functional magic that was the central power of these psychokinetic supermen who needed little else; everything vast, endless, bright . . . so bright that it blinded my sight and my mind . . .

With a scream I ripped the device from my perspiring skin. "This is madness!" I said, putting my head in my hands. "It can't be really true. The SS religion . . . no!"

Dietrich put a comforting hand on my shoulder, much to my surprise. "Of course it is not true," he said. There must have been tears in my eyes. My expression was a mask of confusion. He went on: "What you have seen is no more true than one of your motion pictures, or a typical release from the Ministry of Propaganda. It is more convincing, I'll admit. Just as the first cylinder allowed you to peer into the contents of one mind—my own—this other one has given you a composite picture of what a certain group believes; a collaborative effort, you could say."

"Religious fanatics of the SS," I muttered.

"They have a colorful prediction there, a hypothetical history, a faith. Of course, it is not as worthwhile as my autobiography."

"What has one to do with the other?" I asked. "What does your story have to do with theirs?"

Dietrich stood, and put his hands behind his back. He was appearing to be more like Dr. Mabuse all the time. His voice sounded different somehow, as though he was speaking to a very large audience: "They have hired me to perform a genetic task. In this laboratory a virus is being developed that will spare only blonde, blue-eyed men and women. Yes, Dr. Goebbels, the virus would kill you—with your dark hair and brown eyes—and myself, as readily as my Japanese assistant. It means your son would die also, because his current appearance is, after all, only cosmetic. It means most members of the Nazi Party would perish as not being 'racially' fit by this standard.

"I am speaking of the most comprehensive genocide program of all time. A large proportion of the populations in Sweden and Denmark and Iceland will survive. Too bad for the SS that virtually all those people think these ideas are purest folly, even evil. You know that much of the world's folk have rather strict ethical systems built into their quaint little cultures. That sort of thing gave the Nazis a difficult time at first, didn't it?"

I started to laugh. It was the sort of laughter that is not easy to control. I became hysterical. My concentration was directed at trying to stop the crazy sounds coming out of my mouth and I didn't notice anything else. Suddenly I was surprised to find myself on the floor. Arms were pulling me up and the professor was putting a hypodermic needle in my flesh. As the darkness claimed me, I wondered why there were no accompanying pictures. Didn't this cylinder touching my arm have a story to tell?

It felt as if I had been asleep for days but I came to my wits a few minutes later, according to my watch at least. I was lying on a cot and *he* was standing over me. I knew who he really was: Dr. Mabuse.

"Goebbels, I thought you were made of sterner stuff," came his grim voice.

"You are a lunatic," I told him hoarsely.

"That's unfair. What in my conduct strikes you as unseemly?"

"You said you had been anti-Semitic. Then you told me that you had rejected racism. Now you are part of a plot that takes racism farther than anything I've ever heard of!"

"You've been out of touch."

"The whole mess is a shambles of contradictions!"

"You hurt me deeply," was his retort, but the voice sounded inhuman. "I expected more from a thoughtful Nazi. My sponsors want a project carried out for racist reasons. I do not believe in their theories, religion, or pride. This pure blonde race they worship has never existed, in fact; it was simply a climatological adaptation in Northern Europe, never as widely distributed as Nazis think. It was a trait in a larger population group. I don't believe in SS myths. My involvement in the project is for other reasons."

"There cannot be any other reason."

"You forget what you have learned. Remember that I came to hate all of the human race. This does not mean that I gave up my reason or started engaging in wishful thinking. If the Burgundians enable me to wipe out most of humanity, with themselves exempt from the holocaust, I'll go along with it. The piper calls the tune."

·"You couldn't carry on your work. You'd be dead!"

Sometimes one has the certainty of having been led down a primrose path, with the gate being locked against any hope of retreat, only *after* the graveyard sound of the latch snapping shut. Knowledge has a habit of coming too late. Such was the emotion that held me in an iron grip as soon as those words escaped my lips. Dr. Mabuse could never be a fool. It was impossible. Even as he spoke, I could anticipate the words: "Oh, I *am* sorry. I forgot to tell you that a few people outside the fortunate category may be saved. I can make them immune. In this sense, I'll be a Noah, collecting specimens for a specialist's ark. Anyone I consider worthy I will claim."

"Why do you hate the human race?" I asked him.

"To think that a Nazi has the gall to ask that question. Why do you hate the Jews?" he shot back. I could think of nothing to say. He continued: "There's little difference between us, morally. I know what you advocated during World War II, Goebbels. The difference between us is that I've set my sights higher. So what if Nazi Germany is annihilated? By what right can a Nazi criticize me?"

I remained insistent on one theme: "Why do it at all? You won't have destroyed all mankind. Burgundy will remain."

"Then Burgundy and I will play a game with each other," he said.

"What in God's name are you talking about?"

Another voice entered the conversation: "In Odin's name. . . ." It was Kaufmann, walking over to join us. I was pleased that he had a bandage on his head, and his face was drained of color. I wanted to strike him again! He made me think of Himmler at his worst.

It is my firm belief that the mind never ceases working, not even in the deepest slumber. While I had been unconscious the solution to the last part of the puzzle had presented itself. I didn't need to ask Mabuse about this part.

It is certainly understandable that expedient agreement is possible between two parties having nothing in common but one equally desired objective. There was the pact between Germany and Russia early in the war, for instance. The current case was different in one important respect: I doubted this particular alliance could last long enough to satisfy either party. I was certain that this was the Achilles' heel.

A comic-opera kingdom with a mad scientist! If my daughter had known of this, why had she not told me more? Or had she only been guessing in the dark herself?

The knight in armor and the man in the laboratory: the two simply didn't mix! Since the founding of Burgundy, there had been an anti-science, antitechnology attitude at work. Even French critics who never had good things to say about the Reich managed to praise Burgundy for its lack of modern technique. (The French could never be made to shut up altogether, so we allowed them to talk about nearly everything except practical politics. The skeptics and cynics among them could always be counted on to come up with a rationale for their place in postwar Europe, stinging though it was to their pride. What else could they do?)

Here was a geneticist more advanced than anyone else in the field making common cause with a nation devoted to the destruction of science. That the Burgundians trusted his motives was peculiar; that he could trust theirs was even more bizarre.

The explanation that had come to me was this: unlike scientists who belonged to the humanist tradition and believed that genetic engineering could be made to improve the life of human beings (naive healers, but useful to a statesman such as myself), Dr. Mabuse wished to find the secret of manipulating the building blocks of life so that he could create something nonhuman. This creature he had in mind might very well be mistaken by a good Burgundian as one of the New Men or *Übermenschen*, and viewed as an object of worship. Where others might oppose these new beings, the Burgundians—trained from birth in religious acceptance of superior beings in human form—would present no obstacle.

As for the Burgundians, such leaders as Kaufmann had to believe that wicked modern science had produced at least one genius who was the vehicle of higher mysteries: a puppet of Destiny.

I looked in the faces of these two men, such different faces, such different minds. There was something familiar there—a fervor, a wild devotion to The Cause, and a lust to practice sacrificial rites. As Minister of Propaganda I had sought to inculcate that look in the population with regard to Jews.

It was evident that I had not been made privy to their machinations carelessly. Either I would be allowed to join them or I would die. As for the possibility of the former, I did not consider it likely. Perhaps the forebodings engendered in me by Hilda were partly to blame, but in fact I knew that I could not be part of such a scheme against the Fatherland. Could I convince them that I would be loyal? No, I didn't believe it. Could I have convinced them if I had inured myself against shock and displayed nought but enthusiasm for their enterprise? I doubted it.

The question remained why I had been chosen for the privilege. The message Hilda had shown me was rife with unpleasant implications. I took a gamble by sitting up, pointing at Mabuse, and shouting to Kaufmann: "This man is a Jew!"

I could tell that that was a mistake by the exchange of expressions between the two. Of course, they had to know. No one could keep a secret in the SS's own country. If they overlooked Dr. Mabuse's ideas and profession, they could overlook anything. This was one occasion when traditional Jew-baiting would not help a Nazi! I didn't like the situation. I didn't want to be on the receiving end.

The voice of Mabuse seemingly spoke to me, but the words appeared to be for Kaufmann's benefit: "It is too bad that you will not be able to work with the new entertainment technology. I was hoping we could transfer your memories of the affair with Lida Barova. As she was your most famous scandal, it would have made for a good show."

Before I could answer this taunt, Kaufmann's gruff voice announced: "Don't keep your son waiting."

"He should wait for me, not the other way around!"

Kaufmann was oblivious: "He is with his fellows. Come." Mabuse helped me get off the cot and then we were marching down the corridor again. I was dizzy on my feet, my hand hurt, and my head felt as though it were stuffed full of cotton. So many random thoughts swirling in my mind, easily displaced by immediate concern for my future welfare . . .

Twilight was fast approaching as we entered the courtyard I had noticed earlier in Kaufmann's office. The large funeral pyre was still there, unused. Except that now there was a bier next to it. We were too far away to see whose body was on it, but with every step we drew nearer.

A door beside the pyre opened and a line of young men emerged, dressed in black SS regalia. In the lead was my son. They proceeded remorselessly in our direction. Helmuth gave Kaufmann the Nazi salute. He answered with the same. Quite obviously I was in no mood to reciprocate.

"Father," said Helmuth gravely, "I have been granted the privilege of overseeing this observance. Please approach the body."

Such was the formality of his tone that I hesitated to intercede with a fatherly appeal. The expression on his face was blank to my humanity. I did as requested.

Not for a moment did I suspect the identity of the body. Yet as I gazed at that familiar, waxen face, I knew that it fit the Burgundian pattern. It had to be his body. Once more I stood before Adolf Hitler!

"It was an outrage," said Kaufmann, "to preserve his body as though he were Lenin. His soul belongs in Valhalla. We intend to send it there today." My mouth was open with a question that would not be voiced as I turned to Kaufmann. He bowed solemnly. "Yes, Herr Goebbels. You were one of his most loyal deputies. You will accompany him."

There are times when no amount of resolve to be honorable and brave will suffice: I made to run, but many strong hands were on me in an instant. Helmuth placed his hand on my shoulder. "Don't make it worse," he whispered. "It has to be. Preserve your dignity. I want to be proud of you."

There was nothing to say. Nothing to do but contemplate a horrible death. I struggled in vain, doing my best to ignore the existence of Helmuth. It was no surprise that he had been selected for this honor. It made perfect sense in the demented scheme of things.

They brought out an aluminum ramp. Two husky SS men began to carry Hitler's body up the incline, while Helmuth remained behind, no doubt with the intention of escorting me up that unwelcome path.

"The manner of your death will remain a state secret of Burgundy," said Kaufmann. "We were able to receive good publicity from your Ministry when we executed those two French snoopers for trespassing: Louis Pauwels and Jacques Bergier. This is different." He paused, then added: "Soon publicity won't matter anymore."

My options were being reduced to nothing. Even facing death I could not entirely surrender. The years I had spent perfecting the art of propaganda had taught me that no situation is so hopeless that nothing may be salvaged from it. I reviewed the facts: despite their temporary agreement Kaufmann and the new Mabuse were really working at cross-purposes. If I could only exploit those differences, I could sow dissension in their ranks. Mabuse held the trump card, so I decided to direct the ploy at Kaufmann.

"I suppose I'm free to talk," I said to Kaufmann's back as he watched the red ball of the sun setting beyond the castle walls. The sky was streaked with orange and gold—the thin strands of cumulus clouds that seemed so reassuringly distant. There were a million other places I could have been at that moment, but for a vile twist of fate. There had to be some way of escape!

No one answered my query and I continued: "You're not a geneticist, are you, Kaufmann? How would you know if you can trust Dietrich?" He was Dietrich to them, but to me he would always be Mabuse. "What if he is lying? What if his process can't be made specific enough to exclude any group from the virus?"

Mabuse laughed. Kaufmann answered without turning around: "For insurance's sake he will immunize everyone in Burgundy as well as his assistants. If something goes wrong, it will be a shame to lose all those excellent Aryan specimens elsewhere in the world."

"Nothing will go wrong," said Mabuse.

I wouldn't give up that easily and struck back with: "How do you know he won't inject you with poison when the time comes? It would be like a repetition of the Black Plague that ravaged Burgundy in 1348."

"I applaud your inventive suggestion," said Mabuse.

"We have faith," was Kaufmann's astounding reply.

"A faith I will reward," boomed out Mabuse's monster voice. "They are not stupid, Goebbels. Some true believers have sufficient medical training to detect an attempt at the stunt you suggest."

In desperation I spoke again to my son: "Do you trust this?"

"I am here," came his answer in a low voice. "I have taken the oath."

"It's no good," taunted Mabuse. "Stop trying to save yourself."

They had Hitler's body at the top of the ramp. The SS men stood at attention. Everyone was waiting. The setting sun seemed to me at that moment to be pausing in its descent, waiting.

"Father," said Helmuth, "Germany has become decadent. It has forgotten its ideals. That my sister Hilda is allowed to live is proof enough. Look at you. You're not the man you were in the grand old days of the genocide."

"Son," I said, my voice trembling, "what is happening in Burgundy is not the same thing."

"Oh, yes, it is," said Dr. Mabuse.

Kaufmann strolled over to where I was standing and craned his neck to look at the men at the top of the ramp with the worldly remains of Adolf Hitler. He said, "Nazis were good killers during the war. Jews, Gypsies, and many others fell by the sword, even when it exacted a heavy price from other elements of the war program. Speer always wanting his slave labor for industrial requirements. Accountants always counting pennies. The mass murder was for its own sake, a promise of better things to come!

"After the war only Burgundy seemed to care any longer. Rulings that came out of New Berlin were despicable, loosening up the censorship laws and not strictly enforcing the racial standards. Do you know that a taint of Jewishness is considered to be sexually arousing in Germany's more decadent cabarets of today? Even the euthanasia policy for old and unfit citizens was never more than words on paper, after the Catholics and Lutherans interfered. The Party was corrupted from within. It let the dream die."

The kind of hatred motivating this Burgundian leader was no stranger to me. Never in my worst nightmares did it occur to me that I could be a victim of this kind of thinking.

Kaufmann gestured to men on the ramp and they placed Hitler's body on top of the pyre. "It is time," mourned Helmuth's voice in my ear. Other young SS men surrounded me, Helmuth holding my arm. We began to walk.

Other SS men had appeared around the dry pyramid of kindling wood and straw. They were holding burning torches. Kaufmann gestured and they set the pyre aflame. The crackling and popping sounds plucked at my nerves as whitish smoke slowly rose. It would take a few minutes before the flame reached the apex to consume Hitler's body . . . and whatever else was near. My only consolation was that they had not used lighter fluid—dreadful modern stuff—to hasten the inferno.

Somewhere in that blazing doom Odin and Thor and Freyja were waiting. I was in no hurry to greet them.

I wondered at how the SA must have felt when the SS burst in on them, barking guns ripping out their lives in bloody ruins. Perhaps I should have thought of Magda, but I did not. Instead all my whimsies were directed to miracles and last-minute salvations. How I had preached hope in the final hours of the war before our luck had turned. I had fed Hitler on stories of Frederick the Great's diplomatic coup in the face of a military debacle. I had compared the atom bomb—when we got it—to the remarkable change in fortunes in the House of Brandenburg. Now I found myself pleading with the cruel fates for a personal victory of the same sort.

I was at the top of the ramp. Helmuth's hands were set firmly against my back. To him had fallen the task of consigning his father's living body to the flames. They must have considered him an adept pupil to be trusted with so severe a task.

So completely absorbed was I in thoughts of a sudden reprieve that I barely noticed the distant explosion. Someone behind me said, "What was that?" I heard Kaufmann calling from the ground but his words were lost in a louder explosion that occurred nearby.

A manic voice called out: "We must finish the rite!" It was Helmuth. He pushed me into empty space. I fell on Hitler's corpse, and grabbed at the torso to keep from falling into an opening, beneath which raged the personal executioner.

"Too soon," one of my son's comrades was saying. "The fire isn't high enough. You'll have to shoot him or . . ."

Already I was rolling onto the other side of Hitler's body as I heard a gunshot. Out of the corner of my eye I could see Helmuth clutching his stomach as he fell into the red flames.

Shouts. Gunfire. More explosions. An army was climbing over the wall of the courtyard. A helicopter was zooming in overhead. My first thought was that it must be the German army come to save me. I was too delighted to care how that was possible.

The conflagration below was growing hotly near. Smoke filling my eyes and lungs was about to choke me to death. I was contemplating a jump from the top—a risky proposition at best—when I was given a better chance by a break in the billowing fumes. The men had cleared the ramp for being ill protected against artillery.

Once again I threw myself over Hitler's body and hit the metal ramp with a thud. What kept me from falling off was the body of a dead SS man, whose leg I was able to grasp as I started to bounce back. Then I lifted myself and ran as swiftly as I could, tripping a quarter of the way from the ground and rolling bruisedly the rest of the way. The whizzing bullets missed me. I lay hugging the dirt, for fear of being shot if I rose.

Even from that limited position I could evaluate certain aspects of the encounter. The Burgundians had temporarily given up their penchant for fighting with swords and were making do with machine guns instead. (The one exception was Thor, who ran forward in a berserker rage, wielding an ax. The bullets tore him to ribbons.) The battle seemed to be going badly for them.

Then I heard the greatest explosion of my life. It was as if the castle had been converted into one of Von Braun's rockets as a sheet of flame erupted from underneath it and the whole building quaked with the vibrations. The laboratory must have been destroyed instantly.

"It's Goebbels," a voice sang out. "Is he alive?"

"If he is, we'll soon remedy that."

"No," said the first voice. "Let's find out."

Rough hands turned me over . . . and I expected to look once more into faces of SS men. These were young men, all right, but there was something disturbingly familiar about them. I realized that they might be Jews! The thought, even then, that my life had been saved by Jews was too much to bear. But those faces, like the faces that I've thought about too many times to count.

"Blindfold him," one said. It was done, and I was being pushed through the courtyard blind, the noises of battle echoing all around. Once we stopped and crouched behind something. There was an exchange of shots. Then we were running and I was pulled into a conveyance of some sort. The whirring sound identified it instantly as a helicopter revving up; and we were off the ground, and we were flying away from that damned castle. A thin, high whistling sound went by— someone must have still been firing at us. And then the fight faded away in the distance.

AN HOUR LATER we had landed. I was still blindfolded. Low voices were speaking in German. Suddenly I heard a scrap of Russian. This in turn was followed by a comment in Yiddish; and there was a sentence in what I took to be Hebrew. The different conversations were interrupted by a deep voice speaking in French announcing the arrival of an important person. After a few more whisperings—in German again—my blindfold was removed.

Standing in front of me was Hilda, dressed in battle fatigues. "Tell me what has happened," I said, adding as an afterthought—"if you will."

"Father, you have been rescued from Burgundy by a military operation of combined forces."

"You were only incidental," added a lean, dark-haired man by her side.

"Allow me to introduce this officer," she said, putting her hand on his arm. "We won't use names, but this man is with the Zionist Liberation Army. My involvement was sponsored by the guerrilla arm of the German Freedom League. Since your abduction the rest of the organization has gone underground. We are also receiving an influx of Russians into our ranks."

If everything else that had happened seemed improbable, this was sufficient to convince me that I had finally lost my sanity and was enmeshed in the impossible. "There is no Zionist Liberation Army," I said. "I would have heard of it."

"You're not the only one privy to secrets," was her smug reply.

"Are you a Zionist now?" I asked my daughter, thinking that nothing else would astound me. I was wrong again.

"No," she answered. "I don't support statism of any kind. I'm an anarchist."

What next? Her admission stunned me to the core. A large Negro with a beard spoke: "There is only one requirement to be in this army, Nazi. You must oppose National Socialism, German or Burgundian."

"We have communists as well, Father," my daughter went on. "The small wars Hitler kept waging well into the 1950s, always pushing deeper into Russia, made more converts to Marx than you realize."

"But you hate communism, daughter. You've told me so over and over." In retrospect it was not prudent for me to say this in such a company, but I no longer cared. I was emotionally exhausted, numb, empty.

She took the bait. "I hate all dictatorships. In the battle of the moment I must take what comrades I can get. You taught me that."

I could not stop myself talking, despite the risk. I sensed that this was the last chance I would have to reach my daughter. "The Bolsheviks were worse statists than we ever were. Surely the War Crimes Trials we held at the end of hostilities taught you that, even if you wouldn't learn it from your own father."

She raised her voice: "I know the evil that was done. What else would you expect from your darling straight-A princess than I can still recite the names of the Russian death camps: Vorkuta, Karaganda, Dalstroi, Magadan, Norilsk, Bamlag, and Solovki. But it has only lately dawned on me that there is something hypocritical about the victors trying the vanquished. You didn't even try to find judges from neutral countries."

"What do you expect from Nazis?" added the Negro.

My daughter reminded me of myself, as she continued to lecture all of us, captors and captives alike: "The first step on the road to anarchy is to realize that all war is a crime; and that the cause is statism." Before I could get in a word edgewise, other members of the group began arguing among themselves; and I knew that I was in the hands of real radicals. The early days of the Party were like this. And whether Hilda was an anarchist or not, it was clear that the leader of this ad-hoc army—enough of a state for me—was the thin, dark-haired Jew.

He leaned into my face, and vomited up the following: "Your daughter's personal loyalty prevents her from accepting the evidence we have gathered about your involvement in the mass murder of Jews. You're as bad as Stalin."

My dear, sweet daughter. Reaching out to embrace her, I not only caused several guns to be leveled on my person, but received a rebuff from her. She slapped me! Her words were acid as she said, "Fealty only goes so far. Whatever your part in the killing of innocent civilians, the rest of your career is an open book. You are an evil man. I can't lie to myself about it any longer."

There was no room for anger. No room left for anything but a hunger for security. I was ready to happily consign my entire family to Hitler's funeral pyre, if by so doing I could return home to New Berlin. The demeanor of these freelance soldiers told me that they bore me no will that was good.

Hilda must have read my thoughts. "They are going to let you go, this time, as a favor to me. We agreed in advance that Burgundy was the priority. Everything else had to take a back seat, including waking up about my . . . parents."

"When may I leave?"

"We're near the Burgundian border. My friends will disappear, until a later date when you *may* see them again. As for me, I'm leaving Europe for good."

"Where will you go?" I didn't expect an answer to that.

"To the American Republic. My radical credentials are an asset over there."

"America," I said listlessly. "Why?"

"Just make believe you are concocting another of your ideological speeches. Do this one about individual rights and you'll have your answer. They may not be an anarchist utopia, but they are paradise compared with your Europe. Goodbye, Father. And farewell to Hitler's ghost."

I was blindfolded again. Despite mixed feelings I was grateful to be alive. They released me at the great oak tree I had observed when flying into Burgundy. As I removed the blindfold, I heard the helicopter take off behind me. My eyes focused on the plaque nailed to the tree that showed how SS men had ripped up the railway and transplanted this tremendous oak to block that evidence of the modern world. It had taken a lot of manpower.

How easily manpower can be reduced to dead flesh.

Turning around, I saw the flowing green hills of a world I had never fully understood stretched out to the horizon. With a shudder I looked away, walked around the tree, and began following the rusty track on the other side. It would lead me to the old station where I would put in a call to home . . . to what I thought was home.

POSTSCRIPT BY HILDA GOEBBELS

SPIRIT STATION
(THE CHARLES A. LINDBERGH
EXPERIMENTAL ORBITAL COMMUNITY)

JANUARY 1, 2000

From this point on my father's diaries become incoherent. He must have recorded his Burgundian experiences shortly after returning to New Berlin. However much he had been the public demagogue he was surprisingly frank in his diaries. It must have been galling to him when they assigned psychiatric help. They knew what had happened. They sent in a full strike force to clean out Burgundy. They also came down on the underground shortly after I escaped. What a time that was. When the dust settled, Father had lost his influence.

Sometimes I try to decode Father's final entries, scrawled out in the last year of his life. He was a broken man in 1970, unhinged by the Burgundian affair, afraid of reprisals by the underground, unable to fathom why his favorite child hated him so. One consistent pattern of his last writings is that his recurring nightmare of Teutonic Knights had been displaced by a Jewish terror: an army of Golems concocted by Dr. Mabuse, who, after all, would work for anyone. Although there was no reason to believe that Dietrich survived our attack that afternoon, Father went to his grave believing the man to be immortal.

Images that crop up in these sad pages include a landscape of broken buildings, empty mausoleums, bones, and other wreckage that shows he never got over his obsession with The War. As for Mother leaving him at long last, he makes no comment but *das Nichts*. Even at the end he retained the habits of a literary German. One moment he is taking pleasure from the "heart attack" suffered by Himmler on the eve of Father's return—and there are comments here about how Rosenberg has finally been avenged. This material is interspersed with grocery bills from the days of the Great Inflation, problems he had with raising money for the Party in the mid-thirties, and a tirade against Horbiger. Before I can make heads or tails of this, he's off on a tangent about Nazis who believed in the hollow earth, and pages of minute details about Hitler's diet.

Those of my critics who believe I am suppressing material are welcome to these pages any time they ask. The only material of value was made available in the first appendix to *Final Entries*; to wit, Father's realization that they had substituted another body in Hitler's tomb—hotly denied by New Berliners to this day.

After all these years it is a strange feeling to look at the diary pages again. He accurately described me as the young and headstrong girl I was, although I wonder if he realized that I was firmly in the underground by the time I was warning him about Burgundy. If he could only see the crotchety old woman I have become.

I would have enjoyed speaking to him on his deathbed, as he did with Hitler. The main question I would have asked would be how he thought Reich officials would ever allow his diaries, from 1965 on, to appear in Europe? The early, famous entries, from 1933 to 1963, had been published as part of the official German record. The entries beginning with 1965 would have to be buried, and buried *deep*, by any dictatorship. Father's idea that no censorship applied to the privileged class—of his supposedly classless society—did not take into account sensitive state documents, such as his record of the Burgundy affair, or his highly sensitive discussion with Hitler. If the real *Final Entries* had not been smuggled out of Europe as one of the last acts of the underground, and delivered to me in New York, I never would have been in a position to come to terms with memories of my Father. Nor would I have had the book that launched my career. Americans love hearing of Nazi secrets.

Now as I begin a new life of semiretirement up here in America's first space city, haunted by equal portions of earthlight and moonlight, I wish to reconsider this period of history. Besides, if I don't write a new book, I believe I will go out of my mind.

Yesterday they had me speak to an audience of five hundred about my life as a writer. They wanted to know how much research I had put into the series about postwar Japan and China. They wanted to know how I deal with writer's block. But most of all they wanted to hear about Nazis, Nazis, Nazis.

A handsome young Japanese boy saved me by asking what I considered the greatest moment of my life. I told him it was that I had been a successful thief. Once the audience of dedicated free-enterprisers had stopped gasping like fish out of water, I explained. Back in the eighties, the specter of cancer was finally put to rest, thanks to new work derived from original research by Dr. Richard Dietrich. Yes, the most pleasant irony I've ever tasted was that "Mabuse's" final achievement was for life instead of death; I made it possible. It was I who delivered his papers into the hands of American scientists.

I must take repeated breaks in writing this addendum. My back gives me nothing but trouble, and I spend at least three times a day in zero-g therapy. How Hitler would have loved that. After the last bomb attempt on him his central concern became the damage to his *Sieg Heiling* arm, and his most characteristic feature—his ass. To think my Father literally worshiped that man! I guess if Napoleon had succeeded in unifying Europe he'd be just as popular.

Now I'm reclining on a yellow couch in Observation 10A. There is a breathtaking view of Europe spread out to my right, although I can't make out Germany. The Fatherland is hidden beneath a patch of clouds. What I can see of the continent is cleaner than any map: there are no borderlines.

Who could have predicted the ultimate consequence of Hitler's war? Certainly not myself. I recognized what Nazi Germany was, because I grew up there. It was an organization in the most modern meaning of the word. It was a conveyor belt. Hitler's ideology was the excuse for operating the controls, but that mechanism had a life of its own. Horrors were born of that machine; but so were fruits. Medals and barbed wire; diplomas and death sentences—they were all the same to the machine. The monster seemed unstoppable. In the belly of such a state it was easy to become an anarchist. The next step was just as easy—join a gang of your own, to fight the gang you hate. None of us on any side, not the Burgundians, not the underground, not the Reich itself, could see what was really happening. Only a few pacifists grasped the point.

Adolf Hitler achieved the exact opposite of all his long-term goals, and he did this by winning World War II. Economic reality subverted National Socialism.

The average German used to defend Hitler by saying that he got us out of the Depression, without bothering to note that the way the glorious *Führer* paid off all the classes of Germany was by looting foreigners. This was not the friendliest method of undoing the harm of Versailles. But as Europe began to remove age-old barriers to commerce, economic benefits began to spread. A thriving black market ensured that all would benefit from the new plenty, and ideology be damned. While the Burgundians actually tried to implement Hitlerian ideas, the rest of Europe enjoyed the new prosperity.

Father was intelligent enough to notice this trend, but he carefully avoided drawing the obvious conclusion: Nazi Germany was becoming less National Socialist with every passing decade. For all the talk of Race Destiny, it was the technical mind of Albert Speer that ran the German Empire. Our sideshow bigots provided the decoration. Hitler was going to achieve permanent race segregation; his New Order lasted only long enough to knock down the barriers to racial separation, and economics did the rest. There is more racial intermarriage today than ever, thanks to Adolf Hitler.

Today Germany is seeing a flowering of historical revisionists who are debunking the Hitler myth. They are showing his feet of clay. They are asking why Germany used a nuclear weapon against a civilian population, while President Dewey restricted his atomic bombs to Japanese military targets in the open sea. Even a thick-headed German may get the point after a while. The Reich's youth protests against the treatment of Russians by Rosenberg's Cultural Bureaus, and they are no longer shot, no longer arrested . . . and who knows but that they may accomplish something? If this keeps up, maybe my books, including *Final Entries of Dr. Joseph Goebbels*, will become available in the open market, instead of merely being black-market bestsellers already. America is still the only uncensored society.

More than anything else I am encouraged by what happens when German and American scientists and engineers work together. The magnificent new autobahns of Africa demonstrate this. But nothing is more beautiful than the space cities—the American and German complexes, the Japanese one, and finally, Israel. I've received an invitation to visit. I'm looking forward to setting foot inside a colony that proves *Der Jude* could not be stopped by a mere *Führer*. They have returned to their Holy Land, but at an unexpected altitude.

What would Father make of this sane new world? His final testament was the torment of a soul that had seen his victory become something alien and unconcerned with its architects. His life was melodrama, but his death a cheap farce. They didn't even know what to say at his funeral, he, the great orator of National Socialism. Without his guiding hand, they could not give him a Wagnerian exit.

The final joke is on him, and its practitioner is Dr. Mabuse. Father sincerely believed that in Adolf Hitler, long-awaited Zarathustra, the new man, had descended from the mountain. This, above all others, was the greatest lie of Joseph Goebbels's life.

The new man will ascend from the test tube. I pray that he will be wiser than his parents.

Hilda Goebbels

Paul Joseph Goebbels
Born October 29, 1897
Died March 15, 1970

About the Editors

HARRY TURTLEDOVE was born in Los Angeles in 1949. After flunking out of Caltech, he earned a Ph.D. in Byzantine history from UCLA. He has taught ancient and medieval history at UCLA, Cal State Fullerton, and Cal State L.A., and he has published a translation of a ninth-century Byzantine chronicle, as well as several scholarly articles. His alternate-history works have included many short stories, the Civil War classic *The Guns of the South*, the epic World War I series The Great War, and the Worldwar tetralogy that began with *Worldwar: In the Balance*. He is a winner of the Sidewise Award for Best Alternate History for his novel *How Few Remain*.

MARTIN H. GREENBERG is a veteran anthologist and book packager with over 700 books to his credit. He lives in Green Bay, Wisconsin, with his wife, daughter, and four cats.